A KINGDOM OF CURSES

OF

THE EMERGENCE

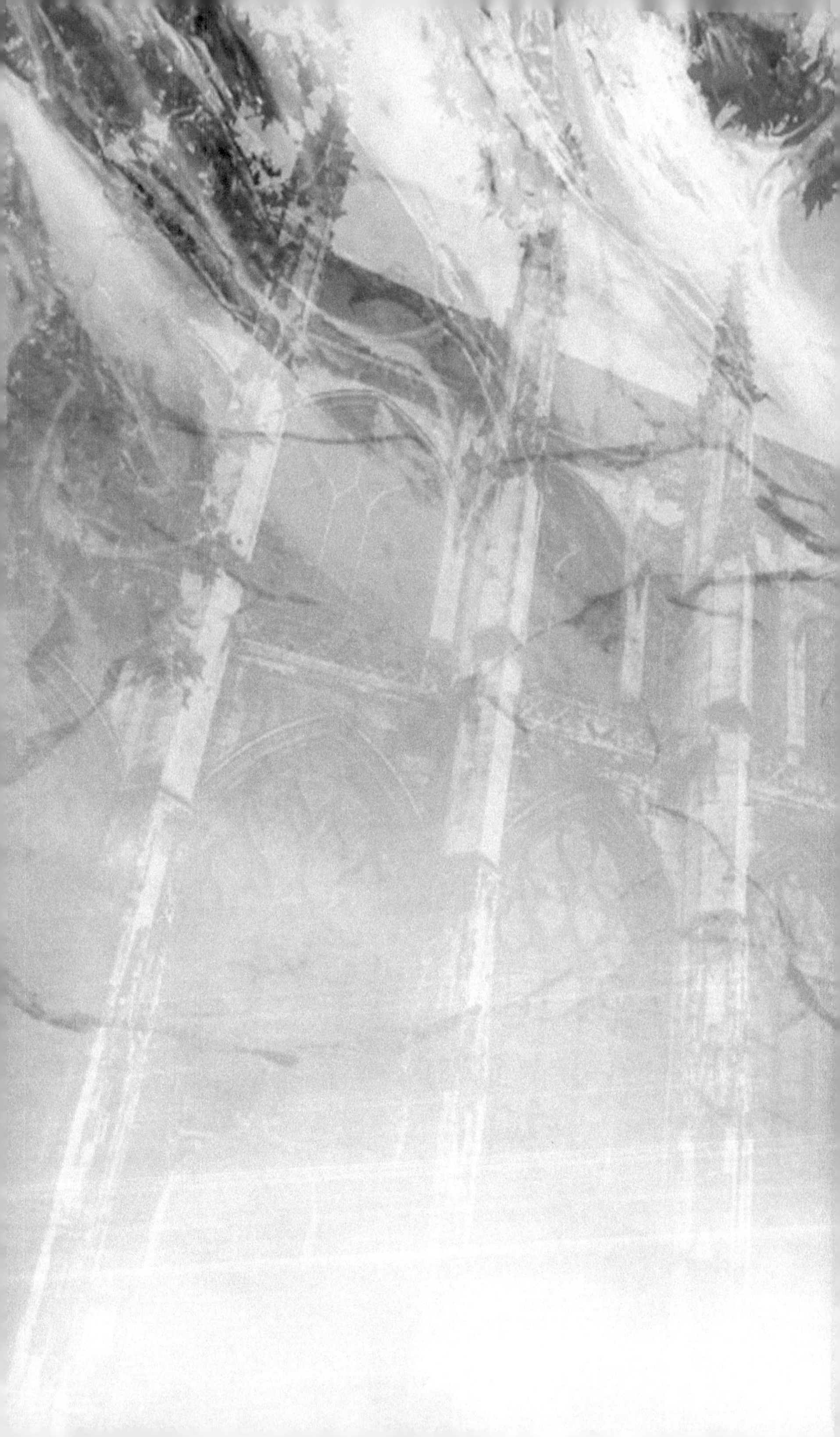

An Original Sin Novel
Book 1

A
KINGDOM
OF
CURSES

THE EMERGENCE

Danielle D. Drummond

Cover Art by Lexie at Selkkie Designs

Hard Cover and title page artwork by Juniper Hartmann

Interior art by Juniper Hartmann

Interior art by Aanastasia Mirolubova

Interior design and formatting by Danielle D. Drummond

Map design by Winter Cutt

Editing by Charla Ayers

PAPERBACK ISBN: 9781763765108

HARDCOVER ISBN: 9798307336069

HARDCOVER D/J ISBN: 9781763765115

Authors Note and Content Warnings

A Kingdom of Curses, The Emergence is a book of fiction. Any description or representation of any person or place in this work is fictional, and any resemblance is purely coincidental.

This book contains heavy themes of emotional abuse and manipulation, drug use, violence, kidnapping, branding and death, both on and off page. The FMC goes through a lot of trauma in this book and it is not entirely dealt with. Your mental health matters so please take note and use your discretion before choosing to delve into the world of Elyndria and please be kind to yourself while reading this. This book also contains explicit sexual content.

Playlist

When I daydream about the world I'm creating, music becomes my muse, inspiring me to breathe life into my characters. It helps me tap into deeper emotions, visualize scenes as they unfold, and find the creative energy to tackle even the most challenging chapters. If music resonates with your creative process too, or if you simply enjoy listening while you read, hop over to Spotify and explore the incredible artists who helped shape the world I've brought to life for you.

STAR-BORNE
ACADEMY
THALASSIA
DYTHALIS
ORPHELIOS
Fe
RIVER PYVE
NEOPOLIS
SERPENT'S SEA
ARCHANOR
VALSTROME
FENRIERA
WELVERYN
QUESPELIA
OKSANA
ACREA
N
LOURNE

MOUNTAINS OF G'PHEN
OWENSTOWN
DEAD FOREST
WHITE FOREST
EDRUS
THE BARRONS
BLETHYN SE
WYSTRINE
DOR DESE
ELYNDRIA

To the man who showed me the stars and told me to reach for them.
I will forever love you.

Prologue

S o much blood. There was so much blood. Salty puddles crested in her eyes as she took in the carnage before her. The Hallowed never left the sanctity of their island. But earlier, each one of them was violently ripped from their slumber. When the screams and cries of the family pierced their peaceful minds as they were brutally murdered, they had no choice but to answer their prayers.

But they had been too late.

Hera's hand shook as she brought it to her aching chest and placed it over her heart. A tear rolled down her ivory face. The glow of the crescent moon rippled through the window, casting a soft light around the expansive room. Halexander laid beside his wife, Vaelencia. Both still in their night clothes. The babe still cradled in her arms. The athame still buried in her bloodied chest.

The haunting chants from the garden where her sisters remained bounced eerily through the halls to the bedchamber where she stood in an inky crimson pool, drowning out the ringing that grew louder and more intense between her ears. Why did they not get the warning, Hera asked herself.

There had been signs something was coming. Hera and her sisters knew the gods were angry. Zyphera's winds had been funnelling and racing across the kingdom. Tidryn's ocean tides had been rising with fury, drowning those who dared to cross the seas. Fissures formed along Terra's Earth, separating cities and species. Pyrrhia's volcanoes spewed lava into the northern skies, lighting it up like Isra's exploding stars. But the Hallowed's usual sight had been blanketed. Hera and her sisters saw nothing.

Not until it was too late.

And now, Edom's blood flowed like a crimson river of life and death.

Hera knelt beside their lifeless bodies. She gently placed a hand on Vaelencia's chest and pulled the athame from her heart. Vaelencia's eyes snapped open at the movement, and a gasp was pulled from Hera's mouth.

"My babe?" Vaelencia rasped as she took a rattled breath, her emerald eyes blinking erratically.

"I'm sorry," Hera replied, and she quickly glanced to the lifeless babe in the female's arms. Nausea built at the sight, but she could not fall apart. She would not fall apart, but Gods, he was only a few months old. He had his mother's soft features but his father's golden hair. Darkness seeped into Hera's light. She didn't care.

"My babe," Vaelencia whispered again. She coughed and rocked her head to the side, letting it fall into the sanguine liquid that pooled around her. Her glassy green eyes settled on the large mahogany armoire behind Hera, and a tear fell from the crook of Vaelencia's eye. "Please," was all she said before her eyes closed again, and the life permanently left her body.

Hera stood, hitching her blood-soaked white gown and cloak with one hand and clasping the bloodied blade she pulled from Vaelencia's chest in the other, then walked on shaky legs to the armoire. Aside from her sisters' melodic chants, the room was completely silent as she padded across the cool stone floor that bit into her bare feet. She should join her sisters, but Hera was sure she needed to open this door first.

She looked back to the family, swallowing her tears. Who would commit such an atrocity? It seemed the Israykiel Guards did not even fight. This was their one true duty. This was what they were created for. So, how did they fail? Most of them had died a bloody death, and those who didn't probably wished they did. The family, everyone, had been asleep. They had all been completely helpless. She turned her attention back to the armoire and sucked in a deep breath. The coppery tang of blood assaulted her senses. Grounding herself, she grabbed the handle and twisted.

And when the door flung open, her next breath caught in her chest.

Present Day

CHAPTER 1

Standing in front of the large crimson door, the pit in my stomach growls, and it sends a shiver crawling down my spine. I've always been intuitive. Intuition is one of my gifts. The growling is not something I have experienced before. Not until a few weeks ago. So, I heed the warning, contemplating if coming here is the best choice.

Do I *really* need to know what my future holds?

When I left my apartment earlier, my plans were simple: go to work as usual at my second job at The Pit, where the best live music in the Neopolis is played. The ale is cold, the liquor is strong, and the crowd is unruly. Best of all, the music is loud.

I wanted to be there.

I *needed* to be there.

It's the one place in this world that makes me feel like I belong. Where I can forget about all my troubles and just be me. But with my Sacred Birthday fast approaching, I feel like my life has been lacking direction. I've spent the first twenty-four years of my life spinning in circles, unsure of where I belong or how to fit into this world.

I suck in a breath, trying to ease the pounding in my ears. Abrasive metal bites at my skin as I wrap my fingers around the large brass ring positioned in the centre of the door. I knock. One, two, three times.

The eyepiece slides open, and a golden, marbled eye greets me, darting around in an avine manner. "What is your purpose for visiting this warm autumn eve? For me to read your future and tell you what I see?" the voice behind the door asks in a whimsical chorus.

"I request a sitting with the Seer—before my Unification," I reply, hoping the mention of my Sacred Birthday gets me seen. But the reality is, this is not the only reason I am here.

Silence fills the air between us for a long moment. The large red door finally swings open into a tiny dark room filled with iron trinkets, candles, books, and crystal balls. Upon a white throne, on the far side of a large, round wooden table, sits a petite middle-aged Witch. The Seer. Her translucent crepe paper skin exposes violet-blue veins that somewhat resemble a vine-like tattoo spreading throughout her frail frame. It's unusual yet striking.

She smiles, revealing a mouth full of angular teeth. Each one is etched with intricate rune engravings, and one jewelled canine shimmers faintly under the soft glow of the candles, radiating an aura of ancient mysticism rather than malice.

"Come in," the Seer instructs in a melodic voice as she gestures over the table that is almost too big for the room. It's covered in a thin, black-lace cloth that reminds me of my mother's fabrics, and I feel a tug at my lips as I exhale the breath I held with anticipation.

As I cross the threshold, her wide-set eyes dart around erratically, and I can't help but wonder if she was the one who answered the door. Intrigued, I open my senses up, but I don't feel another Being inside. Not that I expected that to work.

"Thank you," I respond meekly, and the mass of butterflies that reside in my belly begin to stir. I cross the room to take a seat in one of the three sumptuous wingback chairs opposite her. The smell of cedar and sage dances in the air. I lean back into the supple cushions. The chair's inky wings wrap around me, encasing me in a velvety cocoon of shadows. The candles that litter the entire space ignite instantly, and the Seer's golden eyes burst with light, creating a marbled effect across her irises that spark a flickering reflection in the gemstones and crystals around us.

And the shadows come to life, dancing across the room.

"Don't be nervous, my dear," she sings, looking down at me over her beaked nose. "For you have no reason to fear." Her words instantly take effect, and I feel the growling inside subside, and the butterflies begin to settle.

Every word she speaks with her wispy tone lands like poetry as she draws out and over-enunciates every word, sounding every bit as wise and old as legends say.

There are many rumours about who she is. One thing everyone seems to agree on is she has been around for over five hundred years and is well respected in the Neopolis as one of the eldest Witch Seers in the kingdom of Elyndria. She takes a moment to look at me, and I mean really look at me. Studying my features closely, her head bobs sharply as she eyes me up and down. It should make me feel uncomfortable, but it doesn't. I am used to it by now.

"You are not like the others," she muses.

She is right. I am not like the others at all. I am a demi-Fae: a half-Fae, half-Human hybrid. My mother, Synthony, is Fae. My biological father was a Human warrior who fought and died in the Human war. He was apparently very brave and noble for a Human. I never met him, though. He was isolated from the Humans when the wards went up around our kingdom, keeping the mortals out, and died before I was born. My mother doesn't like to talk about him. She's never even told me his name. Or how he died. Which I completely understand, and to be honest, I don't need to talk about him because, as far as I am concerned, Amerax, my stepdad, is one hundred percent my father.

I swallow down the lump that's forming in my throat as I push the thoughts about my bio-dad aside and answer, "No, I am not."

The Seer blinks once, twice, and continues to look me up and down. Is she waiting for me to say something?

After a few minutes, she raises a brow and speaks again, "You are *really* not like the others."

I get it. I'm different. I've spent my entire life dealing with Beings judging me, pointing, and gawking. No wonder I don't feel like I belong anywhere. The only Being, aside from my family and close friends, who makes me feel like I'm not different is Sylas. Who, ironically, is also the one that makes me feel insignificant and confused.

And if I am being honest with myself, he is the real reason I am here.

"But you are not here to talk about that, are you, young Fae? You have more pressing matters of the heart to understand," she says, drawling out her words even more, turning poetry into song.

Finally, we are getting somewhere.

With her words, I sit forward, and the butterflies in my stomach become restless once more because all I have ever wanted is to feel accepted. For someone, anyone, to not treat me differently. To belong. And Sylas has never been phased that I am a demi-Fae. Does he treat me poorly? Yes. But he has never looked at me the way the others do. In his eyes, I have never been *different*.

So, I want more than nothing else for things between us to change. For all of it change.

"Yes, that is true," I say, looking down at the table. This table *is* ridiculously large. This whole situation is ridiculous.

Paege, what are you doing?

Walking over here, it felt perfectly normal to want to get my cards read. Because who doesn't want to know if their future is written in the stars? But now that I'm here . . .

Blood rushes my ears, and a warmth prickles my cheeks. Gods, I feel stupid wasting my time and my money on this.

Looking up, I find the Seer's eyes fixated on my face. Her head cocks slightly to the side as if trying to read my thoughts, the expression on her face otherwise indifferent. I suppose I would feel even more stupid if I were to leave now.

I sigh. "My Unification is in five months, and I have spent the last two years with a male who somehow makes me feel everything yet nothing at the same time."

The Seer cocks her head to the other side, her long white hair cascading over her shoulders like silken curtains. She grabs her tarot deck and shuffles the cards. Her fingers move swiftly.

"He is the only male who's ever truly accepted me for who I am—for *what* I am," I correct myself. "But is that enough?" I exhale sharply, and the question lingers in the air like shadows in the recesses of this dark room. It's a question I have asked myself a lot lately, and I honestly can't come up with an answer.

Things between us have been feeling especially off these past few weeks, and it's been making me anxious. Who am I kidding? My relationship with Sylas has always felt a little off. I've never been able to quite put my finger on it. I love him so much, this I know, but sometimes I don't understand why he treats me the way he does. Or, more importantly, why I put up with it. The confusion over why I stay has been mounting like snow on a cliff, ready to avalanche at the slightest whisper of truth. A truth that never comes.

She stacks the cards in front of me, and like a magnet, my hands are drawn to the spellbinding tower. Without thought, I cut the deck into three. Blinking away whatever emotion that's threatening to build inside, I look up at the Seer. Her face wears a kind and heartfelt smile full of warmth. One that a mother would give her child.

The Seer gracefully lays out five tarot cards in the middle of the table in the shape of a pentagram. The cards are exquisite and unnerving. It almost feels as though each card is watching me with an eye of its own. Like they peer into my murky future themselves. Intricate artwork of golden filigree patterns glistens atop the black-based cards, and bold colours of deep royal greens and blues weave through the contrast. Each one is slightly different from the rest.

Without a word, the Seer turns the first card over and reveals a group of stars.

"Pentacles, hm, of which there are five." Her head twitches again, short and sharp, in that bird-like manner. "This card represents loss but one you'll survive. Possibly a lover?" She raises an eyebrow, and my heart sinks at the words. "It suggests a deep loneliness and feelings of isolation. Maybe even ones of rejection. This is your current situation, where you are in your life right now," the Seer confirms, but her eyes soften with what I'm assuming is sorrow because she and I both know her words couldn't be truer. "But do not worry, it will turn around."

The Seer immediately turns a second card over, and it reveals the Moon card.

"Hm, the Moon, and it's upside down," she sings as she cocks her head again. "An interesting card—young Fae do not frown."

Jolting upright, I self-scan my face and feel my brows pulling together.

"The second card in this spread is simply looking ahead to see where you will end up if you follow the current path you are on. The Reversed Moon symbolises confusion and unhappiness; however, it also symbolises the end of darkness."

I force a smile, willing my face to relax, and she continues.

"It seems your current predicament may come to a resolution sooner than you think, regardless of your actions, young one." She pauses, and I try not to shiver as the blood in my veins chills. Leaning down, she grabs a pot of tea and two miniature mugs from somewhere under the table and places them in front of her. My brows furrow at the sudden interruption.

"Would you like a drink?" I shake my head, watching curiously as she pours herself a cup of tea, the lump forming in my throat keeping me from using my words. "Alright, well, I suggest we continue with the reading and see where it leads."

I nod in silence, trying to make sense of what she is saying, her words crawling through my mind and how they apply to my current situation.

"The third card in this spread represents what you need to do to resolve this problem," the Seer continues as she turns the third card over and reveals golden swords clouded in darkness, all pointing toward a rainbow.

"Six of Swords. Just as I expected. The message here is simple and direct. You must walk away, let go, and release. Leave your past behind, and you shall find peace. This burden you carry is not yours to own, but as you move on, the truth shall be shown," the Seer sings in her whimsical tune.

More muddy thoughts attempt to push themselves forward, but before they succeed, they evaporate into darkness like a dream upon waking. My paralysis impedes their emergence like an insurmountable barricade.

Unable to think clearly through the thick, hazy fog that's seeping in from every far corner of my mind, I rub my clammy hands along my pants in an attempt to clear my overcrowded yet vacant mind.

The Seer gracefully turns the fourth card over, and as she does, I let out a gasp as a chill slithers up my spine, for what I see scares me to death. The irony does not escape me as I stare at the face of the Death card. My heart plummets to the darkness inside my stomach, and the lump in my throat grows, completely restricting my breath. The Death card cannot be good.

Zephyra, save me now.

The Seer's eyes soften as if she can see the fear in my own. "Don't fear, young Fae, for the Reaper is not what it seems," her songbird voice soothes me enough to release a breath. "This card represents the end of a cycle and a transition to something better, more powerful with greater meaning."

Her revelation raises my brows. "But how is that possible? Isn't it the . . ." I stutter, "the Death card?" My voice rattles as my body begins to shake. Resisting her song's calming influence, my fear swells like a turbulent tide.

"Why yes, it *is* death, but it is the death of something old to reveal something new. Like when a serpent sheds its skin." She smiles. "A new life you shall begin."

An ache blooms in my jaw from the pressure of my teeth clenching, and I press my fingers into my temples, massaging gently. Yet the attempt to dissolve the anxiety throbbing through my veins fails while I process what she is saying. But I suppose it makes sense. Before I can question her further, the Seer turns the fifth and final card over to reveal a single female warrior-like Goddess, and my breath catches. My Gods, she is the epitome of femininity, beauty, strength and grace. Everything I have always wanted to be.

And everything I am not.

The Seer warmly smiles. "This card holds immense power, and I'm happy to advise, as the fifth and final card drawn, it represents your final destination. Where your heart's true desire lies. The Empress is an embodiment of all the elements of the kingdom. Air, Water, Earth, and Fire. The key to ultimate freedom." Her wispy, whimsical voice seems to harden slightly, becoming more affirming. "Now, do not let your eyes deceive you, for in this mystical tapestry, the image of pregnancy may not signify the conventional bearing of a child. No, it speaks of a different kind of nurturing: a role as a mother figure to all, embracing the world with care and wisdom."

She blinks rapidly and stands in a disjointed manner before shuffling over to me to take a seat in the empty chair to my left.

"This is a perfect closing card if I have ever drawn one." She closes her eyes momentarily and hums. "Death and rebirth," she muses to herself before reopening her eyes. "It's as if Amara herself is blessing you. Young Fae, you needn't worry about your future, but I have a message you must heed. This male who you think you know is not who he seems."

The Seer dips her head, and her marbled eyes widen when she notices the gold charm resting between my breasts. With one hand, she reaches out and wraps her spindly fingers around it. My muscles tighten, and I resist the urge to sweep her away. The Seer inspects the long golden dagger and Fae wings that encase a dark ash-coloured gemstone with pearlescent blues swirling through it hanging from a delicate chain. As she does so, she whispers something to herself in a tongue that is vaguely familiar, yet I can't place.

"Pardon?" I ask, trying to make sense of what she mumbled.

"You are such a lost, little winged one. But," she gently releases the charm, allowing it to fall back in its place between my breasts, "I think you will find, you will be just fine. It is clear the Gods have great things planned for you."

CHAPTER 2

Although it has passed, summer's warmth still lingers in the air long after the sun has gone to bed. But the coolness of the evening threatens to infiltrate the streets, leaving a refreshing feeling against my skin as I wander back to my apartment, rehashing my time with the Seer. Contemplating her every word. Revisiting every card drawn.

The Five of Pentacles: the loss of a lover.

The Upside-Down Moon: unhappiness and confusion.

The Six of Swords: walk away.

The Reaper: death.

The Empress: rebirth.

It's not even up for interpretation. The Gods really supplied me with an answer. A divine intervention, perhaps.

If it was any other night, I would stop at any of my favourite bars for a drink and to listen to some amazing music. But tonight, I have no such desire. I want to walk in silence. I need to focus, to think. I need to reflect. I don't want the distraction.

Deep down, I know what I must do. I think I have known for months. But every time I try to leave him, something happens, something changes, and I question everything I think I know.

The memory of our first encounter wraps around me like a warm blanket. The smell and feel of him haunts my every step. I tug at the charm hanging around my neck.

"Sorry," I said through chattering teeth to the hard body I slammed into. I can be really clumsy sometimes. But to be fair, after the deluge of rain that washed me out on my way home from breakfast with Lumeilia and Mhelodie, the last thing I was thinking about was where I was going. I was too busy walking the halls of the gallery, trying to warm up, waiting for the rain to stop.

A low grumble caused me to raise my gaze from the floor, ready to defend myself, but golden eyes met mine. Soft and friendly golden eyes paired with a charming smile that lifted ever so slightly on one side.

I apologised again, heat flushing my cheeks as I stepped away from the beautiful male who stood before me. But he reached out an arm and laid it gently on mine, halting me from moving.

"No, I'm sorry," he said, his voice warm and smooth like hot chocolate. "I was distracted by the most beautiful vision and wasn't paying attention to where I was going." He gently tipped his head, "Please, forgive me."

"That's alright," I murmured in response. I was so Gods-damned cold and wet that it took every bit of energy to not let the shivers overcome me. All I wanted to do was keep walking through the heated gallery until the weather cleared enough to walk home.

"You look cold. Here, take this," the tall male said as he shrugged off his jacket and handed it to me.

I didn't take it. I eyed him up and down, my brows arching high, unsure how to take this charming gesture by the tall, mysterious, and very handsome male.

"Please, I must insist. I promise I won't ask for anything in return. Except maybe an escort to help pass the time," he smiled.

"You want an escort?" I considered his proposal for a moment. He was very handsome and looked harmless enough. Maybe the company wouldn't be so bad?

"What piece were you so interested in?" I queried, looking around the gallery. The male continued to hold his hand out, but still, I didn't take the jacket off him.

"Well, you see, it was this charming little piece of the most beautiful female I had ever laid eyes on." I continued to scan the room, looking for the piece he was referring to. "Her emerald eyes were quite exquisite. Like nothing I have ever seen. From the moment I entered the gallery, I couldn't take my eyes off her."

My eyes shot to his. Warmth enveloped my entire body, and suddenly, I was shivering for a whole other reason.

Oh, he is good, I thought to myself.

I wish I'd never fallen for those damn golden eyes.

Strolling through the half-empty streets, still ruminating on things, a distant laughter distracts me from my ever-changing thoughts. I still. The sounds of insects and distant music quiet, and the bustle of the city night's chatter slowly fades into the background as a cloud of unease rolls through the pit of my stomach. It growls, and my Fae ears hone in on a siren's song of hypnotic musings.

That laughter, it's so familiar.

Sylas.

He thinks I'm working at The Pit. I never told him I took the night off. The last thing I need right now is his twenty questions and a guilt trip about why I didn't tell him I wasn't working. I sigh, but keep on walking, my body tensing as I brace for him to exit the alley ahead and step directly in my path. One I know I cannot avoid.

But something's not right.

Ice slithers down my spine as the anxiety I feel coils around my body like a viper, tightening its grip with every breath I take. Another voice mingles with his, one I don't recognise. My brain scrambles for any sign of familiarity yet registers nothing.

Oh, fuck.

My heart stops momentarily then sinks deep into my core. I take in the situation in front of me. One that I can only describe as my worst nightmare. One second, I'm walking down the street, contemplating my future with a male I *love,* the next, I find myself face-to-face with him. His arm wrapped around the shoulders of a much younger, exquisite-looking Fae. Her long, elegant arm reaches up toward her shoulder. Her pedicured hand in his. Their fingers entwined.

Comfortable. Familiar. *Together.*

A blink interrupts my sight, and I take a long breath in and hold it as my mind empties, refusing to allow my lips to speak. My eyes study them both, searching for an explanation. Sylas breaks his fit of laughter, his bottom lip twitching where his scar rests, and he slowly unclasps her hand. Sliding his perfectly muscular arm back to where it belongs—attached to only him.

The weight of their stares has me shifting my body in an attempt to stand tall, and I expand my chest. It's a feeble attempt to make myself seem bigger. Stronger. Unwavering. An intense heat rises through my body, prickling my skin like thousands of tiny insects injecting me with their poison.

Speak, Paege, speak.

But nothing comes out of my quickly drying mouth.

Just say anything.

With nothing but sheer determination and will, I release my locked jaw and finally manage a word.

"Hi," I exhale.

Silence.

Narrowing my eyes, I scowl at him. "Who's this?" I nod towards the perfectly proportioned red-haired Fae he had his arm wrapped around.

"I, ah . . . what are you doing here, Paege? I thought you were working tonight?" Sylas asks, but it's not really a question; it's more of a statement. His words grate on me as they creep through my mind. His faultless pronunciation of every single word annoys me to no end.

"I have a headache, so I'm going home." Not an entirely untrue reply as a dull ache begins to bloom behind my eyes. "Sorry, who's this?" I ask again as my eyes study the beautiful female standing before me.

Nice try to deflect. Another typical Sylas move.

"This is," he pauses and his eyes to the younger female before continuing, "Nikita. We are friends."

I nod, my focus remaining solely on the male standing before me.

Sylas' golden eyes burn into mine, challenging me like a game of Russian Roulette. Who is going to blink first? I swear I can see a hint of fear flicker in his beautiful golden eyes.

He blinks first.

I return my attention to Nikita and force my lips to arc, revealing a saccharine smile and concealing the humiliation that swells like a rising tide in my tightening chest. Her khaki eyes widen at my brazen attempt to undermine her, illuminating the flicks of gold and bronze that shimmer under the warm street-lights.

But my effort to stand tall and unaffected is short-lived. She releases an insulting laugh from her strawberry lips, and suddenly, I feel small and inferior because I am the exact opposite of her.

The. Exact. Opposite.

"You are friends?" I spit my words between clenched teeth. "It looks like a lot more than just friendship."

Sylas glares pointedly at me, his face and golden eyes expressionless. Clearly, he has nothing to say. But why? Why won't he say something? Why won't he try to explain what's going on or give me anything? He is supposed to love and care for me. He is supposed to be the one who always has my back and wants what's best for me. At least, that's what he always says. So why isn't he doing what is best for me right now and telling me this is all one big, horrible mistake?

It seems no amount of wishing is going to make him speak. He purses his lips as if trying to stop the deceitful words spilling from his venomous mouth.

Darkness weighs down on me, and I gag as a thick glue-like nothingness coats my mouth.

Guilt.

Not mine.

Nikita's.

My heart sinks further, and it steals the breath from my chest as Nikita's emotions betray her, confirming to me what I thought I already knew.

Holding his gaze, I feel a new wave of heat burn through my body as the raging inferno building in my gut intensifies from the betrayal. Sylas blinks, and his lip quivers, suggesting he is finally about to speak. His lips part, and he draws in a short breath, but I don't let the words fall out of his mouth.

I raise a heavy arm towards them, waving it in front of their faces. "I can't!" I exclaim. "I can't do this right now. I don't understand exactly what is going on here, but I think I've figured out enough to know I can't deal with whatever *you're* about to say."

Nikita flinches and steps back.

Blood rushes in my ears, and my body begins to shake. Salty tears sting my eyes as they start to fall, sending tiny tickles in the tracks down my cheeks. My eyes drop, and the forced smile I try to retain quickly turns in the same direction as my world—upside down.

Sylas reaches out to grab my hand, but I yank it away.

"Don't!" I caution, baring my teeth. A clear warning that whatever he tries to do or say next will not end well for him.

Quickly, I turn on my heel, my shoulders rolled back, and I pull my spine tall, walking away. It's not even one hundred lengths to the next corner. I just need to keep moving and keep my head held high. *Just. Keep. Walking. And whatever you do, do not look back.*

CHAPTER 3

I make it around the corner without him following me. Without him catching up to me.

To be honest, I am not too sure what I will do if he does catch me. Will I fold and melt into him like I have done so many times before, or will I finally wake up and knee him in the Godsdamn balls?

Opening myself up to the world around, I don't feel him anywhere near, and that's when it hits me—the reality of the situation.

He isn't trying to stop me at all. He just let me go.

As I reach the next corner, I veer left into the deserted street where suddenly, something inside breaks like the snapping of a string wound far too tight, releasing everything I held in all at once. And I run. I run as fast as I possibly can.

My mind clears with every step. My body propels forward as if it's leaving the past behind me—just like the Seer said I should. Pain jolts up through my legs with every stride as my feet smack against the pavement violently. My steps find a rhythm with every beat of my racing heart, and as it beats faster, so do my feet. The city streetlights fade into blurry lines as I pass through block after block after block, and when I no longer feel the wild beast thrashing inside, I allow myself to slow, coming to a gradual stop.

Fuck.

I knew it. I knew something was wrong. I've had this pit in my stomach for weeks. This overpowering anxiety that I couldn't shake has kept me awake, and my intuition has been screaming at me that something was not right.

He has been distant.

He has been moody.

He has been mean—meaner than usual.

That's the reason I went to the Seer in the first place. I knew something was wrong, and I needed reassurance that it wasn't all in my head. And Sylas, a master at shielding, has blocked me from reading his emotions. But here it is, right in front of me—all the reassurance I need.

My shoulders slump as the most contradicting feelings I've ever felt roll through me in waves. Hurt that he betrayed and discarded me with so little consideration or guilt. Relief that it's over. It's finally over. The understanding that I wasn't going crazy at all. That my intuition was always right. I should have trusted myself—given myself more credit.

How did I always end up questioning myself and never him? How did I always end up confused and apologising? Anger joins the party as my thoughts spiral further. Blood rushes my ears, and the world around me tilts.

Breathe, Paege.

Every inhale burns as the air travels down my constricting chest, and my legs wobble. No longer capable of holding myself up, I descend to the ground. Like a lead anvil falling from the sky, my ass finds the pavement with a solid thump. My warm face receives the cool air like an unexpected gift. Shocking yet pleasant as it penetrates my damp skin from the beads of sweat and tears that continue to trickle to my chin.

"Nikita," I say to myself. I can't compete with her. Not with her unblemished porcelain skin, curvy hips, and perfectly full breasts.

Not with her effortlessly styled dark auburn hair that falls to the apex of her round ass. No wonder he didn't chase after me.

I wouldn't chase after me, either.

I sit on the side of the road and put my head between my knees, trying to catch a steady breath as I fight off the tears that keep streaming down my face. An unhelpful rush of panic causes my chest to tighten, my breaths to sharpen, and everything starts looking distorted.

Just breathe, Paege.

I remember what Amerax taught me during our training. How breathing, when done right, can calm the heart and reduce stress, grounding you. I continue to focus on every breath.

Breathe in, breathe out.

I want to go home.

Breathe in, breathe out.

To my safe place.

Breathe in, breathe out.

To my bed.

Minutes pass, and I feel the rhythm of my heart slow to a deep, heavy bass, and the erratic voices in my head become a sluggish whisper of nothing.

Thank Zephyra herself.

When I eventually have the strength to do so, I will myself to stand and look around to get my bearings. Instinct kicked in, and I ran without thought of where I was going.

Scanning the empty cobblestone streets, my eyes catch on a rusted sign up the road from me. Blaxheild Metalworx. The hairs stand up on the back of my neck. Blaxheild, the south side of the Neopolis. I must have run at least five miles— much further than I thought.

Blaxheild is one of the districts that the Wolves run. Illegal drug dens, prostitution, and underground fighting rings are just some of the rumours told around the Neopolis of what goes on in the various abandoned warehouses. Not that I would know for sure; I've never actually been here before. In fact, like most Fae, I usually make a conscious effort to avoid this area at all costs.

Rumours or not, it's not something I want to find out first-hand.

Backtracking the way I came, I hear an unexpected but familiar voice call out my name, and a heaviness settles in the depths of my stomach.

"Paege?" he calls. "Paege Vailenbyrg, is that you?"

I turn to see two males accompanied by two barely dressed yet extremely pretty females heading my way.

Guy Braxtion and Quentin Ishaan.

Two of the hottest but most arrogant males I know from the Neopolis Collegium. Also, Wolves.

To be honest, I'm a little surprised they even know my name. Yes, we went to the collegium together, and yes, I'm the half-Human Fae girl everyone talked about, but the Wolves and I never spoke. We hardly had a few classes together. Wolves stick with Wolves. They don't care much about Fae business unless they are implementing more rules and policies that keep us in check. And these two never so much as glanced my way.

Or so I thought.

"Oh, hi. Yes, it's just me," I say as my hand nervously reaches for the charm that hangs around my neck. "Sorry, I would stay and talk, but I'm just walking home." My voice squeaks in an extremely embarrassing way as I zip the charm back and forth along the length of the chain.

My heart quickens as I realise my attempt to brush them off becomes futile. The four of them stroll over, surrounding me like a pack of wild animals around their prey. Surrounding me like the pack of Wolves they are, making it impossible for me to escape.

Ugh. This seriously can't be happening to me right now. As if my night hasn't been bad enough, now I need to deal with this.

"Shouldn't you be at the library, *Books*?" Quentin teases with a cheeky smile on his face, and his grey eyes glisten in the streetlight as he wraps his arm around the pretty platinum-blonde female. She leans in and whispers something into his ear, and they both chuckle.

I get it. I worked in the collegium library. I spent most of my days reading, and my name is Paege. He couldn't have come up with something even remotely original?

After my internal diatribe comes to an end, I shelf my irritation and let go of the charm. "No, not the library."

My cheeks flush with warmth. These two must have paid some attention to me in the collegium. How else would they know all of that? But why pay any attention to me? I am a nobody.

Quentin whispers into his female companion's ear, holding her sleek shoulder-length blonde hair behind her neck. His lips graze her lobe as they move, and she seductively bites her ruby-red bottom lip, the piercing sliding between the small gap in her two front teeth. I must admit, she is striking. Hels, sexy even. And she knows it. Quentin knows it.

Her dark brown, almost black eyes dart to mine, narrowing, scowling, and her lip twitches as she holds my gaze. An uncomfortableness washes over me in waves, and my heart fires off loudly. Too loud for my liking, especially when I'm alone at night, surrounded by Wolves.

Shit—Wolves can smell fear, right?

"I would love to stay and talk, but I really do have to get home," I repeat, swallowing hard.

"Are you alright?" Guy asks with a genuine look of concern on his face, his large emerald eyes softening at the edges.

Stay calm, Paege.

"Of course, why?" I ask nervously. Yes, I just broke up with my boyfriend and ran five blocks in sheer embarrassment, but they don't need to know that.

The dark brunette that stands next to Guy gestures to her grey eyes and then points my way. I rub under my eyes, revealing black kohl covering my fingers. It seems to have run down my face. Great! Just what I need, black eyes, when two ridiculously good-looking Wolves and their equally attractive dates are talking to me.

Typical, Paege!

"Oh, that. Um . . . yes, I'm fine," I stammer. "It's been a rough night."

"Anything you want to talk about?" Guy asks as I glance away, pathetically trying to wipe away the kohl that's painting my face, and I swear I catch a glimmer of compassion in his eyes. He seems to be genuinely worried, which is a strange trait for a Wolf. And although I can't feel a grain of emotion pulsing from any of the Wolves, somehow, I can tell he wouldn't hurt me. Quentin, on the other hand, I'm not so sure.

"Not really, no."

Then Guy says something I never would have expected. "We can walk you home if you like. It's not safe out here tonight in this part of town."

"Would not be good if a *halfling* ends up dead . . . or worse," Quentin interjects as he brushes the stray hair that's fallen into his eyes from his face, his wicked smirk looking more wolfish than ever. His girlfriend tugs at his arm, looking extremely bored and a little irritated by Guy's offer, and she laughs again at his comment.

My nose scrunches up at hearing the word *halfling*. It's such a derogatory term. It means dirty, insignificant Being. Everyone can tell I'm a demi-Fae, but Beings mostly just stare, gawp, and snicker behind my back. Not many would ever call me a halfling to my face. But Wolves are arrogant and conceited, and these two Wolves, especially with who their fathers are, know they can get away with just about anything.

And they do.

"Since when are you two in the habit of walking a lowly Fae home?" I try to joke, my eyes shifting nervously between the Wolves as I place my shaking, sweaty hands in my pocket.

Quentin laughs as if he understands my bad attempt at humour. He and his girlfriend turn around and start walking up the street, snickering among themselves. The brunette follows a few steps in their shadow. Guy, however, remains behind, silent. His large emerald eyes meet mine again, and there is something oddly quiet, calming, and familiar about him. I've never noticed it before, but why would I? This is probably the most we have spoken in our twenty-four years of life.

"Come on," Guy smiles and nods as he strides past me towards the Central Business Quarter, hands buried deep in his pockets, bumping his hard muscular arm into my shoulder affectionately so I know he isn't a threat. "Let's get you home."

CHAPTER 4

The tears I had been holding back erupt from my eyes, and a sob cracks from my chest as my body falls through the front door of my apartment. My knees crack against the polished concrete floor, but the pain shooting through my bones is nothing compared to the pain exploding from my constricting chest. Darkness floods my veins as I continue to ride the tempest of betrayal until a gentle touch pulls me back from the brink.

It's over. It's really over.

My mouth opens, but the muffled sounds that spew from my lips make no sense whatsoever, even to me.

"Sh," a soft voice whispers into my ears. "We've got you," she continues as two sets of hands pull me to my feet. I peel open my swollen eyes, and through the blurry haze of tears and pain, I see the golden curls and strawberry waves that outline the faces of my two best friends, and they quietly guide me through my dark apartment to the place I crave to be so badly. My bed. My safe haven.

Loving hands brush my matted hair from my face as I sit down on the edge of the bed. Lumeilia's large mahogany eyes meet mine. Boots are pulled from my feet, and the mattress behind me groans as my denim jacket is wriggled off my body.

"Lie down, Paege," Lumeilia whispers.

I nod. My body falls to the side, and I curl my knees into my chest. Tears continue to cascade down my face, but at least the uncontrollable sobs have subsided.

"Scoot," Mhelodie's voice quietly requests, and I shuffle myself to the middle of the bed and roll over. Through my tear-soaked lashes, golden cat eyes filled with love greet mine. She smiles and tucks my hair behind my ear. "We love you, Paege."

A blanket of warmth cocoons me, accompanied by a soft light that curls around my soul, trying to find a weakness in the wall of darkness surrounding it, and my body trembles as I relax into the arms of my friends.

Lumeilia's long arms stay wrapped around me, and Mhelodie continues to lay soothing strokes down my hair. A soft tune that my mother used to sing to me when I was just a babe hums from my lips. Gradually, the tears start to dry, and my heavy lids fall to a close as a sliver of relief bursts from my aching heart and stressed body.

For the first time in years, no soul-crushing thoughts plague my mind. No emotional torment weighs heavy on my chest. I am grateful for the mind-numbing emptiness that accompanies the darkness around me because without it, I wouldn't be able to fall into the deep, dreamless sleep I so desperately need.

Chapter 5

"Who walked you home?" Lumeilia jumps up abruptly like a serpent bit her in the ass.

"I don't think that is the point of Paege's evening, Lu-Lu," Mhelodie exclaims, brushing her gorgeous curls out of her face.

She gets it. It's really not.

"I have to side with Lumeilia on this one," Asheron chimes in. "Those *Wolves* are dangerous."

"They didn't walk me home, per se. They more like, followed me," I clarify.

"So, they stalked you?" Asheron retorts, and I shake my head, trying to ignore the disapproval and worry coming from my friends.

I woke up this morning to Lumeilia and Mhelodie curled up with me in bed. For one second, I completely forgot about my horrible night. All seemed normal. But as the world slowly came into focus, I registered why they were lying in my bed, and like a floodgate that had burst open, all the memories and emotions came flooding back, drowning me like a tidal wave.

"I just can't believe it," I whisper into my coffee mug, feeling every watchful eye of my three closest friends huddled around me. The warm, bitter aroma of the coffee fills my senses, and my mouth salivates, inviting another sip.

"I can," Asheron responds, tucking silver strands of hair behind his pointed Fae ears. "Sorry, Paege, but Sylas is bad news. He always has been, and we've all been worried about you for so long now. I hate to say it, but I honestly think this could be the best thing to happen."

"It wasn't all bad," I counter, but deep down, I know he's right. When I think back on everything that's happened between us, of what I forgave, of what I put up with in the past, shame crawls its way through my heart.

I lay my head back against my pillow headrest and close my eyes for a moment. I breathe through the ache that blooms behind my eyes and allow the scent of caffeine to steal my harmful thoughts.

A bevy of emotions ripples over me, and my stomach churns at the unsavoury concoction as it swirls inside.

One of them is concerned.

One of them is angry.

One of them is relieved.

All of them are sad.

As if aware of the debilitating effects of the emotions rolling through me, one suddenly slams shut and eases the dizziness and nausea building.

Asheron.

He is the only one here who can shield himself so easily. He is the only one who has had his Sacred Birthday. Asheron had his Unification nine years prior. And while some can master the act of shielding before their Sacred Birthdays, most cannot. Grateful for his reprieve, I smile. The emotions of two are easier to handle than three.

Some days, I wish I was not an Empath.

While it's hard to feel their pain, especially when I'm struggling to handle my own, they all have every right to feel what they are feeling. My relationship with Sylas has not been the easiest. It's been very turbulent, and they have been there for all of it. Watching me spiral out of control, unable to intervene. Helpless. They have all been helpless, too—caught in his web of deceit and lies just like me.

He went from being attentive and charming to distant and cold in a matter of months. A master at shielding, I could never get a read on his emotions. His detachment fed my anxiety, driving me to the brink of exhaustion and craziness, only to pull me back to sanity with small acts of kindness and warmth once more.

I take a large gulp of my coffee, finish it off, and set the empty mug on the nightstand. I lean back, laying my head against the suede-cushioned headboard, and reach for my pendant. I close my eyes for a moment. Memories from my last birthday come rushing through my mind.

"He said he would meet us here," I confirmed with Asheron as I continued to pace the apartment. "I'm not leaving without him."

"Maybe you should send him a message?" Lumeilia suggested. "If we don't leave soon, we'll miss the show."

"I know, I know, these tickets cost a fortune." I rolled my eyes and immediately regretted it. Lumeilia did nothing wrong. It's Sylas, who was once again late. "Sorry. If you want to go on without me, I understand."

"Paege, it's your birthday. We aren't leaving without you," Mhelodie said shaking her head, and some golden curls free themselves from their binds.

"No, it's alright. I don't want you to miss the show. I'm sure he isn't too far away. We'll catch up. I promise." I placed my hand on my chest in true Vailenbyrg style and smiled at my friends, urging them to go on without me. I can't believe he was late on my birthday. Especially after he insisted we all buy tickets to this damn stage show to celebrate. Tickets none of us, except Asheron, could really afford.

I grabbed my scribe and sent him a message.

Me: How far away are you?

Nothing.

"I'm sorry," I said to my friends once more. "Please go on. I won't be far behind you."

Eventually, my friends apprehensively departed the apartment and left me alone to wait for Sylas. I sat on the couch in silence, anticipating his arrival. But it never came. The winter sun set fast, plunging the apartment into an eerie darkness as the early evening turned to night, and with no word from Sylas, tears built in the wells of my eyes.

I couldn't believe I was here again.

Bang, bang, bang.

"Paege," he called through the door. I peeled my puffy eyes open, waiting for them to adjust to the darkness. It was late into the evening then.

"Paege, open up. It's me." Like I didn't know who it was. The urge to ignore him grew. Fuck him. He left me here. He abandoned me on my birthday. Again.

Bang, bang, bang.

But what if it wasn't his fault? What if there had been an emergency? No. He could have sent me a message. But amid the war that raged inside my head, that small nugget of doubt started to glow brighter.

Fuck.

I stood and walked to the door. Opening it a small amount, I peered through the gap, looking at him but not looking at him. "What do you want, Sylas?" I asked, not bothering to hide the annoyance I felt.

"I'm so sorry, Paege. Please let me in so I can explain?"

"What could have possibly happened that not only had you standing me up on my birthday, but you couldn't even send a message?"

"If you would let me in, I can explain everything."

"Go home, Sylas." I huffed, trying to close the door, but he stomped his foot against the jam and pushed it wide open. My eyes widened at his forcefulness, and I tried to step back, but his hand grabbed my arm, halting me from moving away. He cupped my chin and raised it, forcing my eyes to meet his.

"Little one, you know I wouldn't do anything to intentionally hurt you." The tightness that had been coiling around my chest loosened at his words. "You know you want to let me in so we can forget about all this and go back to the way things were. I'm here now; that's all that matters."

He was right. I did want to let him in and forget about all this drama. I hated feeling the way I felt for the past few hours. Insecure and alone. But he was here now. He came. That was all that mattered.

I sighed at the sudden relief that washed over me, knowing it was going to be fine.

"Come in."

How is it that every time I tried to leave, I ended up forgiving him, believing him, and going back to him? Over and over again. I can't explain it.

There's just something about him I am drawn to, and I can't imagine being without him.

I love him. I know I do.

Gods, this hurts. It hurts like the Hels.

I open my eyes, releasing the tears pooling in my eyes to run down my face, and a sob cracks from my chest. Lumeilia leans over and hugs me tight as if she knows exactly what I'm seeing in my mind. So, I close my eyes again and lean into her embrace, allowing her lightness to gracefully waft around me. A floral bouquet bathes me in her compassion, and I hope it will bring me some peace from the wild storm that brews inside my head.

Moments later, Lumeilia lets go, gently brushing my matted hair from my face, and smiles. "Do you need anything?" she whispers, her brown eyes still burning pure love into my soul. I shake my head and lean back into the pillows behind me. She leaves to join the rest of my friends in the kitchen. The clattering of dishes is a dead giveaway that someone is trying to cook. Please let it be Asheron.

Looking at my nightstand, a sudden moment of responsibility floods my numbing brain, and I reach for my scribe to contact my boss, Blaire, to tell her I will not be in today. In my two years of working full-time as an assistant archivist at the Neopolis History Museum and Archives, I have never taken a day off. But if I ever needed one, today is the day.

Switching the scribe on, a gasp rips from my chest. I count the flood of messages that chime through the silence of my room: one, two, three, four, ten, seventeen, twenty-three chimes.

Fourteen text messages and nine missed voice communications. What in the Hels?

Sylas' name flashes across my screen, sparking a flurry of confusion within my chest as my heart thrums to a heavy rhythm. Mindlessly, I stare at the scribe, and my chest tightens and tightens and tightens.

Maybe he is sorry. Maybe he is trying to explain himself. Maybe it's not what I think. Maybe . . .

Reluctantly, I open the message thread and read. I never thought it could get any worse than a moment ago, but it does. And my world feels like it's going to implode.

The first three messages read:

Sylas: This was never going to work. You're emotionally unavailable. You never let me in.
Sylas: I needed more.
Sylas: It's over. Sorry.

Followed by two missed voice communications and then two more text messages.

Sylas: If you want to catch up for drinks to talk about things, let me know.
Sylas: I'm sorry, Paege. Can we talk?

Another two missed voice communications and four more text messages.

Sylas: Paege? Answer the damn scribe!
Sylas: Stop acting like an immature little halfling and reply to me!
Sylas: This is why it will never work. You're not adult enough to have a conversation about our future.
Sylas: It's over! Don't bother replying.

Three more missed voice communications followed by two more messages.

Sylas: I'm sorry. You just make me so angry, Paege. Please answer the scribe.
Sylas: Fine, be that way. I'm done!

Two more missed voice communications and three final text messages.

Sylas: I'm sorry. I love you. Please reply.
Sylas: You could have been the one.
Sylas: Goodbye.

What the actual fuck? Is he kidding me with this shit? Is he really blaming me for this? I'm emotionally unavailable, so he cheated?

This is how it always goes, though. He hurts me, I get upset, and he finds some way to make me responsible for it. He twists the truth around and around until I end up confused and disoriented, apologising to him for my reactions to his *shitty* behaviour. It's tiresome. And although every part of my being knows I am not overreacting, not to blame, and I should just leave, before too long, I end up right back where I started.

I look back over the messages he sent during the night, and a new wave of anger rushes over me.

He loves me.

I could have been the one.

I'm acting like a childish halfling.

My jaw tenses, and a growl rumbles deep inside for the first time today. My fist closes tighter around the scribe in my hand, my muscles twitching, and before I even realise what I'm doing, my scribe is flying across the room and out my door. Landing in the living area at the feet of my friends, it smashes into hundreds of pieces, just like my heart.

One by one, they all shift their gaze to my shattered scribe on the polished concrete floor and then back up at me.

With tears streaming down my face like an open faucet, I turn my head to the pillows behind me and scream like a banshee—wild and full of fury—into the soft mound, muffling the haunting sounds my body makes as I bellow out my cries. When I remove my face from the pillows, I sit up straight, a dark numbness slinking through my body, and watch Lumeilia and Mhelodie wordlessly bend down and pick up the pieces of my scribe. Asheron's beautiful violet eyes turn dark with rage.

He storms over to me, his iridescent black wings flaring. "That's it, Paege. What did that fucker do now? I'm going to break him. I swear to the Gods I'm going rip his wings off and feed him to the Wolves."

Asheron grabs hold of my arms, and I flinch as the touch of his skin against mine jolts my body awake like a bolt of energy, thinking he is going to shake some sense into me, literally. Instead, his eyes begin to soften, the black receding, and he pulls me in close, enveloping me with his strong masculine arms. I bury my head into Asheron's chest and let the tears flow again. Every ragged breath fills my nose with sandalwood and tobacco, and my heart slows from the calming scent of the friend who always seems to be able to ground me. I stay, buried in his chest, until the tears no longer flow from my burning eyes or my broken heart.

Once my heart beats a rhythm that is more akin to an emotionally stable Being, I pull myself back from Asheron's embrace enough to cock my head and look up at his beautiful porcelain face. His eyes are soft, full of concern and worry. A smile tugs at his lips, and he places a gentle kiss on the top of my head.

In a soft yet harsh tone, he asks, "What the fuck did he say to make you get so angry and upset that you went and broke your scribe?" His eyes quickly dart to the mess at the end of my bed.

I don't answer for a long moment, the fire inside returning like a raging inferno, but I take a few measured breaths, and then on one of the exhales, I blurt out the context of the messages, unable to show him the messages because stupid me threw my scribe in a fit of rage.

Good one, Paege. Always so impulsive.

"He *blamed* you?" Asheron exclaims and jumps up off the bed. "He blamed *you*?" he repeats even louder, pacing the room "And he called you a halfling?"

Pure, white rage washes over his face, his eyes turning black once again, and his wings flare with such force that my curtains blow open. While I hate the thought of my friends being hurt because I hurt, I can't help but feel a little proud that my friend, this beautiful male Fae, is so protective of me, a *halfling*.

Before I register what is going on, Asheron has pulled his scribe out of his pocket, his fingers moving erratically across the keypad, and Lumeilia launches herself at him, snatching the scribe out of his hands.

"Don't you dare, Asheron!" she scorns. "Paege does *not* need us rescuing her. Nor does she need us getting involved and making things worse."

She is right. A message from Asheron would only escalate the situation right now, and I need to de-escalate things.

"Right! What are *we* going to do?" Mhelodie interrupts, throwing her hands into the air. "I mean, I am all for moping around the apartment and trying to dissect the *coward* that is Sylas." She isn't wrong; he is a coward. "But I say, as we've all taken the day off, let's do something crazy with it and try to forget about this sadness for a bit. Because I hate to break it to you, Paege, but this," she waves her hand towards the fragments of my scribe sitting on the end of my bed, "*is* Sylas. It's always been him. You just haven't noticed because you have been so blindly in love with him." Her voice softens. "And that's alright. But now you get to see him how we see him."

"You get to see him for who he truly is," Lumeilia adds.

Mhelodie sits at the edge of my bed next to me, places a hand on my leg, and continues. "I'm so angry he hurt you, we all are. And I am not saying you need to forget about it and move on. But I am saying, let's try and get some happiness back in your life, even if it is only for a night." Mhelodie's mouth slowly creeps upwards, like she is fighting to hold back the smile, and her golden eyes dance with mischief.

"So, what do you say, Paege? Do you want to blow off steam with your besties and go a little wild?" she asks, raising her eyebrows at me, her lips now pulled into a full cheeky grin as her golden eyes playfully dart between the three of us.

My eyes meet the gazes of all my friends. Their grins are larger than they should be considering the circumstances, and something bubbles up inside, popping like a VineMist bottle as I realise the reason for their mischievous expressions. I know exactly what they have in mind.

Chapter 6

Asheron saunters into my apartment, after being gone for a few hours. He casually hands me a basic white box before placing the three bottles of alcohol on my kitchen bench. Two VineBrew—a fermented drink made from grapes—one blood and one dew, and a bottle of DesertFyre—a sweet and spicy spirit made from a succulent plant found in the Aridor Desert. Also, my favourite.

It's going to be a big night.

Inspecting the hand-sized box nervously, I shake it. There are no markings on it to give away what's inside, but it's got some weight behind it.

Asheron sighs loudly. "Don't break it, just open it."

"What? You shake it, you break it?" I chuckle, and Lumeilia bursts out a laugh as Mhelodie clasps around her neck a leather choker adorned with ruby red jewels that match the colour of her tight knee-length dress. She looks gorgeous. But she always does.

It's a stark contradiction to the grungy look I portray.

"Aren't you a little firecracker this afternoon?" Asheron chides in return as he strolls back over to me and plants a gentle kiss on my cheek. "Glad to see the Paege I know and love is back." He winks. Warmth lingers on my cheek from where he planted his soft lips, and something inside my chest flutters. But it always does when Asheron is around. I don't know if it's because he might just be the most attractive male to ever walk the kingdom or if it's the little things he does that make me feel extra special, but my heart and soul secretly crave that sort of attention. Our friendship is undeniably platonic, but he certainly knows how to make a female feel treasured.

"Something like that." My lips tug upward, and I pull open the lid off the box to find a brand-new scribe. Music fills the apartment, and I bring my gaze up from the box. Mhelodie dances across the room from where my music box now spins. Her white and green floral wide-leg jumpsuit swishes around her body as she swings her hips to the sound of the music. Her tight golden-brown curls hang loosely, framing her face in a soft but lively way, bouncing along in rhythm. She always looks so fresh and natural, a true embodiment of Terra—the Goddess of the Earth—herself.

My eyes settle on Asheron while he pours four glasses of VineDew and then four DesertFyre shooters. He wears his typical outfit of black pants and black shirt, never fully buttoned to the collar, and his silver hair curtains his porcelain face. He lifts his violet eyes from the drinks and they land on me. I mouth *thank you* to him across the room. He lifts the shot glass filled with the golden liquid and mouths *you're welcome*, and he knocks it back before sliding the other glasses across the bench.

"You can all get your own drinks after this. I'm not your server," he jokes, and Mhelodie barks a laugh as she hugs Lumeilia and grabs two shot glasses, one for each of them.

"Hm, keep telling yourself that," I call out in jest over my shoulder as I take my new scribe to my room and install the information card that I rescued from my broken one.

In the Territories, the Fae and Witches still live by the old ways, using traditional magic as their source of power. The Neopolis, though, is progressive. The magic buried in the land not only provides power for lights and appliances, it's also used to create a technological network that sends and stores information between people and places. Access to this technology and culture is not only utilised here, it's worshipped. Technology mixed with magic has taken the Neopolis to a whole different level, progressing quickly.

When I re-enter the living room, the three of them are standing around the kitchen bench, laughing and having another glass of DesertFyre. Pausing for a moment, I bring my hand up to my chest to grasp the pendant that hangs around my neck, and my heart swells with a radiant warmth as I cherish the view of my wonderful friends. I certainly lucked out with them. When I came to the Neopolis for collegium, I was alone and scared, but a hopefulness born of innocence lived deep within my heart, carrying a quiet belief that the Neopolis was where I would find my place in this world.

And what better way for me to learn more about the other half of me, my Human half, than at the collegium that houses the largest library in the kingdom—apart from the Neopolis History Museum and Archives? All those books. All that information. All that history. All that lore. There wasn't any other option, in my opinion, much to the dismay of my parents.

My first day on campus was overwhelming. I hadn't prepared myself for the onslaught of emotions I would feel. I had not considered for one moment that most of the campus students would not be able to shield themselves. I'm sure my parents had mentioned it a time or two before, but as bull-headed as I can be at times, I probably dismissed them as being overprotective or paranoid.

The students on campus wreaked emotional havoc on my senses the first day. My body and mind felt abused and raw, and I needed a reprieve. To find a haven. I was too weak to make it home. I found the closest empty bar, ordered a drink, and gave myself time and distance to manage and heal the emotional and psychological distress of the day.

That's when I met them. It's where our friendship started.

And that is where we are headed today.

To Slynx.

To take Psyloxin.

To forget about Sylas.

"Paege?" The sound of my name pulls me from my memories. "Are you just going to stand there like a creep watching us all afternoon, or are you going to come and join us?" Lumeilia teases.

I cross the room, join my friends, and shoot back the Desert-Fyre waiting for me.

"I still don't know what my Fae gifts are going to appear as, but I'm not worried," Lumeilia says to Asheron, who is running a palm across the silver star on his forearm. "We need to get through Mhelodie's Ascension first, then I can focus on me," she finishes.

Mhelodie smiles, placing her drained glass on the dining table before getting up to grab the DesertFyre bottle. She refills our glasses, and I can't help but smile at the empty fogginess that rolls through my mind. My own gifts are smothered by the alcohol I've consumed this afternoon, and I've never felt more free.

Asheron pulls down the black sleeve over his forearm, covering his mark. "It's going to be glamour. Look at your art," he replies casually.

The Fae gifts are all diluted magic descended from the Lesser Gods, yet some Fae are gifted more powerful magic than others. Only the Star-Borne are gifted a pure, elemental magic. No one understands how it's decided, it just *is* during the Unification. However, it's usually connected to some other gift or skill the Fae possesses, and Lumeilia is a particularly skilled artist.

The four of us slam back another DesertFyre shot, and the sudden realisation that we will be heading off to Slynx soon has a surge of panic rippling over me.

Palms melting from the heat that burst to life under my skin, I turn to Lumeilia for help or some sort of reassurance. "Lumeilia? I don't know if I can do this," I whisper to her, trying not to draw attention to myself as Asheron and Mhelodie continue to discuss all things Unification and Ascension. "How about we stay in, drink VineBrew, and chat all night instead?"

She doesn't respond. She just blinks at me as if trying to understand my unexpected surge of anxiety about heading out.

"I mean . . . what if we bump into Sylas?" I add in a whisper.

Her mahogany eyes widen with realisation "Paege, come with me a moment." She grabs me by the arm and drags me off toward my bedroom.

Lumeilia swings open the bedroom door, sits on my extra-large bed, and pats the navy blanket, gesturing for me to sit next to her. I do so hesitantly, suddenly disappointed by the amount of alcohol I've consumed as I try to read her emotions, unsure of what she is going to say. Nothing but a blissful purple haze.

"If you truly don't want to go out, we don't have to. I'll support you. I always will. But you can't let Sylas control your life. If you never leave the apartment again for fear of bumping into him, he wins."

Nodding, I agree with her. I understand what she is saying. She has seen me go through this a few times with Sylas now. And it's never been pretty. It's always been messy. But it's different now. I know for certain this is the last time. So, I won't let it destroy me, no matter how much I want to allow it to.

Lumeilia leans over and wraps her arm around me, pulling me in close to her. Her soft scent of cherry calms the racing traitor in my chest.

The door opens gently, and Mhelodie peeks her head around the door. "Lu-Lu, is everything alright in here?"

"Yes, it's fine. Paege was having a Sylas crisis, but we are alright, aren't we?" She tucks her strawberry waves behind her Fae ears, and looks at me with the most caring and concerned eyes ever, the mahogany in them warming me with their kindness. She wants nothing but the best for me. She is always so patient, and sometimes, I wonder why she even puts up with me. I'm a hot mess most of the time. Certainly not an easy friend by any means.

I nod. "Yes, I'm fine. Just a bit anxious."

"Well, I can fix that," Mhelodie says with a cheeky grin. "How about a little sneaky-sneaky before we head off? Sh, don't tell Asheron!" She laughs while closing the door behind her.

Mhelodie pulls out three little perfectly round pills of Psyloxin from her purse and hands us one each. In complete synchronicity, we all place the pills in our mouths and swallow, chasing them down with VineBlood.

The door bursts open, and Asheron stands there with a devious grin on his face. "Oi, what's this? The secret sisters club?" he yells, then sticks his tongue out. Sitting there in the centre of his tongue is a little red pill.

He swallows and winks before laughing the most mischievous laugh I have ever heard, and we all join in.

Oh, Gods, it's going to be a messy one.

CHAPTER 7

My skin hums from the Psyloxin's effects as we reach Slynx. The line to get in is non-existent, and I feel like we are early to the party. But it is midafternoon, so I am not too sure what I was expecting.

Looking at my friends, we all sheepishly grin at each other, knowing full well how silly it is feeling this high on a Friday afternoon, but also, part of me thinks, fuck it. You only live once, and I sure as Hels deserve to let off some steam. The good thing about this place is that no matter the day or time, the music is always good. Today is no different.

Once in, we dance our way across the floor to the secluded velvet booths that line the wall in various regal shades of green, blue, and red. We take residence in our usual red booth. I place my hand in the centre of the wooden table. Closing my eyes, I think back to when we first met, and I trace my fingers idly over the roughly carved initials.

LF, AM, MR, PV.

Regardless of my state of mind, that day still shines clearly in my mind. I remember how the illuminated sign behind the bar buzzed the word Slynx in a deep red colour that mirrored the hue of the velvet booth that moulded itself to my body as I finished my second DesertFyre shot.

Slamming my empty glass down, I closed my eyes and drew in a long breath. The offensive stench of piss and stale ale mixed with the DesertFyre and the emotional remnants of today had my stomach churning. Maybe one more DesertFyre shot? Unexpectedly, a floral sweetness in the air replaced the rancid odour. I opened my eyes to find a beautiful strawberry-blonde Fae with the darkest brown eyes I had ever seen seated across from me.

She smiled widely. "You must be the infamous demi-Fae everyone keeps talking about? Paegence is it?"

Disappointment sat heavy in my gut as I forced a smile in return. "Everyone calls me Paege," I replied, wishing everyone would just leave me alone.

"Paege, alright. Well, I'm Lumeilia Faulksing." She lifted a hand and pointed to her right. "And this is Mhelodie Ravenswood and Asheron Millenford."

My gaze followed the direction of her pointed finger and noticed two more Beings standing beside Lumeilia. One was a darker-skinned, petite Witch with tight, long golden-brown locks and golden cat-like eyes to match—she radiated warmth and sunshine. The other was the most attractive male Fae to have walked this kingdom, and looking at him made my cheeks flush with a warmth I immediately regretted.

Mhelodie reached out a hand and introduced herself in true Witch style: friendly and bubbly. "Hi. You sure are pretty. I bet you had all the males falling over you back in your village."

Ha, I wished.

I took her hand in mine, and a warm and welcoming feeling rippled over me. Her power was strong, and she was kind.

The male with shoulder length silver hair and bright violet eyes nodded at me and said casually, "Hi, I'm Asheron." He leaned into Mhelodie and whispered something into her ear.

I rolled my eyes and braced myself for the surge of emotions to batter me once again, but the battering didn't come. All I received was a light and airy freshness that continued to gently curl itself around my heart while Asheron and Mhelodie scooted into the booth next to Lumeilia. And it was oddly comforting.

A minute of silence shrouded the group as I watched the three Beings seated across from me. All smiling widely, staring back at me with an equal curiosity. Mhelodie was the first to move, reaching into the pocket of her winter jacket and pulling out a silver tin. She pried it open and poured out some of the contents right onto the old sticky wood table between us. Bright red powder, which I knew of as Psyloxin—a legal but heavily controlled drug made by the Witches that could only be bought and sold in Medela Circle—was heaped in a pile on the table.

Asheron laughed wickedly. "Alright then." Amusement at his friend's bold actions cut through the edges of his jovial words. "Who wants to party?"

One by one, we all licked our fingers, scooped up some of the red powder, and rubbed it in our mouths and along our gums, and before I knew it, Lumeilia, Asheron, Mhelodie, and I were dancing and laughing and talking and drinking right up until the sun rose the next day.

I can't believe how lucky I am that they chose me. *Me.* My lips stretch, and I lift my gaze to find three sets of eyes all fixated on me.

"What?" I query as if they don't know exactly what I'm thinking about.

"Who wants to party?" Asheron shouts, and we all laugh.

We are one of a few small groups of Beings here. There is one red-haired female by the bar, two males sitting with two females over by the music master's booth in the far back right corner, and a group of five Sirens standing by a tall table by the back door. You can tell they are Sirens because of the distinct brandings on their wrists that bind their powers of compulsion and persuasion. It's illegal to possess such powers. Sirens get their compulsion powers bound by the Elder Witches as soon as they manifest. If ever caught using compulsion, it's punishable by death. It seems harsh, but the damage one could do if they could compel the entire kingdom to do whatever they wanted, whenever they wanted, without consequence is unimaginable. We have enough of that with the Wolves. Murder, corruption, control.

Scary.

The music master seamlessly transitions to a dark and heavy bass tune, and my skin seems to purr in response as warmth radiates from my body. I lean back, relaxing into the booth, and gently close my eyes, listening to the music. My head and body fight a raging war over whether to get up and dance or melt into the booth. Unsure of how the battle is won, I snap open my eyes. I look at the two girls in front of me, and without having to say a word, we all nod and stand in complete synchronicity. Like a perfectly timed choreography, we move—no, we float—to the dancefloor.

"I love you all!" Lumeilia yells above the music with a big smile on her face.

"I love you, too!" I yell, lips parted, exposing a toothy grin.

Mhelodie blows us both a kiss.

Surrendering myself to the music's rhythmical ebbs and flows, I close my eyes. Hidden secrets of the harmonies fill my heart and soul, freeing me from all my inhibitions. Although the Psyloxin has numbed my empathy gift, I become an unbound creature of pure emotion. And it's euphoric.

Time passes in windows of songs and broken beats, leaving me unsure of how long I've been dancing. Tiny beads of sweat grace my brow, and long, wet strands of brown hair stick to my face, reminding me that I'm in dire need of some fluid. As I refocus my attention from the blissful state, I manoeuvre myself around the bodies writhing on the dance floor to get to Asheron, who is sitting at our booth with a table full of drinks, watching us.

"Where did you go earlier?" I ask Asheron, shoulder-bumping him as I slide into the booth next to him. With every heave of my chest, as I draw in stale, sweaty air, further drying my mouth.

"Have a drink," he says and slides a clear drink in front of me. "You must be thirsty after all that sexy dancing," he adds in a teasing tone.

"Knock it off, Asheron." I laugh and roll my eyes at his attempt to be smooth.

I take a sip of the icy drink, discovering it to be CrystalFyre, a smooth, clear spirit that burns as it travels down my throat. I shudder as it settles into my belly, the trail of warmth a stark contrast against the coolness of the liquid. I glance back over to the girls who now dance even closer than before, hands entwined, smiling and laughing.

"They are so lucky they found each other."

"Lucky?" Asheron responds. "How do you figure? You know Fae and Witches can't bond."

"I know, but Lumeilia doesn't have to accept her FaeMate bond if she ever finds her FaeMate. You, of all people, know that better than anyone else. And it's not like they can procreate, so there's no chance of any crossbreeding happening there," I finish sarcastically.

Cross-species relationships are frowned upon for the most part for fear of any cross-species breeding—which is strictly prohibited by the Crown. Forbidden by the King. It's an attempt to ensure bloodlines don't mix and power isn't shared among the species. It's an effort to keep the Wolves as the most powerful Beings while ensuring the rest of us remain as powerless as possible.

The only exception to this ludicrous rule is the Fae and Star-Borne—and me, the *halfling*. But as a demi-Fae with a Human father, I'd say there is little to no chance my power would exceed anyone. So, I'm guessing that is why I was allowed to survive.

The whole thing is absurd. As far as we all know, there hasn't been a recorded case of any cross-species breeding in the history of our kingdom, except for me. Regardless, in situations like Mhelodie's and Lumeilia's, the Crown looks the other way. And I'm certain it's for no other reason than the fact they can never procreate.

Asheron nods, and he closes his eyes for a long moment. When he opens them again, even in the darkness of the bar, I can see the black emerging in them like shadows stealing the light, and I know when I mentioned the FaeMate bond that I hit a nerve.

"Have you spoken to her recently?" I ask, taking another sip of my CrystalFyre.

"No, she won't answer my messages."

"Give it time, Asheron. She will come around. I'm sure."

"It's nearly been twelve months, Paege," he answers, swallowing down a mouthful of his drink and placing it heavily on the table. His hand wraps tightly around the glass, and his knuckles whiten. "I don't think I can salvage it. I don't deserve . . ." My hand reaches for his, and I lever his grip from his glass. I can't imagine what it must be like for Asheron or Remi, his FaeMate. None of us could believe it when he rejected their FaeMate bond. He refuses to discuss why—with any of us. We can only guess it has something to do with his lineage. But the day he rejected it, Remi disappeared, and none of us have heard from her since.

"Why?" I begin to probe, hoping the Psyloxin or alcohol has lowered his inhibitions just enough to possibly open up.

"What about you? Are you doing alright, Paege? I'm worried about you," he interrupts, shutting me down.

Got it. Still not ready to talk about it.

I smile. "You don't need to be worried about me. I'm great . . . I'm out, high with my three best friends." I shake his hand that's still held in mine.

Asheron slides his hand out from mine and tucks his silver hair behind his ear. He forces a grin, one that doesn't reach his eyes. While the girls continue to dance, we end up talking for hours, even though it feels like minutes. Psyloxin does that. Time-thieving party drug it is. The bar has slowly been filling up, and the makeshift dance floor is littered with heaving and writhing bodies as another powerful song booms across the room.

"Come on, let's go dance." I gulp back what's left of my drink, grab Asheron's arm, and he doesn't hesitate to follow me to the dance floor.

We find Lumeilia and Mhelodie in the middle of the dancefloor, and we all start moving as a group. The music is all kinds of dirty. It's dark and sexy. My hips sway, and I bring my arms up above my head, twisting and curling, folding and shaping myself to the beat of the music. Every crescendo cradles a promise of transcendence, whisking me away to another reality and getting me completely lost in the moment.

Asheron motions for me to come closer to him, and I do without hesitation. He brings his hand to my mouth and brushes a finger over my dry lips. His touch sends electricity racing through my body. I can feel his touch everywhere. My skin tingles, and my lips part ever so slightly . . . And he pops a little red pill inside.

Oh, Gods, here we go again.

Then we dance. Our bodies sweat, moving in rhythm, in sync with each other. Energy shifting, the true bond of friendship echoes between us all with every smile, touch, and hug.

CHAPTER 8

Gods know how long we have been here for. My senses from the Psyloxin are on overdrive, reacting to every touch, and the music still sends jolts of unchecked energy racing through my body. I need to sit and take a moment—catch my breath. I leave the group without saying a word and hastily manoeuvre my way back over to our booth. The table has another round of drinks on it. I grab a glass and take a sip. Closing my eyes, I invite the CrystalFyre to awaken my mouth as the icy liquid bites into my throat and travels to my very empty stomach. The assault of the burn causes it to rumble.

A chill suddenly spider-walks up my spine, and my chest tightens as I feel a slight brush of air against my cheek. I snap my eyes open, sitting upright, but no one's there. After a long moment of feeling unsure, I resign myself to the fact I felt a trickle of emotion starting to infiltrate my senses. The Psyloxin must be wearing off. Closing my eyes once more, I prepare myself for the influx of emotions, but oddly, none come. But I can't shake the feeling that someone is watching me.

Feeling too uncomfortable to remain at the booth, I finish a drink and head back to my friends, ready to ask for another hit of Psyloxin. As I approach the group, the next song the music master seamlessly weaves together is one of my favourite songs. A female

Fae with an angelic voice, singing about love and loss, plays over the top of a heavy bass with one of the most euphoric climaxes ever. It's unique, and I've never heard it here before. I've only ever played it for Sylas. Not even my friends have heard it before—that I know of.

I close my eyes and let her voice cascade through me.

Gods, take me now!

Each beat is a pulse reverberating through my body. A rhythmic spell. Her voice is a melodic elixir, and it fills me to the brim, infusing every atom of my being with its rich timbre. As each note flows into the next, a symphony of ecstasy floods my senses, sending my body into a state of pure, unadulterated bliss. The Psyloxin has all but gone now, and what I am feeling is *all me*. This room, the world—everything—falls away, leaving only the hypnotising echo of her lyrics, cradling me in a cocoon of pleasure.

As I continue to move my body in unpredictable ways, a sticky mess of sweet and spicy heat swirls around my core, and my skin pimples in response. I open my eyes and turn my head to look behind me. Asheron dances close to me, his eyes closed, and his body is *almost* touching mine. But with the emotions emanating from him, he may as well be. I can feel his every desire. And he wants to be touching *me* at this moment.

Confusion weaves itself through the recesses of my mind with deceptive tendrils that curl and twist around each uncertain thought.

What is going on?

Every attempt to grasp clarity is like trying to catch smoke—fleeting and elusive.

It's Asheron. He is your friend. You are vulnerable. Do not do it, Paege!

Against all reasoning, in true Paege Vailenbyrg style, I let go of all self-control, my innate impulsive nature rearing its head, and I find myself stepping back and leaning into his body.

He doesn't flinch. He wraps his muscular arms around me, and when our bodies touch, it sends energy pulsing through every molecule of my being. Hot, electric energy. As I sway my body in rhythm with his, a sultry beast awakens within me, its head rising with a primal yearning. Its urges stir with each teasing step. It whispers to the darkness of my soul, a seductive echo of desire, begging me to draw nearer. Wanting, needing to be closer, to take what this beautiful Fae is offering.

I turn to face him, and his hands take mine. Our fingers entwine as he steps toward me, closing the gap. I peel open my heavy lids and collide with dark violet eyes full of . . .

Confusion.

That sweet scent turns dark and thick. It turns bitter. I can feel it brewing in the pit of my stomach as it knots and twists, thrashing to escape. Heat builds inside, and my stomach growls as it erupts like a volcano, scalding my body in a flash, and it instantly snaps me out of my trance.

Anger.

Rage.

Jealousy.

I rip myself away from Asheron, violently pulling my hands out from his as I curl my fingers into my palm, lengthening the bones in my arms straight down my side.

"Paege?" Asheron calls over the music as he tries to take my hands back, but I withdraw them further, the rage still burning deep inside me. "Are you alright?"

"What was that?" I snap, unsure of what is happening around me.

"What do you mean? We were just dancing." Asheron runs his hand through his hair, tucking it behind his ears, and his brows furrow. His eyes roll back for a moment, and he licks his lips before shrugging and closing his eyes again. Clearly, he's still full of Psyloxin. He must have taken another one, the cheeky ass.

Trying to find the source of these intense and conflicting emotions, I pivot, frantically scanning the bodies nearby. Was the lust that fuelled my stupid and embarrassing decision even from Asheron? The rush of anger certainly didn't come from him, so who? I can't tell. There's . . . well, there is nothing.

Guy walks across the dance floor, and my gaze locks on him as he passes me, tracking his movements. He either doesn't see me, or he pretends not to, as he shows no signs of recognition. He stops as he reaches Quentin, who stands with two female Wolves. Two different Wolves from last night. Gods, they do get around.

I can't help but watch them for a minute, talking and laughing. Then all four of them, in complete synchronicity, turn their heads to face me as if they heard every unsettling thought scrolling through my mind, and something inside me startles. I want to pull my eyes off them, to turn away, but I can't. I seem to be entranced by Quentin's stare. A wolfish grin crosses his face, and he holds up his glass before gulping it back. Guy casually cocks his head back to Quentin and says something, prompting Quentin to wrap his arm around the shoulder of the blonde and take off, heading for the exit.

I suck in air and swallow hard, trying to push down the remaining remnants of anger, or possibly fear, which coils around my chest, tightening with every moment that passes. But still, something doesn't feel right. Something doesn't add up, and the blood in my veins chills.

I felt the burning desire. I felt the need. The hunger. And then I felt that rage.

Without consulting my friends, I leave the dance floor and head toward the booth. Asheron has already turned to some other Fae and resumed dancing like nothing happened. Lumeilia and Mhelodie are still too enamoured with each other to notice anything going on around them, which is fine. They deserve this.

But I need to go.

As I'm about to exit Slynx, Lumeilia unexpectedly catches up with me, stopping me in my tracks. "Are you alright?"

"No, I'm not. Not really. Something isn't . . . ah . . ." I trail off before I finish my sentence because I'm so confused, and everything feels so muddled in my head. I take one deep breath and start again. "Something isn't right. I need to get out of here."

"Let me get the others, and we can go." Lumeilia begins to head back to get the others, but I stop her. I don't want anyone with me right now. I'm coming down off the Psyloxin, and my empathy gift seems to be on overdrive. I need to be alone.

As she walks away, I grab her by the hand, spinning her back towards me. She does a cute, little dancing step, and a laugh bubbles out of my mouth unexpectedly.

"Please don't. I am alright, honestly," I lie.

Lumeilia cocks her head to the side, lips pulling thin, and puts her free hand on her hip. She isn't believing a word I'm saying.

"I mean, it's been a long couple of days, and I just want to go home—alone—and try to get some sleep." Silver tendrils radiate from Lumeilia, her concern trying to envelop me in its comfort. I need to reassure her. "Honestly, stay. I'm fine. I promise." I smile and place my hand on my heart in a pledge-like manner. It's how my Mum and I make promises to each other. It started when I was younger when she would tell me things would get better in life because it was hard for me sometimes growing up, being a demi-Fae. A half-breed.

Mum would say, "Things will get better, I promise," and put her hand to her heart. But then, as I got older, we started doing it for other things, silly things like, "I won't try to sneak the horses into the house again, I promise," or "I will clean my room, I promise." And now, it's a habit that I do whenever I promise anything to anyone. I place my hand on my heart in true Vailenbyrg style.

"The Psyloxin is messing with my gifts. That's all, I swear," I finish, hoping she believes me and lets me go.

"Are you sure? I don't want to stay and be the shitty best friend who let you go off into the night alone. Plus, the streets . . ." she trailed off.

There is no way I would ever think that of her. She is the best friend anyone could ever ask for, and I will not let her feel guilty for something she hasn't even done. For something that I want. And Gods, do I want to go home.

I smile. "You could never be the shitty friend."

We hug, and I can feel she is still apprehensive about letting me go, but I also know she won't fight me because that is the type of friend she is. One who trusts me and takes me at my word. "Tell the others I left? I'll message you when I get home."

She nods. "I love you, Paege. Be safe."

"I love you, too," I reply.

And I truly mean it.

Chapter 9

Confusion drifts aimlessly through my mind as I wander the streets home, shrouding my awareness like phantom shadows in the recesses of my consciousness.

What was that? Who was that?

My gift certainly seems to be getting stronger as I approach my birthday. But it also somehow seems to be more unpredictable, more out of control. Or maybe I'm the one who is out of control. I haven't exactly been the most emotionally stable Being of late. I bite at my bottom lip, hoping my Unification will offer more control over this damn gift than I do now. An unease settles heavily in my stomach like a sinking rock, and that pressure building inside doesn't relent.

The cobblestone streets of Lockswick are eerily quiet, save the few party stragglers further up the block. Tall stone buildings adorned with pointed arches and intricate tracery tower high above, piercing the dark moonless sky. Their spires and steeples contribute to a skyline that feels both awe-inspiring and slightly foreboding. It's an intriguing blend of old-world architecture, inspired by basilicas and historic structures of ancient Elyndria, combined with the brisk pace of rapidly evolving technology.

A phantom laughter echoes down an unoccupied alley, and the ruckus of metal clanging and rolling fills the unnerving emptiness, and my heart jolts.

We've all heard the news. We know there have been random Witch killings, and many others have gone missing these past few months. The speculation is it's all been Wolf gang related. Every one of them seem to be someone of importance. But no one knows what's going on, and I suspect this is why the streets are quieter than usual.

Almost home, I sigh to myself as I cross over the border from Lockswick into Forte Darthic, the popular living quarter of the Neopolis. The chilly bite of the iced cream I just bought feels so nice against my humming skin as I cradle the container in my arms.

I've been walking for a while, and I can't wait to take these Godsdamn heels off and sit and eat my peanut butter iced cream in peace. I can't believe I let Lumeilia talk me into wearing such inappropriate shoes. I wanted to wear my signature boots, but *no*, tonight was about me *shedding my old skin—Sylas—and showing off my new.* Which also meant wearing clothes I don't feel completely comfortable in. She wouldn't let it go until I took a pair of crimson red heels out of my wardrobe, which I own purely for special occasions, and put them on. The ache in the ball of my feet now has me truly regretting ever listening to her. At least she let the leather pants and crop top go.

A blanket of comfort envelopes me as I relish in the stillness of the Forte. There's a distinct quiet in my body and mind. It's like the world around me doesn't exist here. I welcome the relief that thought brings.

The Forte is a mix between apartments, townhouses, and warehouse living. The closer to Lockswick, the grander. The high-rise apartments are enthralling. They stand at least twenty stories, and the stone facades are decorated with gargoyles, statues, and intricate carvings. Each apartment boasts a large open balcony that spans the entire side of the building. Owning, or even renting, an apartment in one of these prestigious buildings requires considerable wealth. Some of these are worth hundreds of sparks. A level of affluence I'll never achieve in my lifetime.

In Midtown, classic stone townhouses dominate the landscape. Their large bay windows and iron-fenced stoops portray the historical significance of the Neopolis, a stark contrast to the newer, more modern buildings scattered throughout Lockswick. Further out, the vibe shifts to a more edgy and affordable part of the Forte, offering options that appeal to a broader demographic.

I live on this side of the Forte, the poorer side. Though to be fair, none of it is really poor. It's just not as opulent.

A shuffling of feet behind me has the hair on my neck standing, and my adrenaline skyrockets. I glance around to scan my surroundings, hoping to see a trash can rat or alley cat, but instead, I find Guy and Quentin walking directly toward me, and my heart tumbles deep into the pit of my stomach.

Fuck. My. Life. Not again.

"Hi, Books!" Quentin calls out, wearing a grin so wide his pearly white canines glisten. He's dressed casually—dark, tight pants, an unbuttoned white shirt, and a black jacket to match—but everything about him still exudes that Heir Apparent allure. "Wait up." They both do a little shuffle run to catch up to where I stand.

"Hi," I reply, trying to sound polite but refusing them any real attention, as I pivot back and continue to walk in the direction of my home. I *really* don't have the patience for these two.

"Hi, Paege," Guy says as he catches up to me, also grinning. Although, his smile doesn't feel so conniving. "Are you heading home?" he asks. He is dressed a lot more casually than Quentin. In fact, Guy's attire blends right in with us *normal* folk. Denim pants, black boots, and a casual knitted top. There's also something odd about him. Odd, yet familiar. I can't quite put my finger on it.

"Twice in two nights. This must be my lucky week." I retort, sarcasm lacing every word.

"I was *just* thinking the same," Quentin replies, still with that annoyingly smug grin on his face.

"Where are your girlfriends?" I ask for reasons that escape me entirely. Like, I really care where they are? I am aware those Wolves tonight, or last night, are not their girlfriends but probably some random girls they picked up.

"They went on to meet some other friends. Also, not our girlfriends," Guy responds as he huffs out a little chuckle in amusement.

"Hm, why didn't you go with them?"

"We were on our way with some others when we saw you walking alone, so we told them to go on ahead without us," Guy replies.

"Jealous?" Quentin chides, and blood rushes my head.

I snort. "Ha. Don't flatter yourself."

Quentin shrugs, still grinning like a scheming viper, and I want to slap the damn smile off his face.

"We'll catch up with them later," Guy says. "Are you alright?" he asks, shoulder bumping me, a complete repeat of last night, and a fire ignites in my gut.

"I don't need an escort home," I snap, stilling in the street as a familiar feeling of frustration creeps across my body.

"I know, but some company is better than none." Guy slides his foot across the cobblestone street in front of him, lips gently tugging upward, revealing one single dimple.

"We told you it wasn't safe on the streets at night," Quentin intercepts a little abruptly.

"No, you told me it wasn't safe on the streets in Blaxheild, and we are nowhere near Blaxheild. We're only a few blocks from where you left me last night."

Guy grins. "Fine. I'll give you that. But it's becoming less and less safe out on the streets at night, Paege. You shouldn't be walking alone. Especially at this time of night." He looks around. "Allow us to walk you home, and then we'll leave you to enjoy the rest of your evening with your iced cream."

"Where are your friends anyway?" Quentin looks around, searching for them as if they are hiding behind a trash can or something and will appear any moment.

"Not here," I snide.

He hums and nods. "Well, I'm sure you've heard about the attacks around town." Quentin moves fast, circling me, and I realise it isn't so much a question as it is a statement.

I nod anyway and pivot, following his movements, my chest tightening with every slow, measured step he takes.

"Well, the King," he pauses and winks, he actually winks, "asked us to keep an eye on things, you know, while we're out and about, just to make sure things stay . . . *safe.*" He has such arrogance in his voice, and it grates me. He stops and brushes the hair falling across his brow away and then inspects his nails casually. "So, that's all we're doing—just trying to keep you safe."

Whatever fear that was building up inside quickly turns into pure white rage.

"You mean your *dad,* who hates Fae."

A sound grumbles from Quentin's chest as a canine flashes, and not in the cheeky kind of way.

My hand swings up and covers my mouth.

What the fuck Paege. You can't speak like that to the fucking Heir Apparent.

"I'm sorry," I mumble through my hand, and my eyes drop to the ground.

"No, no, by all means, tell us how you really feel," Quentin mocks sardonically. That annoying fucking grin resurfaces, and this time, it's laced with an entertaining arrogance that would even have Edom, the God of Blood, proud of his legacies.

I shake my head.

At the Neopolis Collegium, no one treated Quentin with any true royal formality. I've never seen any of the Wolves address the Heir Apparent in any other way than casually. But still, I don't think I, a demi-Fae, should be testing any theories on how to address or talk about the royals.

Guy puts a hand on Quentin's shoulder. "Be nice, Q."

"Sorry, I just meant . . ." I start.

"It's fine, Paege," Guy interrupts me. "He is just being a royal ass."

"I'm sorry, and thank you for the offer, but *no*, I don't need *you two* keeping me safe. I'm perfectly capable of walking home by myself and keeping myself safe. Thank you." I nod to Guy and turn on my heel to walk away, but Quentin laughs and leaps in front of me again, blocking my way.

"You don't know what you're talking about, Books. He doesn't hate Fae. He's trying to keep Fae safe. All Beings safe." Quentin shakes his head and brushes his sandy blond hair out of his eyes *again*. His hypnotic, piercing grey-blue eyes glisten in the moonlight. "But hey, if you don't want our help, then who am I to stop you?" He holds up his hands in mock surrender as he turns and strides off up the road in the direction of my apartment.

"Isn't that what I *just* said," I yell after Quentin, who pretends to ignore me as he paces up ahead.

Gods, he is so arrogant.

"Sorry. Don't listen to Q, Paege. He's in a bad mood because his night was cut short. He'll get over it when he gets back to the den."

A huff escapes my lips. "He's free to go whenever," I mumble under my breath.

Guy clears his throat at my little retort.

I meet Guy's emerald eyes, and something tugs in my chest. I can't help but think how conflicted he looks. He wears all the typical traits of a tough, brooding Wolf; however, if possible, he also looks a little softer than most. There is something so very different about him. His emits a sense of calmness, one that drills into my very soul, and it feels *weightless*. It's not usually attributed to any normal Wolf-like behaviour. Although I don't feel any emotions pouring from him, I know exactly what he is feeling. His angst and sadness is right there at the surface, exposed for all to see. How did I ever miss it before?

And he also has a grace about him. A grace that Quentin Ishaan certainly does not have.

Guy's father was, however, the original King of Elyndria, so I don't know why that surprises me.

"Speaking of, you looked like you were having fun tonight?" Guy interjects my thoughts. Shit, I've been staring at him like a creeper. "Feeling better after yesterday, then?"

My heart sinks to my stomach, and I force a smile. I have managed to keep thoughts of Sylas locked away, out of reach for the past few hours, but that simple question has a familiar sting biting at my eyes. I turn away, trying to ignore the pain unfurling in my chest, and walk toward Quentin, who is now leaning casually back against the wall of a building a few hundred lengths up ahead, waiting for us to catch up.

"Sorry, I don't mean to be nosy." Guy follows, falling into step beside me.

"It's fine," I say, dismissing the knot twisting tighter inside. "I *was* having a great night until—" Wait, what am I thinking? Talking to Wolves like this? "Never mind." I shake my head. "You wouldn't understand. You know, being a . . ."

"Wolf?" Guy finishes for me.

I don't respond. Is it rude to think that because he is another species, he wouldn't understand? Is it any different to how others treat me for being different? I sigh, but before I can conclude my internal debate, Guy continues, seemingly unphased by the notion Wolves are different; therefore, they wouldn't understand.

"You *can* talk to us, Paege," Guy urges. "We won't bite. I promise." He holds his hand up to his heart, and I smile at the familiar gesture.

"Speak for yourself, *Braxtion*." Quentin laughs flippantly.

"Don't pay any attention to him," Guy says sarcastically, shaking his head from side to side. Then, more softly, he continues, "I may be a *Wolf*, but I'm a pretty good listener."

He pauses, waiting for a reply, but I'm still hesitant. The silence between us thickens like a fog of unease with every passing moment. However, it's certainly less awkward than last night. "Plus, I'm guessing we have a few blocks to walk, and I'd rather not have a repeat of last night. That silence was deafening," Guy chortles, and I can't help but wonder if he can read my mind.

My chest collapses, allowing the tension I was carrying to slowly float away. Why do I feel so relaxed around him?

Maybe I can trust him.

And just like that, as we walk through the streets of the Forte, I tell him about the last couple of days: the Seer, Sylas, and my chaotic empathy gift.

"When's your Sacred Birthday?" Guy asks.

"Winter's middle." Guy nods and digs his hands deep into his pockets.

"Mine too," he replies, his face going white as a ghost. I think I understand why. If a Wolf hasn't merged by the age of twenty-five, they are forced to during an Emergence ceremony, which includes taking a life. I'm guessing Guy hasn't merged yet.

Quentin snorts again. He's kept a casual few lengths ahead of us the entire walk, eavesdropping on our conversation and dropping little huffs, snorts and sighs along the way.

"How much further, Books?" Quentin asks, still ahead of us. He refuses to turn back to look at me, and it triggers a chain of irrational thoughts.

Books? Could he not come up with something a little more original? Does he think so little of me that he won't even look at me when he talks to me? Glad he finds amusement in my life drama.

But still, I can't help but feel a little giddy at the idea that Quentin Ishaan, son of King Ruhaul Ishaan, has a nickname for me. So childish, I know.

Checking myself, I inhale slowly. "Not much, I'm just a few gates up." I nod toward the large complex ahead. "You don't need to walk any further with me."

Quentin finally turns to face me. "It's not a problem, Books." He smirks as if he knows exactly how irritating that nickname is to me, then turns back on his heel and continues walking toward my building.

"It's fine, Paege." Guy shakes his head. "We'll walk you to your gate and then head off. I promise." Guy smiles, and he places his hand on his heart again. The familiar gesture pulls at something inside.

When we reach the brick archway with large iron gates to the complex, I punch my code into the keypad, and the gate unlocks, swinging open automatically. I turn back to the Wolves, both idly standing, watching me as I slide the red high heels off my throbbing feet. Losing my balance, I clutch the brickwork, almost losing my iced cream. Quentin smirks. Neither reach out to help.

Hands full of shoes and half-melted iced cream, I smile awkwardly at the two Wolves, then pivot and head under the brick archway and through the open gate toward my apartment.

"At the very least, you could have said goodnight, Paege," Quentin yells as I cross the garden.

"Goodnight, Paege!" I yell back, waving my hand with my shoes in the air, and I hear the iron gate click shut behind me.

Chapter 10

The raven mural under the breakfast bar that my friends and I painted one night high on Psyloxin usually makes me smile the second I enter my apartment, but not tonight. Something is not right.

As I step through my front door, I sweep my eyes across my room. I don't see anything out of the ordinary. But I can feel it. I can feel eyes watching me like a hawk, and the weight of their presence presses against my chest, filling me with a sense of unease. Something thick and heavy rolls through me, and my stomach tightens.

Someone's in my apartment.

My hands splay, my iced cream and shoes fall to the cold, hard concrete flooring with a smack, and I pivot and run out the front door back through the gardens. My hands shake as I fumble to open the gate. Relief washes over me as I fall out onto the street where I left Guy and Quentin, and I let out a long breath. They haven't got far.

Thank the Gods.

"Guy?" I call out.

My voice must emit the fear that's rushing through my veins because, without any hesitation, both Guy and Quentin turnaround and run toward me as fast as I've ever seen a Wolf run.

"What is it, Paege?" Guy asks as soon as he reaches me.

Quentin doesn't stop running, bolting straight past us into the complex. Unable to speak, I point a shaking hand toward my apartment. Guy moves before I even have a chance to blink. I follow them both.

Both the Wolves are inside when I get back to my apartment. Quentin's eyes are wide, and his face is taut and intense as he scans the room. Guy tries to open the glass bifold doors at the back of the living space, but they don't budge. He rattles the lock. It's secure.

Quentin lifts his head into the air and sniffs.

I had heard Wolves have a strong sense of smell, and they can track scents. Very helpful, but it's super weird and a little creepy to watch. Guy and Quentin exchange a look, and they both nod at each other like they are having some sort of telepathic conversation.

This whole situation feels unreal.

"You had a visitor tonight," Quentin says, and the blood in my veins turns to ice. Quentin looks over to me. I still stand outside my door while fear coils around me, preventing me from stepping into a place that should be a haven. "You can come in, they're gone," he reassures me.

My teeth clench. "Are you sure?" I ask as I hesitantly step through the threshold into my apartment, stilling before I venture further in. "It felt like someone was in here when I opened the door. I could feel their emotions."

Guy turns to me and says, "You said earlier that your gift is acting up." This is true, it is. But I can't feel emotions if there is no one around to feel them from.

"My gift doesn't work like that. If I felt them, they were here." Meaning there was someone here when I walked into my apartment. They only just left.

My chest tightens as I try to suck in air.

Breathe.

Guy nods as if he understands what I am saying. "Well, whoever or *whatever* was here, they are gone now."

"Anything missing?" Quentin asks.

"I, uh, I don't know," I say. And I honestly don't know. I ran out to get help as soon as I opened the door.

"You should have a look around." Quentin suggests.

"We can stay for a bit if you want. You know, until you feel a bit safer," Guy adds as he makes his way to my grey velvet couch and sits down, making himself a little too comfortable for my liking.

"Or calmer," Quentin adds. He strolls toward me, and without taking his mesmerising grey-blue eyes off mine, he bends down, allowing his sandy blond hair to fall over his face. He picks up the sad-looking tub of iced cream I dropped that also miraculously didn't spill anywhere, and his lips pull up into a wolfish grin that causes my stomach to do a flip worthy of a gymnast.

What the fuck?

I watch the two Wolves as they settle into my apartment. Guy turns the vision box on and starts watching some Witch sporting event while Quentin sits at my breakfast bar with my melting tub of iced cream and starts scooping it out with a spoon—which he also helped himself to.

What is going on here? I now have two Wolves in my apartment who seem to be dead set against leaving any time soon.

"What are you both doing?" I ask calmly, trying not to show my concern and unease.

"Weel kweep wou shafe, Bwooks." Quentin grins at me with a mouthful of iced cream. "Dis is gwood." He points his spoon to the tub.

As if I don't know that. It is *my* tub of iced cream.

Guy nods, not taking his eyes from the vision box. "Exactly, we're here to keep you safe, Paege. Does this thing show any other sports?" he adds, flicking through the frequencies with the remote, clearly looking for something more interesting to watch than Witches playing their broom-sweeping sport—a game I have never quite grasped—so I completely understand his request. Yet, I still don't understand what the Hels is going on here.

I throw my hands up in the air and huff loudly, walking off to my bedroom, and I hear both Guy and Quentin laugh.

It takes me minutes to have a good look around to see if anything is missing, but everything appears to be where I left it. My bed? Perfectly made. My dark mahogany dresser drawers? Closed. Even the trinkets: the phoenix, pegasus, and dragon eggs that my mother and father gave me still sit perfectly arranged atop.

The rest of the apartment is the same. Nothing seems to be out of place.

I retreat down the stairs from the mezzanine to stand between the two Wolves who are sitting on the couch and roll my eyes. This has got to be the weirdest night ever.

"Um, I think everything is where I left it; nothing seems to be missing or out of place. I honestly don't think anything was taken." I pause, looking between the two Wolves. "So?" I drawl.

Quentin shifts his gaze from the game of Batton Ball playing on the vision box to me and gestures to the empty space next to him on the couch. "Sit," he commands. "It's been a long evening." His grey-blue eyes burn into mine, and the heat of his stare has me shifting my weight between my feet nervously. He doesn't blink or move.

"Sit? What am I, your lap dog?"

He chortles but senses my unease because when he speaks again, his voice has lost its harsh edge. "Just come sit with me and Braxtion for a bit. Take your mind off things. We'll be out of your way as soon as you feel safe. I promise, Books." He smiles, and this time, it's genuine. *I think.*

Looking at the Wolves, I hesitate a moment longer. It's ridiculous how good-looking they both are, and something tugs at my core thinking about myself sandwiched between them on the couch.

Zephyra, help me!

Quentin smiles, his brows arch, and he slides an arm along the back of the sofa, waiting for me to move. He has the same crescent moon tattoo that Guy has on the back of his hand, but he also has a second tattoo that extends from his wrist up his arm and disappears under the sleeve of his shirt. I wonder how far up it goes and where else it covers.

"See something you like?" he chides, and my cheeks flush with an unwanted warmth.

Fuck.

I roll my eyes, trying to hide my sudden burst of embarrassment. I know the Wolves are supposed to be dangerous, and I should not be alone with them in my apartment, but to be perfectly honest, as scary as the Wolves seem, these two are just not giving off any menacing vibes.

Annoying? Yes.

Entitled? Definitely.

Dangerous? Well, Guy isn't anyway.

Quentin, I haven't made my mind up about him yet.

But they did just kind of save me. So, I take a deep breath and think, fuck it.

We twirl around each other, the sun beating down on us as our wooden swords smack together in unison. Clank, clank, clank. I gobble down air and take a small step back, lowering my sword for a moment as I regain my strength. We've been playing this game all afternoon, and the weight of the wooden sword is becoming heavy in my little hands.

"Are you too tired to continue, Princess?" he taunts, his single dimple just like mine appearing with his grin.

I hold my sword back up, using both hands like Amerax taught me.

"Never, Prince! I will fight you until my last breath." I lunge for him, but he jumps out of the way, bringing his sword up to meet mine again with a clank.

"When I best you, I will lock you in the dungeons to be forgotten about forever," he laughs.

"You will never be able to best me, Prince," I reply with a giggle. "I am too fast." I swing at him again, and our wooden swords smack. "I am too skilled." Another smack. "Too smart." Smack . . .

Bang, bang, bang.

"Are you in there, Paege?"

I stir. Remnants of the recurring dream I've not had since I was a child fade into the dark recesses of my mind, where it resides, as I attempt to pull myself into a conscious state. My bed feels harder, warmer than usual. Silence fills the air around me, and I nuzzle myself into the hard pillow as I melt into the warmth that surrounds me, pulling me back into my slumber.

"Paege?"

"Who is that?" a familiar male voice growls, and I stir once more.

An arm, yes, I'm certain it's an arm, pulls me in close again, but before I can register where the voice came from or whose arm is pulling me in for snuggles, another male voice fills the room.

"Sh."

It takes me a long moment for my memories to come crashing back from last night. The club, the Wolves, the break-in. My eyes snap open, and I push myself off Quentin's body.

Guy is sprawled out on the floor of my lounge, my rug wrapped around him and his head on a couch cushion. Quentin and I slept on the couch, apparently snuggling, me laying across him with a blanket over the both of us. I must have sought him out in the middle of the night. Or he sought me?

What the fuck?

"Paege?" Asheron yells again as he rattles the door, trying to get in. If he wanted to, he could easily break that door down—Star-Borne strength and all.

Shit, shit, shit. What do I do, what do I say?

"Ah, one moment, Asheron," I yell back as I push myself up and off Quentin's warm body. Asheron cannot find me like this with the Wolves. Asheron hates that he will one day have to serve the King, Quentin's father, and the Fae and Wolves don't get along at the best of times. It still makes no sense to me why they are even talking to me, let alone why they helped me last night. By the way Asheron is rattling my door, I don't have time to think about that now.

"Guy, Quentin," I whisper, "you both have to go." Guy shushes me again and rolls over. "Now," I demand.

Quentin yawns and stretches himself out. "Relax, Books."

I yank the pillow out from underneath Quentin's head and throw it at Guy. "Get up!" I whisper-yell at them both. "Can you go hide in my room, please?" I point toward my bedroom door. I need to get them out of here. There is no way Asheron will understand the Wolves being here, no matter what I say. And to be honest, I wouldn't even know what to say.

Quentin smirks, sitting up and sweeping sandy-blonde hair away from his eyes. His brows arch. "You want us to leave the lounge room where it's completely innocent, just the three of us casually relaxing, to go hide in *your* bedroom, Books? Where all sorts of naughty things—"

"*Do not* finish that sentence," I demand. But he has a point.

"Fine, stay here. But please, *please,* be quiet."

At a snail's pace, I walk to the door and open it, barely cracking it enough to see Asheron's silver hair curtaining his face, and keep my foot jammed hard against it.

"Gods, Paege, we were so worried about you. You didn't message Lumeilia or Mhelodie when you got home and didn't answer any texts last night or this morning. We thought something bad happened." I haven't even looked at my scribe since arriving back at my apartment last night. I look down to find my bag still on the floor by the door where I dropped it.

"Fuck, sorry, Asheron. Honestly, it was a bit of a crazy night, and by the time I settled on the couch, I just fell asleep." I yawn. "But I'm fine, I promise."

"Ah-ha. You going to let me in?"

"Now's not a good time. Can you come back later?" Anxiety sweeps through my body like a flood. I swallow hard, trying to keep myself composed.

"Paegence, what is going on?" Asheron demands. I flinch. Using my full name like that, he reminds me a lot of my father right now. I understand his concern. I just broke up with Sylas, and I've been emotional and impulsive. I left Slynx abruptly, walked home alone, and made no contact afterwards. The last being very unlike me. So, I truly understand he is worried, but even this is a bit excessive.

"Nothing."

"Paege, can you please just let me in? I can tell something isn't right."

Gods, he is persistent.

"I'm—" Before I finish my sentence, Asheron uses his Star-Borne strength, pushes through my foot jam, and swings the door wide open.

Hey, that's not fair! My foot stings at the impact of Asheron's force.

"What the fuck, Paege?" Asheron's violet eyes widen, and shadows seem to swirl behind his pupils.

"It's not what it looks like," I protest.

"Really? So, you don't have two Wolves sitting in your living room, half naked, who, by the looks of things, spent the night?"

"I'd say it is exactly what it looks like, Books," Quentin chimes in.

"Not helping," I bite back through gritted teeth.

Quentin holds his hands up as if to surrender, and he flashes a canine. I roll my eyes, unable to deal with the Wolf situation, and I turn my attention back to Asheron. "Honestly, it's not what it seems."

"What is it then?" Asheron storms over to the counter, arms folded against his chest, and his eyes dart between me and the Wolves, waiting for one of us to respond. I can't help feeling a little irritated by this alpha-male bullshit.

Guy casually stands and walks toward the guest bathroom, ignoring the commotion unfolding in front of him. I wonder what it must be like to be completely unphased by a male challenging dominance. I suppose because Asheron is the only male in our group, I rarely see this side of him. Where was this side of him when I was with Sylas? That was when I needed to see this version of him. That would have been appropriate.

I watch as Guy enters the bathroom, and I realise for the first time since waking that he is shirtless. My cheeks heat. I shift my attention to Quentin and realise he, too, is shirtless. My eyes scan the room. Jackets, shirts, belts and shoes are strewn across the table and floor, making things look every bit as provocative as Asheron is thinking.

Holy mother of all things beautiful. Kill me now.

Quentin's tattoo covers a lot more skin than I first imagined. And it's beautiful. The intricate artwork travels up his arm and across his . . . *Focus, Paege!*

"Paege, what the Hels is going on here?" Asheron asks again, interrupting my thoughts, this time with a little less aggression and a lot more concern.

Asheron and I sit at the kitchen table, and I rehash my evening. Every. Single. Detail. By the time I finish, Asheron's mouth hangs open, his brows knitted with worry.

"Shit, Paege. Do you need to get a message to your dad? Have you contacted anyone?" Asheron pulls his scribe from his pant pocket.

"No, by the time I sat down to think and take a breath, we must have fallen asleep."

"*We* fell asleep?"

Is that contempt I hear?

"You heard her," Guy chimes in to defend me. My eyes flash back to him as he exits the bathroom. Fully clothed. Thank the Gods.

I cannot say the same for Quentin.

"Yes," I repeat, looking back at Asheron. "*We* fell asleep."

I pause, unsure of what to say next, but Quentin beats me to it. "No offense, Books, aren't you a bit old to be asking for *daddy's* help?" he mocks. "And what's your dad going to do anyway?"

Says the male who still does as his daddy commands.

"Quentin, is it?" Asheron says sardonically, and his knuckles start turning white as he clenches the scribe still held in his hand. "Her dad is the Imperial Strategist of Israykiel Guard," he defends.

Both Guy's and Quentin's jaws drop.

Israykiel Guards are Star-Borne. A superior Fae warrior species. Their speed and strength are unmatched. Their access to the magic outperforms that of any other Fae, and their ability to control the elements makes them downright scary—even to the Witches. Little is known about their history, but they are believed to be a direct descendant of Isra, the God of Stars. Their secrets are heavily safeguarded, even to me, one who has been surrounded by Star-Borne's my entire life. But I am not a Star-Borne. I'm not even full Fae. They are the guard of our kingdom, and they are not to be messed with.

"I thought your dad was Human?" Guy asks, but not in a condescending way; he sounds genuinely confused.

"My bio-dad *was*, yes. My stepdad is Star-Borne."

Quentin nods, unimpressed.

"Those Fae are badass!" Guy says approvingly.

"You do know that Asheron—"

Asheron interrupts. "You *are* going to get a message to your dad now, aren't you?" That wasn't a question; it was more akin to a demand.

"Still a bit of an overkill, don't you think?" Quentin chides. "It was a break-in, not exactly a concern for Elyndria's Guard."

And while the sarcastic tone in Quentin's comment makes me want to slap that fucking smirk right off his face, I have to agree. It *is* a bit much. This is one area of my life I do not need them worrying about any more than they already do.

"Asheron, I appreciate the concern, but I think we can take it from here."

"You can, can you? All three of you?" He pauses, his eyes darting around the room. "You and the Wolves?" He stuffs his scribe back in his pocket.

Quentin interrupts, "We have Books' back. She's in safe hands with us."

"See, I'm in safe hands." Oddly, I completely believe the words as they spill out of my mouth.

I step toward Asheron, taking his hands in mine, and I squeeze them gently. We have been friends for years. He has always treated me with so much love and respect, but he has never been overprotective or unreasonable. And the last thing I want is for him to spend his weekend feeling like he needs to look after me.

"Seriously, I don't want you to worry. Please go back to your carefree day. It's Saturday, for Gods' sake. It's your favourite day of the week."

"Paege," Asheron's voice softens, "do you honestly think I would care more for my Saturday than I would for you?" He seems genuinely hurt.

"Sorry, Asheron, I didn't mean to suggest you don't care. I just don't want you to worry. But of course, if you want to help, then fine. The four of us can figure this out *together*." I swallow, trying to hold the anxiety that's been creeping through my flesh at bay because this couldn't be more awkward even if I tried.

The veins under my skin lightly bubble with amusement, and tiny bumps chase a shiver across my body. I press my lips together, but a giggle escapes them anyway. I turn back around. Quentin still occupies my couch, half-naked. A wolfish grin washes across his face, clearly entertained by this encounter, and he winks. *Asshole.*

Guy, on the other hand, is nowhere to be seen.

CHAPTER 11

"Where did you disappear to?" I ask Guy as he casually re-enters the apartment, trying to break the uncomfortable silence we have been sitting in for the last fifteen minutes or so.

"Checking the perimeter. Seeing if I could find the way they got in."

"And?" I stand eagerly, hoping with all my heart that he found out how my intruder got in. If he did, we can fix it, and everyone can leave, and life can go back to normal. Or as normal as it was. Which wasn't that normal. But still . . .

"No, nothing. Everything is secure here. Anyone else hold a key?"

I sigh. "No one, aside from Lumeilia," I say, disappointed. I trust all my friends, but I need my privacy. Lumeilia is the only person I could trust to not use the key without reason. If Asheron had a key this morning, he would have let himself in, no question. I bet he would not have even knocked first.

I steal a glance at Asheron. He pulls his lips tightly, concealing a sheepish grin, and he tucks strands of silver hair behind his ears.

Of course, I bet he tried to get the key from her this morning.

"Lumeilia, Mhelodie, and Asheron all know my access code, though. Even Sylas," I add.

Quentin chimes in, "The ex?"

Asheron's brows furrow in confusion as his eyes dart between the Wolves and me.

"Yes, Fae, she told us about the ex. We walked her home when it happened, remember?" he adds sarcastically.

For fuck's sake. This isn't a pissing contest.

Quentin continues. "I suggest you change your code and make it difficult so no one can guess it."

"And only give it to a select few. There's a chime, so maybe start using that," Guy adds.

"Right. Chimes, change code, no keys. Got it!" I repeat. "Anything else?

"Well, I think me and Guy should bunk here for a day or two. Just to make sure," Quentin responds. My body tightens, and blood rushes my ears. I draw in a sharp breath, ready to protest, but Asheron beats me to it.

"No way, Wolf!" Asheron barks, baring his teeth.

"Just for a few days," Guy adds, too eager to agree to Quentin's outrageous and completely inappropriate plan.

"And if there aren't any more problems, she's all yours," Quentin adds sarcastically.

"I don't know," I question, my eyes shifting between all three of them. Isn't this all a bit much? I am perfectly capable of looking after myself. I don't need a bunch of babysitters. I don't even know the Wolves. Why on earth would they want to spend time here with me? I am a nobody. So, what is their angle? For some reason, I don't voice my concern or my disagreement. I keep it all bottled up.

"What are your other options, Books? Is your dad sending Guards to the apartment? Stalker weirdo coming back? Asheron staying here and *protecting* you?"

Wow, low blow!

"Excuse you! Asheron is . . ." I start to defend my friend, but once again, Asheron interrupts.

"Maybe it's not such a bad idea, Paege." What is going on here? "I hate to say it, but Quentin's right, they may be the best for the job."

What job? Am I a job now? Still, I don't object. I don't question it. I keep my mouth shut.

"Besides," Asheron approaches me and takes my hands, "I will check in daily, make sure you are safe and that these two aren't causing you any problems." Asheron moves in closer, his warm breath brushes against my cheek as he whispers, "Not that you need it. I know you can totally kick their arses if needed." He smirks and winks.

"This is crazy!" I exclaim, ripping my hands from Asheron. Nothing has even happened to warrant any of this. They're all acting like they are over-protecting alpha assholes.

I storm to my room, slam the door, and don't return for a long, long while.

Determined not to let the drama ruin the rest of my weekend, as the sun starts to set, I exit my room.

I spy two Wolves sitting on my couch and Asheron sitting at my breakfast bar, his violet eyes pinned to them, watching their every move.

At the sound of my steps, Guy looks over to me, his eyes tracing me up and down, studying my outfit—a short denim skirt, white crop t-shirt, chunky black knee-high boots, and matching leather jacket. My lips are painted red, gold powder sweeps across my eyelids, and my long, boring brown hair is pulled into a high-top tail.

"Where are you going?" he asks.

"To work," I say sharply, not in the mood for any of their antics.

"And where is work?" Quentin replies, and while I stand here feeling very judged, I notice they are all still dressed in last night's clothes . . . even Asheron.

"You know where my work is." *Jackass.* "The Pit." I roll my eyes. They have both been there plenty of times while I've been working.

Fair enough, before this weekend, these two Wolves had barely ever glanced my way. And at The Pit, it's not like I pour the drinks or wait on anyone, so I can see how I'm easily overlooked. Still, it stings a bit when they don't remember. I float around, clearing empty glasses from the tables, and I've cleared their tables many times over.

It's not a glamorous job by any means, but I get to watch all the amazing bands play there for free, and the extra coinage, whether it's drops or clays, well, that's just a bonus.

"Nope," Quentin responds, shaking his head, his sandy blond hair spilling across his eyes. "You can't be serious?"

"What now?" I sigh, irritation dripping from my words, and I place my hands on my hips.

"You do remember you thought you had someone following you last night, and your place was broken into, possibly by the same someone?"

"And?"

"*And*," he drawls, "I think it's best you stay in tonight, Books, and not get yourself into any more trouble."

"Excuse me?" I drawl. "Trouble?" I huff and stomp toward the door. "I did not get myself into any trouble, thank you very much." My hand shakes as I grab my door handle to open it, my anger rising with the situation at hand. "I'm not a bloody child, and I can go to work if I damn well please. I can go anywhere I want!" I yell over my shoulders as I violently swing open the door.

Guy laughs and shrugs at Quentin and says, "Q, you feel like heading to The Pit tonight?"

"Read my mind, Braxtion," Quentin replies with a huge grin on his face.

"Sounds like a great idea. I just need to cancel my plans," Asheron adds.

Fuck. Am I going to have two Wolf escorts for the next few days? And Asheron? Can my life get any more complicated right now?

I slam the door behind me and storm out of my complex. I'm not waiting around for them. They can bloody well catch up or find their own way there.

Twenty minutes later, with my frustration still simmering at the surface, we all walk into The Pit together, and I can't help but think this is the start of a really bad joke.

Two Wolves, a Fae, and a halfling walk into a bar . . .

Asheron sees some of his friends the second we walk in and leaves us to talk to them. The Wolves take a table in the middle of the seated area right behind the dance floor. I'm guessing for its viewpoint advantages.

I check my temper at the door and head straight to the bar to get a tray and start work.

The Pit is lively tonight. The band is new, not one I have ever seen before, and they seem to be playing covers of old rock music from the Human kingdom.

I don't know why it surprises me that Humans can make such good music, but it does. The Humans haven't walked our lands since before I was born—after the Humans revolted and tried to war against us. That was when the wards between our realms were put up, and now Humans cannot access our realm or visa-versa. We tell ourselves it's for our own protection against further invasions, but really, it's to protect the Humans from themselves. Their obsession with waging a war against us over and over cost them more lives than when we all had free passage to travel between the realms, according to history. While most of them would like to forget all about the Humans, some Human remnants still linger, like their music.

I'm grateful for it because, to some degree, it gives me a connection to a side of me that is greatly looked down upon in our kingdom, that's deemed inferior. A side of me that feels lost and forgotten, but one I so desperately want to find and hold onto and need to understand. Because no matter how much Amerax loves me, no matter how full my life has been, I still feel like a part of me is missing, I feel I am not whole. So, I will take any connection I can find to the Humans. No matter how small and insignificant it may seem.

I go behind the bar to grab a tray and scan the room before I set off on my rounds. It's a full house, but strangely, I don't feel any emotions from the throngs of people around me, which is nice. Hallie, the younger Centaur bartender, prances over to me and grabs a bottle of DesertFyre and four shot glasses. She pours the drinks and sets them in front of us. Our tradition.

"One Fyre, two Fyre, three Fyre, four," she sings, pointing between the shot glasses, back and forth. Two shots each.

"Don't mind if I do." I smile, grab one of the glasses, and pour the liquid gold down my throat. The spicy warmth of it hits me instantly, and I don't wait before taking my next one.

Hallie takes hers in sync with me. All four drinks are consumed within seconds.

"I see you came in with those two yummy Wolves." She nods over toward Guy and Quentin. "What's the deal there?" she asks as she grabs four ales for the two male Fae waiting at the bar.

"Oh, nothing. They are both *friends*." I think.

"And Asheron?" She winks.

"Also, *just* a friend, Hallie." I roll my eyes. Everyone always asks about Asheron. Yes, he is flirtatious with me, but he is flirtatious with everyone.

"Alright, just checking. I mean, I know you have a sexy Fae lover, but you never bring him here anymore, so I was curious, that's all."

My heart sinks. It's been a good few hours since I have even thought about Sylas. "Sylas and I are no longer together."

"Since when?"

"A couple of nights ago."

It was here at The Pit when he asked me out for the first time.

We were friends for almost a year before we admitted it was more. One night, I was here at work, and he sat at the bar, as he had done so many times before, but this time, when he arrived, the first thing he did was ask for a whole bottle of AmberFyre, a malt spirit aged in barrels, and a glass.

Then he poured himself a drink and asked me on a date. He said he wasn't leaving until I said yes, and he would have a drink for every time I turned him down.

At first, I thought he was crazy, but as the night progressed and his bill increased, I realised just how serious he was. So, I said yes. If for no other reason than to save him from a ridiculous bill.

"Oh shit. Sorry P, my bad," Hallie says, pity rolling off her in waves.

"All good. You didn't know," I say, pushing away her emotions. I grab a tray and wave it in the air. "I'll be back soon for another drink," I say, needing to get out of here and forget about the male that just shattered my heart.

"No problem, you sexy Fae." Hallie whips me on the ass with a towel, laughs, and goes back to the tending bar. She is nosy as Hels, but she means well. And she is so much fun. Her company is exactly what I need to forget about my problems.

I make four trips around The Pit, emptying tables, before I have an overwhelming urge to go sit down with the Wolves. I grab three glasses of DesertFyre from the bar, walk over to the table, and set them all down. I slide one to each of the Wolves and hold my glass up. Guy grabs his, and Quentin, not taking his eyes off the band, slides his back toward me. The lead singer is a Wolf and mesmerising at that. Short, choppy brown hair with red streaks, bright red lips to match, a short black leather skirt, and a grey ripped t-shirt across her rib cage and belly, exposing what looks like a rose vine tattoo along her ribs and a belly piercing. She stands on the stage barefoot, belting out a dark rock song, and I have to say, for a Wolf, she is pretty amazing.

"You're not drinking tonight?" I ask Quentin, cocking my head, trying to get his attention. Because, *rude!*

"Nope, not while on duty!" Quentin responds, face completely devoid of any expression.

"Duty? I'm not a job," I snap. I shoot my DesertFyre back and slam the glass on the table.

"Yes, you are. For the next few days at least."

"No, I'm not! I didn't ask you to do this shit. If you want to have a good time, have a good time." I push the DesertFyre back toward him.

"Will you stop acting like a selfish child for one second, Paege, and realise that we are trying to help you?" Quentin bites, sliding the DesertFyre back to me for a second time.

Stop acting like an immature little halfling and reply to me!

I wince, Quentin's words striking their true mark.

And he called me Paege.

Pushing back the tears that are threatening to swell, I bare my teeth, and the beast inside my belly growls loudly. Quentin shifts slightly in his chair, his eyes leaving the Wolf on the stage for a quick moment, but he still won't look at me. My skin flushes with heat.

Gods, I hate him.

I take a steadying breath in, remembering what Amerax taught me, and as quickly as it comes on, the anger fades, and I feel myself gain control of my emotions—for the first time in a long time.

Wow, that technique works.

"You sure know how to make a female feel good about herself." I stand, "Your loss, though. The night is on me." I lean down closer to him and whisper in his ear, "And I've got access to all the good stuff." I grab his glass of DesertFyre and slam it back, banging the glass upside down in front of him. I turn on my heels and saunter away, leaving all the empty the glasses on the table and swinging my hips in rhythm to the music. Because damn him if he is going to make me feel guilty for his inability to have fun.

I didn't ask for this shit.

When I reach to the bar, I pivot around to find Guy standing behind me. He smiles kindly.

I sit on a high chair, and Guy sits next to me. "What's his problem?" I shout, hopefully loud enough that his Wolf ears hear me above the music.

"It's not you, Paege. He always gets grumpy when Juno's around."

"Who?" Confusion and tipsiness swirl around in my head, making me feel more lightheaded than I care to admit.

"Juno, his ex. She's here tonight, which means her WolfMate is most likely going to turn up at some point." He looks up to the band. Holy shit, the mesmerising Wolf singing is Quentin's ex-girlfriend.

"Oh," is the only word I can find to say. I don't know if I will ever be mated. Being half Human means there's a chance the FaeMate bond won't ever happen for me. But all Fae and Wolves *can* mate, and some even hold out having any type of long-term relationship in wait for the mate bond. Many don't hold out, though, because meeting your Mate can take centuries. It would suck to fall in love only to have your lover bond with another. My heart unexpectedly hurts for Quentin. Because I, too, understand what it's like to have your heart broken.

Maybe Asheron has it right, reject the mating bond and screw everything that walks? Not that he actually does that. He sure does like to tease about it. But I've never actually seen him take anyone home.

I reach over the bar and grab the bottle of DesertFyre and two new glasses.

"What about you, Guy, any Wolf you're interested in?" I pour two drinks and hand one to Guy. Guy shakes his head and drinks his DesertFyre without a flinch. "Not even one of the females from the other two nights?" I ask. Then drink mine, too.

Guy snorts. "Who Monella and Immojen from Slynx? No, they're just good friends. Alpha pack members. They're like sisters to Q and I."

"Oh," I respond. My face suddenly feels a little warm, and it's not from the DesertFyre.

"And the girls from the night before, not my type. Q is trying to keep his mind off Juno," he adds sarcastically. He nods towards his empty glass, motioning for another. I oblige.

"And what about you, Paege?"

"What about me?"

"Any potential males out there?" Guy smirks and looks toward Asheron.

"Oh, Gods, no, we are *just* friends." I laugh, taking my next shot. *Honestly, why does everyone keep asking me that tonight?* "Asheron is mated, but he rejected his mating bond because . . . Well, we don't know why, to be honest."

"Huh." Guy takes his shot, and his brows knit as if he is contemplating what I said. "Interesting. So, tell me more about this Fae gift of yours."

"What do you want to know?"

"I don't know, what's it like? How do you control it?'

"Ha, control it? You don't, or I don't anyway. I haven't been able to master mine yet, but after my Unification, I'll be able to control it more. *Hopefully.*"

"Hopefully?"

"Well, we don't know," I continue. "I'm only a demi-Fae. No one knows what to expect. We didn't even know if I would even develop any gifts. Empathy came on strong a couple of years ago, but before that, I had zero magic, unlike the rest of my Fae peers, and I still have no idea if I'll get any other Fae magic."

"Others?" Guy's eyebrows lift, curiosity glistening in his eyes.

"What we experience before our Unification is only a spark of our magic, but during our Unification, if we are deemed worthy by the Gods, we are gifted with our one true magic gift. And in rarer cases, some Fae manifest lesser elemental magic or other active magic."

Guy's brows raise.

"Telekinesis, Dream Walking, or Portal Creation."

"Portal Creation?" I nod. "So, they wouldn't need to use the portal halls?" I nod again. "Cool." Guy mutters to himself under his breath

Yes. Yes, it is.

"And lesser elemental magic, like the Star-Bornes?" he asks.

"They're rare gifts, very rare. Not many possess them, so I doubt a demi-Fae will."

Guy nods his head, and he stares off toward the crowd, his eyes wide with wonder. I ponder if this is the first time he's learned about Fae and their gifts—or paid any attention to it. *Probably the latter.*

"So," I drawl, "my gift might manifest into precognition, but for now, it's only a heightened sense of my surroundings and feeling others' emotions."

Guy snaps his attention back to me. "Seeing the future? Like Witches?"

"Not really like the Witches. It's more like random visions when you touch things or people or when you dream. Again, Fae magic is a lot weaker than Witches'."

Guy nods but doesn't say anything else; he just watches me as if waiting for more information.

"Empathy, as a gift, really sucks though," I continue. "Feeling everyone's emotions with no warning can be overwhelming and pretty confronting. I mean, I feel their disgust, fear, curiosity, anger, sadness, guilt."

"Lust," Guy adds with a smile playing around his lips.

I feel my face grow warmer. "Yes," I gulp. "Lust".

"What does it feel like?"

"Lust?" I chuckle, unsure where he is going with this.

"No," he snorts. "Your gifts. Empathy. How does it work?"

His question startles me. No one has ever asked me what it feels like before. Yes, everyone's been intrigued about what emotions I can feel, but not how I feel it.

I pause for the longest moment, trying to figure out the best way to answer his question. "It's different for every emotion. A taste or smell or some other physical reaction. It's uncomfortable and painful at times. But I've learned over the years what different reactions mean. The more emotions or the more intense the emotion, the worse it is. Even positive emotions."

Guy hums, considering the information I just shared with him.

"It's strange, though," I continue. "Because my gifts don't always work. Like tonight, I don't feel anything." I hold up the DesertFyre bottle. "This helps, too, I suppose." I laugh before putting the bottle back behind the bar.

"That's how you handle it?" He raises an eyebrow, not hiding his disapproval of my coping mechanisms.

"Not always," I scoff. "I am used to it by now. But yes, sometimes a Fae's got to do what a Fae's got to do." I chuckle, and Guy chuckles, too. And thank the Gods because I already have two overbearing parents who disapprove of my coping mechanisms. I don't need another.

It's nice to see him laugh and loosen up a bit. He isn't a bad Wolf at all. I have a sense that he's mostly misunderstood, probably because of his lineage. There's something about him, something familiar and warm I can't quite put my finger on. Maybe we'll become good friends after all.

Suddenly, hair stands on the back of my neck as a brush of a warm breeze tickles against the skin of my cheek, and an uneasiness grows deep in the pit of my stomach. Guy straightens his back, tall and strong, and his eyes start darting around The Pit. My stomach growls, sending icy chills spider-walking down my spine. I heed the familiar foreboding warning, looking around the bar, searching for any sign of trouble, but I don't see anything or *anyone* unusual.

Quentin turns in his seat, looking over at Guy and me. He stands abruptly and marches to us. "Come on. We need to go," he says. He grabs my arm and pulls me from my seat, sending me stumbling to my feet.

"Hang on, what's going on?" I try to pull my arm from Quentin's bruising grip and steady myself.

Guy and Quentin exchange a glance. "We can smell the scent from your apartment."

That is all I need to hear Guy say.

I no longer fight them. I no longer argue. We leave The Pit without as much as a goodbye to the others.

Chapter 12

The second we step outside The Pit, we are instantly surrounded by a group of Wolves. Blind-sighted.

"Well, if it isn't the betrayer's son and the halfling," an older Wolf says. He rubs his hands together, and a scorpion tattoo on the back of his hand catches my eye.

The Scorpion Wolf pack. The scariest Wolf pack in the kingdom. They pretty much own Blaxheild with their prostitution and illegal drug dens. They steal and ransack. They kidnap, start street brawls, and pretty much take the laws into their own hands. They are thugs, total outlaws. And somehow, they always get away with it.

No doubt it's because they are Wolves. And in the king's eyes, the Wolves can do no wrong. The Pit was nearly shut down with allegations of it turning into an illegal strip club after installing poles for dancing. Yet Blaxheild continues to survive and thrive.

"What do you want, Ric?" Guy says, annoyance lacing his words.

"Nothing, we're here for the show." Ric smirks. I presume he is the High Alpha. He stands at the front of six Wolves. Four males and two females, looking strung out, their bloodshot, vacant eyes staring at us. No, not at us. Right through us.

"Let's go, Paege." Guy grabs my arm and tugs me to the left of Ric, but Ric grabs my other arm and yanks me toward him, causing my stomach to lurch at his touch. He probably would have been a handsome younger Wolf, but his face is now covered in several long scars. I'm assuming trophies from fighting.

"Is that what you want, darlin'?" He smirks, and my skin prickles as if hundreds of invisible bugs are scattering over my body. "To head off with these pups, or do you want to come play with a real Wolf pack?"

"Excuse me?" I ask in disgust.

"Shut up, Books." Quentin urges under his breath in a warning to not start something that is out of my league. And they are. These Wolves are nothing like Quentin and Guy. The royals may be asses and make my blood boil at times with their selfish and entitled ways, but these Wolves . . . These Wolves are entirely different. They make my stomach churn. They make my skin crawl.

"I said, why are you leaving in such a rush, darlin'?" Ric repeats himself as he tightens his grip on my arm.

A snarl pulls at my lips. "I'm not your *darling*," I snap back, yanking my arm out of his, clearly forgetting Quentin's subtle warning as a ball of anger starts to unravel inside.

Guy pulls me in behind him, keeping me close, protecting me from the pack that has us surrounded and outnumbered. As I fall into the refuge that Guy's body provides, the anger fades, calming my trembling heart.

"Oh, she's a bit of a feisty one." Ric and his pack laugh, and my body shudders at his words.

"Why don't you leave these pups? Come join us." Ric licks his lips. "I can guarantee you a good time. So good you won't ever want to leave. Just ask Juno." Ice fills my veins at his words. He looks around at his pack, his smile wide, clearly proud of himself. But before I have a chance to fully comprehend what I heard, Quentin sucker punches Ric in the side of his face.

He moved so fast that no one saw it coming.

It's a hard enough punch to startle Ric. His feet shuffle, trying to regain his balance, but not hard enough to drop him to his knees—which I'm guessing was Quentin's intention.

Ric stretches his jaw widely, and his hazel eyes scowl. "You'll pay for that, you bastard," he snarls, blood running down into his mouth from his nose.

"Go on then!" Quentin opens his arms wide, welcoming a hit from Ric. But Ric doesn't bite. He stares Quentin dead in the eyes. Not blinking. Not moving. Then, in a disgusting move, he licks the blood from his upper lip and swallows, seeming to revel in the taste.

"Just as I thought." Quentin grins. "You're too chicken shit to fight back. You're not a real Wolf."

"That's not what Juno says when she has her pretty little lips wrapped around my cock." Bile stings my throat. So, this is Juno's WolfMate. No wonder Quentin sucker-punched him. I probably would have, too.

Silence fills the thick air around us while we all await Quentin's reaction, but there is none.

"You know where to find us." Ric winks at me.

Quentin's mouth drops open as if to say something, but he closes it again when Ric tsks him.

"I'd bite your tongue, boy." Ric spits blood on the ground in front of him. "I may not be able to harm a hair on your pretty little head tonight, but that doesn't mean I can't find another way to break you." He smiles, exposing his sharp but disgusting teeth. "I'll say *hi* to Juno for you."

Ric whistles to the pack like he is rounding them up, "Let's move everyone. We got some damage to do." Ric motions the pack to move into The Pit.

An icy shiver crawls uncomfortably down my spine, and my hair rises.

Something's not right.

A growl releases from deep within my core as the beast inside me awakens. My fingers curl, nails biting into my palms. Something thick and heavy rolls through me. My chest tightens, and tears sting my eyes.

Hunger, but not for food, not for sex, for something else entirely.

Blood.

Fear unfurls within.

"Guy?" I turn to face him. "Asheron and Hallie are in there. We need to warn them!" I plead.

"On it, Paege!" Guy hands me off to Quentin like I'm some prized possession and then rushes to the door. He speaks to the Centaur security, who opens the doors and goes inside. Guy follows.

As soon as Guy steps inside The Pit, all Hels breaks loose. A roar booms from behind the door, and a macabre chorus of cries and blood-curdling screams follow. Oh, Gods. I've never heard anything like it before. The Wolves must have shifted when they walked into The Pit, and from the muffled sounds coming from inside, it sounds like they are ripping everything and everyone apart.

Quentin pushes me behind him and yells, "Run!"

But I don't, I can't. My bones are like steel. My muscles are like stone. I can't move. I can't leave. Not when my friends are inside.

"Asheron and Guy?" I plead with Quentin. He pivots to face me, his eyes a raging inferno. He blinks once, surprised that I am still standing here. Then he scoops me up in his arms, throws me over his shoulder, and runs.

"No!" I yell as I fight his grasp, but it's no use.

I hit and kick him as hard as I can, begging for him to let go, to turn back. He doesn't relent.

"Please, let me go back," I plead, but my words fall on deaf ears as he continues to run through the streets of Lockswick with his arms wrapped firmly across my legs, holding me in place.

"We can't leave them," I sob.

Over and over again, I cry for him to let me go, to put me down. But he doesn't. No amount of screaming or pleading distracts him. No amount of hitting or kicking deters him. He doesn't stop. He doesn't even flinch with any of my blows. Not until we finally reach my apartment.

I don't even pause when he eventually lets go of me. I turn on my heel and run, heading back toward The Pit. I make it maybe twenty lengths before Quentin is back in front of me, blocking me, and he has me by the arms, holding me still.

I stop fighting, and my eyes drift up toward his, studying the angles of his face, the hard and sharp lines, as they make their way up to greet his grey-blue eyes. Our gazes collide for one moment before I feel it rise inside me. My heart cracks as the anguish I feel ripples through my body, and salty tears begin to rain from my eyes.

"Why? Why did you do that?"

I struggle with him again, but it's no use. His Wolf strength is exponentially stronger than my demi-Fae strength.

Quentin stares at me. His rugged face is stoic as he brushes his hair away from his eyes. "You need to stop, Paege. You need to come with me inside right now."

He pulls me by the arm and drags me to my security gate with a bruising grip. My mind empties. Numb and exhausted, my body burns as fatigue takes over. I used every ounce of energy my little body possessed, fighting him on the way here.

I can't fight anymore.

I don't fight anymore.

He enters the new code into my security gate lock, and when the gate opens, he ushers me toward my apartment, still holding my arm tightly. He takes the keys out of my jacket pocket and unlocks the door. Swinging it wide open, he gently nudges me inside. I take one, two steps inside, two steps away from him when my body gives way, and I fall to the ground and let out an almighty scream.

Quentin kneels beside me and scoops me up off the ground, and without saying a word, he carries me to my bed. He gently lays me down and covers me with a throw. Then he sits at the edge of my bed and stares at the wall.

Neither of us talk.

Neither of us move.

So, I close my eyes and let the darkness consume me.

Commotion outside my apartment, in the gardens, has my eyes snapping open. I sit upright, heart beating fast, adrenaline kicking in once again. Quentin does the same, and our eyes collide. Steel grey eyes burn into mine. Eyes, which are usually so full of mischief, are now drowning in grief and sadness. His sandy blond hair is dishevelled, swept across his brow, and his face is drawn and exhausted.

I hadn't even noticed Quentin lying beside me in the bed. Gods, he is so beautiful, and I hate that I notice that.

My heart kicks in my chest, sending a tingling sensation through my core, and I'm suddenly very aware of the distance between us. So close but not touching.

Another cacophony of sounds outside has our eyes darting to the door, breaking our connection.

"Paege, Q, are you in there? Open up!" Guy's voice yells, sounding frantic and breathless. My stomach flips.

Quentin leaps to his feet and dashes to the door. I follow in his footsteps.

By the time I make it to the door, Quentin has already opened it, and an injured Guy and Asheron spill through my doorway into my apartment, slamming shut the door behind them. They are covered from head to foot in blood and what I think is Wolf fur.

Gross.

I run over to Guy and wrap my arms around him, my guilt tearing at me for his selfless actions and putting himself at risk for me. He winces from my touch. He's injured. I pull back, my hands finding his arms, and I hold on tight while I look him over and mouth, *sorry.* He shakes his head and turns to Quentin.

I release Guy's arms and turn to see Asheron, who appears to be uninjured, and that's when it hits me. Relief floods over me, and my muscles and bones relax as tears start streaming down my face. Asheron strides over to me with determined steps and wraps his muscular arms around me. Enveloping me whole.

"I'm fine, Paege, see?" He releases me from his embrace, steps back, and does a spin, showing me his body ever so gracefully.

"Are you sure?" I ask, coming back in for another hug but this time squeezing him tightly. "I was so worried."

"I'm sure!" he reassures me.

"Hallie?" I ask. Asheron dips his head and shakes it, his violet eyes avoiding mine, and I know exactly what that means. My heart sinks.

"Guy, what the Hels happened?" Quentin asks as Guy limps over toward the couch, wincing with every step.

I head to the spare bathroom to grab all the medical supplies I have—which is a lot because my father, an Israykiel Guard, taught me well. I come back into the room where the males are. Neither Asheron nor Guy have said another word. I don't have the courage to ask about the others. I don't think I have the stomach to learn of their fates.

"Paege, your dad's on his way to the Neopolis with mine!" Asheron says as he walks to the kitchen and then helps himself to my supply before pouring a few glasses of water.

Oh shit, Amerax is going to be so angry.

I walk over to where Guy is sunken into the couch cushions, exhausted and injured. I hold up the first aid kit, and Guy promptly pulls his ripped shirt up over his abs. A tattoo of a wolf's face covers his right muscled pec, and a huge gaping wound travels across his stomach from left to right, top to bottom, and my throat burns from bile. Wolf claws sliced him clean open.

As I inspect his wound, Asheron comes over to us. "Thanks for the backup, Guy. I would never have been able to get all those people out of there alone."

Guy nods in response and opens his mouth like he is going to respond, but then hisses as I pour alcohol on his open wound.

Sorry, I mouth, showing a toothy grin.

He then turns to Quentin. "No idea what the fuck that was. They were rabid! But it wasn't the drugs. It was like they were looking for something. They turned the place upside down, biting into anyone that got in their way."

As I cover Guy's wound with gauze, he turns back to me. "Sorry, Paege." He puts his hand on mine, the one still resting on his wound. "Hallie put up a good fight, but she didn't stand a chance. She was gone before I got to her. The Wolf venom was too strong for her young, Centaur body."

He turns back to Quentin. "Q, we need to speak to your dad. He needs to put a stop to them!"

Quentin objects, "No!" My heart stops, and we all face to look at him. "I mean, *yes*, but *I* will go to him tomorrow. Braxtion, you stay here with Books." He turns to Asheron. "Asheron, you think you're up for the job?"

Guy replies before Asheron gets a chance. "I think we've got it covered." He nods at Asheron, and he nods back like some weird silent code is being exchanged before my eyes.

Guy then smiles at me, grateful for the help even though we both know it's completely unnecessary. Wolves heal fast—even before they've merged with their Wolf. Give it a few days, and it will probably be fully closed up, with nothing left but a surface scar.

I stand up and look around my apartment at the three males who have been here for me over the last few days and everything we've gone through: the attack, the stalker, the break-up.

My eyes dart between the two Wolves who unexpectedly entered my life and who I have started to become very fond of. My gaze shifts over to Asheron, my long-time Fae friend who I love so much and who has put his life on hold to look after me the last few days. My heart swells.

A single tear runs down my cheek.

I can't bear the thought of any of them getting hurt—especially because of me. I think I need them *all* in my life.

Sure, Paege, your life isn't complicated.

Not. At. All.

CHAPTER 13

The sun's harsh light squeezes itself through the small cracks in my eyes as they flutter open. Muffled sounds of chatter in my apartment and the smell of freshly made gridcakes—my favourite—fill my room, and a smile slowly creeps across my face.

I wonder who's cooking.

The sky was changing from an inky darkness to a deep shade of purple when I finally went to bed. The four of us stayed up late analysing the night's events, trying to understand what happened and why. Nothing seemed to fall into place.

What were the Scorpions doing attacking innocent Beings for no apparent reason? What were they looking for? Why were they so careless and brutal? For what possible reason would they act in a way that attracts the Israykiel Guard? The Guard hasn't been called to the Neopolis in many years. There hasn't been a need for the Guard to be here. There has always been a certain level of animosity between the different species, but there hasn't been an attack like this since, well, not since before I was born. And the Star-Borne patrols have been enough to keep the peace. Mostly.

In the new light of day, it seems I still have no clue.

I guess that it must be midmorning. I need to get up and face the day. But if I'm being honest with myself, all I want to do is stay wrapped up in my blankets, bury my face in my pillows, and hide away from everything. Because when I walk out that door, I'm going to have to explain everything to my dad.

Twenty minutes later, I'm showered and dressed in comfy, baggy cotton pants and an equally baggy shirt. Today is all about comfort, and if I'm lucky, I won't have to leave my apartment for anything. Maybe I'll get to read a book or take an afternoon nap. I open my bedroom door to see a room full of people. Lumeilia, Mhelodie, Dad, and Asheron stand around the breakfast bar while Guy stands over the cooker. Or maybe I won't.

Sundays have always been gridcakes day. When I was younger, every Sunday morning, Mum would make them for Dad. She learned how to make them from my bio-dad. They were his favourite food. When I left home and moved to the Neopolis, Lumeilia, Mhelodie, Asheron, and I continued the tradition. I am a hopeless cook. So, Asheron quickly learned how to make them for me, and it's been his job to cook them ever since, but none have ever been as good as Mum's.

A quick scan of the room tells me Quentin isn't here, and my heart sinks a little.

I suck in a breath, preparing myself for the emotional attack, and walk over toward the kitchen. They all stop whatever conversation they were having and look at me. Their faces are full of concern, sorrow, and pity. But strangely, my body isn't assaulted by their feelings. Yet a heaviness still settles over the room.

"Morning, Paege," Mhelodie says in her usual chirpy voice as she skips over to me and gives me a quick hug. Her face is missing its usual glow.

"Morning," I reply to the entire room.

"Are you alright?" she asks me gently. "Asheron told us about Hallie. I'm so sorry," she whispers.

Unable to wrap my head around what happened or articulate a reply, I nod.

"Hi, Dad,"

Dad holds his arms out wide. Things must be bad if they sent Amerax to the city for duty. A smile appears on his lips, softening his appearance. He's wearing his Israykiel Guard uniform: black, leather patched shirt and tactical, armoured vest and pants. It's a uniform that shows off his sculpted muscles from hundreds of years of training. His weapons are sheathed in their various halters strapped to his legs and chest.

I step into his embrace and close my eyes, holding back the urge to cry as his large arms cocoon me in a blanket of warmth.

Safe and protected.

It's how I always feel when in his arms. If I could, I would stay here forever, sheltered from the big bad beasts of the world. I know they have always existed. I just never thought they would come knocking on my door. Quite literally.

"Hi, Pumpkin," Dad replies. He's always called me Pumpkin. I honestly thought he would have grown out of it by now. But secretly, I hope he calls me Pumpkin for the rest of our lives. He may be a badass Israykiel Guard, but he is also a father. My father. He has always treated me like his own. I have felt his love wash over me so many times that there is no doubt in my mind he would lay down his life for me.

I am proud to call him my dad.

"Where's Mum?" I ask, crooking my neck to look at him. His handsome face hides behind a forest of thick facial hair. I don't think I have ever seen his face bare. I don't even know if I would recognise him.

"She couldn't come. The twins are still on break from the academy, prepping for their White-Star challenge."

I was ten when my parents had children of their own. The twins, Nassurah and Kholann, are the most beautiful yet aggravating Fae I have ever met. Always getting into some kind of trouble. So, when they are on break, someone has to watch them. That someone used to be me. Of course I love them, but they aggravate me to no end. Now, I live far, far away, and that responsibility has gone back to my mother. And only the Gods know what kind of mischief they would get into if they weren't under some sort of constant supervision.

"What's the White-Star challenge?" Guy asks casually as he turns to plate up all the gridcakes he's cooked.

"Stars are the Israykiel Guard combat grading system. Children of the Guards attend the Star-Borne Academy, and every two years, they must pass a Star in preparation for their calling," Asheron replies. "There are five grades." Asheron stands tall, his violet eyes beaming with pride. "Starting at white, progressing to silver, and then gold when we are finally activated," he continues. "Training starts their fourteenth year." Asheron shakes his head. "I still can't believe the twins are fourteen this year."

"Neither can I," Dad replies.

Neither can I.

Dad clears his throat. "I must go, but can you spare an hour to spar with your father?" he asks me as I grab a plate of gridcakes covered in fresh cream and syrup and sit down at the kitchen table.

His brows furrow with what I can only describe as concern. Amerax has always been extra worried about me. He is concerned that being half Human makes me weaker than the rest of the Beings and a likely prey—especially because of his position within the Guard. So, he has done what he can to ensure I'm always protected. He even taught me how to protect myself.

"Well, I don't have any other plans," I mumble under my breath before I take a bite of the best damn gridcakes I have ever eaten in my life. *Sorry, Mum.*

"I'll meet you at our usual spot?"

I nod in response, my mouth full of creamy sweetness.

"At noon? I've got a few things I need to take care of. Make sure the legions understand their sector of responsibility. And not only are we searching for the Scorpions, but there's also a missing Seer I have to look into."

"Another one?" Mhelodie asks, and worry etches across her usually carefree features. "How many does that make?"

"Three missing Witches in the past two months, and now the Seer." Shit, I'd almost forgotten about the missing Witches.

He plants a kiss on my forehead. "I love you, Pumpkin."

I swallow. "Love you, too, Dad."

"Where's Quentin?" I ask Guy when Dad's left the apartment.

"Q left after you went to bed. He needed to leave straight away if he was going to make it to see the king today." Guy smiles and takes a big bite of his gridcakes, then motions to my plate as if to say, keep eating. So, I do. You don't need to tell me twice.

"Thanks! These are good," I mumble to Guy with my mouth still full of food. The others nod in agreement as they all scarf down their food like a bunch of starving animals.

"I was really worried about you last night!" I let him know. "I can't believe Quentin did what he did."

Guy glances to me, a flash of anger washing over his face. "Wait. What did he do?"

"You know, carrying me off like that when you and Asheron were trapped inside The Pit."

"What was he supposed to do, Paege? Leave you out there and come in after me? Let you come in after Asheron? Don't be ridiculous."

"I just mean—"

Guy interrupts, "I know what you mean, Paege. But you have to remember, Q and I haven't turned yet. We aren't as strong as the Wolves who have. There would have been no way to protect you from . . ." he pauses, looking down to the wound I patched up last night, "from a fatal bite."

I hadn't even thought about that. I don't know why, but I assumed Quentin had already merged with his Wolf.

"I didn't know," I say sheepishly, my shoulders slumping forward in defeat. "You know, I also didn't thank you for going back in to try and save Hallie and Asheron." I smile, trying to redeem myself. "So, thank you."

Guy smiles in return. "You *also* never said how much of a badass Asheron is?" His eyes widen. "Did you all know he's an Israykiel Guard?"

"No, I'm not. Not yet," Asheron interrupts.

"Whatever. You're still a badass, and I'd happily fight alongside you if ever needed again," Guy responds. "You saved my hind last night."

Asheron doesn't respond. He nods graciously and returns to his breakfast.

He truly is a complicated male. I mean, it's one thing to reject the mating bond to the one you truly love, but to blatantly hide as a Star-Borne . . . it's the most ridiculous thing I've ever heard. And for the life of me, I cannot figure out why.

I arrive at our usual training gym an hour later. The smell of sweat and eucalyptus stings my eyes when Amerax lugs open the large wooden doors and ushers me in. Leather bags slapping, chains groaning, feet shuffling, and loud grunts echo around us as we walk through the heavily padded room. It's where the Star-Borne train when they are stationed in the Neopolis, and we are not alone today.

A tall, dark-haired Guard nods at Amerax as we pass by. A glint of acknowledgment passes between them both, but it's not friendly. One of his direct reports, maybe? He looks much younger than Amerax, but that means nothing. He could be any age.

His tanned stomach ripples as he moves around the mat. A large five-pointed star tattoo across his chest filled with script I can't make out flashes as he swings an arm to take out his opponent. His moves are clean and fast as he dances around the mat, jabbing and hooking. He gets a clean shot, and his opponent, a female with striking silver and purple hair, takes it without complaining.

"Looks like you've got yourself a fan," she mocks as she raises her hands back up in defence and regains her position.

Huh?

The male Guard pivots, his amber eyes colliding with mine, and he raises a pierced brow.

"Can I help you?" he chides.

My mouth snaps close. Shit. I've been standing here, watching this perfectly chiselled stranger move like the lethal warrior he is. Mesmerised like a Godsdamn moron. Warmth blooms in my cheeks, and I take a step away.

Fuck.

"Paege?" Amerax calls my name, and it snaps me out of the hypnotic stand-off with the male, and I swear I see a flame burst to life in those amber eyes as they widen briefly.

I break our eye contact. "Sorry," I mutter and scurry across the mat to where Amerax stands, pulling his long, dark blond hair back and knotting it into a bun. The heavy weight of the warrior's stare still presses against me with every step I take.

He's laid our gym bags down and is unpacking our weapons. Mine from my bag, his from his various halters.

"You know them?" I ask Dad, curious about the encounter between the two Guards when we arrived. Amerax never brought friends to the house growing up. He said it was to protect us. I don't know if I believe that. I've never really seen Amerax with any friends. He always spent all his time with Mum and me. Then the twins when they came along.

"They are a couple of the Guards being stationed around the Neopolis for the next few days. I briefed them this morning. Those two will be patrolling the Forte tonight."

"Ah huh," I respond nonchalantly as I unzip my jacket and slide my shoes and socks off.

"Have you been training?"

"When I can," I reply as I tie my boring brown hair into a messy bun atop my head. It's not a lie. I don't train often, but when I can, I do.

"Weapons or hands?"

"Weapons," I reply, stretching my arms and legs, trying to contain the nerves bubbling up under my skin. I'm not much of a fighter. Amerax has always taken the time to train me, but I don't enjoy it. I'm not a Star-Borne—I wasn't born with an affinity to fight, and my empath gift make it all that much harder. Hurting someone and feeling the pain I've caused is almost unbearable, but it's different training with my dad. He can shield for a start, and it's not real. But Gods, I don't know what I would do if I ever faced a situation where I needed to fight. I'd probably run and hide.

Standing, my dad holds out one of my twin swords. I take one, the cool dragon bone biting at my palm as I wrap my fingers around the hilt and move into position on the mat.

"Now that we are alone, I want to ask about that back at the house?" Dad probes.

"What about back at the house?" I prepare myself for battle, shifting my body weight and the weight of the sword. Finding a perfect balance between the two.

The swords Amerax had made for me are light but deadly. Most long swords are heavy, too heavy for a small demi-Fae like me. Most are made for the Star-Borne to wield. These, however, are made especially for me. A step up from the wooden ones I used to fight with when I was young.

"How do you know Braxtion's son?" Dad starts as he lunges forward.

I meet him, blocking sharply and retracting quickly.

"Guy?" I thrust forward and retract again as my sword meets nothing but air.

"Yes, Guy. I didn't realise you were friendly with the royals." He lunges again, and I block him again. The jarring of our blades sends a sharp pain reverberating up my arm.

"I'm not—or I wasn't until a few days ago," I supply.

I parry his blows, blocking him strike for strike as he moves with a majestic dance. I'm not naïve; I know he isn't putting his full weight behind it, but the fact I can anticipate his movements still has a feeling of pride bubbling up inside me.

"Why all the questions about Guy?" I puff as I move to defend myself from another strike, swinging my sword up with both arms to block a strong blow from above. My chest heaves, and muscles twitch as I hold steady, pushing back against the brutal force of his attack. I'd be screwed if I was in an actual fight.

"You've never mentioned them before." The weight suddenly lifts, and my muscles relax at the welcomed reprieve of his attack.

"Them?" I drop the sword down by my side as I try to draw in air to my burning lungs.

"Quentin, the Heir Apparent. I'm assuming he is hanging around, too." Amerax hasn't even broken out in a sweat.

You are pathetic, Paege.

I raise a brow.

"Where one goes, the other is almost always around," he clarifies, wiping invisible sweat from his brow.

He isn't wrong there. Even while attending the collegium, they were inseparable.

I hum.

"Just be careful there, Pumpkin."

"Careful?" I puff. My body is still trying to take in as much air as possible.

"He has a habit of . . ." Dad breaks off, clearly searching for a less offensive sentence than *'using young females for their pleasure'*. "Just be careful, promise me that," he finishes.

"It's not like that. They helped me. They have been helping me."

He nods. "I suppose that's true, and I wouldn't be here if it wasn't for them."

"What does that mean?" I snap.

"They were at The Pit. Why else do you think we were sent here? The king explicitly sent us to protect his son."

Something in my chest tightens, and a heat starts rushing through my veins. Of course, the king sent the Guards here for his son. Not for the hundreds of thousands of other Beings that reside in the Neopolis. How stupid of me to even consider that.

"Pumpkin?"

Dad's hand covers mine gently. I look down. My knuckles appear as white as the dragon bone they are wrapped around.

"Yes?" I answer, a little perplexed. My aggression got the better of me there. What is it about Quentin and the king that riles me up so much? Shaking my head, I release my grip, and my dad pulls the sword from my clasp.

"What just happened?" he inquires. Worry lines grace his brow.

"I'm alright, Dad, I promise." I raise my hand to my heart, smiling wearily. But something in my stomach twists because I don't know if I truly am alright.

And I just lied to my dad about it.

CHAPTER 14

I sip on my second cup of coffee for the morning, willing the caffeine to work its magical powers and snap me out of the hazy funk I've felt since waking.

Almost immediately after Lumeilia and Mhelodie left last night, I went to bed—much to Asheron's dismay. The past few days have taken a toll on my mental health, and I just needed some sleep. But I didn't get any.

I laid awake in bed listening to Asheron and Guy talk for hours about all manner of things: theories about the Scorpions, demi-Fae, Star-Borne, and FaeMates. Even Wolves and their Emergence ceremonies. If I didn't know any better, I would say they were becoming fast friends.

They must have stayed up until at least midnight before deciding who was going to sleep where. Guy insisted on the couch, saying Wolves can sleep anywhere. Asheron didn't protest. Of course, he didn't. But long after the lights were out and the apartment went silent, I still laid in my bed, awake. Motionless, listening for any sound. Wide, wide awake.

When the birds began to chirp, and other signs of life began to stir outside, I decided it was time to get up and get out of bed. So, I did, with very little willpower needed, and I snuck out through my bedroom window, determined not to rouse the sleeping Wolf from his slumber.

Now it's midmorning, and I'm fast regretting that decision. I felt weirdly energised and refreshed after training at the Star-Borne Gym this morning. The faux energy boost from the murderous boxing session has worn off, and waves of tiredness keep overtaking my body. Caffeine is proving to be a useless weapon against it.

Blaire, my boss at my full-time job at the Neopolis History Museum and Archives, hasn't made it in yet. She left me a to-do list long as my arm and an itemised list of some scholarly articles and books she wants me to collect for a *special project*. As an archive assistant, I do a lot of her grunt work—which I truly don't mind. Working in the archives allows me time to read all matters of information we have documented, including catalogues of the entire museum's exhibits (past and present). Our history. And reading about the rich history of our kingdom excites me. Although, with many different Beings writing very different accounts of what has taken place over the centuries, there seems to be more confusion about our history than knowledge.

The archives are underground, below the museum above. The exposed rock walls keep the space purposely cold in the peak of the summer months. No natural light seeps in to damage any of the records we hold here, and it's completely soundproof.

With music playing far too loudly for a museum—thank goodness for the soundproofing—I've been working my way down the list one by one, perusing vast aisles of manuscripts, books, journals, and tomes.

Today, some of the literature Blaire has me collating is pretty interesting. *Witches: Fall of the Winters Coven. Five Houses of Quespelia. The War of Gods. Gargoyles and Harpies: Can We Save Them?*

I can't help but stop on one in particular. *The Origin Series: The Crescent Wolf Pack.*

Intrigued about my newfound friends and their Crescent Wolf pack, I have an urge to flip through the pages. Blaire allows me read whatever I want down here—anything that isn't restricted—so, I plan to have a sneaky read. Yet as I hold the big red leather book in my hands, something has me hesitating.

When I return to my desk, I turn the music box off and take a seat, studying the dusty old book closely under the dim sconce lights. The leather is heavily worn and cracked, embossed with a crescent moon on the cover. It's part of a bigger series. Volume two of six, but I don't remember seeing any other similar books with this one.

Maybe they were destroyed or lost before we had a chance to protect them?

I wouldn't normally be so nosy about Wolf history, but after spending time with Guy and Quentin, I can't help but be a little curious. I open the book, and a shiver spider crawls down my spine. Hesitantly, I turn the first page, and the beast inside stirs. Unsure if I should continue, I heed the familiar warning sign. What is it about this book that creates so much unease inside me?

Seconds pass, and the uneasiness settles heavier in my stomach with every shallow breath I take.

I slam the book shut.

A shadow moves behind me, and my breath hitches, my body becoming as still as the gargoyle sculptures that protect this building. Silence hangs in the thick air for a moment before the chime of my scribe jolts my heart straight out of my chest. I push myself back from the desk and jump up out of my chair. Spinning around, this morning's boxing exercise overrides my muscle memory, and I take a combative stance. Hands up, fists curled, and ready to tackle whatever is coming my way.

Blaire stands in front of me, casually tapping a stiletto heel, arms crossed across her body. Her siren brand sneaks out from under a rather large gold cuff, and a smile tugs at her lips. Her brows raise above the rim of her fashion eyepieces, clearly finding my stance more entertaining than threatening.

"Blaire, you scared me," I exclaim as I relax my body, grabbing for my chair that is spinning in circles like a carousel.

"Doing some light reading?" Blaire quips as she peers over my shoulder to the book. "Are you expecting a Wolf to jump out of the pages and attack?" She grins.

"Oh, this?" I respond sheepishly, shuffling myself back into my seat and trying to brush out the wrinkles in my pants and straighten myself out while doing so.

Straighten myself out? *Sure,* that's unlikely!

"No, I was just curious. I've, ah, been spending some time with a couple of Crescent Wolves lately, and when I saw this book, it intrigued me," I answer, trying to explain my behaviour. "But then the scribe startled me," I add, awkwardly attempting to hide my humiliation.

"So," Blaire drawls. "You were going to attack the scribe then?" Blaire must be loving this.

I shake my head.

"Have you got what I asked for?" she continues, her voice switching from amused to authoritative in under a minute. She walks to the office where my desk sits outside.

"Yes, it's all on your desk," I call out after her.

"All except that one," she adds from inside her office. "You can bring it in when you're done with whatever it is you were doing with it."

Reclaiming my position at my desk, I grab my scribe. Guy messaged to say he would come meet me at work later today to walk me home.

Ugh, like I need an escort.

I send a quick message back to say I will be finishing midafternoon, so there is no need to escort me, and he sends back an immediate reply.

Guy: I will see you then!

Gah, I should have just ignored that message.

And damn, I'm still intrigued by this book. Without much further hesitation and ignoring all warnings intuition keeps throwing at me, I open the book to a random page and start reading.

I barely get through one page of rather uninteresting information before Blaire summons me to the gates of aisle five for help. I've never been past the gates into the vaults—the restricted vaults. Restricted to assistants anyway. The vaults hold manuscripts deemed too fragile to be exposed to the elements or bound with curses and magic too dangerous for uneducated Beings to handle. One day, I'm sure Blaire will entrust me enough to work in the vaults with her. Until then, the archives it is.

The rest of the day is spent running around for Blaire, not even attempting to complete my initial to-do list, let alone continue reading about the Wolves. When midafternoon rolls around, new waves of tiredness crash through my body, and I decide to leave. As I pack up my desk and prepare my exit, Blaire approaches with a large string-bound paperback book and hands it to me.

"Here, you can take this copy of the book and have a read if you like. I'm not too sure how helpful it will be. The magic has redacted a lot of the content, but it could still make for an interesting read. Just don't let it out of your sight, alright?"

Shocked, I reply, "Thank you. Are you sure?" Blaire allows me to read whatever I want, but the rules have always been clear. Nothing leaves this room, not for anything or anyone. Even the king can't remove the writings contained within these walls. The archives are run by a board of representatives. Two representatives from each species: Fae, Witch, Wolf, and Siren. The Sirens manage the Neopolis History Museum and Archives. Their inability to be coerced makes them the perfect protector of such treasured, albeit manipulated, historical information. Texts must be signed out by each representative and monitored.

"It's just a copy, Paege. We have the original. So, I won't tell if you won't." A flash of something crosses her face so quickly, but then she smiles awkwardly as if trying to cover up whatever it is she feels. And, of course, she is shielding herself, so I can't get a read on her. "Who knows, you may find some answers to whatever it is you were looking for in there. But like I said, don't let it out of your sight." Her awkward smile fades, and her boss face is back.

"Oh, I'm not looking for anything in particular. I was just curious," I respond.

Blaire just nods and walks off, waving her hand above her head. "Goodbye, Paege. See you at a decent time tomorrow, I hope?" And then she disappears behind the corner of aisle ten.

Uncertain about what just happened, I stand hesitantly with the book in my hands, unease snaking its way around my chest. That was weird. Blaire and I could get into a lot of trouble for taking anything out of this room, but . . . Before placing the book in my pack, I flick through the pages, trying to remain casual. Maybe since it's just a copy, the same rules don't apply. Or maybe some texts are exempt? I don't get the same warning from my intuition that I got earlier with the original manuscript, thank the Gods.

Excitement sparks in my stomach, replacing the unease. I can't wait to get started on this when I get home.

 CHAPTER 15

Walking out of the Museum, I find Guy leaning against a tree in the parkland surrounding the Museum, looking a lot calmer than he has in the last few days. His broad shoulders are rolled forward, and he has a foot planted against the trunk.

When he sees me, he pushes off the tree with a wide smile and strolls over to meet me. I must admit, after seeing him standing there, I no longer care about being escorted home. There's something about Guy's presence that calms the constant buzzing under my skin, and I suppose a female could have a worse escort than Guy Braxtion.

"Hi," I greet Guy cheerily, trying to hide my weariness. The caffeine has certainly worn off now.

"Paege," Guy responds, addressing me with a smile that suggests he is genuinely happy to see me. It makes my heart swell because, as it seems, I am happy to see him, too. "You disappeared early this morning. Do you normally start your day so early?" he asks casually. I can't tell if he is acting like a smartass or if he is genuinely curious.

"Not usually, no. I couldn't sleep." He hums under his breath. "So, I decided to train and head to work early." Guy turns to walk, and I follow, falling into step beside him. I continue. "I didn't want to wake you, so I snuck out the window. Sorry, but why should insomnia keep you from getting a decent night's sleep?" I ask rhetorically, forcing a toothy smile. I mean, truthfully, I was trying to spare both Guy and Asheron from being awoken by me, but also, I just wanted to escape from the constant eyes watching my every move. I feel like Guy understands. I can't feel his emotions right now, but the way he nods and continues to walk, not arguing or questioning me any further, makes me think he truly does.

We continue to walk in silence for a moment. The sun beams down on us, and I welcome the warmth as it breathes against my skin, rejuvenating my tired and achy body.

Guy abruptly stops and faces me. The sun reflects thousands of golden specks through his dark green eyes, and it's kind of mesmerising, to say the least. They're unlike any Wolf eyes I've ever seen. Not that I've seen a lot.

"I do get it, Paege. Having Q and I around must feel like an inconvenience, but we truly are just trying to help." He no longer wears a smile on his face. Instead, his face is expressionless. "But if you're going to keep fighting us, maybe we should reconsider our strategy." He turns away and resumes walking.

I'm a little stunned. Does this mean I will get my life back? I hope to the Gods I do.

"I don't mean to be ungrateful," I call out after Guy. Because I really don't. But my mum and dad have always been overprotective of me. Always watching me with careful eyes. Even as an adult, they attempt to tell me what I can and can't do because I'm a demi-Fae and need to be more careful than others. That's half the reason I left Orphelious and came to the Neopolis. To be free of the constant scrutiny. I suppose I'm just feeling a little triggered and a lot suffocated.

Taking a few long, running strides after Guy, I catch up with him and continue, "But Quentin treats me like a child, and it's infuriating. A week ago, my life was mine. Now, I have three babysitters watching me around the clock, and I feel like I have zero freedom.

And for what?" Guy doesn't respond, so I continue, "I never asked for this. I am truly grateful for you both when my place was broken into, but The Pit . . ." I swallow. "That was not about me. That was the Scorpions. And there are thousands of Beings in this Neopolis that need protecting more than me—if that's what you both want to be doing."

Guy stops in his tracks, but he doesn't look at me. Instead, he drops his gaze and kicks his foot forward, loosening a stone from the street beneath him. I gently take Guy's hand and squeeze it. He tilts his head and faces me. His green eyes are fierce, and his brows pull together. He appears to be fighting a war in his mind.

"We don't need to make any changes right now," I say reassuringly. "To be honest, I just want to go home and relax." I smile warmly. "Present company is more than welcome to join me." Asheron messaged earlier to say he was staying at his, so I have the house to myself for the afternoon. But truthfully, I don't mind Guy's company, so why the Hels not?

Guy smiles warmly, and nods his head, and we continue to stroll through the streets, a comfortable silence stretching between us.

"That's interesting," he states, pointing to the necklace hanging around my neck.

I look down at the charm that rests between my breasts. The pearlescent blue gemstone that's embedded in the gold dagger bursts with flecks of gold under the afternoon sunlight. Not dissimilar to those exploding in Guy's emerald eyes.

"What is it?" he asks, and I look back up to him.

"Oh, just a necklace my mum gave me on my sixteenth birthday." My hand clasps the dagger, and I look down at it once more, studying the intricacies of the wings, and I feel my heart starting to thump heavier in my chest.

"My bio-dad gifted it to her before he died. I think the dagger represents something about him, a Human warrior perhaps, and the filigree guards represent my mum, Fae . . ." I trail off because, truthfully, I don't know. Mum won't ever discuss it, so that's the story I made up and what I've always liked to believe.

"Athame," Guy blurts out.

"Huh?"

"It's not a dagger. It's an Athame."

I have no idea what that is, but alright. Athame.

"And the stone?" he asks, his eyes widening as he takes in the intricacies of the *Athame*, the wings, and the stone.

"Probably something from the Human lands." It's not like anything I've ever seen before. The greyish-blue stone has swirls of lighter blues and whites with freckles of golds and red that sparkle brightly in the sun's reflection. "But I love it. It's the only thing I have of my bio-dad's, so I wear it every single day to remind me of the man who gave me life."

My eyes fill with tears, and I feel that familiar lump forming in my throat.

"I know it's unusual," I continue. "Amerax is my dad. I've never gone without the love of a father, but I have always felt like a part of me is missing. Like I'm not whole." My hand releases the charm as I set it back against my shirt. I look back up at Guy, trying to hide the pain I suddenly feel inside, the hole that seems to have been ripped open by this conversation, the pain of a daughter who hasn't met her father.

"I think wearing it brings me closer to feeling complete." I turn my head to blink the tears away and take a few large, deep breaths.

Guy nods in response and whispers, "I understand."

He sighs and runs his hands through his hair. "I never met my mother," Guy adds. "She died not long after I was born . . . I know nothing about her, not even her name. My dad never got a chance to tell me." I look up at Guy, and his eyes are glassy. He swallows hard, as if he's trying to push the emotions down. "Well, you know the story. He was killed when I was young, too," he pauses. I study his face, and I see the pain of two lost parents unveil with every word he speaks.

"Like you, I was never alone though." His eyes shift uncomfortably, but he continues, "I had the pack. The king—" he clears his throat. "Q's dad," he clarifies. "He has always treated me like family. His mum always cared for me before she died."

My heart lurches at this news. Quentin's mum had died. How did I not know that? I suppose he never *really* talks about himself. I can't even imagine Quentin and I walking down the street, hearts open, speaking freely. Nope. We are not *those* friends.

"I didn't know. I'm so sorry, Guy." I take his hand again and squeeze it gently.

"Q's my brother, you know. Fight or die. His family's mine. The pack, they're family, too. But it's not the same . . ." He trails off for a moment, eyes burning into mine, and I swear tears prick at his eyes. "When you lose a parent when you're young, I think a part of you gets lost." He shifts his glassy eyes down, glances at the golden charm hanging around my neck, and smiles. "So, yes, Paege. I do get it."

CHAPTER 16

The rest of the walk home is shrouded in silence but not full of uncomfortableness like the last couple of times. It's almost as if an unspoken agreement between the two of us has formed. A recognition of our past trauma—the death of our parents—lingers between us, bridging the gap of our differences.

"Stay behind me, Paege," Guy instructs suddenly as we approach my apartment complex, and his arm forces me behind him. I push up to my toes and lean over his shoulder to see what the fuss is about, and my chest compresses like a sea of serpents encasing themselves around my ribs.

The gate lock is covered in blood, the mechanism scorched, and the large iron gates ajar. Drops of blood stain the footpath, trailing through the garden up to the apartments.

What the Hels is going on?

Guys ears twitch, his Wolf senses bursting to life, and he sniffs the air. Then he runs, yelling at me to stay behind.

But of course, I don't.

Without any hesitation, I follow him, running toward my apartment and hot on his heels, both of us eager and anxious to figure out if my unwanted visitor has returned. But when we get close, I don't see anything suspicious. I don't find anything at all. My front door is closed. There is no blood. No signs of damage. No distress from my neighbours.

Guy reappears from behind my apartment, shaking his head with wide eyes and knitted brows.

"What's wrong?" I ask. Worry instantly overcomes my adrenaline rush from moments ago.

"Nothing!" Guy says, shaking his head again. "Absolutely nothing."

My chest collapses. "I don't understand."

"Neither do I. There was blood and a clear scent, and then nothing. It's like they disappeared before they even got to your apartment."

"If that's where they were headed." I take a moment to catch my breath. "There are fifteen apartments. They could have been going to any one of them."

"After everything that's happened the last few days, it's naive to think that," Guy says. His words drip with frustration, and I suppose he isn't wrong. It's true. I immediately thought this was my intruder returning, but a small part of me also can't believe that it would happen to me. Who would possibly want to stalk me, and what could they want?

"Aren't *you* being a little paranoid?" I retort.

Guy's eyes darken, and a flash of anger appears. But just as quickly, they return to their normal striking emerald, and his face softens. I don't often wish I could feel the emotions of others, but at this very moment, I wish I could read his. The sudden shift in his demeanour has me wondering what he's thinking and sensing, and it's not hard to tell something is wrong.

But I don't ask. And he doesn't tell.

"Come on," he says and takes me by the hand, ushering me toward my front door.

When we enter my apartment, Guy releases my hand and walks away almost instantly. Without another word, he sits on the couch and puts his feet up on my coffee table, staring out the window into the garden.

Taking a deep breath in, I try to ignore the sudden coldness that fills the space. I retrieve my reading material, dumping the bag by the door, and I climb the stairs to the mezzanine. Dropping my new book onto the daybed, I take a moment to look outside over the gardens.

My skin prickles as the warmth from the sun caresses me through the windows. The garden fountain erupts with water in unpredictable patterns, and a flock of tiny birds flies around, darting through the spurts of water, playing and chattering away. It reminds me of a game of chase, and a smile tugs at my lips. I can't help but think how much fun it would be to be that free and happy. The green and golden leaves of sap trees sway gently in the breeze, and it all looks so peaceful. For a moment, I forget all the craziness of the past few days.

Minutes later, I make my way back down the stairs to the lounge area to find Guy also staring out the window. He turns to face me when he realises I am back in the room with him.

"How well do you know Mhelodie?" he asks, his voice a little shaky.

"Why?" Curiosity burns through my veins at his sudden interest in my friend.

"No reason—it doesn't matter," he dismisses me, trying to end the short but strange conversation.

I respond anyway. "I met Mhelodie the first year we started at the Neopolis Collegium. She is one of the sweetest and kindest Beings you will ever meet. After her Ascension, she'll likely become a healer," I say, pride beaming from me with every word I speak. Mhelodie is going to be one of the most gifted healers in our time. I'm sure of it. Her magic is strong for a Witch that hasn't yet ascended. I can't even fathom what her magic will be like once she has. Her mentor, Enderlene, is one of the most revered healers in all of

Elyndria, and the fact that she has chosen Mhelodie to mentor speaks volumes about how gifted Mhelodie truly is.

Guy nods.

"Why?" I ask again.

He doesn't answer. Instead, he mumbles about how he must be wrong about something and returns his attention outside.

I take the silence as an opportunity to freshen up, grabbing my bag to head to my room to change.

Feeling much more comfortable, I return to the living area wearing my baggy fleece pants and a cropped shirt. Guy's in the kitchen with remnants of grated cheese, vegetables, and eggshells strewn across the kitchen bench as he whisks what I assume are the ingredients together in a large bowl.

"Eggfolds?" he asks with a big grin on his face, clearly in a better mood than a moment ago. "Then maybe we can watch your vision box this afternoon."

"You act like you've never watched a vision box before?" I laugh out loud. His obsession with watching it is absurd.

"I have, but we don't have one in the palace or the den. Ruhaul won't permit it."

I jump up from the couch at his admission. "King Ishaan won't permit it? Why? He doesn't have a problem with technology. You and Quentin have scribes."

"Yes, but a vision box is not a necessity," he supplies as he pours the egg mixture into the pan on the fire stove top.

I suppose it's true. After our Sacred Birthday, both Fae and Witches have means to communicate using magic and their gifts, so the use of scribes becomes almost redundant. But as far as I am aware, Wolves don't. I often wonder if these modern methods of communication and information sharing were born from the Wolves' requirements or desires to communicate like that of the Fae and Witches. So yes, a scribe is probably considered a necessity by the king. A vision box certainly is not. It's for our entertainment only.

Not that I spend much time watching it. I prefer to waste my time reading a good book or listening to music on my music box. Now, *that* device is a necessity. I can't even imagine what life would be like without it.

Guy settles in for the afternoon watching a group of Witch healers navigating their way through life, love, and learning. From the flashbacks, it seems someone dies, or someone's heart is broken in almost every episode. I settle in next to him with my journal, trying to ignore the tragic and cheesy entertainment. Yet it's somehow compelling, and I find myself sucked into the chaotic world that is Varusha's Healers.

Hours pass with no word from Quentin and no further word from my dad, and life somehow feels normal again. I must say it's a relief. Mondays are hard enough as it is.

With the sun starting to set, a stillness settles within, relaxation gently taking hold. I close my eyes for a moment, and I feel the pull to sleep almost instantly. But as I fall into a slumber, there is nothing relaxing greeting me. I find myself clawing back to the edge of consciousness, trying to escape the visions of what I can only describe as war that continue to pull me under.

I stare at the male standing with his back turned to me as a ring of fire dances around him. The heat of the flames licks at my skin as I watch in horror as the crimson sea seeps from the edges of the ring and snakes closer and closer to my feet. When it finally reaches my toes, I step back.

"Guy?" The whispering plea falls from my lips, and he pivots to face me with his hand placed against his heart.

"Sorry, Paege, I couldn't stop them," he says calmly, and a gasp escapes me as I focus on the blood leaking between his fingers—the blood that fills the crimson pool expanding across the ground. I shake my head in disbelief, and I reach out for him on instinct alone. But I retract my arm just as quickly as the flames that separate us flare to life and bite into me, scalding me in a dire warning to keep back.

"I promise I will always be by your side," he swears, and he drops his hand, revealing a gaping hole in his chest. His emerald eyes, bloodshot and teary, widen, and his knees buckle. Unable to move, I watch in horror as he sinks to the bottom of the pool, his very own life force drowning him as he unsuccessfully gasps for air.

An evil yet familiar laughter echoes through the fire, and a blood-curdling scream volleys back in retaliation, the two sounds fighting for a freedom that seems impossible to attain. The flames dance wildly, casting grotesque shadows that flicker and twist as if the very darkness itself is caught in the struggle.

"No!" I scream, and from somewhere deep within, I manage to free myself from the shackles holding me captive, and I lurch forward.

Like a Godsdamn war drum, the pounding in my chest vibrates through my entire body, and I suck in air as I try to gather myself.

A dream.

It was just a dream.

Guy bolts upright next to me, his brows knitting with confusion as his eyes find mine.

"Sorry. I didn't mean to startle you," I apologise quietly, realising I woke him when I jerked awake.

He shakes his head, scratches behind his ear like a pup, and rests his head back against the couch. He closes his eyes once more, drifting quickly back off to sleep.

Well, that must be nice.

An overwhelming urge to hug him washes through me, his body emitting nothing but the epitome of a calm and gentle aura. I resist because that would be weird, and I'm pretty sure I've already used up my weirdo quota for the week. So instead, I cover him with a blanket, turn the vision box off, and quietly climb the stairs up to the mezzanine to lie on my daybed and watch the sun set over the Neopolis.

Once the sun has put herself to bed, I grab my scribe and send Quentin a quick message:

Me: Just checking in to see how everything is going. Guy and I miss you. - P

I wait for a minute to see if he messages back, but nothing comes through. So, I turn on the lights, grab the book, and start reading about my new friends, the Crescent Wolf pack.

The scribe's chime startles me, and for the briefest of moments, I have no idea where I am. As I roll over, I begin to get my bearings and remember.

I'm on the mezzanine. I came up here to read the book. I must have fallen asleep.

I grab my scribe and see Quentin and Blaire have both sent me a message. It's past midnight.

Quentin: Books, tell Braxtion I'm on my way back. I've got some news.
Blaire: Paege, don't come into the office tomorrow. The Museum will be closed. We had a break-in. Will send more information in the morning.

The Museum is heavily guarded with magic It would be near impossible for anyone to break in without some sort of inside knowledge or without the magic of an extremely powerful Witch—or Heretic. But the Heretics had been banished to the foothills of the Mountains of G'phyn, the unmagic lands, hundreds of years ago to stop them from siphoning magic from the kingdom. They are still heavily safeguarded by the Lupa-Centaurs.

Whoever broke in must be powerful. I wonder what they stole, if anything, or what they were looking for. As all these thoughts and more start swirling around my head, my scribe chimes again.

Quentin: I miss you both, too.

Huh? The arrogant, charming, self-obsessed Wolf does have feelings after all? I can't help but feel a little chuffed that he admitted he is missing us.

I retreat to the ground floor to find Guy is no longer on the couch asleep. Tiptoeing, I creep over to the spare bedroom and inch the door open, just enough to see a semi-naked Guy sprawled across the bed. He's face down, shirt and jeans removed, lying only in his boxer briefs. It takes every bit of self-restraint not to sneak into the room and cover him with the quilt that's bunched at his feet. I hesitate as I notice multiple silver marks across his back that shimmer against his sun-kissed skin. I wince at the sight of them. Not because of their ugliness, no, but because of the pain they must have caused. An ache blooms in my chest, and I question what terrible things must have happened to this gentle, caring, selfless Wolf to inflict such scars.

Heartbroken for Guy's past, I gently close the door and walk to my bedroom, forgetting any attempt to be quiet. As I lay my head down in my own bed, I can't help but wonder who did it. Because if I ever come face to face with them, I will make them wish they had never been born.

CHAPTER 17

We twirl around each other, the sun beating down on us as our wooden swords smack together in unison. Clank, clank, clank. I gobble down air and take a small step back, lowering my sword for a moment as I regain my strength. We've been playing this game all afternoon, and the weight of the wooden sword is becoming heavy in my little hands.

"Are you too tired to continue, Princess?" he taunts. His single dimple, just like mine, appears with his grin.

I hold my sword back up, using both hands like Amerax taught me.

"Never, Prince! I will fight you until my last breath." I lunge for him, and he jumps out of the way, bringing his sword up to meet mine again with a clank.

"When I best you, I will lock you in the dungeons to be forgotten about forever," he laughs.

"You will never be able to best me, Prince," I reply with a giggle. "I am too fast." I swing at him again, and our wooden swords smack. "I am too skilled." Another smack. "Too smart." Smack.

We still, our swords kissing. Neither one of us move. His emerald eyes glisten in the sunlight, and a small bead of sweat drops to his brow.

"Honey, it's time to go."

"Paege, it's time to go to work."

My eyes flutter, light slowly spilling into my sight as Guy leans over me. His brows furrow as he rests a hand on my shoulder, gently rocking me back and forth, back and forth.

"Paege, wake up! You've slept in."

"Huh," I mumble, still half asleep, still half in my recurring dream. Gods, it's almost impossible to sleep in around here. Always someone waking me up.

"You've slept in. It's midmorning. Don't you need to be at work by now?" he gently asks.

"No," I say sluggishly, sitting myself up and rubbing my eyes to slowly gain my awareness. "I'm not going in. Blaire messaged last night to say the museum was broken into, so it's not open today, and we're all to stay home."

"What?" Guy says abruptly. "Your work was broken into?"

"No," I huff, "Not *my* work. I work in the archives. The *Museum* was broken into."

"Did she say what was taken?" Guy seems frantic, pacing the length of my room, his eyes darting around as his brows knit like he is trying to solve a puzzle or something. For the life of me, I have no idea why he is so intrigued about the Museum being broken into. Yes, it's bizarre. That place is locked up with so many spells and wards it would be impossible to break into, but I never thought of Guy to be the type that would be all cut up over stolen artefacts. Besides, the Star-Borne will figure it out.

"No." I shift in my bed, finally starting to feel awake.

Guy pulls out his scribe as he leaves my room.

"Uh, why the sudden interest in the museum?" I call out after him, totally confused by his over-reaction.

He doesn't answer.

Well, I'm awake now, so I may as well get up.

After I'm freshened up, I go to join Guy in the living area; however, I don't find him there.

"Guy?" I say loudly, wondering if he just left. However, I'm not fully opposed to it. It would be nice to get my home back to myself.

"Up here," he calls out.

Not so lucky, then.

I climb the stairs up to the mezzanine to find Guy lying on the daybed, the Crescent Wolf pack book in his hands, casually flicking through the pages.

"Doing some light reading?" he asks, not taking his eyes off the pages in front of him.

"Truthfully, I haven't had a chance to look at it yet," I respond and sit next to him. He's freshly showered. His wet, brown hair falls flat against his brow, and the smell of soap still lingers in the air around him. It settles something deep inside my chest.

"I found it at work yesterday and was intrigued. Do you know much about the pack's history?" I ask curiously.

"I suppose." Guy looks up from a page he has landed on. "Q's mum used to share some stories. But it's always been a bit of a contentious subject with me, you know, being the child of the original king, the *Betrayer*." He runs his hands through his hair, pulling it off his face. "Q's dad's always been a little reserved in what he shared around me." His eyes return to pages of the books.

Blood thumps between my ears. Hasn't Guy been through enough already? He lost his entire family and was stripped of his title. Yes, the king took him in, and Q's mum took care of him, but this doesn't sound like the actions of a man who treats him like family. Equal to the rest. But of course, he doesn't. The king doesn't treat any of us as equals. His methods of oppression seem to extend much further than that of the other species he deems beneath him and his precious Wolves.

"You can read it if you want," I offer. Maybe this book could answer some of Guy's questions about his past, his lineage, and his pack. Maybe this book could give him some closure. "But it can't leave the apartment. Oh, and you can't tell anyone I'm letting you read it," I add, remembering what Blaire made me promise.

"No problem. It will be our secret," he smirks, his single dimple making a brief appearance, and an emerald eye winks at me.

That may be the cheekiest Wolf grin I've ever seen.

"Oh, Quentin messaged last night. He says he's on his way back." I stand to leave.

Guy doesn't look up from the book but replies, "Hm, he messaged me, too."

"I'm going downstairs to make some breakfast. Let me know if you want anything," I point to the book, "or if you find anything interesting in there."

"Uh-huh," he responds, but I'm sure he isn't paying attention.

"So," he drawls as I reach the stairs. "You miss Q, huh?"

I snap my head up. Guy's grin appears even wider, if that is possible, but his eyes don't leave the page he's reading.

"Oh, shut up," I chide and stick my tongue out at him.

Bloody Wolves.

After breakfast, I message Lumeilia, Asheron, and Mhelodie, letting them know about the Museum break-in and that I have the day off. Both Mhelodie and Lumeilia respond with some sarcastic commentary, wishing they, too, had the day off. Asheron replies, saying he already knows. Apparently, Guy texted the group message.

What group message?

I send a reply asking about the group message, and Asheron responds immediately.

Asheron: The one Quentin set up before he left. For updates on the situation.
Me: Why didn't I know about this?

No reply.

Me: What is this? Some alpha male-only group?

Still nothing.

I stare at the scribe for what feels like hours before a message appears with the heading *"Paege's Security," which conveniently changes to "Updates" r*ight before my eyes.

What the actual fuck?

"Guy?" I yell upstairs. The annoyance at how far they have taken this situation unfurls within me like a tightly coiled spring. Each moment of their antics has been winding me tighter and tighter and tighter.

"Paege?" Guy sarcastically responds.

"Guy!" I snap back.

"What?"

"Can you come down here, please, and tell me what the fuck this *group message* is all about?" I hold my scribe up and shake it in the air like he can actually see me from up on the mezzanine.

Guy appears at the top of the stairs. "It's nothing, Paege." He sounds annoyed or maybe distracted, I can't quite tell. "Can we talk about it later? I found something rather interesting about the Crescent Wolf pack."

With rage still brewing inside me, I take a deep breath and try to settle myself. "Fine, but we *are* discussing this!"

"Of course, but later. Are you coming up, or shall I come down?"

"I'll come up." I sigh in defeat. He better not be avoiding this.

The mezzanine is much nicer than the living space. It's open and bright with a beautiful view, and its effects are instantly calming, even if it is currently inhabited by one-third of the population of the most irritable males in my life right now.

Once I'm settled on the day bed next to him, Guy starts telling me about the information he just read.

"I'm not too sure I'm reading this right. A lot's redacted with magic, but I think . . . I think the Crescent Wolf pack is one of six, not five, Origin Wolf packs."

"What?" I was not expecting that.

Guy continues, "The book isn't clear about it." His voice sounds disappointed, "But that's not even the craziest thing I found. The Crescent Wolf pack was not always bound by the moon. Hundreds of years ago, we could change at will like the other packs, but something happened." Guy swallows, his eyes roving over the pages. "Something happened and changed our fate."

I know this. The Crescent Wolf pack can only shift during the crescent moon phases, unlike the rest of the packs, which can shift at will.

"The crescent moon curse," I mutter under my breath. It's a phrase thrown around loosely by the Fae and Witches, taunting the Crescent Wolf pack about their inability to shift like the other packs. None of us believe it was a curse, but I have to admit, I often wonder why they couldn't shift like the rest. "Did you know any of this?" I ask Guy. "I mean, if not, this is wild."

"I had no idea."

"What do you think this means? Do you think Quentin knows?"

"I don't know," Guy pauses. "I don't think so, but I think we should ask him."

"I might ask Mhelodie, too. See if she knows anything about it?" I add, trying to be helpful.

"No. Don't."

My brows shoot for the stars, and confusion fills my mind. "Huh, why?" I ask. He's been acting sketchy about Mhelodie for days now.

"Well, we don't know anything, and what if it's some curse the Witches put on us? We need to be careful."

"That's crazy; the Witches would never. Mhelodie would—"

"No, Paege," Guy abruptly cuts me off. "Please. Let's just talk to Q when he gets back, and once we know more, we can revisit it."

"But . . ." I try to protest, but Guy shuts me down once again.

"No, Paege, this is Wolf business. Just stay out of it," he snaps.

Anger born of nothing but the fire that's been simmering in my gut since earlier erupts. My mouth spews words like molten lava. "Seriously? You have no problems sticking yourselves into my business, taking over my life, invading my privacy, reading *my* books." I rip the book from Guy's hand. "But Gods forbid I try to get involved in any of yours. Typical. Fucking. Wolf. Behaviour!"

And it *is* typical Wolf behaviour. They keep their secrets about their packs, controlling the educational system and cultural narratives to guarantee their Wolf supremacy goes unchallenged and to ensure their weaknesses cannot be exploited by us *lesser Beings*.

"Now, what the fuck are these *Paege's Security* group messages all about?" I snarl.

Guy retreats. Flashes of regret and remorse fill his green eyes.

"I'm sorry, Paege. I didn't mean to." He dips his head.

"No, of course you didn't." I'm on a roll now, and I don't want to stop. I've been pushed around far too many times this past week, and I am done. "You never think—none of you do." Guy opens his mouth to speak, but I hold up a hand to stop him, and I keep going, "You all assume I'm this weak, fragile, little female, and you keep making decisions for me. About me. You talk about me like I don't exist, but I do. And I have feelings. I have opinions." I consider for a moment what I want to say next. "And they matter," I finish more softly than the rest of my verbal word vomit.

Oh, the Gods, Paege.

"And *none* of this is my fucking fault!" I yell.

Right, now I'm done.

Salty tears I didn't even feel coming roll down my cheeks. I'm so caught up in my rant that I have no awareness of the plethora of emotions that flood me. Guy's? I don't know. Mine? Absolutely. They are powerful, and there are many.

Guy stands and storms over to me. His large hands tightly wrap around my upper arms. The bruising grip extracts an involuntary flinch, but his face remains motionless. His emerald eyes burn into mine, and a vein pops through the skin above his brow. He looks pissed, and his chiselled jaw ticks.

But instead of yelling, pushing, or shaking me, he suddenly releases his grip, wraps his arms around me, and pulls me in for the biggest hug ever. He whispers in my ear, "I'm sorry."

I don't want to forgive him. I don't want to forgive any of them. They have made my life miserable over the last week, and I've had enough. But regardless of the fight inside my mind, my body sinks into his. The traitorous bitch that she is.

"You've been saying that a lot lately," I can't help but bite back.

He doesn't protest. Instead, his hug becomes tighter, like he's scared I'm going to pull away. I feel my heart slow. All that anger and rage dissipates while the iciness I so badly wanted to portray thaws.

Finally, he pulls back and tucks a rogue strand of my ash-brown hair behind my ear, then smiles. "Feel better?" he asks. And damn if I don't melt away into a river right there on the spot. How does he always do that?

"Yes, I do," I respond, wiping away the tears.

"Good." He tugs the book out of my hand and marches back to the daybed. "Now that you've gotten that out of your system, let's try to find out more about this *curse*—together." He smiles.

"You knew about that?" I ask sheepishly.

"Of course we did, Paege," he jests. "Now, come sit." He pats the bed as if ordering a pup to follow—a command. "And help me." And damn the Gods, I do.

Is he sure he isn't part of the Silver Tongue pack?

CHAPTER 18

"**I**s everything alright, Mhelodie?" I ask gently, moving in for a hug as she walks through the door with Lumeilia—hoping I can squeeze out whatever discomfort she felt about coming here out of her. I invited them over after a bit of a head-to-head with Asheron, and while Lumeilia has been her normal eager self, Mhelodie seemed distant. Uninterested.

Asheron arrived a little earlier to apologise for the whole *Paege Security* group message thing. I may have gotten over it by the time he had apologised, but I wasn't going to let him think it was that easy to gain my forgiveness. So, I made him work for it. I pouted, stomping my feet like a Pegasus, and squeezed out some Harpie tears, trying desperately to rehash my rant to Guy from earlier. But when I couldn't remember what I had said and got stuck for words, Guy, not-so-stealthily reminded me, and blew the whole charade.

Wolves!

"Nothing, I'm fine," she replies, pulling away from my embrace and forcing a smile that doesn't reach her beautiful golden eyes. Her usual bubbly persona is dampened. The sparkle behind her eyes is completely missing, now replaced by solid dark rings.

"That bad, huh?" I reply, trying to open myself up and feel whatever is going on, but I find nothing. Damn gifts. I suppose I'm doing this the old-fashioned way. "It's fine if you don't want to talk about it, but if you do, I'm here." I smile warmly, giving her hand a reassuring squeeze.

She winces immediately.

"Sorry!" I look down at her hand, and my brows pull together as I see the bandage across her palm. "What happened?"

"Nothing," she pulls her hand from my grip. "Just a blood spell I was learning, and I haven't fully healed yet."

"Oh," I respond. I didn't realise that blood spells were even a thing. But if they are, that could explain the absence of life inside one of the liveliest Beings I know. I can't imagine anything good coming from blood spells. Why Enderlene is even teaching that sort of magic is beyond me, but I don't pretend to know what goes on within the Witches' covens. I look to Lumeilia, and she shrugs, her mahogany eyes revealing nothing. Either she is unsure of what is going on herself or unbothered by it. I suppose if it was anything bad, Lumeilia would know.

"Like I told Lu-Lu earlier, I'm fine. I'm just drained," Mhelodie reconfirms, and this time with more of a *real* smile on her face. "Can we please drop it? Anyway, weren't we summoned here to bring some life to the party?" I flinch at the word *summoned* like I've somehow forced her to come tonight against her will, but the smile on my friend's face that seems to grow with more genuineness as time ticks by says otherwise, so I let it go.

She moves gracefully over to the dining table where Lumeilia has taken up residency on Asheron's lap, and she sits between them and Guy. I follow, my eyes darting between Guy and Quentin and the absence of free chairs, trying to figure out where I am going to sit. Not on any of their laps. Before I decide where to place myself, Guy stands to offer me his chair, which I graciously accept so I can be seated with my friends. He then promptly jumps up, seating himself on the kitchen bench behind me.

"You didn't want to sit on my lap, Books? I'm wounded," Quentin jests, placing his hand on his heart, and I roll my eyes at him. Since he returned, he's been acting like a real jerk.

Guy suddenly moves, jumping down from the bench and throwing himself into Quentin's lap, wrapping his arms around his broad shoulders and snuggling into his neck. My mouth opens, watching in disbelief.

"What the fuck are you doing?" Quentin tries to shove him off, but Guy hangs on tighter.

Is this some sort of weird Wolf pack thing?

"Brother, you seemed hurt that no one was sitting on your lap," Guy jokes as Quentin still struggles to push him off. They tussle for the briefest moment, the table sitting in silence, and I can't help but smirk at the odd interaction unfolding before me. Eventually, Guy relents, and Quentin shoves him up. Guy shrugs as if it were nothing, ruffles Quentin's sandy blond locks, walks into the kitchen, and starts pulling out food from my chiller as if nothing happened.

"Q, did you get any updates from your dad?" Guy asks casually as he starts rummaging through random drawers and cupboards. Guy has made himself at home these last few days, but I won't complain if he keeps buying and cooking me food. The Gods know I am the kingdom's worst cook. Sometimes, I wonder how I even manage to keep myself alive.

Quentin clears his throat, flattening his hair back down, and then flicks his fringe out of his eyes. "The king is not doing anything more than placing some Israykiel Guards around the Neopolis. He believes The Pit was a one-off attack, and the presence of the Guard should be enough to deter them from causing further carnage."

"So that's it?" My brows shoot to the sky, not hiding my surprise that there isn't going to be any formal investigation. But of course, there won't be. It's the Wolves. They get away with everything.

"It is what it is, Books. Dad said he has spoken to the Guards, and they don't believe there is a greater threat."

"Asheron?" I ask, turning to the only person in the room I can truly trust when it comes to the Guards, in complete disbelief at what I am hearing.

"He's right, Paege," Asheron supplies. "I spoke to the Guards, too, and there isn't much more they can do but patrol the streets for now."

"So, what does that mean?" Lumeilia asks. "I've got my exhibition this Friday." Her mahogany eyes dart nervously around the room as her hand reaches out to take Mhelodie's, whose face is once again sullen and lifeless. I need to get to the bottom of what is going on with her.

"It means stay out of trouble," Quentin says sharply, his eyes narrowing as he looks toward Lumeilia. She scowls back at him, not showing any sign of submission to the alpha Wolf, and she goes back to eyeing Mhelodie.

Gods, I hope she is alright.

"Don't talk to them like that," I snap back to him. He is in a crabby mood, but I have a sneaking suspicion that my mood might be darker.

"What are they even doing here? None of this has anything to do with them."

"They are here because they are my friends, and I asked them here. The question is, what are you doing here? You've got no information to provide, and you've done nothing but be a whining little Wolf baby since you got here," I snap rather rudely, but fuck it. He has done nothing but insult me and my friends since he arrived. I don't care who he is. He is in my house, and I expect him to treat my friends with the respect they deserve while here.

Quentin's eyes widen with disbelief or maybe irritation at my sudden outburst. Then, a wolfish grin tugs at his lips. *Fuck.* What I would give to smack that smile right off his face right now. I hold his stare, refusing to bow down to this alpha male or royalty shit in my own home. He may be the Heir Apparent out there in the world, but here, I am the alpha. This is my domain, and I will not surrender it. Or that is what I am going to tell myself. I might not truly believe it, but I refuse to let him see that weakness. Wolves smell and thrive off fear, after all.

With our eyes locked in a game of combat, the silence stretches on between us for a long, awkward moment, neither of us flinching. Then Quentin clears his throat and bows his head in what I can only hope is a conceding gesture. Breaking our eye contact, he looks at Guy. The second our eyes disconnect, a gaping abyss appears, the missing weight of his attention prying some sort of longing out of me.

Ouch, Asheron mouths to me, his lips pulling into a thin line, and Lumeilia smiles awkwardly.

"Books, Braxtion told me about your work. What happened?" I reluctantly return my attention to Quentin. His icy blue eyes burn into me with . . . *concern*? I shrug, trying to hide the heat that suddenly fills my cheeks. Without a doubt, I think he is the most irritating male I have ever met in my life, but something inside me stirs, and molten heat pools deep within my core, turning me to putty as he continues to look at me like *that*.

I swallow thickly—and loudly.

"Shouldn't you know? Didn't daddy dearest give you an update?" I'm treading a thin line here, but the monstrous irritation that is building up inside me doesn't want to be suppressed; it wants to be released.

"Books," Quentin warns, and I can't help but feel a little sense of achievement knowing I can get under the Wolf's skin like I do. But is that really the smartest move? I know he is a royal pain in my ass, but I suppose he is trying to help me out. They all are.

Glancing around the room, I make eye contact with all the males, one by one. My very own personal security team. However, now it feels a lot less like a security team and more like a panel of the most complicated males in my life.

Quentin, the Heir Apparent, is the next High Alpha to the pack. A Wolf that wants to avoid his royal obligations unless it's on his terms. A Wolf whose girlfriend ended up mated to another Wolf from a different pack. A vicious and brutal pack responsible for the murder of dozens of Beings. He does look tired. I wonder when he last slept. No wonder he is cranky and being a right jerk.

Guy, the Wolf who never met his mother and whose father's past transgressions plague his conscience. While he was brought up with the pack and Quentin as his family, I now know more than anything he misses having a real family of his own. I also know he is eager to share the news about the pack, but he hasn't brought it up yet. If I'd have to guess, he is likely waiting for Asheron to leave, being that it's Wolf business and all.

Stop it, Paege!

And Asheron. I think he may be the most complicated of them all. He has spent years ignoring the fact he's kin to an Israykiel Guard, always hiding his Star-Borne mark under clothes so the Beings in the kingdom wouldn't find out and pre-judge him. A Fae that rejected his FaeMate for only Gods knows what reason. Maybe all this drama is making him reconsider his views toward his Israykiel Guard calling. Who knows?

So, here they all are in my apartment on a Tuesday night. A stupidly good-looking bunch of males broken in ways that even I, a demi-Fae who doesn't truly belong anywhere, can't fully understand. As I continue to study the three of them, I feel an unexpected sense of pride and belonging. While it's been a heck of a ride the past week, and they have all irritated me to no end, these three beautiful males have done nothing but try to look out for me. Not that I asked for any of this, but maybe I should stop being an ungrateful little brat.

I've done nothing but bitch and complain about it. *Damn it, Paege!*

Swallowing down the emotions pushing their way to the surface, I answer Quentin, "I know nothing more than you do. Blaire sent a message for me to return to work the day after tomorrow. She is also being kept in the dark about the whole situation, so she has very little information to pass on. Except, whoever did it was looking for something specific. Nothing was stolen, but plenty was disrupted. What they were looking for, or who, is anyone's guess."

CHAPTER 19

"I told you, Q, it's probably nothing," Guy interrupts as he places the world's largest and cheesiest doughwheel in the oven. I didn't even know I had the space for something that big in there. I really must learn how to cook.

"Yeah, well, I don't believe in coincidences," Quentin says at the same time a chime rings through the air. He pulls his scribe from his pocket and places his attention firmly on the device in his hands.

"Well, I don't believe in your paranoid delusions, yet here we are," I retort under my breath but still loud enough for everyone to hear, unable to contain my frustration that we are still discussing the Museum break-in and treating it like it's somehow connected to me.

Quentin doesn't bite; he doesn't even react. It's as if he didn't hear me at all. Which is fine, I suppose.

Guy places a few glasses and a bottle of VineBlood on the table, pours himself one, then jumps back onto the bench, resuming his casual position from earlier. Nothing ever seems to ruffle that Wolf.

I pour myself a glass and sink back into the chair. As I do, the room becomes thick with an uncomfortable silence.

"Guy," Lumeilia asks, breaking through silence with her upbeat and cheery tone. "What's Quespelia like? I have an idea for my next exhibition about all the different territories, but I've never been." I thank the Gods for the change in subject.

Asheron and I have heard the stories from our fathers. Lumeilia and Mhelodie only know what has been taught at the Neopolis Collegium or from what they've read about it in books, but none of us have ever been lucky enough to witness the place firsthand.

"No one has unless you're invited or work for the Crown," Quentin interjects as he puts his scribe away and pours himself a VineBlood. "But what do you want to know? Maybe we can organise a trip one day," he adds, and I almost spit my VineBlood back into the glass.

Did Quentin Ishaan just invite us to Quespelia?

Lumeilia eagerly asks the Wolves about Quespelia, the royal territory, and Quentin happily obliges her.

It sounds so beautiful hearing about it from Quentin. His eyes light up talking about it. The picturesque green gardens filled with flowers that bloom year round, the enormous palace and the grounds, the exquisite original art that fills the walls, the statues, and the gargoyles.

Guy and Quentin tell tall tales about running through the woodlands and swimming in the lakes that surround the palace when they were young. As they reminisce, both their faces grow lighter, less troubled. I can't help but think how amazing and freeing it would have been to grow up in the Royal Territory.

Quentin explains how all five Origin packs also reside in Quespelia, though not in the palace itself. Palatial mansions for the High Alphas and expansive houses for their packs lay at the foot of the palace hill, and all the omega alphas and their packs reside in Welvyren.

That I knew from what I had been told by my dad.

It sounds magical, but I can't help wondering how the Scorpion High Alpha and the Origin pack can live in Quespelia yet be so defiant right under the king's nose. Why is he not banishing them from the Territory? How can he not know what they are up to? These are all questions I'm burning to ask but not sure I will get an answer for. I leave it. Filing it away for another time . . . if there ever is another time.

After reading about the Crescent Wolf pack earlier, I'm also eager to learn about how the pack hierarchy works. Feeling intrigued, I throw the question out and hope the Wolves are open to sharing.

"Guy, how do the omega packs work? I've never really understood," I ask as he places the cooked cheesy doughwheel on the table. Gods, it smells so delectable and looks even better.

I grab a slice and smile at both the Wolves, hoping they are relaxed enough to share. Surprisingly, Quentin's grey eyes widen with eagerness, and he smiles.

"Well, to understand how the omega packs work, you need to understand how the alpha packs work." He scans the group and smiles. He must see what I see. He has the full attention of every single one of us, even Guy. Quentin may be obnoxious, but when he wants to, he can be charming. Right now, he is putting on the charm.

"An alpha pack is pure blood. Its pack members are only those born of a mating bond or other relations that occur within the alpha pack. This ensures the pack's magic remains untainted and dominant." He pauses for a second, then continues. "There are many bloodlines within an alpha pack, but there are only five alpha packs."

Or so we thought.

I smile at Guy, but his face stays emotionless. He isn't giving anything away about what we learned earlier.

"Each pack is unique in their gift, our venom."

The group falls silent as Quentin demands our full attention. Asheron leans against the table with his chin cradled in his hands. Lumeilia's eyes widen, taking in every word. Mhelodie wears a child-like smile, her demeanour reflecting a young Witch being told a story before bed. And me? I am in shock that Quentin is so forthcoming with all this information.

"All packs except our pack—the Crescent Wolf pack—can shift at will at any time. The Crescent Wolf pack is bound by the crescent moon."

Guys' eyes shift toward me, and I try to contain my excitement about what we uncovered earlier. It's not my place to bring it up or reveal this information. That is one thing Guy was right about. This is a conversation he needs to have with Quentin himself. Guy shifts his gaze uncomfortably towards Mhelodie, and I can't help but wonder if he is considering asking her about the curse. Or is he blaming the Witches for all of this?

"The Silver Tongue pack is eloquent, cunning, and quick-witted. Their ability to influence and negotiate is unparalleled."

Well, that could explain why they tend to hold positions of great power within the crown and other large businesses.

"And according to your younger sister, rather charming," Guy adds, smirking at Quentin.

What the Fuck? Quentin has a younger sister? He's never shared that before . . .

Shit, focus, Paege!

"They can be very persuasive," Quentin continues, ignoring Guy's taunt. "Their venom lowers your inhibition and acts like a truth serum, making whoever is bit unable to lie.

That could come in handy.

"The Shadow Walker pack can camouflage themselves in the shadows while in their Wolf form. They are swift and stealthy. Their venom knocks you out and gives you nightmares. They can trap you in your dreams." Mhelodie gasps, and I don't blame her. Being trapped in your nightmares would be one's worst nightmare.

"The Dragon Hide pack, when in their Wolf form, have a scaly hide atop their head at the nape of their neck and across their chest. An armour, if you will, that's impenetrable to anything. Their venom neutralises magic in their victim for a period of time." Quentin's eyes light up, and his lips arc high, revealing a canine. Of course, he is loving this. He is essentially telling us how the Wolves could immobilise us. He's flexing his muscles, showing us just how strong and undefeatable the Wolves are. Proving exactly why the Wolves sit at the top of the food chain. And while I know I should be fearful of the Wolves, there is this kernel of doubt glowing inside that tells me this is just as much of a show as it is a warning.

Then Quentin's smile disappears, and he takes a drink of his VineBlood, emptying the glass. A look of remorse and sorrow washes away his excitement. He takes a long breath in and looks directly at me. "The Scorpion pack," his eyes and tone drop, "is composed of outlaws and thugs. There is no other way to describe them. Their venom is like a scorpion sting, fatal."

Blood rushes my ears, and my vision turns spotty. Flashbacks of our last night at The Pit appear in my mind's eye, and I swallow down the nausea threatening to rise. My eyes dart erratically around the group, but everyone else's eyes are upon me, the weight of their stares drowning me in my grief.

Lumeilia holds out her hand across the table, and I take it. Her gesture brings me a small amount of relief but not nearly enough to calm my pounding heart or heal my heavy soul.

"That leaves us, the Crescent Wolf pack. We are the royal alpha pack. Our Wolf strength and speed are more powerful than other packs, and our venom paralyses our victims."

Note to self: Stop pissing off the Wolves!

Guy chimes in, "An omega pack is formed when a cross-pack WolfMate bond materialises. The female Wolf leaves her pack for the male's pack. When they breed, their kin will be destined to either start a new omega pack or join an existing omega pack. Unlike that of an alpha pack, the hierarchy can be challenged in an omega pack because their bloodline isn't pure. When two packs crossbreed, their magic is sometimes diminished, and only the males' magic is carried down the line."

"So let me get this straight: you lot can crossbreed, but the rest of us . . ."

"Technically, we are all still Wolves, so it's not crossbreeding," Guy interrupts before Lumeilia can finish her thought.

Guy continues to discuss the crossbreeding argument with Lumeilia, and I can't help but realise how quiet Quentin is. His demeanour completely changed from a moment ago, the light in his eyes extinguished. Then suddenly, it clicks like a door unlocking. The truth of the situation is revealed. That's why Juno left Quentin and the Crescent Wolf pack and joined the Scorpions. She didn't even have a choice. She was mated through a bond and *had* to leave. But surely, they can reject the bond like the Fae can? Just because they are mated doesn't mean they *have* to be together.

"Can you not reject the bond?" I blurt out. The table falls silent, and the blood drains from Asheron's and Quentin's faces as they turn to face me, slowly. From the darkness that consumes their eyes, damn, I wish I could take it back.

Quentin pushes his chair out and stands, his mouth forming on a word.

"Is a bond ever truly severed?" Guy interrupts before Quentin speaks a word.

Asheron shakes his head in disbelief or disappointment. Maybe both. I don't blame him. Insensitive, that's what that was. Completely insensitive. Before I can apologise, Quentin leaves the table, casually strolling to my back door as if we weren't just speaking about his ex-girlfriend and he isn't trying to escape the uncomfortableness by exiting into the gardens.

The table returns to their previous argument about the crossbreeding.

"How are *you* feeling, Paege?" Mhelodie asks over the argument that's ensuing between Lumeilia, Asheron, and the Wolves about breeding. I honestly have no idea why any of them are concerned with this law. I understand how absurd it is, but it doesn't affect any of us at the moment. Can't they just let it go for one night?

But amidst all the crazy, I can't help but smile. "I'm alright," I answer truthfully because I am.

"I mean about Sylas."

Oh Gods, Sylas. The ex-boyfriend who, in all honesty, I haven't had much time to dwell about. I wait for it. The knot in my stomach, the ache in my chest. But it doesn't seem to come.

"We haven't talked about it since it happened, and I know I haven't asked, but I have been really worried and concerned," Mhelodie adds. I can see the emotion swirling in her eyes, but I can't feel it—not like I usually can. Something is off with my gifts at the moment. Or maybe this is me, finally able to harness more control and shield myself from others.

Control? You have about as much control as a leaf in a hurricane.

"I, um," I gulp. "I haven't had much time to think about it, to be honest. I think I'm alright?" That question was more for me than anyone else.

"You haven't heard from him at all?"

I consider and realise, no. I haven't. Not since the first night when he sent *hundreds* of messages. Usually, he would have made contact again by now, begging to talk, to meet up. He would be apologising and making grand gestures and false promises. He's been so uncharacteristically quiet.

"No," I respond, my voice a little shaky.

"Well, that's . . . *good*?" Mhelodie asks, her brows rising.

Suddenly, the table becomes unusually quiet, and the weight of the silence presses hard against me. The group continues to eat slices of doughwheels, feigning fake attentiveness to invisible lint on their garments or invisible crumbs on the table, but I can tell they have all been eavesdropping on our talk. Especially Lumeilia since she looks anywhere but at me or Mhelodie. I know she despises Sylas as much as Mhelodie does, and she would be genuinely worried that he is up to something. To be honest, so am I now.

"He isn't coming back this time. I'm sure," I say loudly, trying to reassure them all *and myself.* Because I am not too sure how much I believe my own words as I speak them. "It feels different this time. Final! And," I pause for a second to scan my emotions. "I'm fine with that, I promise," I say, putting my hand up to my heart in true Vailenbyrg style, realising I genuinely am.

Losing Sylas, as sad as it was, somehow started a chain reaction that brought the Wolves into our lives. And the six of us seem to be doing just fine together.

Kind of.

CHAPTER 20

"What exactly are you trying to tell me?" Quentin repeats, his voice dripping with frustration. Guy has been trying to explain to Quentin about the curse for over an hour, but Quentin refuses to hear him out.

"I don't see it," Quentin dismisses Guy again. "Brother, I feel you, I do. But I don't believe for one moment we could ever change at will. If we could, don't you think my father would remember?"

I've been sitting upstairs pretending to journal for the past hour, but really, I've been sitting here trying to eavesdrop on their conversation about the Crescent Wolf pack and the possible curse, aimlessly flipping through the pages of my past. No matter how many times Guy tries to convince Quentin that the Crescent Wolf pack could once change at will, Quentin has a counterargument. One, I must say, that has been sound every single time.

"Or maybe it happened before your father—back when the Gods abandoned us?"

My interest peeks at Guy's words. I've never heard the Wolves discuss the Gods ever. It's almost like they truly do believe the Gods abandoned them. It's believed during our Unification, Zephyra, the Goddess of Wind and Air, blesses us for our sacrifice with gifts from the Gods, and invokes our everlasting. The slowing of our aging. As does Terra, the Goddess of Earth, during a Witch's Ascension. But no one truly knows as no one remembers anything that happens as soon as the rite begins.

"You and the bloody Gods. They never abandoned us—no more than anyone else." Quentin's voice lowers, and I strain to hear what he says next. "Edom is still with us, brother."

"Then why must we take a life when the rest of the Beings sacrifice their own?" I can hear the emotional turmoil in Guy's voice, just like I heard it when he walked me home. The thought of taking a life sits heavily in my stomach. I've never understood how the Gods could be so cruel in making the Wolves take a life for their Emergence while the rest of us sacrifice our own. Whose life do they deem so insignificant that they can willingly sacrifice them? Where do they get their victims of such cruelty? The whole ritual is barbaric and completely unnecessary, in my opinion."

"Because we are superior, and the rest are weak." Quentin's words are cold and harsh.

I slam my journal closed and stand. I've always known the Wolves considered themselves superior, and Quentin never shied away in the past from being the arrogant and conceited Heir. But this past week, I've also seen a softer, more caring side, which had me thinking it was mostly an act and that maybe, just maybe, we could all be friends. But hearing these words has reality slapping me in the face with an open palm, and the sting lingers longer than I would like.

"I suppose," Guy replies, sounding very defeated and not like he entirely agrees with Quentin's argument, which surprises me. Guy's father was the true king. He holds the purest royal blood in his veins. I would have expected him to not only agree with Quentin but reinforce his sentiment.

I'm about to descend the stairs and end the madness mainly because I can't stand to hear Quentin speak so cavalier about taking a life when Quentin asks, "Where did you get that anyway?" I still at the top of the stairs, holding my breath, waiting for an answer.

"Paege." Guy supplies.

"Paege?" Quentin asks, almost sounding like he half expected that, and my brows raise.

"Yes, Paege. What is the problem?"

"Guy, you know what the problem is. She's a demi-Fae. You can't trust any information that she or her friends give us about anything, let alone Wolf business. Half of those books are redacted for good reason," Quentin says calmly, and my heart starts hammering away. *Shit.* I know the king controls what information the Fae and Witches have access to, even in our archives. The king sends his guards every so often to do inventory checks, but it cuts a little deeper when I have two Wolves in my home, who I consider friends, talk about it so casually. Guy's lack of response has blood rushing in my ears and my heart sinking into the pit of my stomach.

I stomp my feet violently before I make my descent, warning the Wolves I'm coming down, and I hope my heart racing doesn't give away my emotions.

"I'm going to train," I call out loudly, ignoring the fact I've been eavesdropping on their conversation for the past hour and pretending I didn't just hear them talking about me.

Guy's sitting on the couch staring blankly at the vision box while Quentin's outside in the garden, talking into his scribe in what seems to be a very heated conversation with someone. "Do you want to come, Guy, or are you staying to watch this smut?" I tease, pointing to the vision box.

It's already late morning, and I don't want to waste my day off sitting in front of the vision box. Plus, I promised my dad I would keep up my training.

Guy turns the vision box off. "I'm going to head back to the den and grab some more gear. Sort some life stuff out, you know. So, you go on without me."

Sort life stuff out, I'm sure. He will be right here on the couch when I get back. I'd put sparks on it.

"I'll train with you, Books, if you're looking for a partner?" I flinch, not realising Quentin had re-entered the room.

"Um, don't you have more pressing matters to attend to?" I ask, pointing to his scribe, still gripped tightly in his hand.

"What did he have to say?" Guy interrupts, dragging his eyes from the screen to stare at Quentin.

"Not much. I'll have to head back later today." He shifts his gaze to me. "Pressing matters, yes, but I've got some time before I have to leave."

I'm guessing his pressing matters are Juno. I overheard Quentin telling Guy earlier that she had been brought in by the guards for questioning about the attack on The Pit. They are still trying to locate Ric and the other pack members responsible.

"Alright. I'll take the company," I answer, trying to sound enthusiastic about my new training partner.

"Great!" He responds with keen enthusiasm, something I haven't seen in him for a while. As he's about to head into the spare room, he pauses and turns back toward me.

"Oh, but none of this female Fae stuff you usually do. Let's do some real training. See if we can teach your body to be as defensive as your mouth." He grins cheekily, his lip pulling up to expose an elongated canine. He wipes his annoyingly long blond fringe from his brow in an almost redundant move as it falls straight back into place, and he heads to the bedroom to get changed.

My skin prickles as excitement floods my veins. *Female Fae stuff.* Finally, a chance to get one up on the Heir Apparent. Little does Quentin know, Amerax has been training me in Guard Combat since I was old enough to walk. While I'm not as strong as a Wolf, or a full-blooded Fae, I know I am fast. And I suppose it wouldn't hurt to have a sparring match with a Wolf. Especially as the Wolves are the ones causing trouble around the Neopolis.

Maybe this could be fun.

CHAPTER 21

It's almost midday by the time we arrive at the gym. It's not my usual Star-Borne gym. No surprises there. Quentin wanted to go to his, and I wasn't going to object.

We swing open the doors to the cold and dark arena. Quentin walks straight in, and his footsteps echo through the room with every step he takes. I dump my bag on the ground next to the doors and start feeling the wall, searching for a source of light. The sound of metal chains dragging is met with a gasp from my chest as the sunlight pours into the room, illuminating the fighting arena.

The boxing ring sits off to the right side of the room, and to the left is a wrestling grappling mat or a dojo—I'm unsure which, to be honest. There are four distinct fencing pistes marked out on the wooden flooring that surround the ring and mat. Bleacher-style seats climb up to the high ceiling on the left side of the arena, and I wonder what sort of matches they hold here.

Hot Wolves fighting shirtless? That's a fight I'd pay sparks to watch.

Damn it, Paege, focus!

I scoop up my bag and walk to the middle of the arena toward the mat where Quentin meets me. He smirks. "So, what do you have in that bag of tricks there, Books?"

"Nothing of interest to you, I'm sure," I reply, trying to hide my grin.

"Alright then, so you think you're ready to learn some self-defence?" He asks as he moves further toward the mat. "I promise I'll take it easy on you."

I follow his footsteps, edging closer to the mat. "I'm ready when you are, *coach*," I respond sarcastically, rolling my eyes at him and trying not to give my secret away.

He squares his shoulders and shifts his weight. The hardened muscles in his calves and thighs twitch as they tense. His expression changes, and the jovial spirit I saw no less than a minute ago is replaced with a seriousness that is all too familiar. It's the same expression I saw in his eyes the night of the attack at The Pit.

"This isn't a joke, Paege. There's some serious shit going down in the Neopolis, and Guy and I won't be around to protect you forever." He pauses, his blue eyes catching mine. "You're going to need to learn how to protect yourself." The urgency in his voice burns through me.

Shit, is he genuinely concerned for my safety here? And he called me Paege.

I nod in silence, my hand reaching for the charm that hangs around my neck. I want to tell him I will be fine, that I can look after myself, but something pulls me back. The need to let him have this moment overcomes me.

"Sorry," I mutter, dropping my charm from my grip.

Quentin relaxes somewhat, his shoulders rolling forward, and he lets a small smile escape his lips. He takes one step backward, motions one arm toward the mat, and says, "Shall we?" with a cheeky grin, one I so desperately want to wipe off his face.

I unfasten my hooded top and slide myself out of it, revealing my toned upper body, one that's very unusual for a Fae, then slide off my running shoes and socks, leaving myself standing barefoot in just my shorts and sports crop top.

I feel Quentin's gaze burning into the back of me. I turn to face him and find him standing with his mouth slightly open and his eyes scouring across my body, taking in every inch of my exposed skin. I unexpectedly feel extremely vulnerable and a little shy as his gaze fixates on the wings tattooed across my collar bones. Heat rises through my body, and my heart somersaults in my chest. Excitement, nervousness, and a feeling of wonderment wash over me.

Mine? His? I can't tell, and I don't think I care.

I take a few careful steps toward the mat, but stop, hesitating my next move. The space between us feels intimate, like that night of the attack when he laid on my bed. I inhale a long, slow breath and exhale just as slowly. Quentin continues to watch me, fixed on a target.

"Don't worry, Books. I promise I won't hurt you." As the words escape his mouth, I feel a flutter in my lower stomach. There's something primal about the way his eyes take in my body. I take a few more steps forward onto the mat next to where he stands. I look up at his face. He stands a good half a foot taller than me, and he smiles.

"I trust you!" I reply and manage to find my footing on the centre of the mat.

"Let's start easy. I want to see what we're working with. I'm going to come at you, and I want you to deflect me. Defend yourself. You can't hurt me, so don't hold back," he says.

Splitting my stance, I place my left leg behind me and shift my weight to my back foot momentarily before finding my balance. I bring my hands up, palms open and close to my face, and take a big breath in before exhaling. "I'm ready."

Quentin comes at me. His right arm swings out with a hook, but my right forearm deflects his move, knocking his hand away from the tap he was aiming for against my cheek. I jab my left arm forward and up, clocking him right in the chin. Pain shoots up through my hand, stinging my knuckles. I shake it out.

Holy fuck, that hurt!

"Nice one, Books!" Quentin exclaims, surprise emitting from his voice. He blows a huff of air up, moving his fringe from his eyes.

Nodding, I don't take my eyes off him, thank the Gods, because he comes at me again. This time, he jabs left and right in quick succession. I lean back, dodging each punch without losing my balance before finding my neutral stance again.

He nods in approval, and I feel a sense of pride emitting from him.

Quentin comes at me again, but this time with a left hook, and I duck and swing my right leg around. He jumps, avoiding my attempt to trip him up.

"Books, you got some moves. You didn't tell me you could fight."

"You didn't ask," I pant, regaining my stance. "You just assumed I couldn't." I smile and nod toward him, permitting him to come back at me again.

"How?" Quentin shuffles his feet back and prepares himself to attack again.

"My dad's an Israykiel Guard, remember? Do you honestly think he didn't teach me some basic skills while growing up?" I back up, putting some space between us.

"Basic skills? You've got more than basic skills." The tone in his voice suggests he's impressed, and my heart flutters at the thought that Quentin Ishaan, the Heir Apparent, is impressed by a demi-Fae.

We continue to dance around the mat, Quentin jabbing, hooking, and kicking. His moves are flawless and smooth. I deflect and dodge his attempts, knocking away his jabs and avoiding any connection. The longer we spar, the wider he smiles, and the more complex his moves are, but I continue to anticipate every one with fluid motions.

He comes back at me with another strike, and I deflect, but this time, instead of letting me knock his hand away, he grabs my wrist, pushing my hand down and then twisting it back up behind my back. I have to turn my body fast and away from him as I drive my right elbow back into his stomach. As I make a connection, he wraps his right arm around my chest and over my shoulder, pinning me against his warm, sweaty body.

We pause. My body stiffens against his, and our chests rise and fall in sync. The warmth of his body radiates through mine as he holds me for a moment. Neither of us move away. His warm breath brushes against the skin of my neck, sending tiny jolts of electricity crashing through my body, and I try not to quiver at his touch. Try to keep my feelings to myself, but my damn heart pounds loudly to an erratic beat, and I'm sure he can hear it, too.

Traitorous bitch.

A deep growl comes from his throat, and it turns my mind into a hot mess of thoughts. Thoughts I shouldn't be having. Thoughts I so desperately want to act on.

His grip loosens, "Paege?" he whispers into my ear, and my throat bobs, trying to contain the heat pulsating through me and intensifying between my thighs. I slowly turn to face him. His arms remain caged around my body, keeping us flush against each other. My breasts press harder against his hard, sweaty chest with every breath I take. His icy-blue eyes slowly darken, and a delicious hunger stirs between us. A hunger that he acts upon without hesitation.

His lips crash into mine, and my mouth opens, inviting him in. He paws at me with a wild desperation, a longing. His tongue violently explores my mouth, teeth biting, nipping at my lower lip with every kiss. I can't even form thoughts. This is wrong, so very wrong. He is Quentin Ishaan, a fucking Wolf. And most of the time, I can't stand him. But, oh, Gods, it feels so right. He tastes like rain and smells like the forest. It's all-consuming. It feels amazing. He is amazing. Nothing about the way he claims my mouth is sweet and gentle. It's intense and hot. It's primal. His hands find my ass, and he lifts me with ease. My body moves willingly, and I wrap my legs around his torso, hooking them together to hold me in place.

I slide my hands through his blond locks, knotting sandy strands between my fingers, and I pull his head in closer to mine, my tongue meeting every brush of his inside me. He feels incredible. Kissing him is like a rush of adrenaline. It's dangerous and reckless, but I can't stop.

I need more. I want more. My breasts ache as I arch my back, pressing myself firmly against his body, the pressure releasing tiny bursts of euphoria from deep within. He lets out a breathy moan that reverberates through his body, and I release my mouth from his, gasping for air and whisper, *"Oh, Gods,"* while his mouth finds its way back to my body, tonguing the length of my neck from clavicle to jaw. My eyes roll back, and I close my eyes, completely lost in the moment.

The door abruptly bursts open, and a rowdy group rushes into the arena. I snap my eyes open, and Quentin releases his hold on me, dropping me from his body. Luckily, I land gracefully.

Quentin steps back and looks toward the ground, avoiding any and all eye contact, and the embarrassment of our decision overwhelms me as a blush of heat burns my cheeks. But the young Wolves don't so much as notice the two of us on the mat, let alone in our prior embrace.

I close my bedroom door and walk straight over to my bed, dropping my gym bag on the ground before sitting myself at the foot of my bed. The walk home was insufferable. He wouldn't speak to me. He would barely even look at me, and the second we walked into my apartment, Quentin rushed off to the spare bathroom closing the door behind him.

I sigh loudly. I can't believe what just happened. I have never been so reckless in my entire life. One minute we were sparring, the next we were kissing. And that was no normal kiss. I have *never* been kissed like that before. With Sylas, it was good—really good. But this, this was *out of this world, shoot me to the stars, I'm never coming down* explosive. And it was only a kiss.

Nothing good can come of it. Nothing good at all. He is a Wolf; I am a demi-Fae. Wolves and Fae don't mix. Hels, they barely tolerate each other. There are laws in place that prevent Wolves and Fae, or any species from cross-breading. Not to mention that when Quentin merges, his WolfMate bond will form. He'll just be buying time with whoever he is with, waiting for the moment he meets his Wolf. Because the second he touches his WolfMate, it will snap into place.

And I will get fucked over once more and left broken-hearted.

So yes, Paege, nothing good will come of this at all.

But his scent, his taste, his body. *Oh, the Gods.* When I close my eyes, I can still feel his hands exploring my body and his tongue exploring my mouth.

Fuck.

One, two, three light taps at my bedroom door pull my attention back to the present moment.

"Paege, do have you a moment?" Quentin whispers through the door.

Alright, Paege, you've got this.

I straighten myself out and softly reply, "Come in." Quentin opens the door gently, but he doesn't enter the room. He stands in the doorway with his hands buried deep in his pants pockets. His eyes dart from me to the bed and then quickly to the floor in front of his feet. A sticky mess of caramel sweetness swirls around my core, but my mouth quickly dries out as an ashy aftertaste coats my tongue, sending my stomach into fits of queasiness.

Lust. Shame.

Not mine.

His.

"Listen, Books, I need to apologise for earlier. I took advantage, and I shouldn't have acted the way I did. I'm sorry."

I know what he is trying to do. He is trying to do the right thing. To spare me from the embarrassment of our earlier entanglement. But I can't help the anger that unfurls inside of me as his words climb through me and embed themselves into my heart. Because damn, he keeps treating me like a helpless victim, and I'm completely offended by the implication.

"*You* took advantage?" The tone in my voice harshens, and I laugh. "You did *not* take advantage!" I snap back. "If I remember correctly, we were sparring, and I was holding my own." When will he stop treating me like a powerless little child? "But that's fine, Quentin, you are right, it shouldn't have happened. Don't worry, it won't happen again."

Quentin's mouth opens, and then he closes it again.

"I understand. We can forget about it." I cross my arms over my chest, as if protecting myself, my heart, from the pain trying to worm its way in. "It will be like it never happened." I snap, finishing my diatribe abruptly.

"What could you possibly understand, Paege?" Quentin snaps back, brushing the fringe out from his eyes.

"I understand that you are Wolf, and I'm a demi-Fae. So whatever this is," I shake my finger between us, "can't happen again." A ball of knots forms in the centre of my stomach, because as much as I would love it to happen again, I know it can't.

"Well, it seems like you've got it sorted for the both of us," he bites back. He dips his head, and before I have a chance to say anything more, he steps back and closes the door.

Seconds after the door closes, I drag myself up and walk to the bathroom. I turn the shower on, turning the temperature to as hot as I can handle, and step into the recess fully clothed. The boiling hot water scalds my skin as I sit on the floor under the stream, wishing it would wash away all the shame not only from today but that's been building over the years from being labelled a *halfling*. As the tears well in my eyes and I watch the water swirl down the drain, all I feel is another part of my soul disappear into the pit of Hels that lay deep beneath me, and I start to cry.

I cry like I haven't in years.

CHAPTER 22

Wanting to look fabulous for my friend's big event, I take my time getting ready. I'm not one to usually enjoy getting dressed up, but the excitement that's been rushing through my veins all day has me feeling an eagerness that I can only assume is born from love for my dearest friend. Like many Fae, Lumeilia is an amazing artist. Her specialty is sculpting. Her imagination knows no boundaries, and her ability to bring her imagination to life is inspired. We often wonder if her artistic nature is going to form part of her gift when she unifies. This exhibit is her debut in the kingdom, and tickets sold out within days.

It's early evening when I emerge from my room dressed in a sweeping green velvety dress that matches the colour of my emerald eyes and gracefully accentuates my curves. My long ash brown hair is pulled into a loose tail high on my head, my hair sweeping over my shoulder, showcasing the backless design of the low cut dress that also features a daring split up the leg that ascends mid-thigh. The bust of the dress dips, revealing my wings tattoo. The ensemble is completed with strappy gold high-heels paired with long, gold-plated roped earrings to match my gold necklace.

The apartment is eerily empty. As I stand alone in the living room, a subtle unease grips me as my heart quickens its pace into a chorus of unspoken patterns. However, I can't pinpoint the source of my nerves. It's not my big night, but a creeping anxiety seems to be taking hold.

It's the quiet.

"Guy, are you here?" I call out in a hopeful query. But his name echoes through the apartment, the walls withholding any response, leaving my words to linger unanswered.

My place has been a hive of activity for over a week now, and to be honest, I'm sort of used to it. This silence and emptiness are a little unsettling.

I need something to calm my nerves.

I grab a glass and the DesertFyre from the kitchen and pour myself a drink. Downing it quickly, I welcome the familiar warmth of the golden liquid as it travels down my throat, soothing my quickening heart.

Seizing my scribe, I message Asheron to let him know I will be there shortly, and then I delve into my music archives in search of the perfect song to quell my nerves. My eyes linger on a tune made especially for dancing, and with a decisive thought, my music box becomes alive with pulsating beats. I surrender to the rhythm, dancing on my own around the apartment. The music cascades through the room, dispersing the lingering silence.

I'm about to pour another drink down my throat when the front door bursts open and Quentin storms in with a duffel bag over his shoulder, looking very dishevelled and unsettled. My muscles tense, and I pause, feeling an intense heat prickle my cheeks as Quentin stills in the doorway, his eyes roaming over every inch of me like a Wolf eyeing his prey. His grey eyes widen.

I've not seen him since our earlier entanglement. I suspect he's been avoiding me, and I suppose I've been avoiding him, too.

The song finishes and the silence amplifies the thick tension brewing in the air.

Finally, he shifts his gaze to the floor and clears his throat before walking away to the spare room without saying a damn word.

Then I exhale the longest breath I've ever breathed.

But before he reaches the door to the room, I blurt out, "Want one?"

What the fuck was that, Paege?

"Huh?" Quentin turns around to look at me, his brows pulled tightly together.

"Do you want one?" I hold up the glass and wiggle it in the air for emphasis.

"Yes, sure. Why not?" he says. He drops his duffel on the ground and casually joins me in the kitchen.

Alright, I was not expecting that.

I pour him a drink, hand it to him, and watch him curiously. Without saying a word, he takes it and shoots it back. He motions for another, so I pour it, and he slams that down just as quickly.

"Where are you off to?" he asks, his eyes roaming the length of my gown.

"It's Lumeilia's art showing tonight, remember?"

"Of course. I forgot. Is she excited?"

"Excited, nervous, the usual," I respond, not sure if I'm talking about Lumeilia's feelings or my own at this moment. Snatching my drink up off the table, I supply him with a gentle smile and tip it down my throat. Then pour one, two more.

"You look nice," Quentin says coolly, taking his glass and sliding it nervously around the table in front of him for a moment.

"Are you, *Quentin Ishaan,* giving me a compliment?" I joke, arching my brows at him. We've not spoken since he left my room that day. In fact, I don't even think he's been here. Guy has all but moved in, and to be honest, I'm wondering when this weird unspoken agreement between the Wolves and me will end. Do I even want it to end?

"Yes, Paege. I'm giving you a compliment." He shoots back his DesertFyre and knocks the table with two decisive taps. "Well, I'll leave you to it. Have fun," he states, finishing our awkward conversation and heading back for the spare room.

"You can come with me if you like." I blurt out the words for a second time tonight.

Seriously, Paege! Don't you ever think before you speak?

Quentin pivots. He doesn't speak. He just stands there as if he is waiting for more information. The weight of his gaze hits me with a gale force. There's no denying that there is some weird electricity of epic proportions between us that makes my heart tumble around in my chest every time he looks at me like that.

"I've got a spare ticket. It was supposed to be for Sylas, but clearly, he isn't coming now. So, if you want, it's yours." I shrug casually, but I feel anything but casual.

Just stop, Paege. You're a fucking masochist!

The silence continues, and I feel my heart descending into the depths of my stomach, disappointment unfurling within me. It's not directed at him, but rather a self-inflicted reproach for my foolish assumption that he, too, feels that spark and would share in my desire to accompany me.

Take it back, take it back!

My eyes lower to the brim of the DesertFyre-filled glass before me, and I down it in a single, resolute gulp, bracing myself for the forthcoming dismissal of my invitation. However, before I can fully savour the spicy warmth, Quentin answers with a simple nonchalance. "Sounds good." It cuts through the tense currents, dispersing the chaotic ripples within me.

What the fuck?

I choke on the shot on the liquid, and my heart finds wings and starts to soar.

"Um, alright. Great!" I respond, trying not to stammer my words. "Have you got something to wear?"

"Yes, Books, I've got clothes to wear." He smirks. "I'll just get ready."

He walks off to the bathroom picking his duffel off the ground on the way. As he closes the door to the room, he calls out jokingly, *I think,* "There better be some DesertFyre left when I come back out."

I've always been a sucker for punishment, but this has got to be the stupidest thing I have ever done. Inviting Quentin to Lumeilia's event. What on earth am I thinking? Obviously, I'm not. He made it perfectly clear after the kiss that it was a mistake. But I suppose just because we kissed it doesn't mean we can't try to be friends. Can we?

My scribe's chiming interrupts my dizzying thoughts, and I see Asheron has responded.

Asheron: See you there. Oh, and a heads up, I'm bringing Remi. Please don't make a scene. I promise I will tell you about it later. More importantly, I just heard the king has ordered the Guards to immediately leave the Neopolis.
Me: What? You can't be serious.

I'm genuinely perplexed and concerned by Asheron's message, both about the Guards and about Remi. I didn't even know Asheron was speaking to Remi again. Why wouldn't he share this with me? We talk about everything, and now he is bringing her to Lumeilia's exhibition. This is news to be celebrated, but it's drowning in the background of the news about the Guards. Yes, Remi is a conversation to be had later. The Guards need to be discussed now.

Asheron: I'm serious. There's been no more attacks. The streets have been quiet. The Scorpions responsible have disappeared or gone back to Welveryn. He's even releasing Juno.
Me: But it's the Autumn Festival. It's one of the busiest times of the year. The streets will be packed. Surely, he can leave the guards stationed for a few more days.

Asheron: I'll talk to Quentin. Maybe he's heard something more.

Oh, Juno is getting released. *That's* where he's been the last few days. How can Quentin still care for someone who is involved in killing innocent Beings?

Me: You can ask him tonight. He's coming with me.
Asheron: Paege, what's going on?
Me: I could ask you the same thing.
Asheron: Let's talk about it later tonight then.

I place my scribe away and absentmindedly stare off into the empty room, a blank canvas for the myriad of thoughts swirling within the confines of my mind. Quentin and I kissing. Quentin and I *not* kissing. Ric and the pack missing. The Guards being pulled from the Neopolis. Juno getting released.

How can he go to her defence and help her out? Maybe Quentin really is who I thought he was all along.

And not who I hoped he was.

The door opening tears me away from my thoughts, and Quentin emerges from the bathroom dressed in a snug-fitting, button-up black shirt fastened up to his collar, just shy of the top button. His sleeves are folded up to just below his elbows, exposing his tattoo and highlighting the muscles in his forearm. A regal black jacket with intricate embroidery along the lapels slung over his shoulder. His shirt is tucked into a pair of dark grey fitted pants, emphasising the muscular tone of his legs and his amazing ass. He's wearing his usual black boots and a black belt to finish the look. His hair is left shaggy with his too-long fringe hanging over his left brow, and he's cleanly shaven, revealing his pretty boy looks and making him appear all too heir-like, which is a little unexpected.

Damn, he looks good.

Speech deserts me; I'm utterly immobilised. My cheeks flush with that heat again, and I will for the ground below to open up and swallow me whole.

"I take it you approve?" Quentin says, his hand gently cupping my chin and easing my gaping mouth shut. My focus snaps back as his thumb caresses my cheek. When did he move across the room?

The heat intensifies, flooding my cheeks as a tingling sensation begins to stir in my lower torso, and my heart executes a sudden flip. I suck in a sudden breath, and I swear my body turns to molten lava as the scent of fresh pine, akin to the forest's aroma after the soothing touch of rain, envelopes my senses.

Fuck.

Quentin leans in close, his mouth closing in on my ear, and the warmth of his breath sighs across my warm cheek as he says in a low breathy voice, "You smell good, too, Books."

Where's that hole to disappear into?

A wolfish grin appears. He passes behind me. His fingers lightly skim across the bare skin, dancing along my exposed lower back, and my breath hitches. Unable to speak, I watch as he grabs and downs the glass of DesertFyre I had poured for myself before he entered the room.

Before he blew my world apart.

Before I melted into a big pile of gooey mess.

CHAPTER 23

Tonight is the start of the Autumn Festival, and Centauri-ons—an open air carriage drawn by youthful Centaurs—fill the streets. As we are dressed in our finest, Quentin and I travel by one to the gallery. It feels like the kind of evening for it.

We ride mostly in silence, enjoying festivities unfurling around us. Remnants of the sun's presence splash across the horizon, throwing an orange glow through the sky and matching the colours adorning the streets. It's as if she doesn't want to set today. Windows and store fronts are filled with decorations in different shades of oranges, reflecting the Autumn season. Pumpkins and apples sit on display in shop windows and on doorsteps and stoops. Crickets singing their songs fill the air with music, and laughter from the young children playing in the streets brings life to the city that hasn't been felt in some time.

When we finally arrive at the gallery, it's humming, matching the energy of the streets outside. Fae, Witches, Sirens, Wolves, and Centaurs all fill the room, bustling with life. Chatter and laughter bounce through the air as we enter the art gallery space where Lumeilia's showing is held. We're greeted by a young female Centaur who has a grace about her that only the female Centaurs have. The male Centaurs are brutish and strong, which is why most of them seem to hold jobs in security of some sort. She has long, pure white hair that matches her body and a long plaited tail. She wears a golden head chain complete with pearls. Beautiful. She offers us a glass of VineMist, a bubbly fermented alcoholic drink, and both Quentin and I accept.

I scan the room, taking it all in. The warm sconce lights dimly light the room. Shadows dance across the walls from the fires that burn beneath each sculpture, illuminating the art and giving it a sense of spookiness that I'm one hundred percent certain Lumeilia intends to elicit. The profound sounds of war drums beat in succession, almost replicating a thrumming heart, and some sort of deep windpipe plays. Smoke machines blow a faint mist around the gallery that somehow stays low around the ankles, creating an eerie boneyard vibe. The whole display is enchanting.

"Wow!" I exclaim, completely captivated by everything.

"Yeah," Quentin sighs in response.

I spot Asheron with Remi through the crowd. Both of them are beaming. I motion to Quentin to join them, and without another word, he places his hand on the small of my back and gently guides me through the crowd.

I've finished my VineMist by the time we reach Asheron, and just as I'm about to find myself a replacement, a magical Fae appears before me and fills my flute up before disappearing again.

"Hi," I smile at Asheron and lean in to hug Remi. It's been too long, and we all missed her. She smiles warmly in return.

"Paege, it's nice to see you," Remi says with such kindness in her voice. She looks radiant, a perfect match to Asheron.

Her platinum blonde hair falls just below her breasts, and her face is pale with the longest eyelashes I've ever seen. Her large sapphire blue eyes glisten like the gemstone itself, and her lips are painted a ruby red, matching her nails perfectly. She is elegantly dressed in a cobalt blue silk kaftan style dress paired with a golden belt and corresponding cuff. Graceful is the only word to describe her.

"You look stunning," I reply to Remi, meaning every word I say. "It's so nice to see you, too. We've all missed you," I add.

She smiles again and looks to Asheron, who looks just as elegant as Remi. I really don't understand why he rejected his mating bond with her. He'll never be honest about it, always regurgitating the same old line that he "doesn't want the universe to decide who he spends his life with. It should be his decision." But it broke them both so badly. So, I'm happy to see they are both here together, looking happy.

Asheron leans over to shake Quentin's hand. "Quentin."

"Asheron."

Ugh, males! So simple. So boring. So concise.

"This is Remildiaz," Asheron continues. "My..." They both look at each other for a second, pondering their next words.

"Date," Remi responds.

And Asheron responds at the same time, "mate."

What?

I snap my head around at Asheron, and my brows arch high, questioning what he just said, but he corrects himself. "Date, Remi is my date."

A sudden burst of emotions flows through me, sending my heart racing and my head spinning. As quickly as they hit me, I feel them break off. It leaves my heart feeling like it's breaking apart, shattering, There's an unbearable sadness and guilt that lingers.

Poor Remi. This is brutal and so confusing for her. I wonder if she will ever get over what happened.

Also, note to self: take Asheron aside later to have a private conversation with him about what he just said.

"This is Quentin, Paege's—"Asheron starts.

Oh shit.

"Um, yes, he's my..."

"Escort," Quentin supplies.

"Yes, escort," I confirm as disappointment settles in my core like dust after a storm.

Alright, we have that established. Not date, escort. An escort I want to escort back to my room later.

Stop it, Paege!

"Nice to meet you, Quentin, Paege's *escort,*" Remi replies with a grin. Her brows arch high as if she's not entirely sure she believes us.

I'm not entirely sure I do either.

"Nice to meet you, too, Remildiaz," Quentin responds with a softness to his voice I haven't heard before. Playing every part of the Prince Charming he is meant to be. This is how he must talk to those who don't annoy him.

"If you will both excuse us," I interject, wanting out of this awkward interaction, "I want to find Lumeilia and Mhelodie, and I know there is some art Quentin is dying to check out, maybe put a bid on?" I tug on Quentin's arm, urging him to move.

"Ah, yes." Quentin smiles, confused. "We'll meet up with you later," he adds. "Shall we?" Quentin returns his hand to the small of my back and escorts me over toward a creepy but enthralling gargoyle sculpture.

"What was that?" he questions once out of earshot of Asheron and Remi.

"They felt like they needed a moment. It was getting rather intense," I respond and look over to see both Remi and Asheron in what seems to be a heated and sad conversation. Quentin's eyes follow my gaze.

"Have I ever told you how creepy it is that you can do that?" Quentin adds.

"No, you haven't," I respond coolly, trying to ignore the flutter of emotions stirring in my core. I honestly didn't even think he had ever put any thought to me at all. "But that wasn't my gift. That was just knowing my friends," I clarify. "Come on, let's get another drink." I grab his hand and lead him through the crowd toward a Centaur with a tray of VineMist standing near the enormous daemon sculpture in the centre of the room.

We meander around the gallery, chatting casually, drinking, and eating tiny little parcels of food while we admire Lumeilia's artwork.

"She is quite talented," Quentin says. "I've always admired artists. To be able to put your deepest darkest desires and thoughts into art for all to see; there is something so vulnerable and beautiful about it."

I raise my eyebrows at his admission. I never thought of Quentin as having layers beyond his brooding, masculine exterior. He has always been so guarded, so stoic, never showing any hint of emotion. I watch him curiously as he studies her art. His eyes sparkle, and his face seems to relax.

"Do you draw or paint?" I ask, intrigued to understand more as we walk toward another piece.

"Me? No," he chuckles. "I used to play, but that was a long time ago."

"Play? Really?" I ask. My brows arch, and my heart lightly tumbles at his admission.

"Yes, is that so hard to believe?" he asks, the ridge above his eyes rising slightly.

"No, not at all." I muse for a moment before placing my hand on his arm in support. "I didn't know, that's all."

"As a royal, my mother insisted that we must learn the chordo-grande," he responds, his voice lowering. "But it was a long time ago. A very long time ago."

"Why did you stop?" I probe, not wanting this conversation to end. The thought of Quentin playing music has my head spinning. Images of him as a young Wolf, sitting at a chordo-grande with his fingers running across the ivory and black keys playing some magical piece of music, make my heart swell. It's a stark contradiction to the male who stands in front of me.

Music has always been important to me and my family. Music is where I go when I need comfort. When I need to quiet the voices in my head. Maybe he and I aren't so different after all.

"It was another time. I was young, and things are . . ." he pauses, and I feel regret leech from his heart and shadow over us like a dark and gloomy cloud, "different now."

I realise this conversation is taking him to a place he doesn't want to visit. Guy told me about his mother passing years ago. Maybe that was when he stopped playing—if that is what makes the sorrow bleed from his veins. I wait patiently for him to speak again, giving him space to explain more if he wants, but he doesn't. Instead, he does something completely unexpected.

"Would you like to dance?" He holds his hand out, offering it to me. The music has long since changed from the deep demonic sounds of war. A chordo-bowstring starts playing a beautiful melody. Its tempo swaps between fast-paced and graceful. It feels like first glances and stolen kisses. Like mountaintops and winter's first snow. Like laughter and tears.

My heart tumbles hard against my ribs as I struggle to find my breath, and time feels like it stops for the briefest of moments.

Quentin Ishaan, the king's son, is asking me, Paege Vailenbyrg, a demi-Fae, to dance.

I stare into his starry blue eyes, and he grins broadly, waiting for me to answer. I look around the gallery, my eyes searching for what exactly? I have no idea. A reason to say no? A reason to say yes? I catch the amber eyes of a Star-Borne male standing close by. He lifts a single pierced brow, arching it high as if intrigued by what my response will be. A strange familiarity tugs at my mind, but he turns and walks away.

"Are you crazy?" I whisper to Quentin, who still holds his hand out, waiting for my response.

"It's just a dance," he whispers. "Books, it would be an honour."

I draw in a long breath as my hand involuntarily moves toward his. When my hand reaches his, a sweet and salty feeling rolls through my body, soft and gentle like a cascading river of silk. He graciously takes it and gently tugs me close to him. Those damn butterflies take flight in my stomach as I place my hand on his shoulder, and he rests his other hand on the bare skin on the small of my back. Our bodies barely touch, and my exposed skin tingles beneath his touch, sending tiny bumps scattering across my skin. Finally, he releases a long breath, and I feel his body relax into mine.

As the melody picks up its speed, Quentin steps toward me, gracefully leading the way. The space between us diminishes, our bodies moving as one, and I'm unable to tell where my body ends and his begins. He waltzes me around, the fog wrapping itself around our feet as we make our way through the gallery. His eyes never leave mine. A breath barely taken. A word never spoken. With every step, I feel his heart swell, as does mine. He doesn't twirl or spin me, he doesn't pull me in any closer, and he doesn't even smile. He just guides me around the gallery flawlessly, his beautiful light blue eyes locked onto mine.

When the song stops, so do his steps, but he doesn't move away. *Not just a dance.* He doesn't let go of me, and neither do I. Our eyes continue to burn into each other as he holds me here. There is something so intimate about this moment, something that strips me bare, and I've got nowhere to run, nowhere to hide. It's just me, my defences wide open, vulnerable. It was never going to be just a dance.

My breath shallows, and his chest heaves, but neither of us speak. A fire sparks between us, burning brightly, and it's intoxicating.

He is intoxicating.

CHAPTER 24

I take a small step forward, bringing our hands down toward our chests, and close the distance between us. I feel the heat erupt from his body as I lean into it, into him. Desire burns through my veins, all sweet and tangy, and my heart continues to thunder in my chest. As I tilt my head upward, he dips his toward mine, our mouths so close that I can feel the warmth of his breath brush my lips.

Just as I'm about to do something I *think* is extremely stupid, a chill spider walks down my spine, and I get the familiar feeling that someone is watching me, standing the hair on the back of my neck on end. My blades pinch, tensing the muscles in my neck and shoulders, and I pull myself back from Quentin's embrace, scanning the room, unable to lock eyes with anyone.

The feeling doesn't falter; it intensifies.

I look back toward Quentin, and he slips his hand from the small of my back and strains a small smile as our hands that are still touching interlocks.

We plummet into an eerie darkness. The chatter in the room silences, and my bones stiffen as fear and confusion wrap around the gallery.

Hels, what is going on?

A harsh sound of grinding metal has me and about a hundred other Beings gasping in unison, and Quentin's hand squeezes mine. I blink, one, two, three times as I will my vision to adjust to the foggy darkness surrounding us so I can see whatever evil is about to gate-crash this evening.

When the ear-piercing sound finally comes to an end, my jaw relaxes, and Quentin pulls me in closer to him. "What the Hels, Books?" he rumbles under his breath into my ear.

An explosion of lights and a high-pitched whirring has me shielding myself and ducking for cover. But before I hit the floor, Quentin's hand latches onto my arm, and he pulls me up, motioning toward the centre of the gallery. There is Lumeilia, dressed in a flowing white gown and a golden headpiece like the Centaurs, being birthed from what looks like the fiery devil's pit from Hels. Smiling, she raises her arms high.

The crowd begins to clap, and my anxiety fades instantly. Standing behind her is Mhelodie, dressed in a similar white dress and golden headpiece, clapping so hard I swear she is going to clap her hands right off. And her smile. She's never looked so proud.

My heart swells. She is so talented.

I knew Lumeilia put in a lot of work for this art show, but I wasn't expecting *this*. I feel a rogue tear trickle down my face as pride blooms in my chest. I try to covertly wipe it away with the back of my hand so Quentin doesn't notice, but it's too late. I lift my gaze, and my eyes collide with his, a sea of emotions overwhelming me. Without saying a word, he turns back toward the spectacle and squeezes my hand.

"Thank you everyone for coming tonight!" Lumeilia addresses the crowd. "Your support means so much to me. Twelve months ago, I had a vision. A dream! And tonight, that dream came true. 'Gargoyles, Angels, and Daemons' was inspired by my friendships. It's framework representing different species of our kingdom and of others and how each species is significant in their own way." The crowd erupts in cheers and claps. She waits a moment for the crowd to settle before continuing, "I would like to say a special thanks to—"

As Lumeilia turns toward Mhelodie, glass breaking interrupts her speech, and a grumbling sound has the crowd cheering again in anticipation of another spectacle. But this is not right. My heart starts pounding like a war drum, warning me of the intruders who are about to descend upon my best friend's evening.

Lumeilia doesn't continue, her face now frozen with fear. What the fuck is going on?

I look at Quentin, and his ears are pricked back, and he is sniffing the air. I can see the hair on the back of his neck stand on end.

I scan the room. Everyone's eyes are darting around, looking for some sort of acknowledgment of what is happening. Panic starts to set in as I am assaulted by waves of emotions, dark and thick and oily. Beings start running for the exit. Before many can escape, a large roar echoes through the gallery, and everything turns to chaos.

The Wolves come crashing through the windows and doors, smashing their way in. Some fully shifted, many half shifted, claws and canines fully developed, still retaining their humanoid bodies.

Gagging, a bitter and metallic taste fills my dry mouth. I watch, stunned and confused, as one of the Wolves grabs a young Fae and bites down on her neck, ripping out a chunk of flesh. Bile stings my throat, and she screams in terror as blood spurts from her wound. He throws her to the ground, discarded like trash.

Witches start chanting and casting spells, trying to protect their family and friends.

Lumeilia jumps from her podium and runs toward Mhelodie. I can see Mhelodie murmuring something, her once beautiful golden eyes now black and full of fury. She grabs hold of a crystal flute from the bar table behind her and smashes it against the edge of the table, shattering it into thousands of crystal shards. She takes the jagged edge of the flute stem she still has held in her hand and slices through the skin on her other palm, cutting it open.

What in the Hels is she doing?

Still chanting, she places her bleeding palm on a gargoyle, and it immediately starts shuddering and erupting, coming to life. Its stone wings stretch out and flap, and its clawed hands create fists. It snarls, revealing long, razor-sharp teeth. It then unsheathes a sword it has hanging across its chest, and it charges into the crowd.

Mhelodie places her hand on another sculpture and another one and another one, all erupting from stone, all becoming ferocious as they come to life around the gallery. Upon her commands, they start protecting us. They start fighting the Wolves. She continues to chant and move around the room, dodging Wolves and awakening all the sculptures of gargoyles, angels, and daemons that once sat lifeless in the gallery, Lumeilia in her wake.

I have never seen anything like it.

The sculptures draw swords and prepare to fight the Wolves, their stone bodies impenetrable to a Wolf bite and so sturdy they are impossible to budge with any sort of force. They set up a perimeter around some of the crowd, including Lumeilia and Mhelodie, fighting off any beast that tries to attack.

Asheron and Remi, like us, are not within the boundary of the stone warriors. Asheron has Remi placed behind him, and he is guarding her. Wings fully flared, and Remi by his side, he slowly makes his way toward a room set off to the side of the gallery. I know they will be safe. He has been training for this his entire life—even if he doesn't want to admit it.

I, however, am frozen. My bones seize in place, my muscles tensing. Emotions from everyone drown me. The pain echoes through my body, rendering me helpless and vulnerable. I will myself to move, but I can't. The fear overwhelms me, and the pain of every bite, every cracking bone, and every open wound reverberates through my body, sending me into shock.

Quentin grabs my arm and yanks me hard, awakening me from my zombie-like state.

"We need to hide!" he yells and starts leading me toward a large metal door at the back of the gallery. He drags me through the carnage, ducking and weaving as Wolves are thrown across the room by the terrifying monsters Mhelodie created. Beings are ripped to pieces.

Nausea fills my stomach as I taste death.

From deep within, a primal fury rises, and heat envelops every inch of me. My body begins to violently shake like it's going to explode. I have no control. I let out a bellowing scream. A scream so loud it could wake the daemons themselves from the Hels below, one that borders on otherworldly, and I collapse to the ground. Darkness starts to creep in.

Quentin doesn't even hesitate. He bends down, scoops me up in his arms, and runs for the room at the back of the gallery. My body writhes as the pain from the slaughter pierces every inch of my being. Screams hurl from me as death claims its victims one by one.

"Stay with me, Paege," I hear Quentin yell, but I can't think. My mind is plagued with images of blood and death. The pain of it all consumes me, and I feel like I'm going insane.

Then, like an animal's keen ear, over all the screams and roars, over the chanting and spellcasting, over the crying and begging, I zone in on a familiar voice yelling across the gallery. A voice that churns my stomach as his words slither through me, making the hair on my arms stand on end.

"Turn this place upside down, boys. Don't stop till we find it. The Witch, she tracked it here, so it's gotta be here somewhere. Don't you stop lookin' for nothin'!"

Ric.

I will myself to move, and somehow, I manage to grab Quentin's arm and squeeze. He looks down at me, and I muster up enough strength to whisper the name, "Ric."

Quentin stops dead in his tracks. He heard me. He understands me.

He turns back from where we came, scanning the room just for a moment, searching for the face of the name I just said. That moment costs us. It's just long enough for a large Wolf to crash into us. The collision sends us both flying, knocking me from Quentin's arms, and we stumble to the floor. Lying helplessly, I'm easy prey for any Wolf to rip me to pieces, attack me, and subject me to their fatal bite. I try to pull myself toward Quentin, but my bones have turned to ice, and I can't move.

I watch the Wolf that knocked us down circle Quentin as he stumbles to his feet. Before Quentin gets a chance to regain himself fully, the Wolf lunges at him and shifts mid-flight before landing on Quentin and sending him back toward the ground.

A fight ensues. I watch in horror as Quentin defends himself from the snaps of the Wolf's salivating muzzle, but my brain is incapable of processing what's happening from the pain of all the injured and dying shooting through my veins and compounding in my mind.

A searing heat scores through my body, and beads of sweat run down my face. Or is that tears?

I close my eyes, and I hear a yelp followed by a spine-chilling snap, and it sends more tears streaming down my face and bile in my throat. I peel open my heavy lids, my heart thrashing around in my cage, fighting to search for Quentin, but my vision fades to black as the pain overcomes every particle of my body and soul, and I know I'm losing my fight.

As I start to fade out of consciousness, arms wrap around me. "I've got you, little hybrid," he soothes as he—whoever he is—lifts me from the ground. Pain roars in my head like a ferocious wild beast, and I bury myself in the sweet scent of spices, searching for a reprieve.

"Take her in there, go," the male commands.

Fresh forest and rain wash away the spice, and I feel Quentin's warm and safe body scoop me out of the male's hold. Then he moves.

"Stay with me, Paege."

He cradles me in his arms as he manoeuvres us through the crowd. He isn't running like he was before. It's slower but more determined. I know he is running for that giant silver door again, and this time, he doesn't stop for anything—not until we are safely behind the safe-like steel, locked door.

"Just a little further."

Quentin releases his hold of me ever so slightly as he pushes open the large door and throws himself with me still in his embrace across a small room. We slide across the ground, and he kicks the door shut behind us.

"Paege?"

The second that door closes, I feel an instant wave of relief. Like the door is shutting out all the emotions and feelings from outside this small room. The plethora of emotions and pain starts to wean away, and I slowly start to regain my sanity and my consciousness.

CHAPTER 25

When that metal door slams shut, everything begins to fade. All the pain and anguish. All the fear and anger. All the desperation, excitement, and terror. It all quickly dissipates, and the emotional roller coaster of horror I have been riding finally comes to an end.

I honestly don't know how long I have been sitting on the cold, hard floor next to Quentin in this darkened room before I manage to pry open my eyes. It feels like hours but likely only minutes.

For a moment longer, I stare into the blackness, trying to catch my breath. My eyes slowly adjust to the darkness. It's an empty, metal square room with a faint, dim light that borders the edges. One that seems to dim when movement is stilled. Quentin sits next to me, leaning against the wall. When I find the power to speak, the only word I can muster the energy to say is his name. "Quentin?" I breathe.

"Yes?" he responds quietly, his voice heavy and breathy.

"Thank you."

"Don't," he breathes heavily again, "mention it, Books." *Cough-cough.*

"Where are the others?" I ask, suddenly remembering my friends are still out there, and I lost sight of them when Quentin scooped me up.

"Asheron was getting Remi to safety—*cough-cough*—and Mhelodie had Lumeilia. *Cough.* They were safe within the stone army's barricade. *Cough-cough.*" Quentin responds slowly. His breath is still heavy and shallow, cutting in between his words.

"Remind me to never piss off Mhelodie," he laughs and coughs again.

Although the room is silent, and the large steel doors are keeping the sounds and emotional carnage from the other side out, I'm keenly aware the war on the other side hasn't ended. The Wolves are still attacking, Beings are still dying, and my friends are still in danger.

I sit upright as much as I can, and my muscles ache from the tension they endured. "We have to get out there," I command. "We need to get them all in here—into safety."

"We can't go back out there, Paege. It's not safe," he coughs. "It'll kill you. They will kill you."

"I can't just sit in here and do nothing." Adrenaline floods my veins, and I try to stand, but I'm still unsteady on my legs, weakened by the energy expelled from the overwhelming assault of emotions.

"That's exactly what you're going to do!" Quentin snaps and coughs again.

"And what *exactly* are you going to do if I don't? Stop me?" I bark at him. I'm trying my best to sound commanding, but my voice is shaky, and as I take a couple of unsteady steps toward the door, I stumble into the wall.

"Yes, that's exactly what I will do." He coughs again. "Just—" he takes a laboured breath, "give me a damn minute, will you?" He continues to cough.

Quentin's cough doesn't relent. My brows pull together. Something is not right. He is a Wolf. He should be recovered by now, but his breaths are still short and sharp, as if he is trying to gulp down life itself. Worry tugs at me from deep within. I focus, honing my Fae eyesight onto him. His usual sun-kissed skin looks ashen and pasty even in the darkness, and he leans back against the wall of the safe. No, he is slumped. Sweat beads along his forehead, his lips are dry, and his eyes are barely open.

"What's wrong?" I ask, and I take a few unstable steps over to him, using the wall to hold me up, my legs weak and groaning with every step.

The effects from the intense emotional lashing I just experienced linger, so I completely missed Quentin's pain. But as I open myself up to him, there it is, and it's now hitting me like a torrential storm, battering me from every angle with nowhere to shelter.

"Nothing, I'm fine." He tries to smile. "I just need a minute." He coughs again. He shifts, trying to pull himself up, but his hand slips in a puddle of blood that I didn't even see pooling.

"You're bleeding!" I exclaim, stumbling a few more steps back toward him and falling by his side. My bones jar, and my hands sting as I hit the cold hard floor. But I push the pain aside, as it's nothing compared to what Quentin is feeling. I lift his shirt, but I can't see anything. I start inspecting him over, and then I see the rip in his black shirt on the back of his left shoulder. I unbutton his shirt and pull it down. There it is, a Wolf bite. The blood that was once streaming down his arm is already clotting.

Thank the Gods. But the bite itself looks wrong. It looks infected. It's blackening, oozing, and swollen.

That's when it hits me. He was bitten with the fatal scorpion venom. Shit, shit, shit, shit, shit. Terror sets in. I feel my brain snap awake, searching within for any answer.

"Quentin, you've been bitten," I gasp, a failed attempt to hide the fear and worry I'm feeling.

"Is that what that is?" Quentin coughs again.

"Why didn't you say anything?" My panic rises, and my mind runs through everything Quentin and Guy told us the night at my place about the Scorpion's venom.

"I was kind of busy . . . trying to save your life."

"What do I do? We need to get help, or we need to get you help." I attempt to stand again, but my body protests, and I fall forward into his lap. "Shit, sorry."

"I'm fine, Books. Really." *Breath*. "I just need to sit here a minute," Quentin says slowly, and he chokes on an attempted laugh, coughing some more, and his breathing slows.

"You're not fine," I demand. "We need to get you help." I look around the safe, but there is absolutely nothing in here that's going to help me. It's fucking barren.

"If I can get to Mhelodie, maybe she knows some magic?" I think out loud.

"No, that won't work. There's nothing you can do." *Cough, cough*.

"No," I interrupt aggressively. "Don't you dare say that."

The urgency of the situation is becoming more dire, and I need to get out of this room and get him help. I won't sit here and let him die. I won't lose him, too. I can't.

"If I can just get to . . ."

Quentin grabs my arm and squeezes it tightly. I stop scanning the room and turn back to face him. He appears defeated, eyes pleading with me in silence to just let it go. Let him go. But I can't. I won't. I raise my hand to brush his face, the heat of the poison burning my hand at the touch.

"We need to get you some help!" I beg him. "Please."

He just shakes his head and pushes my hand away from his face. He closes his eyes, and his breath shallows even more. A loud growl emits from him, and his body shudders before going limp.

I shake him violently.

"No! You can't leave me. This is not the end. Quentin, you do not get to give up. You need to fight." He coughs again, and as crazy as it seems, relief washes over me.

Coughing is a good sign. It means he is still alive, but probably not for long.

Quentin coughs again, but his eyes remain closed, and aside from the rattling in his breath, he doesn't make any other sounds.

"Do not give up," I demand. "You. We. We never even got our . . ." I break off. My heart begins to drop. "This is not how it's supposed to go," I whisper to no one.

His eyes flutter open, the emptiness behind them expansive. Lifeless. Gone is the cocky sparkle in his eyes. Gone is the arrogant, annoying Wolf. Instead, here sits a fragile shell of a Wolf, one who has no life left in him, no fight. He has given up already, so easily, so soon. He hasn't even tried. I feel my heart smashing into a thousand tiny pieces, and tears prickle my eyes.

"I thought you said we can't be together?" Quentin tries to joke, but it's no time for funny business.

"We can't. But what the Hels do I know? All I know is this," I wave my hand between us, "can't be the end."

He tries to force a grin, but it doesn't reach his eyes. Then he bellows an enormous growl. I pull his shirt open again and swallow thickly as I spy his veins turning black from the bite mark. They reach for his heart like tendrils of death, and I can feel the pain of the venom seeping through his veins. It's killing him.

Quentin closes his eyes again and places a hand over mine, resting on his chest.

"I don't want you to die," I whisper to him. Gently, I lean down and place my forehead against his.

He squeezes my hand and whispers, "This isn't the end, Books. Trust me."

I cup his face with my hand. I gently stroke his cheek, my eyes never shifting from his. Tears fill my eyes once more, and I swallow hard, trying to gulp down the massive lump forming in my throat.

These feelings take me by surprise. He is going to die here, now, and I won't ever get a chance to understand what it is between us—what I'm feeling. He won't ever get to know how I feel. I don't even know how I feel, but I know that if he dies, a part of me will die with him.

That I know.

That I can feel.

Without another word, my mouth finds his, and I kiss him. It's not like our last. It's gentle, soft, and tender. Slow. His lips are dry, but he tastes like VineMist and strawberries. He kisses me back cautiously at first, but when he realises I'm not letting him go, not yet anyway, he opens his mouth and lets his tongue escape, and it finds the opening of my mouth. I welcome him in. I open myself up to feel his emotions. Buried deep beneath the pain, there it is: the silky caramel marble of lust that I have felt before.

And all rational thought escapes my mind.

CHAPTER 26

I move ever so slowly, careful not to cause him any more pain, and pull myself fully into his lap. I straddle him and bring myself as close to him as I possibly can. I need to feel him. The heat intensifies between us as I tangle my fingers through his matted hair, pulling his mouth in closer to mine. That little bundle of nerves pushes up against his hardness, and I let out a breathy moan as the pressure builds, desire burning deep within my core. He grabs my ass and pulls me in closer, his tongue violently searching, exploring my mouth. I pull myself down onto him harder, and pleasure burns inside, building like a rising tide.

He groans as I rock myself forward against him once more. This is so wrong, but it feels so right. He is dying. My friends are out there, fighting and probably dying or possibly already dead, but I can't stop myself. It's like I'm possessed. I pull my mouth from his, and his mouth finds my neck. He continues to kiss me, licking up to my ear and then nibbling my earlobe, which sends charged shivers down my body.

"Quentin, you can't leave me," I breath into his ear as his mouth sucks on my neck.

Unexpectedly, he growls, and it's not one born of the pleasure that I know he is feeling. It's a growl so feral and animalistic it reminds me of the Wolves that just attacked. He pulls his mouth away from me. His eyes widen, and fear surges through me. I bring my hands to his chest, and he grabs my wrists, pushing me away from him.

"You need to get back," he demands.

But I don't move. I just stare, motionless. With a wild force of aggression, he pushes me in the chest, the palm of his hands hitting me with a bruising force, and I fall off him.

"Go," he roars.

I shuffle myself away and watch in terror as Quentin's face begins to morph into something else. Something animalistic.

He strips his shirt from his body in a fit of rage and starts unbuckling his belt with his one good arm.

Shit, is he shifting?

"What's happening?" I ask a barely humanoid Quentin as he continues to try and strip his clothes from his body.

"Stay back, Paege," he orders. Concern emanates from his voice, and he yelps again.

"How?" I inch closer to him, needing to help him, to ease his pain.

He begins panting and writhing before he manages to get his feet out of his pants.

"I killed that Wolf before!" he snaps at me, anger and pain stemming from every word. "Stay back!"

I shuffle further back and find my way onto my unsteady feet once more. His words sink in, jolting me into realisation of what is happening before me.

He took a life.

He triggered his Emergence.

His shoulders hunch forward, and his legs bend unnaturally until I hear the snapping of bones. His body arches, and he bellows a cry. His mouth and nose become pointed and elongated, and his jaw expands. He opens his mouth with a growl, and teeth pierce through his gums, revealing the longest canines I've never seen before.

I blink one time, and standing before me is the most beautiful grey Wolf I have ever seen in my life. He is magical and majestic. He stretches his front legs out and then stretches his hind legs back behind him, and he lets out a mighty yawn. His eyes meet mine, and I swear I see him smile. He pads toward me, but I back away, uncertain if Quentin even recognises me in his Wolf form. He stills as if acknowledging my anticipation. He bows his head toward me, and he lets his eyes meet mine again, and they are his grey-blue eyes staring back at me. All the panic I felt completely washes away. He is letting me know that I don't need to fear him. I take a couple of apprehensive steps toward him, and he follows suit, mirroring my every step until he is inches away from me. Quentin then takes the final step forward, and he brushes his forehead against my stomach.

I let out the longest breath.

Oh, the Gods.

I kneel, and Quentin nuzzles into me. His massive form towers over me on my knees. I run my hands over his body, and through his soft coat. Then I lean into him. I hold him, embracing this beautiful beast. Once more, I look into his piercing eyes, and I can see Quentin's reflecting in them.

It's him. It's really him! Then, without warning, Quentin swiftly shifts back into his humanoid form. It's more fluid and flawless than when he shifted into his Wolf, and a calmness radiates off him. His body accepted his Wolf that emerged. They merged and are now one.

I realise I'm still holding him—a very naked him. I push him off me. "What the Hels was that?" I shriek kind of in excitement and also in bewilderment.

Quentin stands and smiles playfully at me. "I shifted," he pants.

I look him up and down. My eyes trailing down his bare stomach. The perfect ridges of his muscles flex with every breath he takes and tense, revealing even more of their perfect shape as he stands. Then my eyes fall a little bit further.

Gods.

"See something you like?" Quentin asks as I take in every inch of his hardness.

"Huh?"

"Oi, eyes up here, Books," he commands in a teasing tone, clicking his fingers around his face.

Shit. Heat prickles my cheeks.

"Sorry. It's just—you're naked," I whisper into the room, a goofy smile forcing itself onto my face. I have no idea why I whispered that because it's not like anyone can hear us or see us.

"Yes and?"

"You shifted." I open my senses up, and relief washes over me as I realise there is no more pain, no more sickness, emitting from Quentin. "And you're healed?"

I wait for him to clarify, but instead, he shrugs and turns to grab his clothes, redressing himself.

"Seriously, Quentin, that's all you have to say?" He smiles his signature grin at me as he pulls his pants up and zips himself. He puts away the hard perfection that had me drooling from my mouth not too long ago, and I wonder if I will ever get to see it again.

"You're healed?" I pause, remembering how he growled at me and pushed me back aggressively. He steps toward me as he puts his arms in his shirt, not bothering to butting it up, and I push him away from me. "And you yelled at me."

"I'm sorry about that." Quentin looks away sheepishly and brushes the hair back that's falling into his eyes. "It was my first shift, and I didn't know what was going to happen."

Alright, that's fair enough. *Let that one go, Paege.*

"And healing?"

"That's kind of a pack secret. We are immune to the venom of other Wolves. So, when I merged with my Wolf, I was healed. You can't tell anyone, Paege."

"Did you know that was going to happen?"

"No, Books, I didn't know. I wasn't sure if I was going to die before my Wolf came to me. We never really know how long it can take." Quentin's eyes soften. "I'm sorry, I didn't mean to scare you."

Before he can continue, I interrupt, "So, you were just going to let yourself die? You weren't even going to try to fight even though you knew that if your Wolf appeared, you had a chance to survive? You were just going to let me watch you die in this shitty room. You weren't even going to fight?" *For me*, I add silently. "Gods, Quentin, you're so selfish. Do you ever think of anyone else? I can't believe I was so worried about you. I thought you were going to die. You tricked me."

Gods, I am so angry at him right now. He doesn't get it.

"I didn't trick you, Books."

"No? Then what did you do? Was it just some big ploy? Play dead so the naive *halfling* would feel sorry for you and kiss you?"

"Oh, so that's why you kissed me? Out of pity?"

"No."

Now Quentin interrupts me. "I don't need you to pity me. I certainly don't need your pity kisses, Paege." His grey eyes burn with rage as he stalks forward toward me.

"Well, maybe I shouldn't kiss you again then!" I yell at him, my head so hot with fury I'm sure steam is blowing out from my ears.

"That works for me!" he retorts.

"Fine?"

"Fine!" Quentin sweeps the hair out of his eyes again and then lunges at me. I'm taken aback with shock, but as his lips press against mine, I melt into it. His hands paw at me with a wild desperation. I slide my hands under his shirt and wrap my arms around him, dragging my nails across his back and pulling his body close to mine.

I feel every inch of his exposed, hard body emitting heat against mine. My lips part, and my tongue enters his mouth, searching for his, sweeping and exploring. With every kiss, he sucks and nibbles my lower lip, pulling ecstasy from me with every bite. The heat inside of me is explosive. Quentin's fingers run up the side of my thigh, stopping just before the apex of my legs. His touch sends electricity through my body as the heat between my thighs intensifies. He groans, and I pull my mouth from his. I look deep into his hypnotic, blue eyes and place my hand over his, guiding him ever so slowly toward my centre as I lift my leg and wrap it around him.

Oh, the Gods, Paege, what are you doing?

"We shouldn't be doing this," he breathes into my mouth, but he doesn't stop as he runs his fingers over my underwear. I quiver at his touch, my breasts aching as his fingers find my entrance.

"No, we shouldn't," I reply. "Please don't stop."

"Gods. You. Are. Perfect," he groans as he strokes the entrance to my core.

With these words, I smile, permitting him to enter me. He shifts my underwear to the side, and I close my eyes in anticipation. With one fluid motion, he slips a finger deep inside me, and I open my eyes, moaning with pleasure.

"Paege." The hoarse sound of my name from Quentin's lips sends shivers scattering across my body. Quentin's said my name a hundred times, but this time, it's different. He has never said it like *that* before. He stares deep into my eyes, into my soul, as he starts to slide his finger inside of me again and again and again.

"You feel so good," he whispers.

His touch, his voice, drives me into a wild desperation for more. He strokes the inside of me with raw wildness, going deeper and deeper with every thrust, eventually sliding a second finger in and curling them against my wall, and I know I'm going to explode. I want to make this last forever, but as I buck myself forward in rhythm with his strokes, I can't contain myself. I want more. *I need* more.

With every stroke, the feeling inside of me intensifies. The palm of his hand rubs against my clit and sends my body into fits. I don't want this to end, but I suck in a long breath and hold it, unable to control the sweet release that's rising to the surface.

I moan, or think I do, at the mounting pressure inside that continues to build. Quentin responds to my sound by moving faster against me, his fingers curling deep inside me, and finally, I let myself go, jumping off that cliff of ecstasy, and I soar into the wind of pleasure. I bellow an almighty cry and pull myself in close to him as my body erupts, exploding like fireworks into the skies. My core clenches tight around his fingers before tumbling back down to earth in a euphoric release.

Quentin holds me there for a moment, his face beaming with pride before he slowly slides his fingers out from inside me. As he holds my gaze, he brings his fingers to his opened lips, and with a slight smile, he tastes me off his fingers, and I almost come apart again.

"Books, you have no idea how long I've wanted to taste you."

My legs go weak and give way beneath me as his words flitter through my core, sending my body into more fits. I start to drop, but he catches me. He doesn't say a word. He kisses my little snub nose, and his brow falls to mine. Chest heaving, I breathe in his scent, fresh just like the forest, and my heart thrums, satiated by the pleasure.

"Quentin?" I pant.

"Are you going to thank me again, Books?" I can hear the mischievous tone in his voice, and I know that he is grinning his signature smirk, and I can't help but let a small laugh escape from my lips.

"No," I breathe. "I was going to ask, what is this?" I lift my head, my eyes colliding his.

He takes his hand and runs a finger down my cheek, tucking a stray hair behind my ear, so soft and caring. It's a side to Quentin I never knew existed but one I want to know. One I want to discover. "What do you want it to be?"

But before I can answer, a noise behind me distracts me, pulling my gaze from Quentin's. His eyes dart behind me as another loud sound, like metal scraping, suddenly echoes through the safe room, and I register that the door is opening. My body stiffens, muscles tensing as my heart starts racing and adrenaline surges through my veins. Quentin grabs me and ushers my braced body behind him. Good move because if those Wolves are coming to finish the job, we are trapped in here like hopeless prey. Quentin may be the only hope I have of surviving.

Light starts peeking in, and I brace myself for combat, but instead, I hear my name softly called. "Paege?"

Lumeilia.

As the door opens fully, a metallic odour assaults my nostrils, and I see Lumeilia and Mhelodie standing at the entrance, covered in blood. My heart drops into my stomach as the waves of emotions come flooding into me. Quentin tries to grab my hand to steady me, but instinctually, I pull back from him. I have no idea what made me do it, and it's a decision I immediately regret.

Sadness overcomes me, bringing me back down from the euphoric moment I had shared with Quentin a moment ago. Then nausea fills my stomach as I realise I've been protected in the safe room doing *that* with Quentin while my friends have been living this terror.

I step toward the girls, and when I reach them, I hug them so tightly and think to myself that I will never let them go ever again. As I look up behind them, the carnage I see is heart-wrenching. Then, a heavy weight plummets down on my chest, constricting the breath from my lungs. Tears pool in the corners of my eyes as I catch a vision I never imagined I would see.

Asheron stands behind Lumeilia and Mhelodie, in the middle of the carnage, his face expressionless. Wrath bleeds from his heart.

His black wings are flared, and he's holding a very beautiful but very dead Remi in his arms.

Chapter 27

The moment I see Asheron, everything in the universe fades away.

I've never felt so much wrath and fury from one Being before. It's consuming. A darkness blacker than shadows and thicker than tar seeps from his heart and soul. It's so powerful that I can't keep it out, no matter how hard I try, and Asheron doesn't want me to. He is pushing it out into the kingdom for all to feel. Worry's sharp talons scrape at my mind. Worry for what stupid thing I am sure my dear friend is about to do in revenge for what happened to his FaeMate.

Without a word, Asheron flares his black feathered wings and flaps them so hard he blows a hole in the ceiling above him, and he takes off in one aggressive swoop.

Part of me wants to let him go and exact his revenge. The other part of me, the sane part that knows Asheron is not yet Israykiel Guard, knows whatever power he wields is not enough to stand against the Wolves. It knows I need to stop him. But how? I'm only a demi-Fae—I have not yet got any powers of my own—and he has just taken off in flight before my very eyes, to only the Gods know where.

Then there is Quentin.

This egotistical yet beautiful Wolf who just killed to save me. Who merged with his Wolf in front of me. Who I just let take me to a place of pure ecstasy while my friends were fighting for their lives while my friend was losing the love of his. How could I allow this to happen?

Tears fall from my eyes like a heavy winter's rain. I watch with anticipation and fear as both Lumeilia and Mhelodie turn to view the carnage that lies before us, their hands finding solace in each other's. Masses of bodies and body parts lay among the rubble. A massacre so brutal, a wreckage of war would not even be comparable.

I turn to look at Quentin, a plethora of emotions running through my mind like a kaleidoscope of images, but there is only one I can grab hold of. *Guilt.* Guilt for what I just allowed to happen, and it crawls through me, infecting my soul. It must show all over my face because before I have a chance to say anything, Quentin warily steps to where I stand. He whispers in my ear, "It never happened," sparing me the shame that's taking over my mind. He gently kisses my cheek in what feels like a goodbye and steps past me into the graveyard before us.

Regardless of the guilt and shame I feel, I didn't want *that.*

My heart falls fast, descending beyond my stomach into a fiery pit that's opened up in the ground beneath me, splintering into a thousand tiny pieces, and I know I will never be able to make it whole again.

None of us speak as we try to make our way to the centre of the room where Quentin now stands.

As I find my way next to Quentin, my hand reaches for his to find comfort in the turmoil I'm feeling. To be reminded, even if it's just for one moment, that there is still some light in this dark world. To show him that I don't regret what just happened. But he pulls his hand from reach, and I know it's too late. My heart descends further into the pit below, shattering even more.

More emotions start to overwhelm me as Beings begin to gather on the street outside, looking in horror at what has occurred inside the gallery. I feel myself being pulled and ripped in all directions by the waves of emotions that continue to wash over me.

I need to escape.

I need to get away.

I frantically start to climb over the carnage in front of me, trying to escape the hordes of Beings now assembling outside. My goal is simple. Make it to the street so I can run as fast as I can away from everyone to safety.

But the second I cross the threshold of the gallery into the streets, like a volcano, my emotions erupt, and I let out an almighty scream that sends glass shattering.

I feel the world tilt around me, and darkness curtains my vision, everything slowly turning black.

When the darkness finally takes me, I think I finally find peace.

CHAPTER 28

We twirl around each other, the sun beating down on us as our wooden swords smack together in unison. Clank, clank, clank. I gobble down air and take a small step back, lowering my sword for a moment as I regain my strength. We've been playing this game all afternoon, and the weight of the wooden sword is becoming heavy in my little hands.

"Are you too tired to continue, Princess?" he taunts, his single dimple just like mine appearing with his grin.

I hold my sword back up, using both hands just as Amerax had taught me.

"Never, Prince! I will fight you until my last breath." I lunge for him, and he jumps out of the way, bringing his sword up to meet mine again with a clank.

"When I best you, I will lock you in the dungeons to be forgotten about forever," he laughs.

"You will never be able to best me, Prince," I reply with a giggle. "I am too fast." I swing at him again, and our wooden swords smack. "I am too skilled." Another smack. "Too smart." Smack.

We still with our swords kissing. Neither one of us move. His emerald eyes glisten in the sunlight, and a small bead of sweat drops to his brow.

"Honey, it's time to go."

We relax our swords to our sides as the summer song in my mother's voice carries softly across the garden like the dandelion puffs floating through the air. We both look up, and I see Mum standing with the silver-haired female, one of the two who comes with him every year.

My eyes adjust slowly as I peel my lids open, and an ache blooms behind them as the light violently penetrates my vision. Blinking, I scan the room quietly. Guy sits on the floor in the corner of my room. Worry shows all over his face. His clenched jaw ticks as he flips through the pages of one of my books. The vein above his brow protrudes.

"Guy?" I manage to murmur.

He jumps up, discarding the book like trash, and pounces on me, giving me the biggest hug I've ever received in my life. I wince as he squeezes the life out of me. "Fuck, Sorry. But thank the Gods, Paege. Are you alright?" He looks me over, the worry not shifting from his expression.

"I don't know," I respond hoarsely and honestly because I truly don't know. "What happened?" I ask.

"You passed out on the street after the . . ." He doesn't finish his sentence because, quite frankly, how can he describe what happened? There are no words for it.

I stare up to the ceiling for a moment and blink one, two, three times while all the memories come flooding back in. I close my eyes again, attempting to stop the assault of all the visions of death and carnage, but the darkness just seems to make it worse, so I open my eyes and swallow down the bile that stings my throat.

"What time is it?" I ask as I try to sit up, ignoring the pain searing through my body from, well, everything.

He doesn't answer.

"What time?"

"Midafternoon," Guy responds, shifting his gaze away from me.

"I've been asleep all day?" I say sharply, suddenly feeling the emptiness and fullness in my belly. The need to relieve myself overrides all other needs and wants.

"No, it's, um. You've been in and out of consciousness for two nights," he confirms. "It's Sunday."

"Fuck, it's been two days since?" I gulp. I can't find the words as the images of the attack continue to assault my mind. "Where's Lumeilia?" I croak, trying to stifle down a sob.

"She's been here, and so has Mhelodie, healing you."

"Asheron?"

Guy drops his head and darts his eyes from mine again. "No one's seen or heard from him."

Tears well up in my eyes as worry sets in. He was so angry when I last saw him, and I was sure he was going to do something reckless and foolish. But if no one has heard from him, that could also mean he hasn't done anything crazy, right? So, I tell myself maybe he is safe. Maybe he is just grieving somewhere alone.

I don't even bother to ask about Quentin because if he was here, I would know. He would be the one sitting in my room waiting for me to wake up.

Or Guy would have called him in here by now. Or Guy would have at least mentioned him being here. He hasn't. Which means he has never been here. More tears fill my eyes as that gaping hole in my chest where my heart used to be grows larger.

Guy reaches to my nightstand and hands me a tall opaque glass. "Here, drink this. Mhelodie said it will make you feel better when you wake. Don't ask me what it is, but it smells ghastly."

I take the glass and sniff the liquid. My stomach churns at the foul stench, and I swallow back the urge to vomit. It smells like nothing I have ever smelled before. Sweet like medicine and also acidic like an over-ripe lemon. There is something else I can't quite put my finger on. "I don't think I can drink that."

I place the revolting drink back on the nightstand. I lean back into my pillows and close my eyes for just a moment more, but the emptiness and fullness in my belly have me sitting back up again.

"You must be hungry. Do you want something? Anything?"

"I would love a coffee," I say as I prepare my body to stand.

"And maybe some gridcakes?" Guy suggests.

I nod. "Sure." But truthfully, I am not too sure I can eat anything. I know I have been unconscious for two days, and the emptiness in my stomach is telling me I should be hungry, but food is the last thing I have on my mind.

"How about you try to drink that and then get up and shower? I will make us some coffee and food. You don't have to come out; I can bring it in here if you want. Gridcakes and coffee in bed." He smiles.

The worry shifts from his face, and warmth radiates from him. I have an urge to hug him again, and this time, I don't hold back. I lean over, wrap my arms around his broad shoulders, and bury my head into his chest. He envelops me back and lets out a sigh of relief, allowing me to stay there for a while.

"Thank you," I whisper into his chest. I pull back and plant a soft kiss on his cheek.

"Don't mention it," Guy responds, his cheek flushing a light shade of pink. "Now get yourself freshened up, and I'll be back shortly with coffee and food."

After Guy leaves my room, I drag myself out of bed and make my way to the bathroom. I drink the gross-ass concoction that Mhelodie made for me right before I submerge myself under the cascading waterfall of warm water, preparing for whatever goes down to come back up again. Surprisingly, it doesn't taste half as bad as it smells.

Once I'm clean, dry, and dressed in comfortable clothes—grey loose cotton pants and cropped white cotton shirt—I emerge from my room to find Guy sitting on the couch, talking into the scribe. When he hears me, he quickly finishes his conversation and jumps up with a warm expression, welcoming the sight of me up and alert.

"Sorry, I didn't mean to interrupt."

"You didn't," he says, tucking his scribe away. Looking me up and down, he adds, "You look half decent. Not at all like you've been in bed for days."

"Thanks. Surprisingly, I don't feel half bad either." I give Guy a little smile. "It's amazing what a two-day rest can do for you." I wink and sit myself down at the breakfast bar. "Now, where's that coffee I was promised?" I joke, and I see the relief wash over his face.

"Are you honestly alright? Do you want to talk about it?" he probes gently as he hands me a cup of coffee.

I muse over his question for a long moment, allowing all the variables running through my mind because, honestly, I am not too sure how to answer that.

We were attacked at my work, and I lost a friend.

We were attacked at my friend's art gallery, and I lost a friend.

Asheron lost his FaeMate, and now he is on a revenge mission.

Quentin and I got intimate, and now he wants nothing to do with me.

I don't know why, but I am starting to consider this *is* all because of me.

So, I decide to ignore his question and change the subject. "Have you spoken to anyone to tell them that I am awake?"

Guy seems to understand my sudden shift in the conversation topic, and instead of fighting it, he follows along. "Yes, when you were in the shower, I let Mhelodie and Lumeilia know you were awake. They said they will come by tomorrow."

The dark hole in my heart expands for the second time since I woke from my *comatose* state at the omittance of Quentin's name once more. "Oh, alright," I reply, trying not to sound too disappointed.

"Paege, they wanted to come today, but they mentioned your parents want to see you, too. We wanted to make sure you were alright before your apartment becomes a madhouse full of guests again." He pauses, then adds, "Did I make the wrong decision?" He looks perplexed.

I take his hand and squeeze it gently. "No, Guy. You didn't," I respond because my disappointment is not about my parents or when my friends will come see me. It's about the one other person whose name has not been mentioned since I awoke. The one person I really shouldn't want to see, but for some reason, is the only one I so desperately want to see. "Thank you for looking out for me. *Again.*" I smile and then take a huge gulp of my coffee.

After I've eaten my gridcakes, I try to watch a cringe-worthy show on the vision box with Guy, but my mind keeps drawing me back to one conversation from the other night—what I overheard Ric say at Lumeilia's show. My memory might not be as sharp as usual due to the overpowering surge of emotions that bombarded my mind and body, but I am certain I heard what I heard.

Don't stop till we find it.

The Witch, she tracked it here.

What on earth could he be looking for? And why would he think it was at Lumeilia's exhibition?

My parents will be here soon. I suppose I could talk to Amerax, but being a Guard, I'm sure there is very little he would be allowed to tell me if they're even connecting the Scorpions to this attack. Surely Quentin would have said something? But maybe not. He doesn't seem to care that much at all. Guy is more sympathetic to the welfare of other species. Maybe I could ask him about it, and maybe he could talk to Quentin about it.

"What have you heard about the attack at Lumeilia's gallery?" I ask.

He promptly turns the vision box off and faces me. "Um, not a lot, actually. It's all been kept pretty hush, to be honest. Why?"

"I just remember something." Guy's eyes widen with intrigue. "It's been playing on my mind all afternoon, and I wasn't sure if it meant anything or not," I say casually, trying not to sound too desperate or crazy.

Guy shifts in his seat, and it seems I have his full attention. "What do you remember?"

"Ric, the Scorpion's High Alpha, was there, and he—"

"Ric's not the Scorpion's High Alpha," Guy interrupts.

My brows pull together.

"I mean, yes, he is an alpha, but an alpha of an omega pack. He is not the High Alpha. He was part of the alpha pack years ago, but he was rejected by the pack when he did some questionable shit. So, he made himself an omega pack. Doesn't mean he isn't real nasty, and we can't forget he still has the alpha pack venom."

"Oh, wow." I muse over what Guy just said for a moment. Does this change anything? Does he answer to the High Alpha, then? "What does that mean?" I start, wanting to know the answers to all the questions I now have running through my brain. Then I realise it's not what is important right now, so I shift gears back. "You know what? It doesn't matter. We can come back to that later. It's what I heard him say that's important."

"And that was?"

"'The Witch tracked it here. Don't stop until we find it.' What do you think that means?"

"I have no idea," he muses. "Did you tell anyone that night?"

"No, I was . . ."

"I understand, Paege, it's fine." Guy smiles dismissively, the mental clogs of his brain churning so fast that I can almost hear them. "Let me talk to Q, and I can see if it means anything to him. Worst case, he can take it to his dad."

The strings in my heart pull tight at Quentin's name. It's the first time since I woke up that he's been mentioned. Where is he, and what could he possibly be doing? Or *who* he is doing?

No, Paege, stop it.

Another series of thoughts come together in my mind, and instead of considering what it all means, this time, I just blurt it all out.

"What could they be looking for?"

"I have no idea, Paege, but if they are looking for something, we need to tell the king and let him handle it."

"Hm, do you think it's all connected?" I ask.

"What is?"

"The Pit, The Gallery, maybe even the museum?"

Guy hums, considering my words, then shakes his head. "I don't think—"

"They are looking for something, though," I interrupt him before he can get the rest of his sentence out because something just doesn't add up. "Don't you find it curious that these attacks have happened wherever high-ranking members of the Crescent Wolf pack have been?"

"We don't even know if the Scorpions were responsible for the museum. And there were no Crescent Wolf pack members at the museum."

"You were there. You picked me up."

"I don't know, Paege, it's a bit of a stretch," Guy finishes, running his hands down his face.

"Yes, I know," I concede. Guy does have a point. They had every chance to attack us at The Pit and didn't. It was just a theory—a weak one at that—but something still doesn't seem to fit.

"What about the book?" I ask, trying to change the subject. "Have you learned anything else about the pack?"

"No," Guy admits. "It's too redacted."

Chewing my bottom lip, I hesitate in my reply. The only logical idea I have regarding being able to read the book—one that he was all too proud and cautious to consider last time we discussed this—is to ask a Witch for help. I still believe it's our best shot and probably our only shot.

"I know you were reluctant last time I mentioned this, but I still think Mhelodie might be our best shot." I clench my teeth, waiting in anticipation for the dismissal, but surprisingly, it doesn't come.

"I think you may be right, Paege." Guy sighs, running his hands through his hair, his throat bobbing. "I've had time to think about it, and maybe she can help."

I clap my hands like a small child and sit up straight. Excitement peaks inside me as butterflies start fluttering in my stomach at the first sight of hope I've felt in weeks. It's a nice change from the usual doom and gloom I've been feeling of late. It must be so frustrating to be bound by the moon when the rest of the packs can shift at will. If we can read the book, we can learn about the crescent moon curse. Maybe we can break the curse and give the Crescent Wolf pack the ability to shift at will again. Something I know that Guy and Quentin would love.

"Don't get too excited yet because I think we'll also need to get the original tome, the one that can't leave the archives."

My shoulders slump. The butterflies quickly lose their wings, falling into the shadows of dread slowly spreading throughout.

I swallow down the rebuttal forming on my tongue. I promised Guy I would help him. So, I will. I am, if nothing else, a female of my word.

CHAPTER 29

"It's bullshit, that's what it is. I'm being demoted to a glorified babysitter, and for what?" The male outside my door complains, and I hear Amerax's stern voice reply.

"To look after the one you swore to protect. You made a vow, remember?"

"Sounds like the parents are here," Guy supplies as he stands. "I'll make myself scarce if you like. I need to head back to the den anyway."

"Are you sure? You don't need to leave."

"No, spend time with your family, Paege. It's too important. I will be back later if you want. Just send a message."

"I want . . . I don't want to be alone," I answer.

"Alright, I will come back after. Send a message when they leave."

I follow Guy to the door, and a mix of excitement and anticipation rushes through my veins. It's been months since I have seen my mum, and I miss her so much. I hate that I am seeing her under such stressful circumstances.

"Yes, but this is ridiculous. If I had known . . ." the unknown male says in a growl that has the hair on my skin standing. I wonder who he pissed off to have been demoted. And who is he babysitting?

"If you had known what?" Amerax asks firmly as I swing open the door to my apartment to welcome my parents and see Guy off.

Mum and Dad stand with a tall male Guard. His onyx hair, bounces hues of blue in the afternoon sun, and his bronzed skin glistens. His voice sounds oddly familiar, but I can't see his face clearly. Mum stands in front of him, tall and staunch, with her hands on her hips and tapping a foot. It's almost as if she is the Guard's superior and annoyed at his dissent, which is ridiculous because she is not a Guard. If it were Amerax talking to him, it wouldn't be so alarming. But Amerax is standing next to Mum with a hand on her shoulder as if calming her down from unleashing wrath on the Guard. I'm rather baffled by the scene before me.

"Mum?" I say curiously, and she drops her hands from her hips and spins around to face me. Her blonde hair is braided down her back, and wisps of her fringe curtain her face. We don't look much alike except for our snub noses and the olive complexion we both sport. I've always assumed I look more like my bio-dad.

"Paege," she cries, and she almost breaks into a run to get to me, but she suddenly stops a few steps away from me, her light brown eyes widening briefly as they flick between me and Guy, filling with some sort of emotion that I can't quite read. Worry, no doubt. She knows who Guy is, just like Amerax does. I'm sure Amerax told her that we have become friends. But whatever emotion it is, it doesn't last long as she sets me in her sights again. "Paege," she cries again as she steps forward and wraps her arms around me. "Are you alright? Lumeilia and Mhelodie said . . ." A sob breaks from her chest, and she pulls me in tighter.

"I'm alright," I lie as I melt into her embrace.

"Pumpkin?" Amerax asks, and I look up through bleary eyes to see him standing behind Mum, worry lines creasing his brow. I hold an arm out, and he joins the huddle, and the three of us hold each other like it's the first and last time we ever will.

I'm not too sure how long we stand there in each other's embrace, but when I finally pull away, Guy has disappeared. So has the Guard. No doubt, he's off to fulfill his glorified babysitting duties.

Amerax cooks us some meat with mashed potatoes, pumpkin, and green vegetables while Mum and I sit on the couch, catching up. There is so much that has been happening lately, and I need to fill her in on all of it. The most important being Sylas. I know she knows. Amerax would have told her, but she still acts surprised when I finally confess. Cursing at the right moments, gasping at others. Gods, she is the best mum ever. When it comes time for them to tell me how they feel about what happened, it's not surprising that Mum and Dad's opinion of Sylas mirrors my friends.

When we finish eating, Mum gently asks, "Do you want to talk about what happened at Lumeilia's exhibition?" My heart stills, dead in my chest. I don't know why. I have been expecting the question all evening, and I'm surprised it's taken them this long to bring it up. But it still pulls the floor out from me.

"I don't know what to say," I respond because, truthfully, I don't know what to say about any of it. I can't even begin to process the level of carnage that unfolded in front of us, and for what? Why? Some secret things the Scorpions are looking for?

"How many?" I ask sombrely. My hand finds the charm that hangs around my neck, and I zip it manically up and down the chain.

Amerax answers, knowing exactly what I am referring to, "Thirty-five dead and twenty-seven seriously injured."

I knew the numbers would be high, but hearing it has me choking on my breath and my heart aching for the victims.

"Has anyone heard from Asheron?" Amerax doesn't respond. He looks at Mum, his eyes full of sadness. "Surely he called into the Academy. Or his dad?" I ask Dad, hopeful for some news on my friend.

"Paege, were you hurt?" Mum asks, holding her hand out for me to take. I reach out and take it, but something in the way she interrupts Dad from answering my questions about Asheron has my mind racing. Wondering if he is alright. What trouble has he got himself into?

"No, Mum. Not physically, no. Just . . ." Tears fill my eyes as I try to bite back the emotions rising like a tidal wave.

"Just?" Amerax asks tenderly.

"I felt it all," I gulp. "Every death, every . . ." I whisper at an almost inaudible volume as I choke back a sob, and my Mum gasps, ripping her hand free from mine. She pushes her chair back and rushes around the table, kneeling beside me and wrapping me in her arms.

"I never wanted this for you. I never wanted any of this for you," my mum sobs through her own tears. "I'm so sorry, Paege."

"It's not your fault, Mum," I reassure her.

"I could have protected you more. I should have done more." She was always worried about me leaving our small, isolated town in Orphelious, knowing the Neopolis would cause havoc on my emotional state. Nothing could have prepared me for this. This is not normal. This is something else.

"You didn't choose this for me. I chose to come here. And this gift, it was a gift from the Gods." A shitty, asshole gift from the Gods, I curse silently. And like a cruel twist of fate, my Mum replies, "Paegence Vailenbyrg, you take that back immediately. You know to never talk about the Gods like that," she commands.

"Sorry, Mum, but how about you stay out of my thoughts," I snap.

"You know I would if I could. But, Paege, I've never met anyone who talks so much to themselves with as much intent and clarity as you do. I can't help but hear you."

I bite back a snotty remark, knowing she is probably right about that. I do love a good internal diatribe. She would never listen to my thoughts on purpose. If she was, it's more than justified in this circumstance. She is undoubtedly concerned for me. So, I decide to give her a free pass on this occasion, and I sink back into another hug. Her warmth wraps me up in my own little cocoon of love, and I wish that I could stay here forever, but I know she will be leaving soon. They both will.

Amerax clears his throat, and both Mum and I break from our embrace. "Pumpkin, there is something else we need to discuss." His gruff voice sounds sombre. "Obviously, due to the unfortunate events at Lumeilia's exhibition, the Israykiel Guards are being brought back to patrol the Neopolis."

"That's a good thing, right?" I ask, confused why Amerax sounds so apprehensive to tell me about it. I'm not entirely sure it is enough. The king should be ordering the Scorpion's High Alpha to sort Ric and the omega pack members out. But what do I know? I'm just a demi-Fae.

"It is, but your mother and I were discussing things, and we think it's best if we station a couple of Guards nearby."

"Nearby, where?" I ask. Remembering the Guard out the front complaining about some glorified babysitting duty. Then I realise that glorified babysitting duty, is me.

Neither of them answer, but their eyes watch me with grave concern.

"You're joking, right?" I ask Amerax.

"Mum, tell me Dad is joking."

"It's just for a few days until things settle down," Mum supplies.

"No, I don't need babysitting."

"It's not babysitting. It's just someone watching out for you."

"Alright, I don't need watching," I counter, wishing for the first time in my life that my dad was not a Guard.

"You won't even know they are there. They will be out of sight the entire time."

"No. I already have three unwanted bodyguards; I don't need another." My mum sucks in a sharp breath and opens her mouth as if to speak, but Dad holds a hand up to silence her.

"It's not a discussion, Paege. It is happening whether you like it or not. I will not have any daughter of mine in harm's way because of the Wolves. Until we know exactly why you have been at the last two places this has happened, you will be protected by my most skilled Guards," my father demands, using his best Commander voice. There is a reason he is the Imperial Strategist of the Israykiel Guards. Not only is he one of the strongest and longest-reigning guards, he is by far the scariest. "We still cannot be sure that it doesn't have something to do with at least one of those three bodyguards you are referring to. If my sources are correct, Quentin was also at those two places." He pauses for a moment, his eyes meeting my mother's, and she nods in agreement. "So, until this is over, you will have Guards stationed outside the apartment complex, and they will escort you to work and home and anywhere in between."

"You said I wouldn't even know they are there," I challenge them. Any small abandon in these plans will be considered a victory.

"Fine, they will trail you from afar, but they will be there. Make no mistake." Dad runs his hands through his beard in frustration, and I know this is a battle I will never win.

So, I harrumph and surrender to his outrageous and overbearing parenting. "Fine."

"Thank you for indulging your father," Mum adds, worry lines still gracing her forehead.

"I understand," I say, getting up and hugging them both again. Because although this is completely unnecessary, I can't help but consider Dad's words. Words that mirrored my thoughts earlier.

But of the three, I don't think it's Quentin they are after.

CHAPTER 30

It's been a long week, and it's only Wednesday. Although I've been nervous about tonight, I'm equally excited to find out if Mhelodie will help Guy search for answers about the Crescent Wolf pack. Guy's been pacing the room since I got home from work, unable to hide his nervousness and possible unease about involving a Witch, but she is our only hope now.

The door knocks quietly, and I eagerly jump up, running to it. I swing it open wide without asking who it is and greet my friends with a warm hug as they enter. Gods, it's so nice to see them both. I can't help but wish, after everything we have been through these past couple of weeks, I was seeing them for more of a relaxing evening rather than asking for their help on something as monumental as this. It seems the only time we all catch up these days is because of some drama or trouble I've managed to get myself into. However, I owe it to Guy, after everything he's done for me over the past couple of weeks, to try and solve the mystery of the Crescent Wolf pack by any means possible. I'm sure all this chaos will calm down soon enough, and things will go back to normal.

My friends take their usual seats at the kitchen table, and my heart pangs at the empty seat next to Lumeilia where Asheron usually sits. He is still missing—not been seen or heard from since the night at the Gallery, and I am extremely worried about him. We all are.

Where is he?

What is he doing?

Is he alright?

Of course, he's not alright. Remi is dead.

I turn my focus to Guy, who's pacing my apartment like a nervous puppy, and my thoughts swiftly shift to Quentin, the other missing male in my life. I have the same thoughts swirling around my mind. However, not one person has mentioned his name to me since waking, so I can only assume he is avoiding me on purpose. Maybe Guy is instructed not to tell me.

There goes my heart again, splintering into even more pieces—if that is even possible.

Shifting my thoughts away from the missing males in my life and the pain thoughts of them cause, I gesture toward the dining table, motioning for Guy to sit with us.

If he keeps this pacing up, he is going to leave track marks on my floor.

He sits, shifting in the chair and fidgeting with the coffee mug in front of him, sliding it between his hands and spinning it around. Nervousness oozes from him. I know he is anxious about asking Mhelodie about the book and the potential curse, but I also know he knows it's the only option we have at present.

The four of us sit in silence. The air in the room fills with tension so thick I could cut it with a knife. Lumeilia and Mhelodie's eyes dart erratically between the four of us, and the awkwardness intensifies.

I stare at Guy, urging him to speak, but he doesn't. After minutes of uncomfortable silence, I decide to start the conversation on his behalf, but as I open my mouth to speak, Lumeilia breaks the silence first. "Would one of you please tell us what is going on?"

I keep my eyes pinned on Guy, hoping he responds, but instead, he gets up and strides over to the glass doors.

For a minute, I think he is going to run—slide those doors open and leave me here with my two friends. He stares out into the gardens for a moment and then unexpectedly returns his attention to the three of us and finally speaks.

"I need your help, Mhelodie."

Mhelodie shifts her gaze to me, and I smile, reassuring her to listen to Guy. "You need my help? With what?"

Guy paces back to the breakfast bar, grabs the book, and drops it on the table. "With this." The heavy slap, when leather meets wood, startles us.

Mhelodie and Lumeilia both briefly stare at the book before Lumeilia answers, "I don't understand. You need Mhelodie's help with a book about what?" She leans over the table to where Guy placed the book and reads the title out loud. "*Origin Series: The Crescent Wolf Pack*?" Her eyes widen, and she redirects her attention to Guy and questions, "The pack?"

"No, I need help with a curse."

Mhelodie produces a slight squeak, highlighting her unease about the situation at hand.

"You want Mhelodie to help you with a curse?" Lumeilia clarifies.

"Yes," Guy responds matter-of-factly.

"No," I counter immediately. By the look on Lumeilia's face, I have the feeling she thinks we are asking Mhelodie to curse someone.

"I mean, yes, but no. We don't want you to curse anyone, Mhelodie," I confirm. "We want information on a potential curse and hopefully find a way to break it."

Lumeilia's face softens as she closes her gaping mouth and finally blinks her eyes.

"What would I know about any of this?" Mhelodie questions. Her brows raise so high they almost disappear in her hairline.

"We don't know if you would," Guy starts. "I mean, we don't know if it is a curse or much about anything, to be honest."

"We haven't been able to read much at all," I add. "We do know something changed in history that prevented the Crescent Wolves from shifting at will to only shifting during the crescent moon. So, we were hoping that you could help."

"The crescent moon curse," Mhelodie breathes, "is real?"

"We don't know, but maybe, yes." Guy runs his hands through his hair and sits next to Mhelodie.

"And you're hoping that?" Lumeilia asks, concern lacing her words.

"That Mhelodie could look into it for me," Guy answers, a breath leaving his chest as he does so.

Lumeilia's body straightens, and her eyes widen as silence echoes throughout the room. Mhelodie reaches a hand out for the book, and Lumeilia places a hand on hers in protest. "Mhel?" she whispers, and her brows knot with concern.

"It's fine Lu-Lu." Mhelodie smiles and picks up the book, casually flicking through it. I don't know what's been going on with her recently, but this is the first real smile I have seen on her face in some time. Lumeilia stares at Mhelodie while she peruses the pages, and Guy and I eagerly watch them both, waiting for a reply that doesn't contain a "Hels No."

Minutes pass, and Mhelodie eventually puts the book down and looks at Guy with concerned, understanding eyes. "You need to tell me everything because if I am to even consider getting involved in this, I can't do it with only half the information."

Guy nods his head in agreement and smiles. He quickly shifts his chair over to Mhelodie and sits with her. He opens the book to where, I presume, he first read about the curse. He then proceeds to explain everything he learned about the Crescent Wolf pack and the curse.

While Guy and Mhelodie are discussing the book, Lumeil-ia leans over to me and whispers, "Can I speak to you a second, Paege—in your room?" Her face still conveys the worry she displayed earlier, so I nod and silently get up, walking straight to my room. Lumeilia follows on my heels.

I close the bedroom door behind us, and Lumeilia sits on the edge of my bed.

"What is it?" I ask as I sit next to her on the bed.

"It's Mhel," she responds as she buries her head in her hands, her strawberry locks spilling down over her shoulders like a waterfall of blood rain. Silver droplets track down her cheek, and immediately, my heart sinks. Lumeilia isn't one to normally shed tears. She is strong and brave and wears an armoured shield around. I honestly don't think anything has rattled her much in the past.

"What's wrong?"

"She hasn't been herself at all lately."

"None of us have," I reply. "After everything that's happened, it's bound to affect us all one way or another. I'm sure when Asheron comes back and we all get to heal, she will bounce back," I say reassuringly. I wonder if I am referring to Mhelodie still or if I am, in fact, talking about myself.

"No, it's not that. It's from before the attack." Lumeilia pauses for a moment like she can't find the strength. I put my arm around her to comfort her, and then she finds the will to continue. "Mhel's been losing time, Paege." Lumeilia looks at me, tears now streaming down her face. "Chunks of her memory are missing. She says she has been working hard with Enderlene, and she is sure it's Witch burnout, but I don't know."

Salty waves of icy cold as deep as the ocean come crashing through my chest as Lumeilia's fear and sadness overcome me.

My heart quickens as I try to comprehend what Lumeilia's telling me. Shit, maybe we're asking too much of Mhelodie. If she is burning out, what if asking her to do this puts her in danger? If the Wolves were cursed and it turns out to be by the Witches, would she even be allowed to help us? Could she even help us break it?

"Has she spoken to Enderlene about it?" I ask because if studying Witchcraft is having this sort of effect on her, she needs to sort it out.

"No, and she won't. She is afraid to mention it to Enderlene for fear she will be rejected from the Healers Circle. You know Witches who burn out don't make the cut. Mhel has been studying her whole life to become a healer. With her Ascension coming up . . . it's not the best time." I feel the weight of Lumeilia's concern press down on me harder. "Not only that, with all the Witches going missing, I'm really worried about her getting involved in anything that may draw unwanted attention to her. That poor Seer that's missing is Ms. Mystic."

My heart stops beating. Ms. Mystic is the Seer I visited about Sylas. She was nothing more than a gimmicky old Witch who had been outcast from the covens. According to gossip, she wasn't gifted with the strongest Witch magic after her Ascension, so her ability to contribute to any of the Witch's circles was diminutive. Her visions were strong, but she was unable to wield control of any other magic, so she was deemed a useless asset by the Witch elders.

That's how she ended up reading fortunes in the Neopolis. She saw exactly what was coming that night.

If she was taken, she must be so much stronger than any of us ever gave her credit for. I don't know if I can ask Mhelodie to get involved now. What if it jeopardises her study and her chance to join the Healers Circle? What if all this gets her in trouble—or worse?

Fuck, what have I done?

I jump up from the bed and storm to the door. "I can't let her get involved in this," I mutter to myself as I swing open the door.

As I walk back into the dining room, I see both Mhelodie and Guy smiling. She nods to Guy in agreement of something, and then they embrace. Something in my chest pulls apart. Seeing these two beautiful Beings happy brings me joy. But knowing that Mhelodie is putting herself in harm's way weighs heavy on my soul.

Lumeilia comes up behind me and interjects immediately. "Mhelodie, I don't think it's a good idea to get involved."

Mhelodie lifts her gaze to us and smiles with determination gleaming in her eyes. "I know how much you love me and how much you worry about me, but I also need you to trust me Lu-Lu. I am going to help Guy. I'm going to be fine."

Before Lumeilia or I have a chance to object, a loud thud at my front door has me flinching.

Bang, bang, bang, bang.

The four of us turn our attention toward the door, none of us moving. Another set of bangs land hard, and I take a few slow steps toward the door in response.

"Who is it?" I call out, but get no answer. I turn back to Guy, and he shrugs as if understanding that I was silently asking him if it could possibly be Quentin. But Quentin would have responded. He would have called out and probably scalded me for making him stand outside in the cold like a dog.

I continue my careful approach to the front door. My stomach knots as fear and anticipation run through my veins like a shot of adrenaline, making my heart race uncontrollably.

"Who is it?" I ask again, and again, I get no response. I glance back over my shoulder and find Guy standing behind me. He nods, suggesting he is ready for whatever is behind the door.

I inhale a long slow breath and hold it for a moment, then slowly twist the doorknob and swing the door wide open.

Chapter 31

I close my eyes tightly, forcing the tears to flow freely down my face, wondering if this is some sort of dream.

When I open them again, he's still there. His broken eyes emanate a heartache that one could only feel from losing a FaeMate, and my heart cracks at the sight of him. He doesn't speak, he doesn't move. He just stands there staring at me. His face is sullen and bruised. His clothes are torn. His hands are covered in dirt and blood. His silver hair matted. I faintly hear Mhelodie call out from behind me, but the words are muffled by the paralysing whooshing behind my ears, and any chance of a reply escapes me entirely.

It's not until Asheron says my name that the trance binding me breaks. "Paege," he croaks, and he rushes me, wrapping his arms around me and enveloping me in his embrace. Tears continue to build in my eyes, and the only words that seem appropriate to say at this moment are, "I'm sorry."

I don't move, unsure of how to respond or what to say. A myriad of emotions floods through me: shock that he is standing before me, confusion about where he has been and why he hasn't been in touch, happiness that he is back, anger that he left without any word, and relief that he is alive. All are equally valid and equally powerful.

"Asheron!" I hear Lumeilia call from behind me, and unexpectedly, my body is hit with a force so hard it knocks me off balance. Asheron loosens his grip on me enough for me to pull back from his embrace. Our eyes collide, and the coldness I see in them reminds me of death. Mhelodie and Lumeilia push past me to grab Asheron and pull him into a group hug. He reciprocates the hug, going through the motions, but his heart isn't in it. I can tell.

"Come in," Mhelodie insists, and they both usher Asheron past me into my apartment.

I don't follow. I can't move. I stare out into the gardens, my vision hazy and not focused on anything in particular as my brain tries to fight through the paralysis, processing what's happening around me. A gentle hand rests upon my shoulder, stealing my attention, and I turn to find Guy standing next to me. He smiles but doesn't say a word. He just gently escorts me back inside my apartment and he closes the door behind us.

Lumeilia and Mhelodie fuss over Asheron for a while. I continue to watch in silence as they tell him how worried they were about him, how much they missed him, and asking where he was. They gently try to probe him for information, and I watch curiously as he dances around their questions by answering them with questions of his own. He dodges and darts around their inquisition like a graceful warrior on a battlefield. He never answers one of their questions, doing his absolute best to avoid any real conversation whatsoever.

It dawns on me that wherever Asheron has been and whatever he was doing, he has no intention of sharing it with any of us.

He doesn't mention Remi or the Wolves once. In fact, he doesn't even acknowledge Guy, which is strange as they were friendly before all Hels broke loose. I wonder what has changed. Of course, everything has changed, but what has changed between them? I sense that Guy also notices this as he silently slips into his room, disappearing from the chaos and not returning.

After a couple of hours and too many unsubtle hints from Asheron that he's exhausted and heading home, Mhelodie and Lumeilia decide to go, too.

I walk Lumeilia and Mhelodie to the door, hugging them good-bye, and Mhelodie suggests she'll come back on Saturday to talk to Guy more about the curse. I close the door, turning back to my living room to find Asheron standing by the back door looking into the garden, hands crossed over his chest, and Guy walking towards me with a packed bag thrown over his shoulder.

"I'm going to stay at the den tonight," Guy says quietly as he approaches me. "Looks like you have your hands full here. I will be back tomorrow, I promise." He places his hands on his chest, a familiar gesture that warms my heart. He smiles, leans down, and kisses my cheek. A gentle and sweet kiss. It's not one that makes my heart flutter or legs crumble. No, it's one that stills me on the inside. Calms me and brings me to the present moment. One that could bring clarity to my mind, even on a stormy day.

A soft smile pulls at my lips, and I nod in response, silently watching as he leaves our home. I'm not sure when it happened exactly, but my home has become just as much Guy's in recent days as it is mine.

The second the door closes, Asheron turns to face me. His violet eyes, still void of any emotion, watch me as I cautiously make my way back to the living room and sit on the couch. I think I've said all of three words tonight since Asheron has returned. I'm still in complete shock, and my brain hasn't been able to process anything. I have so much I want to say, and yet nothing has managed to escape my lips all night.

Asheron slowly makes his way over to where I sit. I expect him to announce his departure, but instead, he sits on the other end of the couch. He flinches as he does so.

"You're hurt?" I abruptly ask. He hasn't said anything about what he's been up to or what's happened, but by the blood still smeared across his face and knuckles, I can hazard a guess that it wasn't all roses and sunshine.

"I'm fine," he says quietly, his face squinting as he shifts his weight, trying to ignore the pain. I allow myself to search for his emotions, opening myself up to my gifts, but I feel nothing. Nothing but an empty abyss filled with endless darkness.

"Let me at least clean you up before you leave?" I say.

He doesn't respond. He just looks toward the blank vision box, eyes not blinking. Then a single tear runs down his face. I reach over to him, and I grab his hand, squeezing it gently. He doesn't respond.

I retrieve the emergency first aid kit from the vanity cupboard in my spare bathroom for the second time in as many weeks and return to Asheron. I kneel in front of him and take his hands. I take an antiseptic wipe and start wiping away the crusted dirt and blood from his fingers. He doesn't object. How long has it been there? Surely not since . . . I gulp loudly.

"Where are you hurt?"

Without a word he unbuttons his shirt, revealing the purple and red bruises along his ribs and abdomen. But there's no wound.

"The blood?" I question

"Not mine," he sullenly responds.

I grab another wipe and lean forward, gently wiping away the dried blood, dirt, and grime from his bruised and battered face. He has a small cut above his lip and one on his left cheek, but they are almost healed now.

When I have cleaned him up some, I grab us two shot glasses and a bottle of DesertFyre from the kitchen.

I pour two glasses and rest the DesertFyre bottle on the coffee table in front of us.

"Here, drink this," I say as I hand him one.

He takes the glass from my hand and takes a shot, so I pass him the other, and he chases the first down with the second. Asheron then hands me his empty glass, grabs the bottle off the table, and takes a drink straight from it. Finally, he relaxes and leans back against the lounge, closing his eyes and nursing the bottle on his lap before letting out a sigh.

Unsure whether to relish in the silence echoing through my mind or be gravely concerned, I, in turn, grab the bottle from Asheron, take a couple of large gulps, and hand the bottle back to him. "When you're ready to talk, I'm here," I say, and I sit down next to him. He just smiles and takes another swig.

Half a bottle of DesertFyre later, he finally speaks.

"Paege?" he whispers.

My body tingles from all the DesertFyre we've drank, and my head spins in dizzying, erratic circles. I plant my hands on the couch to stabilize myself as I peel open my eyes. I find Asheron sitting upright, his violet eyes wide with a little bit more life in them and staring intently at me.

"I'm ready to talk," he says, and he hands me back the bottle.

I sit up, trying to steady myself from the spinning room. Instead, the emotional assault incapacitates me. Like a hurricane, I'm hit with a range of emotions so fierce that I find myself swallowing down bile as it violently rises and coats my throat.

Dropping the bottle from my grip, I reach for him. "Asheron," I plead with him. "Stop."

"Sorry, I can't help it. I either feel it all or nothing."

I nod, understanding the predicament we are in, but as I take in a few deep breaths, trying to survive the onslaught, the emotions slowly start to fade, and Asheron regains control, shielding himself from me.

"Thank you," I mutter through laboured breaths.

"Sorry," he repeats. "For everything." He hangs his head. "I loved her." He pauses. "I loved her so damn much. I was stupid and selfish and reckless."

I know he loved her. We all knew he loved her. There was never a kernel of doubt about that. Through all the times he thought he was acting aloof or talking about his freedom to choose his future or bragging about all the *flings* he had, he never really sold it. Sometimes, he would spend so much energy selling his story that his emotional shield would slip, and that sticky, murky feeling of guilt would suffocate me. More often than not, when he saw Remi, he would radiate a fierce love like no other I've ever felt. I never told him this, but I'm sure part of him knew that I knew.

"Asheron, it's not your fault," I reassure him. "You didn't do anything."

"You're right, Paege. I didn't. They did!" A burst of anger slices through his shield, slashing through my soul as savagely as a wild beast, and he looks toward the spare room where Guy has been residing these past weeks.

"What?" I ask, perplexed, "Guy?"

"Guy. The Wolves. All of them. *Q,*" he adds in a mocking voice.

"You can't be serious, Asheron? Guy has done nothing but try to protect me. Protect *us* for weeks. They have sacrificed so much. I know you're angry, but you should be directing your anger where it belongs, not at innocent Beings."

"Innocent?" he roars. "They are far from innocent. Who do you think ..." He pauses for a moment. "Do you think it's a coincidence all this horrible crap started happening around the same time they entered our lives?"

I open my mouth to say something, then close it again. Instead, I muse over Asheron's comments for a moment. He has a point. Ever since I met the Wolves the night Sylas and I broke up, nothing but carnage and chaos have followed. It's not like I haven't had this exact thought myself, but hearing him blame Guy for Remi's death, for all their deaths, has me shaking my head in disbelief. How could I possibly agree that they have had anything to do with it?

It's just not possible.

"No, Asheron, you've got it wrong. They aren't the reason it's happening."

"Then why—" Asheron pauses again. He can't seem to finish the sentence, and I get the uncomfortable sense that he is holding something back. "Look, maybe they aren't responsible for everything, but it's not wise to trust them."

"Why?"

"It's just not, Paege. You'd be best to put some distance between you all, Quentin especially."

My cheeks blush at the sound of Quentin's name. I haven't heard from him since the night of the Gallery, and thinking about him takes me back to the safe room when he took me to heaven, and I exploded into the universe. My feelings shift quickly as anger raises her fiery head. He left me. He said absolutely nothing and left me. He disappeared just like Asheron did.

"Just promise me you will try to put some space between you and the Wolves, Paege. Please?"

I nod, but it's not a promise I'm going to keep. Because Mhelodie and I already promised to help Guy, and well, I honestly don't believe for one second they had anything to do with any of this—no matter how angry I am at Quentin. Asheron is acting paranoid, but who can blame him, when the love of his life, his FaeMate, was so violently ripped away by the very species I am trying to protect?

"Asheron, where have you been?" I ask, trying to change the subject. I don't want to talk about the Wolves anymore. Not tonight. Not while I'm drinking. I might say something I will regret.

"They killed her. I got her killed. She never got to know how I truly felt." He rubs his hands down his face. "She didn't deserve it."

"No, she didn't, but you can't blame yourself for any of it." Asheron's inner turmoil forcefully pushes through his shield again, rushing me so fiercely that my fingers bite into the couch to hold me steady. I've never felt anything like this before. It's raw. Brutal and devastating. It's his brand of poison rushing through my veins. I know I have never felt love like his. I loved Sylas, but it wasn't like the love I felt from Asheron and Remi. I know it's because I wasn't fated. We weren't FaeMates. It wasn't a bond. Even though Asheron rejected his bond, he still truly loved Remi. Rejection doesn't sever the bond. It can only be severed through death.

Fuck. Asheron's grief is magnified because the bond is severed. That explains his complete lack of control. The realisation has a shudder creeping up my spine and tears pricking my eyes.

Silence fills the room as I ride out Asheron's emotional roller-coaster, my hands steadying myself, trying to keep myself strong for my friend in his moment of need. Eventually, it relents, and I feel myself become me again.

I reach a hand out to take Asheron's. It's cool but clammy. "I'm so sorry, Asheron," I whisper.

Something shifts. An unexpected warmth filters through all the thick and murky darkness. I roll my head to the side and my gaze collides with Asheron's. His violet eyes, flickering with a glimmer of life. Bringing with it something I didn't expect.

Something deep inside pulls at my heartstrings, and my heart races in response. My cheeks flush, and I feel a heated burn of desire brewing inside me.

Pull yourself together, Paege. It's just the DesertFyre. Asheron is grieving.

I try to pull my hand back from Asheron's grip, but he holds firm, not relieving me from the growing feeling inside. My stomach tightens as my heart thunders, and a wild heat rises through my body. What the Hels is going on right now?

Like a fountain, lust pours from him all sickly sweet and se-ductive. It floods over me, sending my mind into a tizzy. My body petrifies into stone, and I consider what the heck he is doing. It's the DesertFyre. Or the trauma. Yes, it's the trauma. We've been here before. The night at Slynx when we were dancing. No. That was the Psyloxin. That was . . .

Before I can finish my thoughts, Asheron takes the hand he is holding and brings it up to his lips, kissing my inner wrist ever so gently, and it sends electricity through my body. He closes his eyes and takes one long deep breath in through his nose. *Shit.* I don't take my eyes off him. I can't. I'm frozen, completely at his mercy. Completely unable to comprehend what the Hels he is doing.

But then he opens his eyes and smiles. I let out a long breath as relief engulfs me. The craziness of the moment has passed.

I smile softly in return, but before I can move, he leans in and places his lips on mine.

CHAPTER 32

As soon as our mouth's touch, my mind empties, and all common sense is lost. The space between us diminishes as he shifts his body closer. His lips softly find their place against mine, gently, respectfully. He opens his mouth, inviting me to kiss him back, but I can't.

This is wrong. It's so, so wrong.

Suddenly, he pulls away from me. His eyes widen, and I watch pain wash over his face, and a single tear rolls down the porcelain skin of his cheek.

I lift my hand and gently brush it away.

"Asheron," I whisper.

"Don't," he responds, dipping his head in what appears to be shame.

He doesn't deserve to feel shame. He already feels so much hurt and pain. I know without a shadow of a doubt that he was just looking for something to get lost in, to drown himself in.

I take his hand and stand. His brows furrow, and I nod at him, urging him to follow. He stands without saying a word, and I lead him to my bedroom. I open the door and escort him to the end of my bed. He stops short and watches me, his eyes intense, and I can see he is trying to work out what I am doing. But it's alright. He needs this. We both need this. I sit on the end of my bed and pat the space next to me.

Asheron pauses briefly before following my lead and sitting beside me. His skin glistens from the moonlight that shines through my bedroom window, dancing off his exposed abs. He really is beautiful, but I am not here with him because of his beauty. I am here with him because of his heart. Because he is one of the kindest and most fierce Beings I know, and he would do anything for any single one of us.

Tonight, he needs someone else to look after him, and that is exactly what I plan on doing.

I shuffle myself back across the bed, motioning for him to follow. His brows are still knotted, and he hesitates again, but I hold my arms out to him. "I'm sorry, Paege. I didn't mean to kiss you," he starts.

"I know," I answer. "Do you trust me?" I ask him, hoping that he will allow me to repay a favour owed.

"Yes," he swallows. "You know I do."

"Good, then come here."

This poor, beautiful male is so heartbroken and conflicted and my heart aches for him.

He nods and moves in next to me. I wrap my arms around him, and pull him in close, allowing him to rest his head against my chest. I kiss the top of his head; a mild scent of sandalwood and tobacco meets my nose. He lets out a shuddering breath as he sinks into me. He wraps his arms around me, and a sob cracks from his chest. He's home.

I stroke his messy untamed hair and listen to his breathing finally start to settle.

"Are you alright?" I ask, knowing full well what the answer will be.

There is silence for a long moment before Asheron finally answers, "I don't know." I feel his heart sink to the floor. Tears well up in my eyes, and I blink one, two, three times to clear them away, but they just keep flowing uncontrollably. I know these tears are not coming from me; they are coming from him. Asheron. His heart is shattering into thousands of pieces, and there is nothing I can do to take his pain away except be with him in this moment and let him share his grief with me.

I brush a thumb across his damp cheek, wiping away the streams of tears running from his eyes.

"You will be," I say, knowing my words are just empty promises because what the Hels do I know about losing a FaeMate? What the Hels do I know if he will ever be alright again?

He takes my hand and squeezes it, and I squeeze him back. After a few more breaths, I feel his grip loosen, and I realise that this beautiful, broken, and conflicted male has fallen asleep, probably for the first time in almost a week.

As I lay there with Asheron in my arms, I expect an overwhelming number of emotions to bombard my consciousness and keep me from sleep. Instead, when I close my eyes, I feel myself soaring.

I'm soaring so high it feels freeing. Exhilarating, but there is a weight of something heavy pulling me back down. I look to the ground below and see the beautiful woodlands of Orphelious. The River Plye flows below into an aqua-blue lake surrounded by rocky hills and waterfalls. It's breathtaking.

I've never seen home like this before.

Still, the weight of something heavy pulls me down further, and a knot forms in my stomach. I shift my gaze down myself and see Remi's lifeless body in my arms.

Visions of Asheron and Remi flash through my mind, hitting me with such force I crash to the ground. I curl myself up in a ball, covering my body with my hands as I try to escape the onslaught.

Asheron ushers Remi back toward a room in the gallery.

A Wolf pounces Remi from behind, startling them both.

Remi is pulled from Asheron's arms as he is surrounded by a pack of hungry and snarling Wolves.

Remi's neck snaps in front of Asheron's eyes, and her lifeless body falls to the ground.

Asheron's wings flare, and his razor-sharp feathers slice at their attackers, aiming for a kill.

Rage and fury burst from my body that thrashes violently as I rip myself from my slumber, jolting myself awake.

I lay there panting, the aftereffects of my dream lingering like a bad hangover. As I gradually bring myself to the present moment, I feel fingers stroking the length of my back, slowly but deliberately. There is nothing sexual about it, though.

It's soothing. Comforting. Distracting.

"Are you alright, Paege?" Asheron whispers.

I hesitate to answer. The images of my nightmare continue to pepper me, flashing through my mind. "I don't know," I say. After a long moment, tears fill my eyes once more. Asheron pulls me into his body, holding me tightly, but he doesn't tell me it will be alright. Instead, he plants a soft kiss on the top of my head, lets out a sigh, and whispers, "I'm sorry."

CHAPTER 33

It's still dark when I open my eyes. A heaviness lingers in the air, and the feeling of another's presence in the room has the hair on the back of my neck standing. This unsettling feeling weighs me down into the mattress, and my muscles pull tight.

My eyes take a moment to adjust to the darkness. The moonlight no longer filters in through my window, but as they dart around the room, I don't see anything.

I look over to Asheron. He lies perfectly still, silver hair spilling around him, looking completely at peace. The deep lines in his brow are gone, and his breath is slow and steady. A far cry from the messed-up male from hours earlier.

Something thick and heavy rolls through me, and my chest tightens.

I brush my hand along Asheron's face. Has he let his shield down during his sleep? It wouldn't surprise me. He's been through so much. I don't even know how he is still breathing. But I suppose he isn't, or not well anyway. I vow a silent pledge to myself to make sure he gets through this. To be here for him whenever he needs me and with whatever he needs. But maybe we should go light on the DesertFyre next time.

A creak from my living room catches my attention. I sit up and swallow hard, but a cry is ripped from my throat, and I choke on the air in my next breath. It's like swallowing down scalding razor blades.

Anger, hatred, and jealousy.

The beast inside me awakens with a warning growl as a brush of ice slithers up my spine, causing the hair across my body to stand on end. The residual feeling of someone watching me sleep and the sudden burst of emotions hinder me from moving.

Suddenly, the emotions stop, like the branch in which they flowed was cut off, and it's calm in my body once more. Yet the calmness brings anything but relief. It's unnerving.

"Asheron, wake up," I whisper, nudging him gently, trying to waken him without startling him.

He just rolls over and murmurs, "It can be reversed with the stone."

"Asheron!" I whisper-yell a little louder. "I think there's someone in the apartment." I go to nudge him again, but I flinch back as he lurches upward, his eyes wide open.

"What? Is Guy back?" he asks.

He has a point, Guy may be back, but it's still dark out. I doubt he would come back this early in the morning. He wouldn't want to startle us, especially after everything that's been going on.

"I don't think so, but I felt someone watching me sleep, and then . . ."

Asheron leaps out of bed before I can finish my sentence and turns the light on. There is no one in my room except us. He cautiously stalks out into the apartment, and I can see the lights bursting to life one by one as he searches for the uninvited guest.

He returns after a long moment and stands casually at the door.

"There's no one here, Paege," Asheron confirms.

"Are you sure?" I ask. Because even though it makes no sense for someone to be in my apartment, I still know what I felt.

Or did I? Gods, I think I'm losing my mind.

"I'm sure," he reassures me. "I searched every room. I even went to the mezzanine and checked the doors." He smiles softly and sits at the end of my bed. "Are you sure it wasn't some residual feeling from a dream? Or it could have been me," he finishes, sheepishly dipping his eyes.

He makes another good point. My dreams have been rather intense lately, and Asheron was an emotional wreck last night. I nod accepting his opinion.

"The sun is going to be coming up shortly, so I might head off. I've got to head back to the Academy, and I have a few things to get done before heading back."

My heart drops a little when I hear he is going to leave. I only just got him home, and now he is leaving again. I know that he must, but I can't stop the disappointment from creeping in. I scoot to the end of the bed and sit next to him, resting my head on his shoulder.

"Don't frown. I will check in, I promise." He shoulder bumps me and smiles. "Thank you for being an amazing *friend*, Paege Vailenbyrg. You really are one of a kind, and . . ." He deliberates on his next words, but it doesn't need to be said.

"You know I love you, right?" I ask.

He pauses again before he replies. "I know, and I love you, too." He gently kisses my forehead and stands.

A lightness coils itself around me like fluffy clouds on a warm summer's day. I let my eyes fall close, allowing the warmth to settle my racing heart.

And when the warmth of my friend's love dissolves around me, I open my eyes to the cold dark empty room to find my friend has gone once more.

CHAPTER 34

I spend the weekend with Mhelodie and Guy, trying to work out how we can learn more about the curse. There's been lots of ideas flying around, but everyone seems to be clear on one thing: we need the original book, and somehow, I get roped into stealing it.

I've been surveying aisle five all week, and yesterday, the book was back in its original place. So today, I am going to pull off the heist of the century. Alright, maybe not the heist of the century, but it feels like it. If I get caught stealing this book, I could lose my job. Hels, I might not ever get another job again.

I can't believe they talked me into this.

When the archives door closes behind me, I jump out of my chair and hastily walk down to aisle five, trying to keep myself composed in case Blaire happens to come back. My heart thunders heavily in my chest as I reach the beginning of the aisle, and I steal a quick glance back toward the entrance. No sign of anyone coming back. I suck in a steadying breath, then take off in a hurry, lightly jogging down aisle five.

The book's home is almost at the vaults, so on a normal day, it wouldn't take a while to walk down there. But today, I don't have much time. Blaire's been pulled into an impromptu meeting upstairs, and I have no reason to be down there, so I must find the book, bring it back, and hide it in my training bag—all before she returns.

I'm hoping Blaire won't notice it's gone. She hasn't asked about it again, so maybe she's forgotten all about it. I honestly doubt that, but she barely searches for anything herself. That's why she has me. I just need to hope and pray to the Gods that doesn't change in the next couple of weeks.

Blaire is going to kill me if she ever finds out. No, actually, the king will probably organise that. But I am doing this for *his* pack. For *his* son. And for Guy. Yes, I'll focus on that—instead of the war drum pounding in my head.

I pass by the halfway point, a small opening between all the aisles, and I glance around, making sure no one else is nearby. There shouldn't be. I haven't allowed anyone to enter the archives all day, but every so often, one of the curators or scholars finds themselves down here for research purposes, and they tend to get lost. The aisles are a bit like a labyrinth. They don't follow a straight line. Instead, they weave and twist around in all different directions with study nooks and openings at the quarter and halfway points. If you don't know the way around here, one can easily get lost.

The closer I get to the vaults, the narrower the aisles become. So, while I've got to be quick, I also have to be extremely careful not to disturb any of the books. If I knock one off the shelves, If I damage one, I'll be . . . I really don't know what would happen to me, but I dare say it won't be good. I'm clumsy at the best of times, so I must stay composed and focused.

When I reach the third nook, I slow my pace. I'm close. I fall into a casual stroll, eyeing the books as I prowl closer to my destination. The book is not too far up on the—wait.

My breath catches and my heart punches into my ribs.

Gone.

The book is gone.

It was here yesterday. I spied it when I was working down here. How could it be gone? I scan the shelves around where it should have been and nothing. It's not here.

Fuck.

I don't have time to keep searching, I've been away long enough. I need to get back before Blaire finds me gone. I've got no reason to be down here. She will know I'm up to something.

I'm just going to have to come back another day. Damn it.

I turn to make my way back, falling into a light jog again. As I pass through the first openings with study nooks, a silhouette of a female in a long, flowing dress catches my eye. No one should be down here. I slow my pace and pivot back around.

"Hello?" I whisper-yell into the aisle, my chest vibrating with the increased pressure in my chest.

Nothing. No movement. No sound. There is no one here. A flash of something red under one of the desks near aisle nine catches my attention. As I draw closer to the desk, a breath leaps out of my chest.

The gold cursive writing across the red leather book flickers under the soft sconce lighting, and a smile tugs at my lips. The Crescent Wolf book. How in the Hels did it get here?

As I lean down to collect it, I look around, searching for whoever took it from its home and left it here, but there's still absolutely no sign of life around. My skin prickles with a familiar warning as I pick it up, and the beast inside me stirs. There is certainly something about this book that has my intuition screaming at me to drop it and leave it where I found it. I suppose if I wasn't stealing it for my friend, if we weren't trying to find out some hidden mystery about the Crescent Wolf pack, I would do just that. But I have no time to sit around and think about it. I need to get back to my desk, quick smart, and hide this thing before Blaire gets back. Because Blaire's wrath will be far worse than any uncomfortable feeling this book gives me.

I just hope I'm doing the right thing.

Blues, pinks, and purples bleed together across the horizon as storm clouds start rolling in across the Neopolis. I love watching the sunset over the gardens from the mezzanine. Regardless of how bad my day has been, when I watch the sun disappear, I feel the day's troubles disappear with it. It's done. Put to bed. And when the sun rises again tomorrow, I can start anew.

My eyes trace the outline of the shadowed buildings and trees in the distance. I capture the sight of one of the Guards my dad instructed to watch over me. This is the first I've seen of them since my parents came to the Neopolis.

Suddenly, the Guard moves quickly across the grounds. His wings flare wide, and he takes to the sky, his silhouette passing by the perfect half-moon rising high into the starry night sky. I immediately think of Quentin.

My heart sinks a little, and something tightens in my stomach. Memories of our night together, the night Quentin merged in the safe room, flash so vividly through my mind I can almost taste his lips. Feel his touch.

It's almost been two weeks since Quentin merged with his Wolf, and he hasn't been back to the apartment since. The crescent moon has come and gone, and I never heard from him. Guy hasn't mentioned him either. He would no longer be able to shift into a beautiful Wolf. Maybe that's why he has been gone; he's been spending time with his pack shifting and making the most of the crescent moon. Does that mean he'll come back now?

Stop being silly, Paege. He doesn't belong here. Neither of them do. This is not their home.

A rogue raven, perched in the maple tree outside my window, caws to himself and hops from branch to branch. His antics pull me from my thoughts, and I feel a smile tug at my lips, grateful for the small distraction.

Mhelodie is due to arrive any minute. I have the book, so she agreed to come over. I descend the spiral staircase to find Guy sitting on the couch, watching the start of a game of Batton Ball on the vision box. Seriously, that Wolf is addicted to this thing.

"When did Mhelodie say she would be here?" I ask.

"She said she would be here by sundown, so . . ." Guy looks outside. "Now."

"Huh," I say to myself. It's not like Mhelodie to be late at all. And if she is, she would have let us know. "Has she messaged?"

"Not that I know of." He checks his scribe and then shakes his head to confirm. I check mine. Nothing. I send her another message.

When Mhelodie still hasn't arrived halfway through the Batton Ball game, I send one more message to Mhelodie and one to Lumeilia to see if she knows where she is.

Lumeilia: She left here just before sunset. Has she not arrived yet?
Me: No, not yet.
Lumeilia: I will message her now.
Me: Me too.

By the time the Batton Ball game comes to an end, I'm officially worried. I'm about to start typing another message when one, two, three knocks at the door have my worry dissolving into the night.

Oh, thank the Gods she's here.

I swing the door wide open to find Lumeilia, not Mhelodie, standing at the door, soaking wet.

My heart stops beating for the longest of moments, and dread fills my stomach.

"What's wrong?" I ask Lumeilia as I pull her into the apartment out of the storm. A crack of lightning lights the night sky, and thunder rumbles through the air.

"I can't find Mhel anywhere," Lumeilia exclaims, shivering through her wet clothes. "I'm worried, Paege. It's not like her to not respond to my messages or voice communications." I know my friend is right. Of all of us, Mhelodie is the one who always responds. Tears well up in Lumeilia's distraught brown eyes, and her dainty nose scrunches as she tries to blink them away. Her long strawberry-blonde hair hangs damp and loose around her face.

"Guy, can you grab a towel and a jumper from my room please?"

"It's going to be alright. We will find her. She is probably with Enderlene or something," I say as I wrap my arms around Lumeilia, trying to reassure my friend, but she shakes her head in response, drops of water spraying across the room. I need to get her warm and dry.

Guy approaches us with one of his jumpers and a handful of towels. Worry lines splash across his brow, and that little vein that pops in his forehead when he is stressed is starting to grow.

"Is there anywhere she could be? That Witch coven of hers, did you contact them?" he asks as he wraps her up in one of the towels.

Lumeilia shakes her head in response.

"Enderlene? Can we contact her?" I ask as I watch Guy lead Lumeilia to the dining table. He rubs her arms up and down, trying to warm her up. He takes the towel off her and hands her the oversized sweater. He really is the nicest male with a heart of gold.

"We can't; she's not here." Lumeilia sighs and sits at the table. "She and the coven left for Cedrus yesterday. That's how I know Mhel isn't with them." She buries her head in her hands.

"Is there anywhere else she would have gone? Her parents, other friends?" Guy asks.

"No, I've checked everywhere. She was coming here. She should be here," she sobs.

Guy places a hand on her back. "Don't worry Lumeilia, we will find her. If I have to, I will get the pack to help. If we've got her scent, we can track her."

Yes. I've got the damn babysitter Guards stationed nearby. Maybe if I go outside and call out for help, they'll come out of whatever shadowed corner they're hiding in, and I can get them to aid in the search, too.

"You don't think it has anything to do with this damn curse she has been looking into for you?" she snaps, anger bursting through her worrisome manner.

My stomach knots, and anxiety slithers its way up my spine and coils around my chest, squeezing tighter and tighter until I'm unable to draw a breath.

What if it is? What if all of this is another direct result of the Wolves? Of me?

"No," Guy answers on my behalf, his eyes pinned to mine as if he is also telling me that is not the case. "We haven't even started looking into it yet."

Lumeilia stands, clenching the jumper Guy gave her firmly against her chest like she's holding on for dear life. She nods. "I'm going to go change. Can you reach out to the pack?"

Lumeilia and Guy leave to meet some of the pack members at their house with a plan to pick up a scent to help track Mhelodie. *Creepy.* I agree to stay behind in case she turns up, but the reality is, what good would I be out there anyway? I'm not a Wolf. I'm not even fully Fae. Unless they want me to *possibly feel emotions*, I'm pretty much damn useless in this sort of situation. At least Lumeilia has telekinesis. It may not be fully manifested as she hasn't had her unification yet, but she discovered the night of the attack that she can, in emotionally distressing situations, move some pretty large things with her mind. I'm guessing when the person you love is missing, it could be called an emotionally distressing situation.

Chapter 35

The apartment is eerily quiet while I sit here waiting for word on Mhelodie. Anxiety coils around my chest, and no matter how much I try to breathe through it, it keeps tightening itself around me.

I consider asking the Guards for help, but I'm not sure they would. The Guard I saw with my parents was not eager to *babysit* me, but isn't it part of his job to make sure I'm safe? Mhelodie is my friend. She's an extension of me.

Damn if I am going to just sit here and wait. Maybe I should just talk to them and see. Maybe they would offer to help?

Resolved in my decision, I grab my jacket and scribe and head to the door, determined to find my little stalker friends. The front door swings open in front of me.

I blow out a long breath when I see Mhelodie standing on the other side.

"Mhelodie!" I exclaim. "Thank the Gods you're alright. We were so worried." I start walking over to her, but something stops me in my tracks.

She slowly and disjointedly steps through the door, and tears roll down her cheeks. Her face is different. Her eyes are black, and they're burning into me like a predator's gaze, fierce and unrelenting.

A shudder runs up my spine, chilling and icy, and a knot tightly twists in my stomach.

"Mhelodie, what's going on?" I ask with a shaky voice, and I take a step back.

Dark tendrils of shadows slither across my skin as her fear taunts me, enveloping me in darkness as they wind around my limbs and suffocate me.

She can't possibly be scared of me?

She takes another step toward me, reluctantly. "I'm sorry, Paege," she blurts out, and then, like she has no control over her body, her hand snaps up and covers her own mouth with a bloody hand.

"Sorry?" I ask, truly unsure of what is going on right now. I step back again. "Sorry for what?"

Mhelodie starts shaking her head from side to side, and she takes another step toward me. Her actions seem forced and un-natural. I reach into my pocket to grab my scribe, and Mhelodie clicks her tongue at me in an unnerving manner.

"I wouldn't do that if I were you." She scowls, her voice finding an octave that even a baritone voice would be jealous of.

That's when I see it—the knife she holds tightly in her hand. What in the Hels is going on? The next step I take backward has my ass hitting the back of my couch.

Fear consumes me like wildfire, spreading uncontrollably through my mind. I continue to work my way through my scram-bling thoughts, trying to figure out what's happening. I have no idea what is wrong with Mhelodie, but it's clear she's not here as my friend. She's not here for DesertFyre shots and Friday night laughs. She's not here to help Guy out with the Wolf pack's crescent moon curse.

Mhelodie's lips begin to quiver, and she starts whispering something at me in a language I can't understand.

She repeats the same words over and over, and my head starts to spin. I try to shake off the thick fogginess that rolls through my mind, but my body becomes heavy, weighed down by her words. I try to move out of her reach as she continues to move toward me, but my bones turn to stone, preventing me from making even the smallest of movements. The only thing I seem to be able to do is breathe, and I'm not even sure I'm doing much of that.

I can't stay here. I need to fight. I need to get away, but I don't want to hurt Mhelodie. She's my friend.

No.

I have to move. But how? How do I walk? I need to fight.

Nothing.

It's as if my memories, both logical and muscle, have been stripped from my body, and I'm nothing but an empty vessel made of useless blood and bone and muscle and organs.

I dart my eyes around my apartment, mentally mapping my escape. I'm backed up against the couch, if I move . . . move where?

Oh, I can try to . . . no, that won't work. What about? No, still nothing. But if I could . . .

Damn. What in the Hels am I going to do?

I'm in a game of cat and mouse with a powerful Witch, and not only am I the mouse, I'm locked in a cage like easy prey, and there isn't a damn thing I can do about it.

A warm sigh of wind brushes against the skin of my cheek where my tears now flow freely, and my rapid breathing catches as a familiar feeling overcomes me. The same feeling I had at The Pit. The same feeling I had when Asheron was here. When my home was broken into.

"Mhelodie?" I plead.

Something warm and wet slides up against the length of my neck, and I gasp as my crazy, irrational thoughts start coming to life. The pace of my breath increases, and my pulse beats faster until I'm sure it's about to escape the cage that keeps it contained.

But it's not until I hear my name whispered into my ear that my thoughts become true.

"Paege."

Suddenly, pain explodes across my face as I am hit with an object I don't see coming. I blink, one, two, three times, trying to fight the urge to fall into the sweet darkness that's calling out my name like a siren's song. It quickly engulfs me, and my world tilts upside down, ending this game of cat and mouse.

Drip, drip, drip.

Pain bursts through my body with an explosive force, and I try to peel open my eyes. My head hangs heavily, but as I attempt to lift it, a throbbing pressure builds, and bile rises, coating my mouth before I can swallow it down.

I cough. What is happening?

Visions of Mhelodie and my last moments in my apartment assault my mind, branding me with fear.

"Mhelodie?" I try to call out, but my voice catches, and it barely comes out as a whisper.

Why would she do this? She is my friend.

I attempt to swallow, but my dry tongue sticks to the roof of my mouth as the metallic taste of blood wraps around it. The smell of rancid water and some sort of chemical fills the air, lining my mouth with an acrid taste that has the bile rising from my stomach once more.

In an effort to move, a pain in my arm blooms, and a heavy weight pulls at my shoulders.

I groan.

My feet hang freely just above the floor, and my toes softly sweep across the ground. My arms are lifted above my head, and it's the weight of my own body that is weighing me down. My hands are bound at my wrists with something rough and abrasive, chafing against my skin as I twist my hands. Something cold and smooth rubs against my fingers.

The building ache in my head throbs in tune with my heart's thunderous pace as blood pools in my temples. Each breath is a struggle, my chest constricted by the awkward angle and the unrelenting grip of the bindings.

I'm not blindfolded, but I'm in complete darkness.

Fuck.

I blink hard, my heavy lids tugged by the weight of sleep, unwilling to cooperate. Tears prickle at the corners of my eyes. No matter how much I try to will my vision to adapt to the utter darkness of the cold space that contains me, I have no luck. My heavy, sandpaper-like lids refuse to stay open. Finally, I succumb to the siren's call of slumber and allow my eyes to close again.

 Chapter 36

D rip, drip, drip.

I jolt awake, my eyelids snapping open at the distant sound of a metal door clasping closed. Or opening . . . or . . .

Fuck.

Panic quickly sets in as I remember where I am. Every excruciating memory slams into me like a punch, stealing the breath from my lungs in a sudden swoop. My chest heaves as I gasp like a fish out of water, trying to claim the smallest amount of air.

I'm a prisoner, and I am all alone.

Biting down on the pain, I twist my body around. The sun peeks through one of the blackened windows, providing just enough light to finally see where I'm being held captive.

Through tear-soaked lashes, I study my surroundings. It seems I'm in an old, decrepit warehouse. The room is bare except for a chair to my left, a furnace in the far back right corner, some steel rods lying on the ground to my right, and a shadowed object on the floor by the large metal door. I squint. Sweat drips down my face, stinging my eyes and mingling with the tears of panic and helplessness, but I can't make out what it is.

I need to get out of here.

The ache in my shoulders screams at me while I struggle and wriggle, frantically trying to free my wrists from their binds. The weight of my body pulls mercilessly on my arms, and every slight movement sends fresh jolts of pain through my throbbing limbs. My fingers have long since gone numb, a cold, prickling sensation replacing any semblance of normal feeling. I stretch my muscles long and point my toes to the ground, trying to relieve the weight of my body that rips me from my shoulder sockets. It's no use. My feet dangle uselessly, brushing the air as I twist and turn.

Acid coats my mouth with every putrid breath I take, and my tears, born of pain, born of fear, continue to fall in a constant stream.

I'm nothing more than a hopeless animal caught in a trap, waiting for my predator to claim its prey.

No.

I can't give in. I can't give up.

"Paege, just breathe," I whisper to myself. *One breath at a time, just like Amerax taught you.* I take a shuddering inhale, the motion sending fresh waves of agony through my body.

Angling my wrists to try to loosen the binds, I twist my body again, trying in vain to find any position that offers some relief, but my body cries out as an agonising pain rips through my arm like a jagged knife tearing through flesh.

I bite down on my tongue, stifling a scream.

It's no use.

No.

I refuse to give in. I refuse to give up.

Just breathe, Paege.

Every single muscle in my body aches from the continued tension of hanging here, my torso a constant source of agony, pulled tight and unyielding.

Breathe in, breathe out. Breathe in, breathe out.

I close my eyes and hold onto the rhythm of my breaths like a lifeline. Anchoring myself to the only thing I can control in this moment and not drown in the pain.

Because if I do, I'm going to die here, alone. I am not going to die here, not like this.

I open my eyes again and daze off into the empty abyss while I continue my efforts on my steadying breath. In and out. In and out. Forcing myself to focus, to push past the agony, and to find the smallest spark of courage.

A shimmer of light catches my attention, and the blur of movement scatters my already confusing labyrinth of thoughts. I blink through visions as they pepper my mind. Erratic flashes of Sylas appear and vanish before me like a static mirage. Every time he appears, he appears closer and clearer, gliding directly into my line of sight.

The mirage of Sylas stops before me. His body slowly becomes corporeal, as if he really is standing here, and his cold, hard, empty eyes burn into me.

I'm losing my Godsdamn mind.

He reaches his arm out, and the warmth of his touch sends my body into a fit, and a scream erupts from my fracturing mind.

What the fuck. He's really here.

"What did you do to me?" my raspy voice demands. My tone is unwavering as solid stone.

Silence is my only answer.

"Help!" I scream into the room. "Help me!"

"Your screams won't be heard. I've spelled this place shut. No one can hear you or track you here."

"Why are you doing this, Sylas?" I plead. "Where's Mhelodie?"

He slithers around me, circling me like prey, and then he places a finger over my trembling lips. "Sh, sweet Paege. It's not time yet." His once soothing voice feels slippery as it slinks across my body, and a shudder follows.

"Time for what?" I feel my heart bolting like a startled horse, running to escape this crazy nightmare.

"Don't speak, don't move. You need to save your energy."

I feel my eyes widen. I want to yell and scream, but I can't. I open my mouth, but no words escape me. I try to thrash and free myself, but like a stunned animal, I'm paralysed by fear.

What the fuck is happening to me?

I won't give in. I won't give up.

Every breath is a struggle, and every thunderous heartbeat serves as a reminder of my fragile existence. The relentless pain is a constant companion that whispers despair into my ear.

"There's no need to panic, Paege. Save your energy." His silky-smooth voice cocoons my mind, wrapping it up in a comforting, gentle embrace that shields me from the chaos inside my head.

A disturbingly evil smile parts his lips, "Sleep now, little one."

He leans in, and I try to pull away, but my body still refuses to move. He looks me dead in my eyes and places a soft and gentle kiss on my lips. "Go to sleep," he whispers.

Once again, I find myself fighting the urge to close my eyes, but it's a battle I quickly lose as the need to sleep becomes like the need to breathe air: essential. The darkness I fear slowly consumes me once more.

Drip, drip, drip.

I have no idea how long it's been since I was last conscious. Time loses meaning in this suspended torment. Seconds stretch into minutes, minutes into hours, hours into days, as I sway gently, my body a pendulum of suffering. The world narrows to the throbbing pulse of pain, and the relentless ache that consumes every thought, leaving no room for anything else.

"Focus," I think to myself as I lose track again.

I picture the faces of my friends, Lumeilia, Mhelodie, and Asheron. Their kind faces smile down at me, forging me with their strength to overcome the overwhelming urge to let go.

I picture my family, those who believe in me—Mum, Dad, the twins—and long to feel their warm embraces. I even picture Guy and Quentin rescuing me from this Hels hole. Their images are blurry, distorted by the haze of suffering, but they're there. All of them. They remind me of who I am and why I need to keep fighting.

For now, it's enough. It has to be enough.

I start counting. Numbers are simple, steady. It's the only thing I can control.

I count my breaths. I count my heartbeats. I even count the sound of distant drips that fill the deafening silence. It's a small distraction. A way to keep my mind occupied and away from the despair that threatens to consume me.

One, two, three, four . . .

The sound of a metal door opening shifts my attention from my breaths to the door, and my heart races. For a moment, I don't see anyone, but as I blink to relieve my eyes of the seething pain, I swear I see something move.

"Hello?" I rasp. My lips crack with the movement. The taste of blood coats my mouth as my tongue laps up the only fluid I've had in . . . I have no idea how long.

There's no answer. But, of course, there isn't. There's no one here with me.

I've not seen Mhelodie. I've not seen Sylas in . . . again, I have no idea how long it's been.

A shimmer in the light steals my focus.

A long torturous moment passes, and then Sylas materialises as he casually strolls toward me. Blood thumps behind my ears in time to the thundering tune of my heart. My eyes must be playing tricks on me because I could have sworn when the door opened, no one was there, but . . .

I concentrate, searching for more information, but my memories feel just out of reach, as if they are hiding from me.

No. Focus.

When Asheron stayed, I could have sworn someone was in my apartment. I could feel them, but I couldn't see them. When Mhelodie attacked me, I swear I heard him say my name, but he wasn't *there*. He shimmered into focus once before. I thought I was losing my mind, but what if I wasn't? He just emerged out of thin air, and despite all the pain in my body and terror in my mind, I feel clear about what I saw.

"Sylas? Is that you?" I croak.

"It's me, little one. I'm here to help," he coos, and he strokes my hair.

He's here. He's really here.

"I need to get out of here. Can you let me go?" I plead, desperation coating every word.

"Sorry, Paege," Sylas whispers. He sounds so calm, and there's not a drop of evidence in his voice that says he's ever letting me go. "I can't."

"Please?" I beg.

"You broke my heart, little one. I tried to give you everything. I wanted you more than I've ever wanted another. You have *no* idea. But you kept running around with that Asheron."

"I didn't."

"You can't deny it," he snarls, cocking his head in a predatory manner, and his nostrils flare with anger. "I saw you with him in your bed."

"How?" I ask, determined not to let his anger instil any more fear into me. I need to get answers and understand how this happened. I need to hear him say what I'm sure I already know, even though I can't quite believe it.

I won't give in. I won't give up. I will survive.

"Mhelodie let me in," he smirks. It's cold and emotionless, sending shivers racing down my spine. His eyes burn into mine unsympathetically, like he knows every word is stabbing me like a knife into my back—or my heart.

Mhelodie.

Why would Mhelodie let him in? Why would Mhelodie do this at all? She's my best friend. I love her. I know she loves me. I've felt it. None of this makes any sense.

But what if it does? She would never hurt me on purpose. What if it wasn't on purpose? What if it was out of her control?

No, there are rules in the kingdom that prohibit this. To prevent things like this from happening. It's not possible. There's not been a recorded case. But what if? If he has the gift of—it could make perfect sense.

I need to hear him say it. I need to hear the truth.

"I don't understand, Sylas," I urge him to keep talking, to say the words that will start putting my fractured mind and heart back together again. If he is exactly what I think he is, then none of it was in my control.

"Paege, my gifts." He leans in close. His cheek rests against mine as he whispers in my ear. "Surely a smart Fae like yourself can work it out."

I can, and I have.

Bit by bit, the broken pieces of my past are slowly fitting back together like a puzzle, revealing the truth of exactly who he is. I never understood why I stayed with him, even after all the terrible things he did. But now I can.

The constant feeling of being watched.

Forgiving Sylas for all his transgressions.

Forgetting memories. Being confused.

I lift my heavy head to meet his gaze, resolved in my decision to fight him. Even though I know what he is capable of. "You're a Siren." I breathe.

Sylas smiles.

"You've been compelling me all this time?" As the revelation leaves my mouth, bile surges up from my stomach. None of this has been real. Our entire relationship was a lie. I was under his spell. His compulsion.

"No, Paege, not always. You did love me of your own free will. I just helped you make the right decision about us when you needed the help."

Anger flares a brief but intense fire in my belly, and it cuts through the fog of physical pain and psychological torment. Every second I endured under his spell is a victory I want to claim. I cling to it. I use it to fuel my determination to survive.

"You sick fuck," I spit at him. "And Mhelodie, what was she?"

"She's been extraordinary. That Witch is strong." He sounds impressed. "But I am stronger," he adds almost mockingly. "She has been my eyes and ears these past few weeks. I knew I needed help getting you back when I saw you at Slynx dancing like a slut for Asheron, but then you came home with those Wolves." He spits on the ground in front of me, showing his disgust.

"The invisibility? That's what it is, isn't it? You can make yourself invisible?"

"See, I knew you could figure it out." He pats me on the head like a damn pet, and that fire inside flares even brighter.

"It's not possible. Sirens get bound when they're young to protect us from . . ." I gulp, realising the atrocity of the current situation. "From this."

"I was exceptionally good at hiding my strengths, Paege. You of all Fae should appreciate that, considering your background."

"What the Hels does that even mean?" I haven't hidden anything from him. He knows exactly who I am. What I am. A demi-Fae.

He raises a brow and smiles that evil smile again, and disgust swells like a raging storm inside my belly. I drop my gaze from his, not wanting to look at the repulsive male anymore. As my head falls, my eyes widen at the shiny object dripping in blood in his grip.

"Where's Mhelodie?" I ask with a shaky voice, unsure if I want to hear the answer. She was a puppet, and he was the puppet master. Now, it seems her fate hangs by the same threads that bind my wrists.

"She's fine—for now. She's just taking a little nap outside there." He points the bloodied knife to the door for a moment, and I follow the path of the blade as he brings it up to his face, his knuckles rubbing under his chin.

"I'm sorry, Paege," Sylas says. For the smallest moment, I can almost see remorse in his eyes mixed with the love I thought he once held for me, shining through. He never loved me. I was a toy to him. A game.

He holds the knife up, twisting it in the air like an absolute psychopath. His eyes glisten, and he cackles at the small shafts of sunlight dancing across the bloodied blade.

My stomach twists tightly in knots. I need to escape. I need to get the fuck out of here.

"Sylas, please don't," I plead as he steps around me. "You don't have to do this. I will love you, I promise!"

"Yes, you will," he whispers into my ear from behind me.

"Stop, please, stop," I beg through hysterical sobs. My body is so exhausted I can't even pull enough strength to try to move as the desperation to escape what's coming gnaws at my resolve.

"This is going to hurt me a lot more than it's going to hurt you," he says. Icy air collides with my bare skin as he violently rips my shirt from my back. The cold blade bites when it makes contact. A power so fierce it burns into my back follows the path of the blade as it slices between my blades, from spine to hip. Every fibre of my being cries out for sweet relief as the agony of the wound erodes my will to fight.

I cry out, begging for an end to the torture.

When the blade breaks its agonising contact with my already broken body, I gulp down air. The reprieve doesn't last long. The knife pierces my skin again, carving out a brutal path straight across my spine with an acid burn, not once but twice. The physical pain is matched only by the psychological torment I've endured, and a guttural scream fills the room as the knowledge that I am utterly at the mercy of Sylas finally breaks my will.

"No one will love you like I do, Paege. I need to make sure of that."

Sylas murmurs in a language I don't understand, and the warm trickle of blood that runs down my exposed and wounded back steals my attention. My mind tracks its path as it drips right down the centre of my spine.

The pain of the next cut is buried deep within the first, second, and third, but the feel of my skin splitting open, tearing apart like a delicate piece of paper, isn't lost on me as he cuts from my spine to my right hip.

"Please, Sylas," I beg again, clenching my teeth in anticipation of the next tortured slice, but it doesn't come.

My breaths come in short, sharp gasps. The metallic taste of blood fills my mouth, and bile stings my throat as Sylas steps in front of me. "Now, you are mine forever," he whispers into my ear and kisses my tear-soaked cheek.

Trying to avoid looking at the horrifying male standing before me, I dart my eyes around the room. Two shadowy figures stand by the door, and while I cannot see their faces, there is no mistaking who they are. Their silhouettes have been tattooed into my mind, and relief spills from my heart.

I redirect my gaze back to Sylas, who continues to stare at me with a wicked smile. He's clearly proud of himself and revelling in this moment. He's so arrogant and conceited that he doesn't even see it happen.

I suck in a breath and smile in return, hoping he sees it as an act of surrender. He does. He lowers the blade and relaxes his body, taking a few measured steps away from me, leaving himself vulnerable and completely unprepared.

I am not surrendering. I am not folding.

The two figures waste no time. They move swiftly and silently. Two Wolves in the dead of night, pouncing on their prey.

Guy swings a sword, and it connects with Sylas' neck, cutting his head clean off.

Bile burns up through my throat as thick, warm blood sprays across my already battered face. I stare in terror through blood-soaked lashes as Sylas' body drops to the ground with a thud, and Guy kicks his decapitated head across the room like a child's ball.

Guy lowers his sword slowly, a guttural sound grumbles from his chest, and a muscle in his jaw feathers as he takes me in. Quentin places a hand on his shoulder, and Guy releases the weapon from his grip. The clashing metal and Quentin's touch pull him out of the rage-fuelled rampage he was in. His emerald eyes widen, burning into mine with so much intensity they reflect every bit of terror I feel right back at me.

He reaches for me. "I've got you, Paege."

For the second time in as many weeks, everything starts to tilt. I try to fight it, but it's no use. The darkness slowly takes my sight, pulling me into the sweet call of sleep.

CHAPTER 37

"Paege?" a gentle voice whispers through my mind. It's kind, caressing, and warm.

I stir, and a burning pain blooms in my back. Nausea rushes me, and my eyelids flutter as I adjust to the light. I'm in a white room with people, all eyes focused on me.

"Can she hear us?" I try to move, but my body's weighed down like lead.

"Is she going to be alright?" I try to speak, but the sound catches in my dry throat, and all I can do is moan.

"Paege, can you hear us?" I close my eyes again.

"Sh, don't try to move," a gravely male's voice whispers, and I feel a soft kiss tickle my forehead.

Dad. Tears threaten to burst through my closed lids. Dad is here.

The pain in my body builds like a surging storm, wild and unpredictable. Nausea rushes me again, but this time it fills my mouth. I snap my eyes open and roll onto my side, finding a female dressed in white holding a small bucket for me. I cough out the contents of my stomach and roll back over. My back burns as I lay back down.

A hand gently brushes my cheek, and I flinch away, knocking it back. The touch activates the brutal memories of the warehouse and

269

Sylas. I lift my hands to my face and examine the lacerations around my wrists.

"Paege?" My Mum's soft voice cuts through the violent visions that continue to assault my mind. I turn my head, and through tear-soaked lashes, I see her standing next to me.

I remember being held captive for days.

"Mum?" I croak as a sob bursts from my chest.

I remember him tearing into my flesh like he was cutting into the essence of my being, knowing the scars they'll leave will be deeper than the wounds themselves.

"Sh, you're safe now." She whispers into my ear, her words sounding raspy, like she's been crying and yelling for hours on end.

I remember everything.

"Mhelodie?" I ask. Sylas held her captive, too, but I never saw her at the warehouse. Did they find her?

"She's fine," a stern but equally soft voice to my left responds.

"She's home with Lumeilia," Mum confirms. I nod, swallowing down the razor blades in my throat.

"Here, drink this," that same voice instructs. I turn to see the same female handing me a tonic of some sort. "It will help you rest and speed up the healing so you can go home."

I move to sit up and spot my father by the door, talking in hushed voices with another Healer. Now that my eyes have adjusted, I realise I'm in a Healers ward in the Medelia Circle. The Wolves must have brought me here after they rescued me.

I take the tonic from the Healer, a fresh round of nausea rising at the smell of it. Its stench is just as ghastly as any medicinal tonic I've had before. Seriously, can't they make the smell of these things somewhat less offensive?

I count to three and pour the liquid down my throat. The taste is nowhere near as bad as the smell in the end, and I swallow it all. It tastes sweet like orange and bitter like acid, and there's something else, something that I can't quite figure out that leaves a chalky residue on my tongue.

A warm and calming sensation instantly travels throughout my body, and the pain in my back lessens, drowning out to a distant throb. My tense and achy muscles begin to feel heavy, and limb by limb, they relax. The stress and pain slowly melt away.

"Dad?" I croak, through the haziness. "When can I go home?"

He walks across the spacious white room and reaches down to take my hand. I flinch at his touch, but he doesn't let go. "Soon, Pumpkin," he replies, his usually harsh tone replaced by something I've never heard in his voice before. Fear.

"Yes, very soon," my Mum adds in a whisper, and she takes my other hand. "I promise." She holds her free hand to her heart in true Vailenbyrg style, and a smile tugs at my lips.

As the tonic's properties settle over me, the edges of my vision begin to blur. The room and my parents become distant and unclear. My eyelids grow impossibly heavy, fluttering closed as if being pulled down by tiny, invisible tethers.

I feel a gentle tug at my core as drowsiness weighs me down, pulling me deeper and deeper into the sweet embrace of sleep. Every ache and pain disappear into oblivion, and my racing mind, which has been consumed by fear and exhaustion, begins to quiet. My thoughts slowly soften into a gentle murmur as the last remnants of wakefulness slip further and further away until there is nothing left but an overwhelming sense of peace and tranquillity.

CHAPTER 38

I t's been a week since Sylas kidnapped me, and I haven't left my apartment since I've been home. In fact, I haven't left my bedroom.

It's been tough, but I haven't been alone. There's been a constant rotation of friends and family visiting me, keeping me company, serving as a small distraction from the nightmare I survived, except Mhelodie.

The healers mended all my superficial wounds pretty quickly, but the carvings on my back, they've been harder to heal. Sylas imbued them with some sort of magic, so they aren't responding to tonics the healers made. They have no idea why, but it's something I'm trying not to focus on. If I spend too much dwelling on it, the uncertainty and fear around what that means would consume me entirely, and I'm barely managing to survive as it is.

I take my scribe from the nightstand and send Mhelodie another message.

Me: Can we talk?

Nothing. She's been ignoring me since my return, and I can't exactly fault her. I don't blame her for any of this. Sylas compelled her. Yes, she was his spy, giving him access to my home and life. Yes, she was his Witch, crafting magic and spells for his plan to work. But she was just as much Sylas' victim as I was.

Yet, when she came to visit me in the healer's ward, I could feel every single drop of her murky, dirty guilt as it seeped into me like a cold and unrelenting fog. She was holding onto it for dear life. It was gripped in her embrace, and it enveloped her heart and suffocated her soul.

No matter how many times I told her it wasn't her fault, she didn't relent. She wouldn't give it up.

And the others? They tiptoe around me, asking me if I am alright, if I need anything, if they can any help with anything. But no one dares talk to me about the pressing weight that's keeping me anchored to my bed.

Desperate to get in touch with Mhelodie, I message her, again.

Me: I love you.

I yawn widely and curl back under my covers and bury myself in the little nest of pillows I've made for myself, contemplating my next moves.

I've attempted to leave my room every morning since returning, but every time I get to that door, dread consumes me like a dark storm rolling in over the Blethan Sea. Flashes of the night Sylas took me haunt my memories, and I freeze, unable to take any more steps. So, I retreat back to my warm safe bed, and that's where I stay until I dare to repeat the challenge the very next day.

Maybe today will be different.

I quickly shower and dress in denim pants and an oversized white shirt with the question, *Coffee?* on the front and three check boxes on the back: *Yes. No. Do you have a death wish?*

Today, I am not only going to attempt to step out of this room, today, I am going to succeed. I'm dressed for success.

I casually stroll to the door like I've not a care in the world, but when I reach the threshold, I pause.

It's just one tiny step.

I draw in a long, deep breath and prepare myself to walk out that door. It's open. I don't have to do anything. Just step over the invisible line I've drawn.

It seems my bones are filled with lead and my muscles are made of stone because my body refuses to move. No matter how much I will it to. I try to reach for some inner strength, some reason to push through, and take that final step. But I find nothing.

Transfixed, I stare into the living room. The muffled voices of Lumeilia, Quentin, and Guy talking by the dining table feel distant, out of touch. It's as if I'm a silent observer peering through the veil from another world. They move around my apartment with ease, their conversation flowing naturally, creating an animated tapestry of life. One that I can see but cannot touch. A sense of longing tugs at my heart, but my heavy body is rooted to the ground, and my mind races with a thousand anxious thoughts.

My gaze lands on my couch, and icy fingers of fear tighten around my chest, stealing my breath and caging the herd of wild horses trying to take flight.

Every attempt to move forward is met with a wall of invisible resistance, a force born of my own panic and dread. The idea of stepping into that room, of crossing the threshold and breaking through my invisible wall of security, feels overwhelming.

After what feels like hours, but I'm sure it's only minutes, my body finally starts to move but in the wrong direction. My shoulders sink as the familiar feeling of defeat and frustration consumes me.

Quentin's eyes meet mine briefly before I drop my head, and a muscle ticks in my jaw as I acknowledge my failure. My legs continue to carry me backward toward my bed, one step after another after another. A path well-travelled, etched deep into my mind.

Seven steps back to the haven that is my bed.

When I reach the foot of the bed, I sit and bury my head in my hands.

Disappointment runs through my veins like my very own brand of poison, one I concocted for me and me alone.

How long will I keep myself trapped in my own bedroom?

I don't hear him coming. I don't even smell his familiar forest scent, but I feel his body weight sink into the mattress next to me, and I feel his hand gently rest atop my shoulder. Startled, I flinch, pulling myself away from his touch.

"It's alright," Quentin says gently. The warmth of his voice settles something inside of me, and I let out a sigh of frustration. I roll my head to his shoulder, and he tenderly wraps an arm around me, drawing me closer to his body. The herd of wild horses settle their frantic galloping inside me, gradually slowing to a calm, steady rhythm.

"Paege, what can we do to help?" he asks.

I muse over his question for a moment. It's a question I've been asking myself for weeks. While I tell myself I don't know, that familiar lump that resides in my throat appears. Because while I try to convince myself I don't know what I need, I know deep down exactly what I need. It's all I've ever asked from anyone. It's all I've ever needed in my life.

The truth. *Stop it, Paege, you're being a masochist.*

Against all reason, I push down the inner voice screaming at me to stop, telling me to avoid this at all cost, and I let the question I have been dreading to ask for weeks, but so desperately needing to know the answer to, roll off my tongue.

"Where were you?" Quentin's spine lengthens, and he pulls his arm from around my shoulder. "You left after the attack at the gallery, but then you show up with Guy."

He let out a shaky breath, "Books, I . . ."

"Were you with Juno?" I blurt out, unsure where that came from. Or why I care. I know she is mated to Ric, but Quentin's emotions wouldn't have been shut off as quickly as flicking a switch.

"What? Paege, no." Quentin exhales loudly, and he brushes the long golden hair out of his eyes and shifts his gaze to mine. "I had to go back home. My dad, *the king,* summoned me. I have responsibilities outside of you—of this," he says casually like he didn't just take a blade and stab it into my gut.

"I never asked to be your responsibility," I snap.

"I didn't mean—" he sighs. "That's not what I meant, and you know it, Paege."

We sit in silence for a long moment. The void caused by his absence the last couple of weeks is nothing compared to the canyon-sized hole forming between us now.

"Do you regret what happened at the Gallery?" I ask, my cheeks warming at the stupidity of this situation. I feel like a Godsdamn school girl asking her crush if he likes her too, which is essentially exactly what I'm doing, and I have no idea how I got here.

"No," he says matter of factly. "But Paege, it's not that simple."

"I know," I whisper. Because it's not. There are strict rules against this sort of thing. And even if there wasn't, I'm a demi-Fae. The daughter of a want-to-be artist and a dead Human male. He is the Heir Apparent. The future King of Elyndria. We could never be together.

"No, you don't," Quentin says sternly. "You think you know, but you can't. Gods, Paege, that kiss, your . . ." He shifts his body, angling it toward me and he raises a hand to cup my chin, tilting my face to him. His steely grey eyes are darkened by the storm of emotions rolling through him. "Paege, I don't regret anything except not being here when that asshole took you." His eyes drop to my mouth as he runs his thumb across my bottom lip, and I swear the world stops spinning just for a moment. "Not finding you sooner," he growls in a predatory voice.

My heart pounds violently with a mix of desire and dread. A yearning to belong to him clashes with the terror of rejection. His grip on my chin tightens, and I feel the slight tug of his hand guiding me closer to him. The distance between us closes until his mouth barely meets mine. His lips graze softly along the surface of mine and—

"How did you find me?" I ask unexpectedly, and I pull myself back from the brink of no return. If I kiss him right now, I don't know if I could stop myself.

Quentin's brows shoot for the stars either surprised I pulled away or surprised by the question. Both options are completely viable, but I have no answer for either.

"How do you mean?" he asks.

"Sylas, he . . ."

He draws in a long breath, and his hand drops from my chin. "You know he had Mhelodie spell the warehouse?" He pauses, and I swear I see a sparkle in his eye, and my heart sinks fast into the pit of my stomach. Why would this bring him joy?

I nod, wanting to know where he is going with this.

"She's smart, though. One of the smartest Witches I've ever met. Even under his compulsion, she was clear-headed enough to only block Witch-tracking magic, not all tracking. That probably saved both of your lives. If she hadn't, I don't know if we would have found you. But Guy and I, being Wolves, we could track you—track your scent. He didn't account for that. Stupid prick." he mutters.

"But we didn't have the crescent moon on our side. I couldn't shift, so it took us longer than . . ." His eyes dart away, and his lips form a straight line. His own anguish takes over, and his jaw clicks at the words he doesn't say but that linger in the air like thick smoke after a wildfire.

If they had found me just a moment earlier.

I want to tell him it's alright and that he did what he could. But words escape me.

"I don't know if you remember, but Guy killed Sylas. He merged with his Wolf at the warehouse." Quentin clears his throat and lifts his head. His eyes widen as they find mine. "His Wolf, it's different," he whispers under his breath.

I vaguely remember. It was brutal and horrific, yet beautiful and powerful.

Guy is different from most Wolves. So, it's not surprising. The merge for him was not a joyous rite of passage. He knew that to merge with his Wolf meant he would have to take a life, and that was something he never wanted to do. Never. He'd told me so. My heart cracks open at the thought of him having to do what he did for me, and guilt starts to seep into my already heavily burdened heart.

I shuffle myself back up the bed and return to my nest of pillows as tears well up in my eyes once more.

Damn tears, I've done nothing but cry for weeks.

"Quentin?" I whisper as I close my eyes, releasing the small droplets down my cheek.

"Yes?"

"Thank you," I murmur.

Silence is the only answer for a long moment. The warmth of my room now feels like a stark contrast to the dark chill seeping into my heart, the yawning abyss stretching wider and wider with the lack of response.

The bed trembles, and I snap my eyes open to see Quentin shuffling up the bed next to me. He leans back against the headboard, crossing a leg over the other and lets out a small chuckle. "There you go again, Books, thanking me."

The air whooshes out of my lungs.

 Chapter 39

For the first time in a long time, I wake without being pulled out of a violent nightmare.

A foreign stillness fills the air in my room, its lightness weaving between space and time, and the peace it brings me has a breath slowly leaving my lungs. The afternoon sun trickles through my window, and although I lay here a broken Fae, a smile creeps across my face.

The bed groans, and I roll over to find a sleeping Wolf curled up next to me. I must have fallen asleep after Quentin told me the details of our rescue, and he decided to stay with me.

I trace the lines of his face with my eyes. While he lays here completely vulnerable, I see no sign of the Heir Apparent. No sign of the future High Alpha Wolf. Just a beautiful male who stirs all sorts of contradictory feelings inside me. The muscles in his wide jaw feather, and his eyes flutter at random intervals. Is he dreaming?

His beautiful tattoos are completely on display. I study them closely as I drop my gaze down to his hardened chest and defined abs, watching quietly as they rise and fall with every steady breath he takes.

I've never seen his tattoos up close. What I thought were just random marks are so much more. Intricate lines with dots and feathered strokes form a complicated series of tribal markings that run down the full length of his arm. A series of tattoos depicting a burning sun, a constellation of stars, and a moon transitioning through its phases crown a beautiful but fierce wolf baring its teeth to the sky, all mark his chest and abs. I consider if it's all telling a story.

It's exquisite.

Everything in the world seems to still, including my heart. Something deep inside me, something beyond the physical, calls for me. It's as if his wolf is whispering my name into the breeze, and it transcends the space between us. I need to touch it. I need to connect with it.

Against all reasoning, I reach out to place a trembling hand over the tattoo to unite with the wolf. As my hand touches his soft warm skin, a spark ignites between us. My skin pebbles.

Quentin stirs, and for a moment, I fall still. I quickly try to withdraw my hand, but he snaps his hand atop mine, holding it against his chest as his eyes open abruptly. A wild desire burns heatedly behind his grey eyes. His long, steady breaths quicken, his chest rising sharply in a more deliberate manner.

My breath quickly finds a rhythm in unison with his, and a delicious tightness builds in my core.

"Books?" My name on his lips sounds like a question whispered into the wind, and my toes curl.

But I don't answer. Not with words anyway. I tilt my head, my eyes colliding with his with a desperate plea to be with him. He slowly shifts himself closer to me, bringing his hard body flush with mine, his warmth mingling with my own. His gaze intensifies, tugging at the strands of yearning inside of me, unravelling each thread one by one until he softly rests his lips against mine.

At first, our kiss is slow and gentle. It's soft and tender unlike he has ever been, but it's everything I want and everything I don't.

A heady taste of sweet syrup coats my lips, and I open myself up to him. The lust between us coils around me like soft ribbons of silk binding me in his desire. His tongue sweeps across my lips, and I part them slightly in response. He takes it as the invitation it is and pushes his tongue into my mouth, greeting mine with a sense of urgency. A groan rumbles up my throat, and my mind empties. Every doubt leaves my body, and I melt into him.

Suddenly, he pulls himself away from me, and something twists in my gut at the look of his face. His brows pull, and he runs his tongue over his lips as if savouring the taste of me but also reconsidering our actions. Of course he is.

A tear falls from my eyes as the humiliation of the moment hits me with the force of a gale storm. He runs a curled finger down my cheek, tracing the track of the tear, and then continues down the length of my neck to my collar bone as he strokes his fingers back and forth along my clavicle.

Time slows while I wait for him to tell me he can't do this, to pull away from me again, and leave the room. He doesn't.

"Are you sure you want to do this?" he asks with wanting in his tone that melts my core into a pool of molten lava.

I pause, considering Quentin's question. I have no idea what I'm doing here or why I'm doing this. I don't trust him. I don't even know him. Everything about him screams trouble. But when I'm around him, all the pain Sylas has caused leaves, and it's replaced with something else. I don't even know what it is, but I know that I want it.

Every featherlight stroke of his fingers across my collar bone sends charged shivers pulsating through my body. All traces of common sense escape me.

I am without a doubt sure I want to do this.

A smile tugs at my lips.

"Yes," I whisper into the diminishing space between us as I crash my lips back into his, and I leisurely run my hand down his bare chest, continuing to the depth of his stomach.

He groans into my mouth as my fingers tease the band of his pants, slowly slipping my fingers lower.

His hand finds its way under my shirt, and my skin pimples at the touch of his warm skin against mine. He slowly finds his way to my breast and cups it, his fingers pinching the tip of my pebbled nipple, and my breasts ache at his touch. I groan in response and pull out of our kiss, his lips still grazing mine. Our heated breaths mingle in a hazy need, and I unzip his jeans.

"Fuck, Books," he groans as I slide my hand down into his pants, his fingers still working my nipple, and I take his full hard length in my hand.

I want to feel him come undone for me. I want to turn this alpha into nothing more than a vessel of flesh and blood full of want and need.

I tighten my grip, barely fitting him in my hand, and a smile passes my lips when I feel him twitch and harden more. Then I begin to work him, sliding my hand up and down his cock.

"Quentin." His name barely escapes my lips before his lips are on mine again. His tongue wastes no time entering my mouth. The gentle kiss of earlier is replaced by a hunger to consume. His fingers squeeze around my nipple tighter, and the tiny burst of pain tangles with pleasure has a delicious heat pooling in my core.

He feels so incredible. He tastes so good. I want him. I need him inside me.

Quentin releases my nipple, and his fingers graze my flesh as he travels down to my stomach. His thumb lazily brushes circles around my navel as the tips of his finger press against that little bundle of nerves at the top of my entrance. I buck my hips and grip his cock harder as the pressure against my clit releases a tiny burst of pleasure. He moans between my lips and nips at my lower lip as he eagerly releases the buttons on my pants, and he pulls them down over my ass and slides his hand between my legs, finding exactly how much I want this.

I continue to work his cock, rubbing my thumb across the tip, spreading that bead of moisture across his length.

There's an urgency in his movements as his fingers trace over my entrance and rub my clit, one that I reciprocate as I arch toward him, eager for him to enter me. He spreads my wetness along my core, and I feel myself clench as he slides two fingers inside me. Every brush of his tongue in my mouth and drive of my hand down his hardened cock move into complete rhythm with his fingers inside of me.

The heat intensifies between us, and the want to feel him explode, to bring him to ruin, becomes an intoxicating need. I slide my hand down his shaft and hold it there for a moment. My grip tightens. The throb of his cock beneath my hold brings us both closer to the edge.

The quiver in my core travels through my body, and a warmth blooms across my back. I stop, loosening my grip as the heat in my back begins to burn brighter, hotter.

"Paege, please don't stop," he begs in a heady voice that brings a tear to my eye because I have to stop right *now*.

Heat explodes from my body. The scars from Sylas' markings split me open like the wounds are tearing anew.

"Paege, what's happening?" he asks. The fear in his voice tears my heart apart just like the scars on my back.

This is wrong. So very wrong.

"I don't know," I cry out. I push back from Quentin, and he releases me from his embrace completely. The unnerving pain is a stark difference from the bliss I was riding a moment ago.

A scream erupts from my chest. A wildfire races across my skin, devouring every bit of pleasure and turning it to ash. Quentin moves to touch me, but I flinch back. "Don't touch me," I plead. The pain of my words etch across his face, leaving lasting marks of their own.

New waterfalls of tears burst from my eyes as the realisation of what is happening comes crashing down on me, shattering my heart into a thousand irreparable pieces.

No one will love you like I will, Paege.

Sylas did this to me.

Now, you are mine, forever.

An eternal punishment for rejecting him.

Quentin tries to reach out to me again, but I roll off the bed and crawl across the floor to the corner of my room. I curl myself up into a ball, trying to make myself as small as possible. I need to shrink away. I want the ground to open and swallow me whole.

A sob cracks from my chest. "I'm sorry, Quentin, I can't."

This can't be happening.

I hear Quentin get up from the bed and walk across the room, and a fissure splits my heart apart. I wait to hear the door open and close after he leaves, but it never comes. I continue to breathe through the pain that's slowly subsiding now that I've put space between Quentin and me.

I feel embarrassed and disgraceful, and I just want him to go. But silently, I am relieved that he never does.

The lulling sound of running water calms my sobs and sends me into a mild hypnotic state as I rock myself back and forth while I hum the song that my mum used to sing to me when I was just a babe.

Moments pass before a heavy shadow towers over me. I open my clenched eyes and through tear-soaked lashes, I see Quentin leaning over me with a hand extended out.

"It's alright," he says softly, and he motions for me to take it.

I shake my head. I can't stand the thought of anyone touching me after what just happened.

"Please trust me," Quentin quietly pleads.

I can't look into his eyes. I'm damaged goods. I'm branded, dirty, sullied. I can't be with anyone ever again.

No one will ever be able to love me.

CHAPTER 40

When I open my eyes, I find Quentin on a knee beside me and an arm held out patiently waiting for my approval. I cock my head to the side unsure if I should let him touch me, but I find myself nodding before I make a conscious decision.

I brace myself for the wrath of his touch, and when he gently places an arm underneath my legs and another around my back, I flinch as his body brushes against my wounds, but they don't flare to life.

"Sorry," he winces as he picks me up.

Quentin carries me to the bathroom and gently places me in the clawfoot tub filled with warm, soapy water. The dimly lit room, from the sage and lavender scented candles I keep on the windowsill, creates a relaxing haven just for me.

When I'm fully submerged under the water, Quentin stands to leave.

"Where are you going?" I ask with a shaky voice.

"Nowhere." He kneels back down next to the tub. "I'm not going anywhere. May I?" he motions toward my oversized t-shirt.

I nod and lift my arms up, and he slips it over my head. When it's removed, I slump forward, wrapping my arms around my knees and curling back into that little ball of despair where I find a fragile sense of safety.

The weight of Quentin's eyes roaming over my exposed back reignites the shame in me. My wounds come to life with anger as I feel him tracing over the marks left by another. Marks that scold me when I'm intimate with another. Gone is the lust he had for me at the Gallery. Gone is the hunger he felt for me moments ago. The wildfire of his want has long been doused in water, and nothing remains but the ashy remnants of our lust, disintegrating like the bubbles in the bath at my touch.

"I'm so sorry, Quentin," I mutter into my folded arms.

The tub suddenly shakes, water splashing around me as Quentin submerges himself under the water behind me. His hands gently land on my shoulders, and he pulls me back into him, enveloping me in his arms.

"I told you I am not going anywhere, Books," he whispers into my ear as I sink back into the safety of his arms.

"What about—" My voice cracks, and I don't finish my words. Do I even want to know the answer?

"It doesn't change anything." His chest expands under my weight as he takes a long deep breath. "We will fix it. It will be alright."

I lift my focus from my book at the sound of the door cracking open, expecting Lumeilia to join me for the afternoon, but I'm greeted with the sight of Guy's friendly face instead.

"You want some company? I've got gridcakes."

"Come in," I reply, discarding my book and shifting myself into a more comfortable and modest position.

He enters my room with caution as if he is trying not to startle me, but I haven't cried in almost a day. So, things are getting better. Sort of. I still haven't left my room.

Guy deposits the plate of gridcakes smothered in berries and cream on my lap and hands me a mug of coffee. My stomach grumbles as the sweet and bitter aromas reach the cavernous pit in my stomach. I haven't eaten much this past week.

He doesn't sit. Instead, he towers over me like the gentle giant he is. Golden flecks in his dark green eyes sparkle from the warm sunlight that shines through my window, and I swear I see them dampen the moment they catch mine. A muscle in his jaw feathers, and the vein in his forehead slowly appears, revealing the tension that's building inside him.

"Did I ever tell you how I got the scars on my back?" he starts.

My brows shoot for the sky, and I almost knock my food from my lap. I've seen the scars. Dozens of silver streaks cover his back. I remember how I felt the first time I saw them—the anger that burned deep inside and the sadness that slithered around my body. I remember the vow I made to myself when I saw them, but I never dared to ask.

"I don't like to talk about them," he continues when I don't answer. "I was ashamed of them for a very long time." He sits next to me and idly traces his fingers over the gold stitching across my ruby bed covers as if distracting himself for a moment. "I was taken from my father when he was—" his throat bobs, "overthrown, and Q's grandfather, Kristoff, became the king. He was a cruel, vindictive, power-hungry ass," he snaps, his face looking haunted, plagued by the memories.

Quentin never talks about himself, his family, or his past. I only know what little bits of information Guy has shared when talking about himself, and I know that King Ishaan is a harsh Wolf and an even harsher king, but I never would have imagined him being cruel to his own kind.

"Those Lupa-Centaurs showed no mercy. I was the traitor's son, his blood, his heir." Anger unfurls from the darkened corners of my soul, and my heart pounds hard to the rhythm of a war drum. He was just a child. An innocent child. He had no one.

I place my gridcakes back on the nightstand and sit upright, placing my hand on his knee and giving him my full attention and support.

Trying to keep the fury from rising up, I start, "Guy, you don't . . ."

He cuts me off. "I know I don't." He pauses to take in a long breath and then continues, "I was taken from my father, from the palace, and kept locked in a cage in the chambers underneath the castle. I was just a pup—three, I think." He swallows hard. "I was starved for days, and as I grew older, I was introduced to the cat-of-nine-tails. I was ripped from my life to pay for my father's sins. To be reminded that I was not, nor ever will be, royal again." I swear I can see the vein in his forehead pulsating as he clenches his jaw tight and tighter.

My heart stops dead in my chest and shock fills me to my core. I'm so horrified by the story Guy lays out before me. As he continues to tell me about his childhood, the trauma, the torture, bile crawls up my throat. Blood rushes my ears, the drumming in my head drowning out his final words.

"When Q's grandfather died, Ruhaul was crowned king, and I was finally released. Ruhaul released me, and Q's family took me in. They looked after me."

The fury brewing deep inside my belly, rises and begins to leak at the edges of my seam. I could swallow it down. I could urge it to stay below the surface, but instead, I ball my hands into a fist and close my eyes before bellowing out an almighty scream that feels like it lasts for minutes, releasing the rage that's been suppressed for weeks and months and possibly years. I thump my hands down onto the mattress over and over.

When I eventually stop, my breaths come short and sharp, but surprisingly I feel calmer. I open my eyes and find Guy standing a few steps away from me with his eyes wide and mouth agape.

The bedroom door swings open, and Quentin rushes in, his face wearing a seemingly similar one to Guys. "What the *fuck* is going on the in here?" he cries.

There's silence. Guy stares in shock at me. Quentin's eyes dart between us both, and I'm watching both of them.

Suddenly, a laugh bubbles out of my mouth. Then another one follows before I have a chance to prevent it. Before I know it, I'm laughing like a hyena beast, my belly heaving, and I cannot stop myself.

I don't know where it came from. I'm like a Fae possessed.

I roll around on my bed, my hands clenching my belly as I laugh and laugh and laugh. Tears stream down my face like a faucet, and fog clouds my vision.

"I'm sorry," I giggle between bellows of laughter and gasps for air.

Then of course I snort, and laugh even harder.

"Oh," I sigh as I try really hard to compose myself, and an ache blossoms in my jaw.

Guy's eyes widen, and he opens his mouth to speak. I'm sure he's about to scold me for laughing at his misfortune, but I'm not. I'm not even sure why I'm laughing. So many bad things have happened to all of us and none of it is funny, but it kind of is. Because if I don't laugh, then I'm going to cry again, and I'm afraid this time I'm never going to stop.

But he doesn't speak. Instead, he furls his lips into an O shape and howls at ceiling into the room, into the universe, and then he buckles over and starts hysterically laughing, too.

Guy's outburst brings me back from the edge of my sanity and pulls me back into the madness. I try to howl a few times, and it makes him laugh even harder.

My howl sounds like a sick puppy dog, not at all scary and sexy like the Wolves howl.

Of course, because they're Wolves and you're, well, not a Wolf. Duh, Paege!

Amongst all the madness I feel the weight of Quentin's stare barrel down on me, judging us. I pay him no attention.

Unphased by Quentin's indifference, Guy continues to jump around the room howling and laughing, and I continue to roll around on my bed, kicking my legs around and flapping about like a fish out of water.

After a few more moments, we both begin to control our fits of laughter. Our breaths find a synchronicity, and as they gradually slow, we let out a long sigh in unison.

I catch Guy's gaze, and he winks at me, and I feel my heart settle herself into her cage.

"Are you both done?" Quentin asks, frustration dripping from his words

Quentin doesn't get it. How could he? He has never known the lives that Guy or me have had. He hasn't dealt with trauma. He doesn't know loss like we know loss. So, I don't let his judgement of us get to me.

I know what I must do.

The world around me falls still for a moment while I prepare myself for my next move. I close my eyes and suck in a breath, knowing that today is the day. Guy survived after everything he went through. He was just a child, and he survived. No, he lived, and so must I.

"Not yet," I reply to Quentin's question. I stand up grabbing my now very cold food and coffee from my nightstand.

"Who wants to join me for gridcakes and coffee in the kitchen?"

The Wolves glance at each other, and Guy shrugs his shoulders in response.

I walk tall toward my door. As I pass Guy, I tilt my head up to him and my heart swells as the ocean does for the moon because I am so incredibly proud of him. After everything he has been through, everything he has endured, he hasn't let it harden him. He hasn't let it define him. He hasn't let it beat him like it would most others.

"Thank you for sharing your story," I whisper. "You are resilient and brave, and *you* are my hero." I place a gentle kiss on his cheek, and my heart flutters for a quick moment and then settles still again. "And I chose you as my family. You will always have a safe place here with me."

I shift my attention to Quentin, his eyes burning into me with a fierce intensity, and I see a hint of his signature mischievous smirk breaking free from his worrying look. I wink at him and step over the threshold of my room into the living area. As my feet touch the cold concrete floor, I shed all the weight that's been pulling me underwater, drowning me like an anchor fastened to the seabed. Finally, I break free of the water's surface, breathing life back into myself.

I know, at this moment, I am going to be alright.

We are *all* going to be alright.

CHAPTER 41

This morning, I decided to venture out to the gardens with my book and a coffee to sit under the maple trees by the fountain and relax. The autumn air is cooler, but the sun still holds a radiant warmth. The playful birds darting under the fountain sing in mischievous tones, their songs filling the otherwise silence of the gardens. While I've finally left my room, I still haven't left the complex. But things feel lighter, different, and I'm sure any day now will be the big day.

The sound of rustling leaves pulls my focus from my book. I stare up from the tree I'm sitting under, and a large shadowy figure bathed in the golden rays towers over me.

"Q and I are leaving," Guy supplies calmly, and I rise to my feet to bid him goodbye.

"I know," I say a bit sheepishly and nod my head. I knew this time would come when they would have to leave. It was inevitable that things would eventually go back to normal. But after all the fighting and pushing back, I didn't think I would feel this despondent about their departure. They've become like family to me, and their absence will be felt.

"Come here," he says, and he pulls me into a hug, planting his chin on my head. "I'll be back in a few days to pick you up. We'll all be back together again soon." I nod again against his chest, a tear forcing its way down my cheek.

Damn it, Paege. Get your shit together.

I have never been to Quespelia, so when Quentin and Guy invited me to join them with the pack for Guy's first shift, I jumped at the opportunity.

I close my eyes against Guy's chest and think back to when Guy and Quentin told us about growing up there and how beautiful and magical it sounded. There are old Faery tales that tell of pixies and nymphs who used to live in the wooded lands of Quespelia, and when I read my books, I often find myself wondering if they still exist. I've never bothered to ask about it. Guy would probably think I'm crazy.

I hum. Me with the Wolves in Quespelia. Campfires and laughter and hearing tall tales of the Braxtion and Ishaan brothers. I feel my lips pull up at the edges.

"Are you going to be alright while we're gone?" he asks as I pull away from his embrace.

I nod. "Yes, Guy, I'll be fine. Asheron is coming by later, and I'm feeling much better about everything. I promise." I hold my hand up to my heart in true Vailenbyrg style, and a smile tugs at his lips.

"If you need us for anything—"

"Go," I urge. "I'll see you in a couple of days."

"Quentin is . . ." He looks toward the complex, and his brows furrow, possibly unsure of what to say.

My heart storms to an unsteady beat at Quentin's name. Things between us have been odd, to say the least. Pleasant and polite. But a tension of want coils around my chest, and it pulls tighter and tighter whenever he is near. Neither one of us know how to act around the other. Any possibility of us ever being together has been wiped from the realm of hope. Not that we could have ever been together anyway, but my heart is a traitorous bitch sometimes and a rebellious whore—always wanting what she can't have.

"We've already said our goodbyes," I answer the question he never asked, putting him out of his uncomfortable misery.

"Are you sure you're going to be alright, Paege?"

I sigh and take his hand. "Guy, I owe you two my life. I can't thank you enough for what you have done for me. Do I wish things could be different? Maybe." I shrug, and it's a total lie. I wish things could be very different. "But do I regret anything? No." That is not a lie. "I will be fine."

I step away from him and face the waterfall, those damn playful birds still playing amongst the jets. He steps up beside me.

"Has he said anything?" I ask after a long moment of silence passes between us, the sound of the waterfall spurting water the only sound filling the space around us.

"Huh?" he murmurs absentmindedly, clearly lost in the impish games of our little feathered friends.

"Quentin. Has he said anything?"

"No," is all Guy supplies. And I don't push it any further. I'm sure if there was more to say, Guy would tell me.

"Don't forget to pack those swords of yours so we can keep training," Guy says unexpectedly, and he smiles broadly in excitement.

I roll my eyes and nod in agreement.

We've been sparing together in the garden over the last few days. He found my swords in my wardrobe and has been obsessed with fighting ever since. It's a nice change from the vision box obsession. And he can fight. Apparently, the Guards used to train with him when he was younger. Quentin never joined in.

The things you learn.

"I'm going to miss you. Message me whenever." I reach in for another hug, and he obliges me, his warmth meddling with the warmth of the sun, and my traitorous heart finds herself slowing her pace.

"See you soon, Paege." He retracts from our bubble of our shared warmth and heads to the gates, leaving me to bask alone in the fading fragments of his presence.

But surprisingly, as I watch him leave, his absence doesn't bring me sadness; it brings me hope.

"Oh, and Paege," he yells over his shoulder, not stopping his stride. "Pixies still exist."

I knew it.

 Chapter 42

My home has been uncomfortably empty the last few days with the Wolves gone. So, this trip to Quespelia couldn't have come around fast enough. Every moment alone in the apartment feels like an eternity without Guy's constant need to watch the vision box or Quentin's remarkable ability to annoy me by just existing, but I still haven't been able to leave the complex. So, while I'm excited to see the Wolves, I'm apprehensive about leaving my fortress.

I've been up since dawn pacing around the apartment, my stomach a ball of nerves. We depart at noon, but it's barely mid-morning, and I have nothing to keep me distracted except my restless thoughts that race ahead to the impending journey and what I can expect.

Quespelia is not just the magical mecca of our kingdom. It's the royal territory. It's very rare for anyone to get an invite to the territory. Especially anyone who is not a Wolf. While I know I'm not going to the palace, honestly, I don't think I would ever want to step foot in that place. To visit the territory feels like a real honour.

That's not the problem. The issue is spending the next few days with a pack of Wolves whose sole purpose for this camping trip is to shift and run through the woodlands.

Then there is Quentin.

What the fuck am I getting myself into?

Out of habit, I grab a bottle of DesertFyre from the kitchen and pour myself a shot. I haven't drunk since Sylas tortured me. Do I want to start again now? I don't know. Maybe. It used to ease all sorts of uncomfortable feelings inside, but now, it feels like escaping from reality. Ignoring my truth.

Just as I'm about to decide, my door knocks three times. Guy isn't supposed to be here until lunch. I tip the golden nectar down the drain and hurry to the door. I open it to find Mhelodie in a simple grey knitted dress, holding an armful of books and standing next to a slightly older Witch who I've never met before. Her large chestnut eyes look me up and down as her wavy auburn hair blows around her ivory face.

"Can we come in?" Mhelodie asks as she shuffles the pile of books in her balance without any explanation of where she has been lately and why she has been avoiding me. This is the first time I've seen her since Sylas attacked us. She has spent time with Guy but not me. I was starting to think she didn't want to be my friend anymore, and I never would have blamed her. It was all because of me.

I nod and stand back as the older Witch steps through first, and Mhelodie follows. "What do I owe this pleasure?" I joke, trying to hide my confusion and utter uncomfortableness of the situation, but the knot in my chest twists tightly regardless.

"Paege. This is Sydney, Sydney Helstable," she says as she places all the books down on the table. At the top of the pile is the one book that has been consuming my thoughts day in and day out for weeks now. *The Origin Series: The Crescent Wolf Pack.* I knew Guy had given it to her. But seeing it, my heart plummets through the ground. Of course, she isn't here because of me. It's for Guy.

I awkwardly lift my eyes to Mhelodie. "Guy isn't here," I supply pushing down my disappointment.

"I know, we are here to see you." My brows pull together.

"It's a pleasure to meet you, Paege. Mhelodie has told me so much about you," Sydney says in a thick rounded accent.

"She has?" I ask. Really unsure what all this is about and what is going on. She hasn't even responded to any of my messages yet she's telling a strange Witch all about me.

"Mhelodie, can we . . ." I start, needing a moment to speak with my friend and find out what is going on, but Mhelodie speaks at the same time.

"Paege," I pause, giving her a moment to say whatever it is she needs to say. "I'm sorry," she finishes, her sunshine eyes glistening with tears.

"For what?" I should be the one apologising to her. It was my fault all of this happened. Not hers. If she needed to stay away, I can't fault her for that. I can barely look at myself in the mirror after what happened.

"Everything. Sylas."

"Sylas? What could you possibly have to apologise for? I should be the one apologising to you for getting you caught up in my mess." Somehow, I manage to pick my battered and bruised heart up off the floor. "I love you so much. I've missed you so much. I completely understand why you have stayed away. It was traumatic and seeing me would be a constant reminder of what he did to you. You do not need to apologise for that."

"You think I've stayed away because of you?" Mhelodie's eyes arch high, and she comes around the table to stand in front of me. "Paege, I stayed away because of *me*." She drops her head to look at her toes. "I failed you," she whispers. "I have been trying so hard to remember what Sylas made me do to that blade and what magic he had me use for the brands, but it's like my memories were wiped. I haven't been able to face you. I can't help you." Her voice cracks as a tiny sob bubbles out of her chest.

Blood rushes my ears. *Sylas*. Still hurting people even after he is gone. The carnage he left in his wake is a grim reminder of the darkness that lingered in his shadow, staining the lives of those he wronged.

"You've been staying away because you think I would be upset with you?" I ask, a lump forming in my throat and a fire raging in my belly. Mhelodie is one of the kindest Beings I have ever known. Her love knows no bounds. She loved me when I thought no one else would. When I was all alone and in the big Neopolis with nothing but stars in my eyes and stupidity in my heart. When I thought I could run away from my insecurities and conquer my fears with just a dream. Her, Lumeilia, and Asheron. They all saved me.

She nods and slowly lifts her gaze from the floor between us.

"Mhelodie, I'm not upset with you. I have never been upset with you. I was upset you never came to visit. I'm upset you ignored me, but I knew you had your reasons." I smile cheekily at her, hoping to lift some of her burden. "Turns out they were stupid reasons," I mock.

Life blooms in my friend's face, and her golden eyes sparkle with love as I watch her face soften, and the guilt and shame slowly unclasp itself from her soul and float away.

Wait.

"Mhelodie, did you?" My gaze shifts between her and Sydney, who is sitting at my table with a very large smile and an intriguing look on her face. "I can't feel you," I mutter to myself.

I count the days of the season. It's mid-Autumn. I've been so immersed in my own drama and consumed by my troubles that I completely missed it.

"No?" I drawl. "I didn't." What sort of friend misses their friend's birthday?

Bad, Paege. Very, very bad.

"It's fine, Paege, honestly. It's been such a hectic few weeks, and it's not like I was around myself. I wasn't going to make a big deal of it anyway," she dismisses and turns to take her seat. I grab her arm and tug her gently back to me.

"But it *is* a big deal!" I confirm and wrap my arms around her. "I'm sorry I missed it. An Ascension party is next on my to-do list, right after I return from Quespelia." I pull back from her embrace and place my hand on heart in true Vailenbyrg style. "I promise."

Mhelodie's eyes widen. "You're," she hesitates, "going to Quespelia?"

"Yes, Guy is picking me up at midday. Why?"

"Nothing," she responds and shakes her head. "Are you sure that's wise?" she adds. It doesn't sound like nothing. The vibe shifts in the room. The air around us becomes thick with energy, and my skin tingles from the power being released around me. I dart my eyes between the two Witches, and neither look me in the eyes.

"What's going on?" I ask. The cage in my chest shrinks, squeezing my heart so tightly I'm sure it's about to burst.

Mhelodie lets out a loosened breath and sits in the empty chair next to Sydney and gestures to me to sit, so I do. "We lifted some of the magic from the book, and we got more than what we bargained for. Some of the information is terrifying, and it involves the Hallowed. We think they erased things from our history."

"You didn't?" I ask as I run my hands over the red leather cover of the book.

"I did. *We* did," she corrects. "We've been able to decipher some of the texts. Not just from your book but others from the Coven's collections. Even some of our grimoires have been restored. It's fascinating, but..." she trails off. Her warm smile fades quickly like the light in her eyes.

Sydney stands, brushing her hands down the length of her full burgundy velvet gown, and walks over to me. She places her hand on my shoulder. "Buck up, princess," she says in a thick, rounded accent. "It's going to be a long, few hours."

CHAPTER 43

Hazy memories keep trying to fight their way to the forefront of my mind like a relentless early morning fog, rolling in across the water, but every attempt to grasp them is as unsuccessful as the last.

My hands shakily clutch the glass of water Mhelodie has kindly retrieved for me, and I take another sip, gulping it down audibly. "Fae ruled the kingdom," I say, repeating the words I've just heard out loud to keep my focus.

"Yes," Sydney drawls in her thick accent.

My heart thunders in my chest, drumming to an erratic tune and awakening the daemon that I have become accustomed to feeling in the pit of my stomach, and she growls loudly.

"Are you sure you read that thing right?"

"Yes," Mhelodie and Sydney respond in unison.

"And what you're telling me is," I muse over what I am about to say, the mental clogs of my mind turning over and over and over again, "Fae originally ruled Elyndria, but the entire royal line was assassinated by the Crescent Wolf pack?" It sounds insane. Amerax is one of the oldest Guards, an experienced warrior. If the Fae ruled the kingdom, he would know.

"Yes," they agree again.

"The Royal Family, the Gingerells?" I ask uncertainly.

"Grynderwells," Sydney corrects.

"Right," I nod. "The *Grynderwells*. And *that* triggered the curse?" This can't be right.

"Yes."

"That would be Guy and Quentin's family?"

"Yes."

"The same Guy and Quentin I've had staying in my home?"

"Yes."

"And the Hallowed, the peaceful and isolated priests and priestesses changed or erased all of our history?"

"Yes."

"Will you both stop saying yes!" I snap as the fog in my mind thickens and infiltrates every dark recess of my mind. "I uh," I stutter. "I'm, um, I can't." I place my drink on the table, my fingers tightening around the glass, and I breathe heavily, my lungs surrendering to the pressure of my anxiety.

"It's alright, Paege," Sydney says in a soothing voice as I watch my thoughts fade away like watching pieces of a puzzle disappear right in front of me.

"Sorry, but I can't . . ." I plant my hands on the table, desperately trying to hold onto my sanity, but a cloud rises over my eyes. My memories slip through my fingers like sand, leaving me grasping at fragments of conversations that were there just moments ago. The room tilts around me, and I struggle to anchor myself down. "Mhelodie? What's happening?" I ask, dipping my head, my long ashy brown hair curtaining my face. I breathe deeply as my brain liquifies into a puddle of nothing and tears sting my eyes.

"You've been compelled to forget, princess," Sydney answers softly, placing her hand on mine. "We all have. It's the curse."

The air is squeezed out of my lungs by icy fingers of fear. Memories of the darkest time of my life surge through the hazy cloud of my mind, but these aren't the ones I'm trying to fight for. These are the ones I wish so desperately to forget.

Sylas.

"Paege?" Mhelodie's familiar and soft voice tugs at my attention. I surrender to her pull and look at her. "It's alright, you can trust us." She places her hand on my other hand. "All you need to do is read from this book." Sydney grabs another book from the pile in front of us and opens to an earmarked page. My heart runs to an erratic pace as I try to follow what's going on around me.

Sydney's eyes glisten as if she is enjoying watching me lose my Godsdamn mind. But no, it wouldn't be that. I need to trust Mhelodie.

Releasing a sigh, I grab the book and put it in my lap, focusing my attention to the words on the page.

"Read that?" I ask looking back up at Mhelodie and Sydney as if this is some ridiculous joke. The words on the page are blurry and out of focus, and the text scatters chaotically in all different directions.

"Just give it a moment, you need to open yourself up to hearing the truth. Allow the book to speak to you," Sydney instructs.

She must be fucking crazy.

"Mhelodie, you can't be serious?"

"Trust us, please," Mhelodie interrupts, brushing her hands nervously through her tight golden curls.

My friend's warm face is nothing but a picture of calmness on a sunny summer's day, and I can't help but agree to trust her even though what she is asking of me sounds completely insane.

I stare back at the pages and do as she instructs. I watch and wait. Watch and wait.

"Relax, princess, let the words come to you," Sydney whispers in my ears.

Before I know it, the jumbled puzzle pieces begin to move, letters rearranging themselves and becoming clear, revealing to me the hidden secrets buried within the tangled mess of words. As if a veil has been lifted, clarity washes over me, and fear relaxes his grip. The disjointed text transforms into a coherent narrative, unlocking what looks to be a spell.

The words whisper to me, urging me to read them. To use them. To set them free. As if pulled into a trance, the words roll off my tongue:

A place in time, a time in place,
Memories are not erased.
Deep within, we hid the key,
To protect the royal family.
Nothing's lost, it can be found.
But only when she wears the Crown.

As soon as the last word escapes my lips, a wrecking ball smashes through the brick wall that's been building in my mind. It crashes down in an instant, and memories of my conversation with the Witches come surging forth like a tidal wave.

And more.

Pictures of my mother flash through my mind. I hear conversations with her from when I was a child. I see moments from when I was a teenager and even from when I was a young adult. Even from just a few months ago. Stories she told me over and over again throughout my life about the Fae. About the Israykiel Guard. About my dad.

What the actual fuck?

I let the memories fill my mind. Each detail unfolds like a vivid panorama before me, coming to life inside my mind and disassociating myself from my body.

I can feel my mother's warm touch comforting me as she tells me how my father died. Her tears are so clear I want to lift my hand to her face and wipe them from her cheek. I see her loving smile and her caramel eyes twinkle as she tells me bedtime stories of the Guards, how they were created, and the magic that was used.

I can smell the wildflowers that bloom during spring in Orphelious, and it wafts around us as we sit on a grassy knoll, and she tells me tales of the Fae who once ruled the Elyndria.

A kaleidoscope of emotions blooms in my body, taking root in my soul as they are planted seed by seed. *Joy. Pain. Anger. Love. Hurt. Confusion.* The weight of the stolen memories drowns me in truths and lies. I always thought she never wanted to speak of my dad, but she did. She spoke of him often. My heart blooms with the love she poured into me. The love that my father felt for us. Yet it splinters with pain, knowing I never got to feel that love, and I have lived my life feeling indifferent to him.

Gradually, it comes to an end, and my mind finally becomes mine again.

"Oh Gods!" I look to both Mhelodie and Sydney. "What was that?"

"The memories of what we shared with you this past couple of hours that you have been compelled to forget," Mhelodie answers immediately, her eyes wide with wonderment.

And so much more.

Instinctually, I understand that no one is supposed to know any of this, yet somehow my mother does. How is this possible? Something deep within my core stirs, triggering a warning within, and that beast grumbles in silence. So, I heed the alarm and decide to keep this to myself and hold back the tears that are wanting to fight their way out.

"You are now one of three who remember," Sydney adds and smiles widely.

A wild thought comes crashing through my mind's door, and my heart stills as it forms a coherent theory.

Could Guy and Quentin have known? What if they somehow got their memories back and have known this whole time? Surely, they wouldn't. No, Guy didn't know anything about the curse when I brought the book home. Quentin told Guy to forget about it, and he can be a damn good actor when he wants to be. Why hide it when we said we found out about the curse? Does his father know? Does the king remember any of this? Guy and Quentin, Braxtion and Ishaan? My thoughts spiral into a chaotic storm, and I force myself to breathe to gain control.

Sydney stands as if all this is now boring. She runs her hands down her long burgundy gown and swishes her dark, auburn hair over her shoulder before walking to the kitchen. "May I make us a cup of tea?"

"Tea?" I mouth to Mhelodie, and she just shrugs as Sydney helps herself to the things in my kitchen. I think this calls for something stronger than tea.

"Do you think Guy and Quentin know about any of this?" I whisper to Mhelodie. I'm not sure why. Sydney clearly knows more than I do—than we all do.

"Paege, I honestly don't think anyone remembers anything," Mhelodie answers frankly. "But that isn't to say you can trust them blindly," she adds.

"The magic to break this curse is hidden in some sort of dagger?" I ask, remembering what they told me about the Hallowed cursing the blade that took the lives of our Royal family.

"Yes, the dagger that was used to kill the Grynderwell family, and it's a blood curse."

"Meaning?" I sit back down and close my eyes, waiting for her answer, but I am not sure I want to hear it because I am one hundred percent certain I know what the answer is and what it means.

"It needs the blood of the cursed to break the curse," Sydney drawls from the kitchen.

Meaning it needs the blood of Quentin or Guy.

CHAPTER 44

Melodie and Sydney watch me closely as I flick through the Crescent Wolf book and try to process everything I just learned.

The book describes how hundreds of years ago, the Crescent Wolves were responsible for the assassination of the Grynderwell family and their entire royal bloodline, including their newborn son. All to conquer the crown. Tiergan Braxtion, Guy's grandfather, took the throne, and he assigned Ishaan as his trusted advisor. Together, they abolished all other houses in the kingdom, leaving the Wolves as the sole authority. They established a monarchy.

According to the text, in a desperate bid to restore the natural order of things, the Hallowed drew upon the power of the moon and cursed the Crescent Wolf pack by using the blade that slaughtered the family in their sleep.

Now, the only way to free the Wolves that chain them to the moon is for the dagger to taste the blood of the cursed. Why wipe everyone else's memories? And how in the Hels does my mother remember all of this?

"How did all this happen?" I ask as I look up from the book that's consumed my morning. "Surely the Israykiel Guards would have protected the family?"

"There is more information in this old text." Sydney pats a small brown leather journal. "That details how the Sirens and Heretics worked with the Wolves before they were bound and banished."

I swallow hard. "So, the Sirens weren't always bound?" Is that how Sylas slipped through? Did he come from a line of Sirens that never got their bands? My stomach growls a warning, deterring me from going down this path. Mhelodie takes my hand and squeezes it gently. She smiles kindly, but it doesn't reach her eyes, the colour of warmth in her face slowly draining. I don't know how long this Sylas tragedy is going to haunt us both, but it's going to be for a long while still.

"No, I believe only those that abused their power had their Siren song bound," Sydney confirms as she takes a sip of her cup of tea.

"The Heretics weren't banished to live in the Mountains of G'phen, the unmagic lands?" I ask, my gaze dropping to my lap. My hand reaches for the charm that hangs around my neck, and I zip it anxiously up and down the chain.

"I don't believe they were," she agrees. Mhelodie places the journal in front of me, and I release the charm from my grip. Intrigued, I trace my fingers over the journal, and I recognise it as the book I read to unlock my memories.

"Where did you get that?" I ask. "And how did you know it would unlock our memories?"

"It won't, not to just anyone anyway," Mhelodie says.

"One can't just open the book to read the pages and remember everything," Sydney adds. "It took a lot of magic, blood magic, to break through the locks that kept the words hidden."

"So, how did I manage to read it?" I ask. I am neither a Witch nor able to wield blood magic.

"Sydney suggested it would work because you are an Empath," Mhelodie says in a hushed tone.

My head snaps up, and my brows arch. "What does that mean?" I ask.

"It means you feel the truth of everyone. So, she suggested maybe your gift would allow the book to reveal its truth to you. And it worked." Mhelodie jumps up and down in her seat excitedly at that revelation, and I had to admit, it was pretty cool but also a long shot.

"So," I muse, bringing my focus back to the topic of the Wolves killing the Fae King, his Queen, and their two-month-old son. "The Heretics and Sirens disarmed the Guards so the Wolves could kill the royals, and the Hallowed cursed us all for it."

"How they managed to get close enough in the first place is beyond me," Sydney murmurs to herself as she stands and collects the empty mugs on the table.

For the second time in this conversation, I find the memories of Sylas kidnapping me, tugging at my mind, drawing me back into the emotional torment I've been spending my days trying to escape. There is one way a Heretic or a Siren could get close to the Guards to syphon their gifts and compel them not to protect their charges.

"Not me," I hesitate, knowing the words that follow are going to cause pain for two of us in the room. "Invisibility," I supply, and Mhelodie lets out a tiny squeak.

"Invisibility? But I never," Sydney exclaims, her brows rising with intrigue.

"We have," Mhelodie whispers, and a single tear rolls down her cheek, her golden eyes quickly losing their spark.

"Yes, we have," I agree with a breath. If a Heretic could syphon invisibility from somewhere, they could have certainly gotten close enough to the guards.

"When? How?" Sydney asks.

"That, Sydney, is a story for another day," I answer, and she nods, seemingly like she understands. But she couldn't unless Mhelodie had told her about things.

I hand the book back to Mhelodie and sigh audibly. We got nowhere. In an attempt to help Guy and Quentin with their Wolf pack curse, we have unveiled an illusion so intricate and complicated that we find ourselves deeper in the labyrinth of the problem. Every revelation has only added more levels of mystery and complexity to the curse we all seem to endure, leaving us with more questions than answers.

Mhelodie clears her throat. "Sydney and I are going to leave." She stands, and they both start collecting the various books. "Guy's going to be here soon, and I can't see him. I don't want to lie to him, so it's best I am not here when he gets here."

I nod, completely understanding. Mhelodie and Guy have become close over the past month, and she promised to help him. But now we know this. Given that Guy and Quentin's family is responsible for changing the course of history, we can't share anything that we know with them. And now, I have to spend the next couple of days with them and the rest of the cursed Wolves, trying to pretend I know nothing.

Sure, Paege, you've totally got this under control.

I walk the Witches to the door. "It was lovely to meet you, Sydney," I say as I pull open the door, and she smiles widely at me.

"You have no idea how lovely it was to meet you," she drawls. "May I?" she asks as she drops her gaze to the charm around my neck.

"Oh, um, of course," I offer.

She picks up the charm, inspecting the intricacies of the details. "Curious," she mutters and releases her grip, and I swear I see a hint of a flame ignite in her eyes. "Until we meet again, princess." She pauses and purses her ruby lips before continuing. "And I have a feeling it will be much sooner than anticipated." She cackles, then steps out the door, snapping her fingers as if to order Mhelodie to follow.

I raise a brow at the dramatic exit by Sydney, and Mhelodie just shrugs her shoulders in reply. "Message me when you're back. We have so much more work to do. And please be safe," she implores before kissing me on the cheek and following Sydney out the door.

CHAPTER 45

This trip with the Crescent Wolf pack has my apprehension levels peaking. My heart is pounding with the memory this morning, and I've found myself questioning my decisions more times than I would like to admit, but I want to go, even after everything I've learned.

The apartment complex gate slams shut behind me, and I look up the cobblestone road to find Guy holding some gear and leaning up against a Centaurion.

My heart cartwheels, and a swarm of butterflies flutters in my belly as excitement ripples through me. Even after what I just learned about the Crescent Wolf pack, I feel my smile tug higher as I skip toward him like a child in a playground.

"I thought we were walking?" I question as I approach him. "What is all this?"

"I figured we would take a Centaurion. And this," he holds his arms out to me, "is some travel gear. I figured you might not have the right attire for camping with Wolves, and the portals can be brutal. So, I wanted you to be comfortable." He winks.

My eyes roam over Guy's attire. He wears light blue denim pants, a knitted top, and a black leather jacket with leather boots. Then I look down at myself. I am wearing a dark denim skirt, canvas shoes, and a hooded jumper. Feeling very foolish, I take the gear from Guy: leather pants, jacket, and boots. As I do so, I can't help but notice the garish ring on Guy's finger. One I haven't seen before. Yet, there's something so familiar about the silver band with a sparkling ashy-blue stone set in the centre of a yawning Wolf's jaw.

"I hope you don't mind, I checked your sizes in your wardrobe," Guy says, distracting me from the eyesore that sits on his finger. He flashes a sheepish grin as if he may have overstepped a boundary, but honestly, it doesn't bother me.

"That is perfectly fine," I respond.

Leaving my scabbard and swords with Guy, I run inside and change quickly, cramming my gear into my bag. When I meet Guy by the Centaurion again, he smiles widely.

"Ready?" he asks, and he holds a door open for me. Instead of climbing into the carriage, I wrap my arms around him, trying to contain the excitement that's bubbling up. He pulls me in close, into a warm embrace, and his stoic energy cocoons me. My nerves start to settle, washing away any concerns about our trip so they no longer plague my thoughts.

He always does that, and I don't know how.

We stay like that for a few minutes before the Centaur clears his throat. Eager to get moving, Guy releases me from his embrace and steps aside, and I crawl into the carriage, ready for our trip.

Our time moving through the Neopolis is slow as we manoeuvre ourselves through the cobblestone streets. Though its still early afternoon when we reach the entrance to portal halls on the other side of Lockswick. And once we cross the bridge out of the Neopolis, my nerves are fighting their way back to the surface.

I step out of the carriage, bidding goodbye to the Centaur, and I feel a rush of adrenaline pump through my veins as I stare up at the foreboding portal halls. The afternoon winter sun casts an eery shadow around the portal halls, and I can't help but feel a little intimidated and underprepared for this journey. I have never needed to use the portal halls before. Amerax has portal magic, being a Guard, so he has always travelled with us. Or I have travelled by Centaurion, horse, or by foot. This? This is different. Very, very different.

The massive building stands at least fifty stories high, possibly more. It is one of the tallest and grandest buildings in all of Elyndria. The sharp, soaring spires with gilded accents catch the sunlight as they reach for the sky in asymmetrical angles, giving it a haunting yet somewhat majestic glow. Its stone silhouette looms over the city, a constant shadow watching everything below. Two large angels guard the grand entrance gates, and gargoyles are stationed by the metal doors along with the Lupa-Centaurs that man the portals, checking passes.

No one travels via the portal halls without a prior booking. The halls are home to thousands of public portals, all leading to various locations throughout Welveryn, Orphelious, and Cedrus—even to the Star-Borne Academy. Only one leads to Quespelia, and you can only travel to Quespelia if escorted by an Ishaan, an Israykiel Guard, or have a special ticket signed off by the king himself or his court and, apparently, Guy.

Once in Quespelia, we will portal travel two more times. Once to the alpha manor and once again to the Crescent Wolves usual campsite. I find it strange that a portal exists at a campsite, but I suspect it was put there by the Ishaan's themselves.

"Paege," Guy asks gingerly, his hand lightly grasping my elbow. "Are you alright?"

I turn to face him. Am I? These last few months, my world has been thrown into turmoil. Chaos has exploded all around me, and now, I am about to travel by portal to Quespelia to spend time with a pack that may have been responsible for changing our entire kingdom's history.

My nerves chase away the remnants of calm living behind my chest. But weirdly, looking up at Guy, that very same calmness starts chasing away my nerves.

Gods, I'm an absolute mess.

"Shall we?" I ask, painting the largest grin across my face and throwing my bag over my shoulder.

"We shall," Guy answers, and we loop our arms together as we walk into the building.

Once in the portal halls, we make our way through the large sprawling halls, the air buzzing with excitement where hundreds of Beings frantically swarm around, coming and going from their travels. Yet, despite the busyness, the halls are eerily quiet. It's almost as if the building itself absorbs sounds. Now and then, a Guard's voice travels across the space, or a Centaur calls out to his colleagues, but for the most part, it's bone silent aside from the heavy thud of our own footfalls as we traipse across the marbled floors.

The spiral staircase to Quespelia's portal is relentless. The only reprieve from the burn in my lungs and my legs are the interesting tapestries and paintings that hang from the busy stone walls. I see a collection of paintings called "Welveryn Winter," and I arch a brow as I take in the beauty of them. It's surprising how similar it seems to Orphelious. Isolated villages are separated by beautiful, wooded lands and pine forests. The brick and rock cottages are small with ethereal floral gardens, oak trees, and lots of land. Young Wolves play in the fields and swim in lakes, seemingly unbothered by the fact it is winter.

Breathtaking.

Staring into the paintings, I feel like I'm transfixed in time, watching another world unravel before me as I pass by. I can't help but wonder if Sydney, Mhelodie, and I made some kind of mistake earlier. The Wolves don't seem like they could be capable of such atrocities. Maybe the book is wrong. Maybe it's another concealment spell to hide the truth and deter us. It just all seems preposterous.

"This is us," Guy calls from above me. I look up, and he gestures to me to follow or hurry up. Or both. I drag myself from the mesmerising paintings and bound up the remaining stairs to catch him. Breathless, we enter a grand room and are greeted by a Lupa-Centaur. The Lupa-Centaur nods at Guy in acknowledgment and steps aside, letting us pass and revealing the large archway opening out into the afternoon sky that swirls with blue and reds and golds.

"Are you ready?" Guy asks as he holds a hand out for me, and I shake my head in a firm no as I step toward him, taking his hand in mine. He squeezes his fingers around mine and pulls me to his side. "It's going to feel rough, so whatever you do, don't let go." Then he steps us into the kaleidoscope of colours and shadows, hundreds of lengths above the ground.

I scream. It's like stepping into the atmosphere. At first, it's the most freeing feeling in the world, being completely unbound and moving freely at high speeds. I wonder if this is what flying feels like.

Cool wind whooshes against my face, awakening all my senses. The air thins, and suddenly, I can smell Autumn.

Then the sunset seems to slow. It's as if the sun herself is hanging from the sky, suspended in time, blessing us with her grace to be able to enjoy the picturesque artwork of the portal as images of the world pass us by in a haze.

I'm so transfixed that I don't notice the rapid dip in temperature, but the sudden static charge surging into my chest, zapping life back into my stuttering heart, snaps me out of my hypnotic gaze. I jolt from its impact, and Guy shudders under my grip. Then I feel a slight tug at my core, and everything tilts sideways.

The air around us thickens with magic, and my body hums with energy as it travels through my veins. Then nausea rolls through me in waves. I'm yanked to the side again and pulled into darkness, and I hit the ground with a thud.

Prying my lids open, I meet emerald eyes bursting with light. Amusement seeps through the edges, at my clumsiness.

"Are you ready for that again?" he asks, a wolfish grin appearing across his face, and he pulls me to my feet. Again, I shake my head in a firm no as I let him guide me to the next portal and the one after that until we are finally standing in the middle of the woods.

He is standing in the middle of the woods. *I* am firmly on my ass once again.

After walking a short while, we step out from behind a boulder into a large clearing. There are multiple tents sprawled around the clearing in no particular order and of various sizes. The group of Crescent Wolves sits around a roaring campfire in the centre of the clearing. My eyes lazily roam over the Wolves, and my heart stumbles in my chest when I see Quentin. He smiles, and the flames dance across his sun-kissed skin, igniting a fire of my own. His white canines glows under the moonlit sky.

I close my eyes and draw in a long breath, appreciating the sudden silence as it echoes through my ears. The sound of insects singing and frogs bellowing comes as a welcome relief to the constant roar of the portals.

"Are you coming?" Guys asks, as he strides off toward the pack.

I take a step to follow, but my legs give way, and the world tilts beneath me once more. I stumble for a few steps before I finally find my balance.

Damn it, Paege!

"Are you alright, Books?" I hear the familiar sound of my name, and my heart stumbles in my chest, following the pattern of my feet. I turn around to find Quentin standing a few feet from me. He smiles broadly and holds out a drink for me. "Welcome to our home."

I take a few quick steps toward him, and without any thought, I wrap my arms around his body, burying my head in his chest. He envelops me in his arms, and I feel him let out a long breath. Could he have been as anxious about this as me? No, he doesn't get anxious. He is the pillar of strength. Unphased by anything. He is Quentin Ishaan, the fucking Heir Apparent, the next High Alpha Wolf for the Crescent Wolf pack.

It makes my heart settle all the same.

I let Quentin guide me to the pack. A warmth prickles my skin where our fingers entwine together, and desire blooms in my gut. The sudden pang of pain that awakens in my back relieves me of that feeling, and a knot of remorse unfurls inside.

The pack sits around the fire on makeshift bench seats from fallen trees, chatting and laughing without a care in the kingdom. Guy has nestled himself between two females, and I remember them from Slynx. Immojen and Monella. They all feel free and unphased by life and its responsibilities. It must be a Wolf thing, and I can't help but think how lucky they all are to call this home.

But it's not their home now, is it?

"Everyone, this is Paege," Guy says between words with Monella as we approach the group. Quentin sits next to another young female with sandy blonde hair, just like his, and pats the space next to him. I apprehensively sit myself down.

Heat flushes my cheeks, not from the raging campfire or Quentin's closeness but from the eyes of an entire Wolf pack as they all watch me with great intensity.

Silence explodes around us. Even the insects seem to have fallen still. After what feels like minutes, Quentin finally speaks. Names roll off his tongue as if calling them from an attendance sheet. If it wasn't for Guy pointing toward each Wolf, I'd have no idea who he is referring to.

"Reever, Greyson, Immojen, Monella, Deekon and his brother Slaytar, Harkin, Gilli, and Pippance."

Quentin then turns to the younger-looking girl sitting on the other side of him, and he drops his arm over her shoulder, pulling her in close. "And this little pup is Bridgette, my younger sister." He smiles broadly and then ruffles her curly blonde hair in a brotherly fashion. She rolls her eyes and swats him away.

A cacophony of replies all come at once, but no gazes linger upon me, waiting for me to reply as if it's no big deal that a demi-Fae has gate-crashed their shifting party.

Laughter refills the woodlands as they resume their conversations. I study the pack, watching them as they interact, before my gaze settles on Guy. My brows furrow while a feeling of warmth blossoms in my chest. I observe as he chides with the pack. His laughter bellows from deep in his belly as one of the males tells him something. They joke freely and support each other without thought. A family. That's what I'm seeing. That's what they are. One big family brought together by life, not by blood. I didn't realise how much I've missed him—both of them. But to see Guy smile like this, to see him loved by so many, has my heart blooming with warmth. He deserves this.

CHAPTER 46

The members of the pack seem nice enough, but I've been feeling like an outsider for most of the night so far while they talk and laugh amongst themselves. Every so often, Guy shoots me a questioning smile, checking in on me. Quentin's had his hand on my knee for a while now, squeezing it gently at regular intervals as if trying to keep me involved in his conversations. I have nothing to contribute. They've all known each other for many years. There is no fitting in here. But that's fine. I'm not here to fit in with the Crescent Wolf pack. I'm here to spend time with the two Wolves who saved my life and who I've grown to care about in more ways than I ever expected to.

"How was it seeing your father?" I ask Quentin casually as a gap in the conversation between him and a Wolf with wavy strawberry-blonde hair named Slayter appears.

Quentin shuffles on the log and takes a large gulp of his ale before answering me. "Yes, it was fine."

"Fine?" I raise a brow, a little confused by his nonchalant attitude. Maybe this isn't the time to talk about it, but that little voice in my head is getting louder and louder, urging me to press for more details, needing to know what the king is doing about the Scorpions—if anything at all.

"That's what I said, isn't it, Books?" he snaps.

I bite down a response. I know things between us are strained, and this situation is something no one would have ever seen coming, but his reaction when I arrived told me he was anything but bothered about me being here. So, I continue to press.

"What about the Scorpions? What about—" I stop myself short, realising I was about to say something I am not supposed to know. And one by one, the pack members turn their attention to us. To me.

Shit.

"Sorry, I didn't mean to . . ." I can't find the words to say. I'm not sorry that I asked about Ric and the Scorpions. I'm not sorry that I don't trust the king. But I don't want to cause any more strain between us. I certainly don't want to draw any unnecessary attention to myself from the Wolves. I curl my fingers around my drink tightly, rolling the glass between my hands, and take a sip of the AmberFyre. Its spicy warmth bites at my throat as it travels down into my belly, soothing the beast that wants to rise.

"It's alright. I don't want any secrets between us, Books, but there isn't anything to tell. Ric is in hiding. But I know Father won't give up until he finds them," Quentin responds matter-of-factly. "Let's just enjoy our trip and worry about the Scorpions later."

With that, the subject is changed, and all is forgotten.

Or so he wishes.

The moon sits high in the sky, and I can feel the Wolves are starting to get restless. Immojen and Slaytar have been prowling the edges of the campsite for a while, and Guy's been eyeing the moon all night.

Understanding what time it is, I stand. "I think I'm going to call it a night," I mention to the pack as I stretch my arms high above my head. While I love learning about the Wolf culture, there's only so much listening to new mating bonds forging, Wolves emerging, and omega packs forming, that I can tolerate.

Quentin stands with me, and before I have a chance to ask where I am to sleep, he takes my hand. "Let me show you where we're sleeping."

"We?" I whisper to him. My eyes settle into his for a long moment, and I get lost in the fire reflecting in the large blacks of his eyes. Quentin and I never discussed sleeping arrangements, and I'm not too sure how I feel about sharing a tent with him. On one hand, it's everything my heart desires, but the reality is that it comes with its own set of issues, a myriad of problems that have no solution in sight.

He clears his throat, bringing me back to the present moment, and he smiles, "You, me and Guy," he clarifies. A smile tugs at his lips as if he read every concern I had, and somehow, the three of us sleeping together solves all my problems, I suppose . . . to some extent.

"Come on." He tugs me forward, and I follow into step next to him.

We walk in silence through the site, the warm fire light dimming behind us until it's just us and our shadows standing at the door of one of the largest tents of the lot.

"This is us."

My mouth drops open as I take in the cozy space in front of me, and the more I look around, the higher my smile tugs at my lips.

There are three rooms. The front annex is decorated with a rug on the floor and a heap of pillows, both large and small, surrounding a low wooden table with a lantern flickering a warm, low light, creating a comfy, den-like atmosphere. A few books, a bunch of freshly picked wildflowers in a bottle, and a bottle of my favourite VineBlood are also placed atop the table.

It's clear from Quentin's face that this is all for me.

On the other side are two separate sleeping rooms. I follow Quentin into one, and I notice not one but two separate quilted bed-sacks atop a mattress.

Disappointment settles in my stomach like a heavy rock. I know this is how it must be, but part of me wishes it wasn't so.

"I didn't want to assume," he interjects as if reading my thoughts as they play through my mind. "It's better to be cautious, yes?" he ponders, sweeping his sandy blonde hair from his icy blue eyes.

I resist the urge to say what I want to say. The common sense Paege fully understands and appreciates this kind gesture, but the unreasonable devil inside storms wildly about wanting to unleash all the fury upon the lands.

As if Quentin can see the battle raging inside me, he places a gentle hand on my shoulder and whispers into my ear, "We can join them together. I was just trying to be considerate."

"No, it's perfect," I respond, finding a smile to paint on my face. "It all is." I sigh.

While it's not what I want, it is perfect for exactly what this is—whatever it is—and I couldn't have asked for more.

"Alright," Quentin says, and he places a kiss on my nose, and butterflies stir in my belly. "Me and the pack are heading out, and I've got to take Bridgette home at sunrise, but I'll see you in the morning." He starts to leave, but I reach for his hand.

"Wait, you're not sleeping here?" I ask, panic starting to unpick the seams of my armour.

"Of course I am, but knowing you, you'll be asleep long before I get back, and I didn't want to wake you in the morning."

I want to say more, tell him I haven't had a decent night's sleep since he and Guy left—in fact I've rarely had a decent night's sleep all season—so I'll be awake regardless. Instead, I nod in agreement, ignoring the anxiety that's curling around my chest, making it harder and harder to breathe. "Have fun," I chirp in feigned excitement. "See you in the morning then."

With that, he waltzes out of the tent. I follow him to the tent door and watch as he strides with determination toward the Wolves, who are all gathered by the fire.

One by one, they start stripping their clothes, not one of them bothered by the raw nakedness of their bodies, and they flawlessly shift into their Wolves. It's nothing like when Quentin emerged the first time. No, this is something else entirely. Their bodies morph seamlessly as if the Wolf lives within them. As if the very essence of their beings bleed between the seams of Wolf or humanoid, neither stronger than the other, both wholly them. It's mesmerising to watch.

I take in their forms. Each one as beautiful yet brutal as the next. Their thick coats are mottled with various shades of browns and greys, and their bodies are large and strong, muscular and proud. Their canines are long and razored, and their eyes marbled, reflecting the warmth of the firelight that dances around them. If I hadn't watched them all shift, aside from Quentin, I wouldn't know who is who.

Guy shifts last, and my breath catches in my throat as he stands in his majestic and magical form. Quentin's words about his Wolf form echo through my mind as if trying to piece together the answers to a riddle I'm supposed to know. *It's different.*

His large white Wolf, as white as the moon itself, stands proudly among the rest. Taller and broader than the others.

A gasp falls from my lips, and his snowy ears twitch. He turns, and his piercing emerald eyes, which still explode with stars, find mine.

I freeze, the only evidence of life within me is my still beating heart, racing with the adrenaline that surges through my veins.

One by one, the rest of the pack turn my way.

Shit, what did I get myself into?

Then, unexpectedly, one of the Wolves howls into the night, and the rest of the pack follow suit. Their midnight song, calling for the moon, echoes through the dense woodlands, sending a shiver racing up my spine before they turn in the other direction and run off into the moonlit woods.

CHAPTER 47

Juice from the succulent pear I eat drips down my arm while I swing freely in canvas strung between two trees.

The afternoon sun peeks through the canopy, and my body prickles with warmth as its rays kiss me with their caressing tenderness. I've always enjoyed the outdoors, but camping with the Wolves has almost been surreal. The natural energy of the woodlands has sparked some sort of wondrous healing into my body, and I've never felt more relaxed or at home.

Guy's taking me to Orphelious tomorrow to spend some time with Mum. But as the waxing crescent moon will arise the day after, the Wolves will be here another week, and I may return before heading back to the Neopolis—back to my normal life. I have no idea what that means for us, the Wolves and me, but I don't think they'll be coming back any time soon.

My hammock gently rocks between the trees, lulling me to the precipice of sleep, and I struggle to keep my focus on the book I'm reading and the juice from the pear from smudging it. A ruckus in the woodlands nearby sends a murder of cawing crows taking flight far above the trees, and a small laugh escapes my lips. I can't help but wonder if the crows met the pack. They've been running around the woods all afternoon in their Wolf forms, making the most of the crescent moon, which ends just before dawn tomorrow. I've barely seen them these past few days, but when I have, I've seen way too much of all of them. It must be nice to feel so confident and comfortable in your naked body.

A twig snaps behind me, and I accidentally drop the pear from my fingers. Damn it, I was enjoying that. I cock my head, listening for the cause. An animal of some sort, maybe, but my heart screams a thunderous chant, and I can't help but divert my focus.

Muffled voices suddenly appear, cutting through the serenity, their secrets sweeping upon me by the afternoon wind. I thought they were running with the others. They weren't supposed to be back until sunset.

Curious, I *ungracefully* flip myself out of the hammock, searching for my Wolves. I quietly hike toward their muffled voices. Each step I take reveals more of their conversation, and the beast inside my belly roars to life as I approach the two of them.

"Are you kidding me? I thought I told you not to get involved. Why are you only telling me now?" Quentin says, and I pause. Quentin and Guy stand naked and alone through the thicket, and there's an annoyed tone to his voice that I haven't heard since I met him.

I still. My eyes roam over their bodies. A week ago, I would have been embarrassed by this candid display, but I've seen so many naked bodies this past week that I almost don't even notice it. But watching Quentin stand there, completely bare, has a delicious heat igniting in my belly.

The scars on my back bloom in pain. A warning I've also become all too familiar with, and I bite the inside of my cheek, locking away my feelings.

"I know, I just thought she might be able to help," Guy replies.

"We already have a Witch on it. I told you," Quentin counters.

"You have a creepy-haired Seer that talks in riddles. We needed a real Witch."

"I have a real Witch. She may be old and creepy, but she's tracking exactly what we need."

My heart falls still in my chest. What in the Hels are they talking about?

Memories begin flashing through my mind like a barrage of bolts being knocked from a bow, each word striking me down with startling clarity and intensity, sending shivers slinking down my spine.

The air becomes thick, and I lose my breath. The stark realisation that looms before me turns my world upside down. Not only did Ric have a Witch helping him, but they were also looking for something, and my dad said the Guards were looking into a missing Seer. *My* missing Seer. Ms. Mystic.

It can't be connected, surely? But after everything I learned about the Crescent Wolf Pack, now I can't be so sure.

Not wanting to hear any more, I step backward. My foot lands on a twig, and it snaps beneath my footfall. The sound rings through the woodlands like a sharp crack of thunder, shattering the silence.

Shit.

I draw in a sharp breath. Trapped within the confines of my own body and mind, I'm unable to move. Caught in a web of so many secrets and lies, I am completely paralysed by the realisation that looms before me.

"Paege?" Guy calls out as they both turn to me.

I part my lips on a word, but nothing comes out of my quickly drying mouth.

Voiceless.

Before I know it, they're both standing beside me. Quentin grabs my arm with a bruising grip. "What did you hear?" he demands.

"Are you alright?" Guy asks at the same time, his brows knitting with concern.

I'm not too sure how to answer either of them. Mhelodie and Sydney's visits revealed so much more than I ever would have expected, including that the Crescent Wolf Pack may have been responsible for the assassination of a Fae family and the eradication of all our memories. Not that Guy or Quentin were responsible for that heinous crime, but to hear them talk about having Witches and Seers, after what Ric had said during the attack, sets my pulse throbbing behind my eyes.

"I'm fine," I say as I try to jerk myself out of Quentin's firm grasp, but he doesn't relent.

"What's wrong?" Guy asks again.

"Nothing." I clear my throat, answering both of them at once. "What are you talking about?"

"It's nothing, Books. Nothing to concern you anyway," Quentin responds, finally letting go of my arm and stepping away.

"Nothing?" I retort with a huff. "Does the king usually have Seers kidnapped?"

"Who said anything about a Seer being kidnapped?" Quentin asks, his eyes narrowing at me as if trying to work out something. Trying to work out what I know.

"Old, white hair, and veiny?" I ask with trepidation flooding through my veins, remembering Ms. Mystic's fate. This is all becoming too much of a coincidence.

Guy nods. Quentin doesn't respond.

"She's a Seer that was kidnapped. A very powerful, very old Seer."

Guy blinks at me as my words set in.

"He's working with the Scorpions!" I cry out in frustration and anger, unsure how neither of them can see it.

"Who is?" Guy asks, his head snapping back and forth between Quentin and me.

Quentin steps back from both of us, his eyes wide with fury and what I think is fear.

"The king," I cry out.

"Like fuck he is, Paege. Careful what you're accusing him of!" Quentin's outburst startles me, and I take a step back.

"Sorry, I didn't mean to upset you, but—" I pause because I'm not really sorry I said anything. I need to get them to see the reason. "Guy, even you thought it was possible. You told Quentin what Ric said. He knows about the Witch, and whatever it is they're looking for."

Guy doesn't say anything for a long moment. Then, finally, he dips his head to me, and his eyes soften. "Paege?" he drawls.

"You can't be serious?" I yell at Guy, and then I turn to Quentin. "Quentin, think about this, please?"

"Paege, don't!" he demands.

"Quentin, I know you idolise your dad, and you think he is some great ruler, but—"

"Seriously, Paege, you need to stop!" Quentin warns, baring his teeth, warning me I've gone too far. But how can he not see this? How are they both so blind? The king cares for no one but himself and the Wolves.

But, of course, they are Wolves. All of them are.

The realisation slaps me hard in the face.

I step back from them both. This is bad. This is very, very bad.

"Don't you ever get sick of defending him?" I ask, tears stinging my eyes.

"You have no idea what you're talking about, Paege. If he's so damn horrible, then why would he ask me to look out for you?"

My stomach twists at his words, and the pressure behind my eyes intensifies, black dots exploding across my vision.

What the Hels did he just say?

He wouldn't.

He didn't.

Waves of anxiety rush over me as I stare at Quentin's face, urging him to repeat the words he just said. "He. What?" I ask slowly and calmly.

Quentin clears his throat. "Nothing." He shakes his head and pauses. He darts his eyes from mine, his shoulders roll forward, and his lips tighten. "He is just looking out for everyone's safety, Paege. There is no big conspiracy."

"Quentin?" I bark, my chest compressing from the brutal hit I just took. "What. Did. You. Just. Say?" I demand.

"Let's go back to the campsite and talk about this?" Quentin asks.

"No!" I roar, baring my teeth and taking another step back.

Quentin exhales a long, slow breath. "I said," he swallows thickly, "he can't be working with the Scorpions because he asked me to keep *you* safe, to keep everyone safe."

"Brother? Please tell me you didn't?" Guy demands as disappointment set in in his emerald eyes.

"Didn't what?" Quentin responds casually, like he didn't just admit to spying on me, to betraying me.

"Tell me it's not true. Tell me we didn't bump into Paege that night because you were tracking her?"

"I wasn't tracking her. She was at the bar, and I saw an opportunity."

"An opportunity?" Guy throws his hands into the air. "Don't," he snarls at Quentin as he marches over to me.

"Paege, I swear I had no idea."

I can't believe what I'm hearing. My heart thunders erratically, thrashing around like a wild animal trying to escape its cage. I blink hard, squeezing my lids together, releasing a deluge of tears from the wells in which they were pooling.

I can't be going through this again. Not again. How could I have been so stupid? How could I have been so blind?

The world around me tilts, and the ground is ripped out from underneath me. I find myself free-falling deep into a fiery abyss, careening deeper and deeper with no escape and no one to rescue me. I hit the ground with a solid thud.

I look up to my Wolves. Guy's beautiful green eyes are filled with nothing but the hurt and betrayal I feel, and without a doubt, I trust he didn't know.

I look at Quentin through tear-soaked lashes and study his face. I focus on his piercing blue eyes and trace every line of his handsome face. The curve of his full lips, his annoying fringe that constantly falls into his eyes, *why won't he just cut the damn thing*, and I feel my heart cracking, splintering into thousands of pieces as I take him in. I close my eyes, and I feel the trace of his fingers run across the tenderness of my skin, the warmth of his breath as he whispers my name into my ear. And then, with every ounce of energy, I push all the feelings I felt for him into a safe and slam them behind a solid door.

Opening my eyes, I release a drawn-out breath before finally speaking. "Guy, take me home."

CHAPTER 48

Leaving Quentin standing in the clearing, I walk away without a word. The betrayal clouds me like a shadow with every step I take back to the campsite. His words ring in my ears over and over again, stabbing me in the heart every time I replay them.

He asked me to look out for you.

I saw an opportunity.

The campsite is empty when I arrive. The emerged Wolves are still running through the woodlands, and those that aren't must have gone for a hike, leaving me stranded here with the very Wolves I am trying to avoid.

I spot the tent and crawl inside, choosing Guy's side of the tent to seek refuge and avoid Quentin for the rest of the evening. I curl up in my sleeping bag, with the hope of bringing tomorrow forth sooner by falling asleep. But as I try to drift off to sleep, my mind keeps switching frequencies between Quentin, the curse, and the Scorpions. I ruminate on the same conversations and the same questions that keep playing in my mind endlessly.

Something outside makes me stir. My heart thrums wildly, and I snap my eyes open.

I didn't hear the pack come back, nor did I hear Guy sneak into the tent and curl up next to me. But the heat of Guy's body tells me he is here long before my eyes adjust to the darkness. Every breath I take is a controlled measure of time as I lie here silently, trying not to let the weight I feel on my chest grow heavier. I focus my attention outside the tent, trying to locate the source of my unease, but I hear nothing. It's silent in the woods.

Too silent.

There isn't a frog's song or a cricket's chirp. There's no sound of the crackling fire nor a breeze in the trees. It's as if time stands still.

"Guy?" I whisper into the darkness.

"Sh," he whispers in return.

We lay in silence for a long moment, my chest rising and falling heavily with every bated breath. Listening, waiting for whatever it is.

Movement outside our room has me grabbing for Guy and burying my head into his bare chest, my cheek pressing up against his wolf tattoo. He wraps his arms around me as a naked Quentin, Slaytar, and Grayson come tumbling into our room.

"What the fuck, Q?" Guy says.

I lift my head from Guy's chest and open my mouth to yell at him, but he lurches forward and covers my mouth with his hand.

"Sh."

I look into his eyes and can see he isn't playing games. He shakes his head one, two, three times, then slowly pulls his hand away and lifts a bloodied finger to his mouth to say quiet.

The three of them appear ghastly. All covered in dirt and blood. They rummage through Guy's bag, pulling out pants and shirts for them all to wear. What the Hels happened out there for them to end up so muddy and dirty? And what has us all so rattled?

A snap of a twig outside has my heart marching to the beat of a war drum, and my body turns to stone. Every muscle and tendon strain to keep me perfectly still.

"Come out, come out, wherever you are," a familiar but chilling voice roars through the woods.

Fear stares down at me, its solid weight crushing my chest beneath it. And despite the cold bite of the air, a tiny bead of sweat rolls across my brow.

Ric.

The Scorpions are here. Why?

"I'm looking for the traitor's son and the little halfling. The rest of you can go. I promise we won't bite," he pauses and laughs. "Anymore."

Slaytar closes his eyes, and a tear tracks down his cheek.

Guy grabs my hand, and I look toward him. What on earth does Ric want with Guy and me? What have we got to do with anything? We didn't even know each other before Ric attacked The Pit. Although, he was very interested in me the night we met. Maybe this hasn't got anything to do with me at all. But Quentin? Those two have some sort of feud. I thought it had to do with Juno, but maybe this rivalry goes far beyond that. But what is he up to? I mean nothing to Quentin. That has been made clear.

I turn back to Quentin and whisper, "What the fuck is going on? You better start talking the truth now." He just shrugs his shoulders and shakes his head in denial. I want to believe him, and the look on his face tells me he is just in the dark as we are. But Quentin is a liar and a damn good actor, so why not lie about this, too?

"Speak!" I demand in a whispered yell that is too loud for my liking.

"Paege, I swear I have no idea what is going on right now. I know you don't trust me, but I would never put Guy's life in danger."

Quentin's words wrap themselves around the knife that's been buried in my chest and twist it, driving it further in. While I can't trust a word that comes out of this Wolf's mouth, I do know without a doubt he would never put Guy's life in danger. The Wolf he calls his brother.

Neither would I.

None of this makes any sense to me, so there is only one way to find out exactly what is going on. If he wants me, I'll give him me. As if he can read every single thought playing through my mind, Guy shakes his head, his eyes wide with fright.

I push myself to my knees and crawl past the Wolves into the front annex. Not one of them stops me, but I feel the weight of their stares as they trail behind me. I quickly pull my boots on and grab my swords.

"Here, take this," I say as I hand one to Guy. If it's me he wants, then I'm going out. "Stay here or come. It's up to you, but I am going to end this tonight," I whisper to the Wolves as I fasten my jacket.

"Are you crazy, Paege?" Quentin barks at me, moving in front of the door and blocking my exit. Clearly, we are no longer trying to be quiet.

A soft footfall sounds from just outside the tent, and I know that it's too late. Ric has figured out where we are. I need to go now.

"Fe, Fi, Fo, Fum, I smell the blood of a traitor's son," Ric sings out.

"Quentin, get out of my way now!" I demand.

"No," Quentin snaps, but none of the others protest.

"You do not get to tell me what to do, Quentin. I am not yours to order around. I am not a pack member or your family. I am not your responsibility, regardless of what you believe, and I do not need your permission to go out there."

"No, but I do care about you, regardless of what you think." My heart cracks. I want to believe him. I want to believe it was all real, but it wasn't.

I scoff in response.

"Paege," Guy starts, and I cut him off.

"He wants me, so I'm going." I tilt my head in a pleading manner. I don't want to die, but I won't let anything happen to Guy, so if going out there gives him a fighting chance, then I'm willing to do that for him. For my friend.

"I know," he says, and my brows shoot for the stars. "But it's just before dawn, and the crescent moon is almost done. We can't shift for much longer, if at all." Guy's voice cracks, and he swallows thickly. "I've got your back. I will always have your back. But you need to know."

I reach for his hand and squeeze it. He nods in support and moves toward the exit, veering around Quentin. As I pass Quentin, he grabs my hand and tugs me back, but I can't look at him. Because if I look at him, I might kiss him, and I can't kiss him. I close my eyes and take in a long breath. I want to tell him I will be alright. I want to promise him I will be back for him, but those are promises I can't make because I'm not entirely sure I will be.

Then I remember how I locked it all away. Every bit of lust and want and desire, so I push it back where it all belongs and exhale. Opening my eyes, I tug my hand from Quentin's grip and exit the tent into the campsite and find myself surrounded by a couple of dozen Wolves.

Oh, shit.

I look around the campsite, searching for the pack. Bile stings my throat when I spot Deekon's body slumped over the log by the campfire. No wonder Slaytar was biting back tears. His younger brother must have been taken from him right before his eyes.

Thank the Gods the rest of the Wolves are all alive. Reever, Immojen, and Harkin are standing by a tent. Both Reever and Harkin are armed with some sort of hunting daggers, and Immojen is swinging an axe in her grip. I can't help being a little impressed by the badassness of it. But they are surrounded by a few Scorpions. Gilli's protecting Monella and Pippance by a large boulder, and he's also armed with a hunting knife. They are blocked by one lone Wolf, the remaining surrounding me and the tent.

"Good to see you again, darlin'," Ric says calmly, like he hasn't just ambushed us.

"What do you want?" I ask with a shaky voice, all ounces of calmness fleeing my body.

My hand trembles, and the hilt of my sword slips beneath my grip. I look down as my white knuckles try to burst through my skin from the strength of my grip.

"You have something that belongs to us," Ric answers, a filthy smirk plastered on his scared-up face. What could I possibly have that belongs to him?

A cacophony of sounds comes from behind me, and I lurch forward, closer to the ring of our enemies, as I try to escape the attack from behind. I turn around to defend myself, swinging my blade up high, only to see Quentin, Slaytar, Grayson, and Guy exit the tent. Guy holds my other sword, and the others all have hunting knives.

A sudden wave of relief crashes over me, and I feel my grip relax. While I don't want to put anyone else in any danger, I don't see myself winning against all these Wolves.

Seriously, Paege, you couldn't win against one of them. What were you thinking?

"We don't want to harm any more Wolves. He was an unfortunate casualty." Ric nods toward Deekon. "Leave the halfling and the betrayer's son. The rest of you can go."

My heart charges like a bull at a gate, smashing against the walls of my chest, harder and harder and harder. What the Hels does he want with me or Guy? I am a nobody, like he said, just a halfling. And what the Hels did Guy do except pay for his father's *sins* over and over again?

"No one is going anywhere." I hear Quentin say from behind me. "We do not abandon our own or innocents."

The pack around me stands tall, and they all nod in agreement. They are family regardless of blood. They will do anything for each other, and my heart swells at the implication that they just claimed me as their own.

Then I feel it. A shift in the air around me. My skin hums, and the beast inside me roars to life, her carnal growl resonating through me from deep within my belly. A shiver chases the static energy as it scatters across my body, and my heart slows to a steady thump.

The focus of my eyes widens, and in the corner of my vision, I spy Immojen and the slow rolling of her axe as she drops it by her side. I know that move. I was taught that move by my father.

A saccharine smile tugs at my lips as I stare up at Ric. Suddenly, she whips the axe around and slices through the Wolf standing in front of her, gutting him from side to side.

A deadly silence echoes through the woodlands for the longest moment as the Wolf's entrails disgustingly tumble to earth. Then Ric howls to the sky, "Bitch, I will take back what's ours, and I will kill you in the process." I draw my sword, ready to defend myself, but I have no doubt I am going to die tonight.

Someone yells, "Attack!"

At the same time, I hear the three most important words whispered into my ear from behind me, and the Wolves start charging and shifting.

CHAPTER 49

All Hels breaks loose, and the once peaceful campsite turns into a battlefield.

I don't have time to think about what Quentin just said to me or how it doesn't make sense. He has done nothing but lie to me for months. Used me. I certainly don't have time to process how it makes me feel. All I can do is watch in horror as Wolves shift around me and my new pack friends try frantically to defend themselves.

Chaos explodes all around, and the carnage that follows has me praying to the Gods that we'll all survive before running into the fray. A Wolf starts charging straight at me, and I duck as it pounces through the air. I swing my sword around, and I connect, slicing through his hind leg and tearing it from his body. His blood sprays across my face, and bile immediately bites at my throat. I wipe the blood from my eyes and watch as he shifts back into his humanoid form and writhes across the ground, howling in pain. I've never hurt anyone before in my entire life.

What am I doing?

Immojen charges another Wolf right in front of me with her axe. She swings high, cutting his throat from side to side, and I watch in horror as he falls to the ground with a solid thud.

But that Wolf is a badass, no doubt about it.

Remind me never to mess with her.

I frantically search for Guy and Quentin. I spot Quentin fighting off two Wolves by Deekon's lifeless body, and Guy is defending himself against Ric. No, he is defending me against Ric. *Fuck.*

Movement to my left has me swinging my sword without looking. I miss the Scorpion as he jumps back, anticipating my move. I stumble forward, losing my grip on my sword. I fall to the ground, and pain seers through my palm as I use my hands to break my fall.

Shit, get it together, Paege.

The Scorpion lunges at me, shifting mid-air. I roll onto my back, grabbing my sword, and I swing it in front of me, impaling the Wolf on the pointy end right through his shoulder. He tumbles down next to me, howling, and I scramble back in a mad panic, sliding my sword from his trembling body.

What the fuck am I doing? I've just stabbed two Wolves.

A blood-curdling scream interrupts my manic thoughts.

I turn to see Monella being pulled from Gilli's protection, and a Wolf bites down on her neck.

"Monella!" I scream in pure panic. She hasn't merged with her Wolf. The venom *will* kill her.

The Wolf throws her to the ground and stands between her and Gilli. She's completely separated from the pack. No one can get to her. No one can help her, but I can. I stand and make a run for her. I won't leave her to die alone.

But I'm yanked back by my arm mid-step.

"Where do you think you're going?" Ric laughs. Pain explodes through my face as he connects a fist to my jaw, and my nose stings from the impact. Blood fills my mouth, the metallic taste enveloping my tongue. It's sickening. Disorientating. Incapacitating.

My sword slips from my clasp, clashing to the ground. My body tries to follow, but Ric holds me tight with a bruising grip. I wriggle to break free, but his grip only tightens. He smiles, and the rancid smell of his breath brings bile to my throat.

Suddenly, his body slams against mine, and he lets go. I stagger backward, freeing myself from Ric's reach.

Guy.

I scoop up my sword, stumbling again as I stand. Blood rushes my ears, and my vision fades in waves. My head isn't recovering from that blow.

Guy charges Ric again, slamming into him, and they both go tumbling. Looking around in horror, I can't remember what I was doing or where I was going. Through the carnage, I see Monella, realisation slamming into me. I was trying to get to Monella.

With all my willpower, I propel myself forward and drag her to the other side of a boulder for protection. Her aqua blue eyes stare up at me, completely lifeless, and my heart sinks fast into pits of Hels. I know that face; I've seen it before. We've already lost two. How many more are going to die for this madness?

I shake her and tell her to fight, but nothing.

Loud, solid footfalls have my heart stilling. Quietly, I manage to stand on shaking knees, drawing my sword once more, preparing myself to defend us both. But Harkin steps out from behind the boulder, and I let out a loosened breath.

We exchange glances, and he runs to her side. I want to stay and make sure she is alright, but I know in my heart she's not. She will not come back from this.

Harkin is with her now. Guy and Quentin are still out there.

I need to go.

I need to help.

I need to fight.

I draw in air, pushing the pain in my heart and my body aside, preparing myself to go back out there and fight aside my friends. But no amount of preparation prepares me for what I walk into.

I step out from behind the boulder just in time to see Guy falling to his knees. My body freezes, bones stiffer than steel, muscles harder than stone, as I see Guy impaled by my sword and Ric on the other end of that sword, smiling an evil smile. Ric pulls the sword from Guy's stomach, and he lurches forward, piercing Guy again right through the bones of his chest, right through his beating heart.

Anger erupts from within, and I release a primal scream. One that has birds flocking out of the pine trees from far above, scattering across the newly lit skies, and it releases the restraints that held me still.

I take off, running toward Guy and Ric faster than I have ever run in my life, my legs hitting the ground with such force I feel the impact on every bone and joint in my body.

The Wolves are fighting all around me, being thrown, bitten, stabbed, and slashed. Growls and yelps fill the woodlands surrounding us. The Crescent Wolf pack is trying to protect me and Guy at any cost. I duck and weave the carnage unfolding around me, trying to avoid being hit or killed by a Wolf. Rage boils up inside me as the adrenaline continues to pump through my veins, and I feel invincible as I try to make my way over to Guy.

I duck the claws of a Wolf, one that Reever is fighting to my left as they wrestle for the win. Both snarling and slashing carelessly in an attempt to make any connection with their opponent. A vomit-inducing crack whips at me from behind, but I can't bring myself to turn around. I can't bring myself to face the possible suffering and massacre I leave in my wake, so I swallow hard, and I keep my focus on Guy.

I jump over an injured Scorpion Wolf lying on the ground, making sure I use his body as a springing board to gain momentum, finding enough height to clear Immojen and decimating another Wolf as they are wrestling on the ground in front of me. As I hit the ground, I don't have time to think about if Immojen is going to survive. I don't have time to consider the pain jolting up my legs or my joints screaming at me from the impact. I push it all down and rush forward.

A Scorpion Wolf lunges for me, and I drop, sliding underneath him and stabbing the sword I have upwards in an attempt to stab him before he gets me with his teeth or claws, but I hit the air, missing him by mere inches. He tries to pivot back for a second go, but I anticipate his movements, rolling toward him and swinging the sword across the ground, slicing through his left Achilles, and he falls to the ground, yelping in pain.

I pull myself back up and run faster toward Guy, who is now lying on the ground lifeless, and Ric is leaning over him, whispering something into his ear. My eyes meet with Ric's, and he smirks. I clench my jaw. With pure rage burning through my veins, I lock my eyes onto him, like a bolt of energy, engaged with its target. And I make sure he knows I'm coming for him. Make sure he knows I am going to kill him.

I'm going to kill that mother fucking asshole.

CHAPTER 50

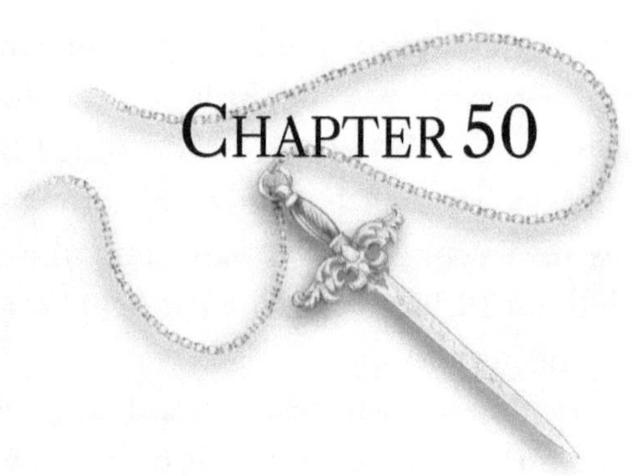

My body aches, but I need to get to Guy at any cost. Every limb burns. My hands throb, and I taste blood. It's that metallic taste swirling around in my mouth that gives me the momentum to keep going because it tastes like revenge, and I've never tasted anything sweeter.

Guy is so close now, so I dive toward him. Toward Ric, who is still leaning over Guy's body, and I brace myself for impact.

As I land, I push Ric off Guy. Ric stumbles back into Quentin, who is suddenly behind him, and I throw my arms out, throwing myself onto Guy, covering his body to protect him. I cock my head and watch as Quentin grabs Ric by the arms, biting down into Ric's shoulder, injecting his venom into him, which I know is slowly going to paralyse him. I finally let myself breathe.

Now that I know Ric is taken care of, I draw my attention back to Guy as panic fills my mind. I try to stop the bleeding by putting pressure on his wounds in his chest and stomach, but he just bleeds right through any attempt I make.

Guy coughs, but he doesn't move. His green eyes darken like a forest after dark, the stars no longer exploding in them, and all I see is his pain. My heart cracks, and darkness starts to seep in like necrosis, eating away at the flesh.

"No, no, no!" I cry as I keep trying to plug the holes in Guy's body with my bare hands.

I grab hold of him and try to yank his heavy, limp body into my embrace. But I'm not strong enough. I paw at him like I'm grabbing for purchase, my anchor, my strength.

Suddenly, he jerks, and life sparks back into his face. He forces a smile, one that doesn't quite reach his eyes, but I still see hope.

"Quentin?" I cry out in desperate need for someone, anyone, to help us.

"I didn't . . ." Guy coughs, his breath rattles as he tries to gasp for air.

"Sh," I urge him. He needs to save his energy, and we need to get him help. But Guy doesn't listen to me. Typical fucking Wolf.

"Paege," *cough, cough,* "listen to me." He takes a laboured breath. "Our love," *cough,* "our connection," he breathes again, "I didn't understand until now."

"No," I whisper to him.

"I wish I got to love you longer."

"Don't you dare. This is not goodbye." Where is Quentin? Where is the help?

"I've never been prouder." He blinks, forcing tears to run down his bloodied cheek. But then he stops. Everything fucking stops.

He doesn't blink again. The tears no longer fall. He doesn't cough. He doesn't take another breath.

He doesn't . . . He doesn't . . .

No, no, no, no, no, no, no.

"Don't you dare, Guy!" I scream at him. I shake him violently. "Wake up, Guy!" I roar. "Wake up!"

His limp, lifeless body doesn't respond. I keep screaming and yelling at him, telling him not to leave me. Begging the Gods for him to stay. But he doesn't listen.

The Gods don't listen.

Tears fall from my eyes like a deluge as the hole in my heart expands rapidly with darkness.

A sob cracks from my chest, the fissure left in its wake so deep it will never be repaired. I finally manage to drag Guy's body onto mine, and I throw myself across him.

Sticky, muddy blood covers my hands. I'm covered in his blood. Oh Gods, there is so much blood. The whole world fades away until it's just me and Guy's lifeless body, and my body trembles uncontrollably.

Rage and fury attack me from all angles, and I see black. But this time, I don't resist. I close my eyes and lean into it, allowing it to wash over me. I bathe in the darkness as it envelops me and cradles me like a newborn baby.

I know what I must do.

I gently place Guy's lifeless body back on the ground, and I stand on shaking legs. I grab my sword and walk toward Quentin, who's holding up Ric's paralysed body. He won't stay that way for long. Without a second thought, my fist tightens around the hilt of my sword, and I thrust it forward right into Ric's body. Gliding it in like butter. I feel my soul turn black, dark as a moonless night, and I relish in the taste of that sweet revenge as his lifeless body falls at my feet. Then I withdraw my sword.

He hits the ground with a thud, and nausea builds inside like a raging storm, but I swallow it down, refusing to succumb to the turmoil. I look up to see Quentin's face, seemingly unaffected by my actions, but I feel a mixture of shock and approval emanate from deep within him.

Unexpectedly, all the Wolves stop fighting. Silence falls around us, and I feel the weight of their eyes staring at me. Floods of their emotions start rushing over me: pain, fear, respect, sadness, anger. I don't care. I ignore it. Bit by bit, I push it all away behind a solid door, and I slam it shut. The calm that follows is a numbing reprieve, settling over me like a thick fog after a storm, murky and chilling.

I turn my attention back to Guy and sit down beside him. I pull him into my arms and hold him against my body, rocking him back and forth, back and forth, and the tears start flowing once again.

Please, Gods, I don't know what to do. Please help me.

"Guy, I need you," I whisper through every sob that leaves my breaking body. "I love you. Please come back to me." I kiss his forehead and hold him tight, hoping, like some fabled tale, that he will wake from his slumber.

He doesn't move.

He doesn't wake.

A gentle hand rests on my shoulder, and I look up to Quentin. "He can't be gone. He can't be gone," I plead with him, with the kingdom, with the universe.

"You need to let him go," Quentin says softly.

"No!" I yank my shoulder out from his grip. "Don't say that!" Fury starts to ball inside my stomach once more.

"Paege, we need to leave. You need to let him go."

"We can't leave him here. We need to take him. We need to give him a proper Wolf burial!" I demand.

"We will. I promise," Quentin says calmly and once again places his hand on my shoulder. "We will come back for him, but we have to leave, Paege. Right now."

Nausea roils through me.

This beautiful, selfless, and caring Wolf who saved my life—who sacrificed himself to save my life—didn't deserve this. He was so kind and generous. He wasn't like the rest. He didn't deserve this at all. And it's all my fault.

"NO!" I demand again through uncontrollable tears falling down my face, hugging Guy closer. "I can't," I whisper through a choke.

"Yes, you can, Paege. Please trust me. I promise I will come back for him, but I need to get you to safety now. We need to get out of here. You killed their alpha, and they will only respect you or me for so long. We need to take our chance, take the pack, and leave now."

"Get one of the Wolves to take Guy with us?!" I plead.

"It doesn't work like that, Paege. But I promise you, we will get him back. The Scorpions will take our fallen, and we will take theirs, and we will exchange our Wolves respectfully."

I understand what Quentin is saying. The Wolves have their rituals, and they must be respected, but my body and mind won't let me let go of Guy. So, I don't.

Quentin leans down and takes my hands gently. "I know you are angry with me. I know I have given you little reason to do so, but you need to trust me, please," he begs. "May I?" he asks, and I nod, permitting him because the only way I will let go of Guy is if he forces me off him.

Slowly and gently, he pries my fingers one by one from Guy's lifeless body, and then he wraps his arms around me. I feel my body relax, and I lean into Quentin's body, burying my head into his chest. Quentin envelopes me, once again scooping me up and carrying my comatose body to safety.

"No." I weep into his chest, and he carries me away.

I don't remember much after that.

Quentin instructing the pack to grab Ric and the other Wolves' bodies. Quentin carrying me through the woods. Quentin travelling me through a portal. Quentin carrying me into a house. Quentin lying down next to me.

For a moment, all I can do is look into his eyes and drown in his grief. I let his emotions pour into me, his love and pain, his hatred and anguish. The pain of losing Guy is breaking him apart, but he's holding it together just for me. He's acting strong just for me. But why? I should be the one staying strong for him. They've been brothers for eighteen years—ever since Guy lost his father. Brothers by bond, not by blood. But brothers, nonetheless. Inseparable.

Tears fill my eyes again. I take in a shuddering breath, then place my hand on his chest, holding it to his heart. His heart beats erratically under my touch. Beating with anger, beating with sadness, beating with grief for a brother lost.

For the first time since leaving Guy's body, I finally find the strength to speak. "I'm sorry I couldn't save him," I whisper to him.

"Don't be sorry, Paege. It's not your fault," he says through gritted teeth. But I don't believe his words. If I hadn't gone rogue, if I hadn't tried to sacrifice myself, Guy might still be alive. Monella might still be with us.

Tears pool in his eyes, and my heart splinters into a thousand pieces. I can't stomach the thought of this other wonderful Wolf, even if he did hurt me, going through all this pain and heartbreak because of me.

I close my eyes and let Quentin's anguish pour over me because that is what I deserve: to feel all the pain that I have inflicted on this Wolf's heart and soul. But I unexpectedly feel something else. A kind of warmth radiating from him, pulsating to the rhythm of his still-breaking heart.

A grumble shudders through Quentin's body, and I open my eyes, hoping to meet his, but I don't. They're closed. Shut tight. Still weeping with tears.

The weight of my guilt crushes me beneath the sadness and anger of Guy's death, and I can't help but close my eyes again, hoping to find salvation in the darkness. But the Gods have other plans. Instead, images of the attack flash through my mind, and Guy's death plays on repeat like my own personal form of torture. Plaguing me until I finally fall asleep.

CHAPTER 51

I'm violently ripped from my slumber, and the beast that lives inside me growls in the pit of my stomach.

Pain erupts through me, detonating like explosives beneath my skin, and an intense heat storms through my veins. My organs twist, ripping me apart from the inside, and my muscles tear apart from my bones. Bile stings my throat, and I swallow hard, trying to push the waves of nausea down. I lurch from the bed in a bid to escape the torture but fall to the ground. My legs give way beneath me, breaking backward as I hit the floor.

"Quentin?" I cry out in desperation.

What's happening to me? What in the Hels is going on?

Confusion sets in as I try to determine what is going on. The unbearable pain takes over my entire body.

Was I bit by a Wolf? I don't remember that happening, but it could have. Is there some sort of curse if Fae kill a Wolf? That wouldn't surprise me. Or maybe this is my punishment for getting Guy killed. That's probably more like it.

Adrenaline rushes through me, my heart pumping it through my body in waves. I try to stand in a desperate attempt to flee this torment, but I fall to the floor once more.

I hear a growl, and it reverberates through my chest. I cock my head. Where the Hels did that come from?

My heart pounds to the beat of a war drum, and my breaths come in short and sharp. I try to focus on what's going on, but everything's a mess. Visions of Wolves baring their teeth at me, snarling and snapping, continue to torment me.

"Paege?" Quentin's voice sounds so close yet so far.

"Quentin?" I plead, reaching out for him. "Help me."

Quentin bolts upright in the bed. "What in the Hels? Paege, what's going on?" Desperation and apprehension lace his words, but he doesn't move to help me, and maybe he doesn't want to.

"I don't know." I try to crawl towards him, but I feel like I'm being crushed from the inside out. My body won't respond to the instructions my brain is sending it. Suddenly, my vision is violently stolen from me, plunging me into a darkness that's both petrifying and comforting, and my heart slows its pace to a calming rhythm.

Breathe, Paege, just breathe, I tell myself, but as I try to draw in breath, it catches in my throat.

My beast sits at attention, and she growls as Wolves, hundreds of them, appear before me as if I'm having some sort of vivid hallucination. They snap at me and howl as I stand before them. A bleak cloud shrouds them, and I know I need to stay away.

I can't move.

A tendril of firelight pierces through the cloud and wafts toward me. I try to fight it off, but it engulfs me, binds itself around my wrist, and tugs me forward through the rows and rows of Wolves. Each one steps back as I'm tugged forward, but I'm not being tugged. My body is freely moving, following the firelight as if it knows it's safe to do so.

Then I see her, and the snaps and howls of every other Wolf seem to fade away.

Her coat is pure white except for a splash of grey colouring at the tips of her ears. Her dark green eyes, reflecting golden specks of starlight, focus on me, and I know.

She is beautiful.

She is Majestic.

She is mine.

Emitting an almighty and powerful howl, she causes all the other Wolves to fall silent and retreat into the shadows. My Wolf calmly pads toward me, her regal nature is mesmerising, and she demands control.

When she reaches me, the firelight evaporates into the wind, and the battle within me completely ceases. The heaviness that I've been carrying these past months is lifted, and I feel a weightlessness I've never felt before. Free. My skin hums with the energy that surrounds us, and I know what I must do. It's as if a silent whisper is instructing me, and I know that voice can be trusted.

I know I will be alright.

I hold out a hand and reach for her, and she graciously accepts it, stepping into my touch. She nuzzles her head into my hand, and I run my hand over her body, brushing my fingers through her thick coat.

A feeling I have been searching for my entire life washes over me, and I let out a loosened breath and sigh.

Home.

I blink, and my vision slowly returns, but it's morphed like I'm looking through a prism. The colours of the world are slightly muted yet somehow brighter. I blink again, and I see Quentin standing by the edge of the bed. Though everything is distorted, I can see his face clearly: eyes wide, mouth agape.

"What's going on?" I ask, but nothing familiar comes from my mouth. Instead, I hear a growling howl-like sound. "Quentin?" I try again, but again, I hear the same sounds.

Perplexed by what's going on, I try to reach for him, but instead, I find myself moving slowly toward him.

I watch as Quentin slowly steps toward me, meeting me as I approach him. He smiles broadly, his eyes widening with bewilderment.

"Paege? If you can hear me, nod."

I nod in response, and his beautiful face relaxes. I see a light emitting from him, glowing around him, and bright yellow tendrils, like rays of sunshine, start extending from him to me. But when they reach me, large, powerful wings casting dark shadows envelop me from behind. I feel myself expanding like my body is calling out for him, reaching for the peace and warmth his light is emitting, but something a lot more primal is preventing me from reaching him. Something I don't understand.

He closes the physical space between us and extends a hand to me, cupping my face. His warmth radiates through me, and the wings retreat. I close my eyes, leaning into his hand, and sigh.

"You. Are. Beautiful," he whispers as he brings his face closer to mine. I look deep into his blue eyes, and I see looking back at me the mesmerising Wolf I saw earlier, reflected in the blacks of his eyes.

"Paege, you're a Wolf!"

A Wolf. I'm not a Wolf. How could I possibly be a Wolf? My Mum is Fae, and my bio-dad was Human . . . wasn't he?

As I stare into Quentin's eyes, the reflection of my Wolf staring back at me has me questioning everything I thought I knew. Her brilliant white coat, her grey-tipped ears, her emerald green eyes. It's undeniable.

My mind begins to spiral as everything I have learnt these past months crashes into me. Of all the answers I have been searching for, this was not one of them. The curses, our memories, the original family, my true heritage, Guy . . .

Wait—

It hits me then. Our wolves. They are—were—the same.

The world begins to tilt around me, the hazy fog lifting, and I stumble to my knees at the same time Quentin reaches for me and pulls me into his embrace.

Hesitantly, I collapse into his body, the scent of pine forest working tirelessly to calm my soul as sobs repeatedly crack from my chest.

I manage to pull myself out of Quentin's hold just enough to tilt my head up, and through teary lashes, I meet his gaze. He brushes the blood-soaked hair plastered to my face out of my eyes and tucks it behind my ears, all while he looks back at me with pity. Its heaviness weighs down on me with every moment that passes.

"Quentin?" I finally manage to speak through hiccups,

"Yes, Books?"

"What's happening?"

Quentin's eyes widen, and then I watch as the pity disappears, the brightness of his irises turn to that steely blue before they completely glaze over. His mouth opens and closes, and I suck in a breath as I wait for the words of my truth, my family, my destiny to fall from his traitorous lips.

THE END

Glossary and Pronunciation Guide

Names
Amarax (AH-mah-racks)
Asheron (ASH-er-on)
Blaire (BLAIR)
Braxtion (BRAX-tee-uhn)
Bridgette (BRID-jet)
Deekon (DEE-kon)
Enderlene (EN-dur-leen)
Gilli (GILL-ee)
Greyson (GRAY-sun)
Grynderwall (GRIN-der-wall)
Guygar (GUY-gar)
Halexander (HAL-ex-an-der)
Hallie (HAL-ee)
Harkin (HAR-kin)
Hera (HAIR-uh)
Immojen (IM-oh-jin)
Ishaan (ih-SHAHN)
Israykiel (iz-RAY-kee-el)
Juno (Joo-noh)
Kholann (KO-Lahn)
Lumeilia (loo-MEEL-lee-uh)
Mhelodie (MEL-oh-dee)
Monella (MON-ell-uh)
Paegence (PAY-jence)
Pippence (PIP-ense)
Quentin (KWEN-tin)
Reever (REE-vur)
Remildiaz (rem-EEL-dee-ahz)
Ruhaul (roo-HAHL)
Slaytar (SLAY-tar)

Glossary and Pronunciation Guide

Sydney (SID-nee)
Sylas (SYE-lass)
Synthony (SIN-thuh-nee)
Vaelencia (vay-LEN-see-uh)
Vailenbyrg (VAY-len-berg)
Vharkus (VAR-kus)

Places
Aridor (ah-REE-dor) Desert
Blaxheild (BLAX-hee-uld)
Blethyn (BLEH-than) Sea
Cedrus (SEE-drus)
Darthick (DAR-thick)
Elyndria (eel-LIN-dree-uh)
Ferinini (feh-REE-nee-nee)
Lochswick (LOK-swick)
Medelia (meh-DEE-lee-uh)
Mountains of G'phen (guh-FEN)
Neopolis (nee-OP-poh-lis)
Orphelios (or-FEE-lee-ohs)
Quespelia (kwes-PEEL-lee-uh)
River Plye (PLIE)
Welveryn (WELL-vuh-rin)

Gods
Aesther (EST-er) Goddess of Elements
Amara (AM-ar-ah) Goddess of Life
Edom (EE-dom) God of Blood
Isra (ISS-rah) God of the Stars
Pyrrhia (PEER-ee-uh) Goddess of Fire
Terra (TEH-rah) Goddess of Earth

Glossary and Pronunciation Guide

Tidryn (TID-rin) God of Water
Zephyra (ZEH-fie-rah) Goddess of Air

Terms
Fyre: A type of alcohol, or liquor, genric
AmberFyre: Whiskey
BlossomFyre: Gin
CrystalFyre: Vodka
DesertFyre: Tequila
VineBrew: Wine, generic
VineBlood: Red wine
VineDew: White wine
VineMist: Champaign or sparkling wine
VineStar: Sweet syrup wine, port
Clays: Currency, low value coins
Drops: Currency, moderate value coins
Gales: Currency, high value coins
Sparks: Currency, highest value coins
Scribe: A device to send written messages or make voice calls
Vision Box: A device to watch entertainment
Music Box: A device to listen to music
Chordo-grande: Instrument, piano
Chordo-bowstring: Instrument, violin
Chordo-strummer: Instrument, guitar
Chrodo-bass: Instrument, bass guitar

Acknowledgements

There are so many people I want to acknowledge. Without them, this would not have become a reality. Firstly, my friends. There are too many of you to name, but without you, I would not have made it this far. Especially my best friend Mel. Our endless voice messages, coffees, and walks and talks, and writing weekends gave me the space and courage to not only complete the novel but take it a step further and share it with the world. Your friendships mean so much to me, and without you, my world would be a very boring place. And this one, would never have come to life. Thank you.

Charla, Rachel, Jordan, Bianca, Hannah, Amelia and Laure-anne, aka my incredible writing group. I don't even know where to begin. It was a fluke we found each other, and I am completely honoured to be surrounded by such inspiring and talented women. Each one of you has been a cheerleader for me since the day we met, and I honestly don't know if I would have had the courage to self-publish without meeting you all. I am truly blessed to be able to call you friends. Even if we all live on opposite sides of the world, I cannot wait to see what you all do, too. But I do know this: we will all be meeting very soon.

My brilliant editors. Firstly, Charla Morgan Ayers thank you for helping me make this book the best it could possibly be, for challeng-ing me, and supporting me, all while spending endless hours editing and fixing my ridiculous grammar without complaint and with a smile on your face. Brittany Gossin, thank you for always answering my questions, not just about editing but about anything related to self-publishing, no matter how silly or what time of night or day, and for giving me the courage to self-publish. And my proofreader, Laura, for making sure my manuscript was completely polished before printing.

A huge thank you to Krystal, I don't even have words to express my gratitude, but I am so happy we found each other. From the second we met, we clicked, and we have been on this crazy ride together, bluffing our way through. Look where we are now!

Juniper, you crazy cat. Thank you for the endless voice messages and chats regarding publishing, art, and life in general. I loved working with you on this project and can't wait to work with you again in the future.

A massive shout-out to all my Alpha and Beta readers. Thank you for taking the time out of your lives to read my manuscript and provide feedback to help me build this incredible world and my characters. Your comments on Paege, Quentin, and Guy still bring me joy to read. I must admit I absolutely loved waking up to see more comments made in the manuscript from one of you staying up for endless hours reading. Your comments were all priceless.

And finally, thank you to my amazing family for always supporting me and staying positive, even when I couldn't. Thank you to my wonderful sister, Jaclyn, who has spent endless hours listening to me drone on about Paege, Guy, and Quentin, your support has been invaluable. And especially my dad, Chris. You showed me what it is to love and be loved. You taught me to dream and to never give up. This book is for you. Please don't read it though.

THANK YOU

Thank you to all my readers out there who have taken a chance on reading A Kingdom of Curses: The Emergence. Without you, this could not be possible.

If you enjoyed Paege's story, please head over to Amazon or/and Goodreads and leave a review. As a self-published indie author, every review counts. And please follow me on my social media pages and/or sign up to my newsletter for exciting updates regarding the release of the next instalment of Paege's journey.

instagram.com/dani.drummond_author

tiktok.com/danielleddrummond_author

facebook.com/.danielleddrummondauthor

Also by Danielle D. Drummond

Book 2 of the Original Sin Series is set to be released late 2025.
A Bloodline of Secrets – The Unification

instagram.com/dani.drummond_author

tiktok.com/danielleddrummond_author

facebook.com/.danielleddrummondauthor

About the Author

Danielle D. Drummond has been spinning tales since she first learned to talk. She wrote her first storybook, about an injured penguin, at around ten years old and has been crafting short paranormal stories and poetry ever since. Today, she writes epic fantasy novels infused with romance—okay, a lot of romance—because she's a sucker for a happily ever after. Based in Perth, Australia, Danielle shares her life with her two beloved dogs. You'll often find her at a local coffee shop or bar, fully immersed in the worlds she's bringing to life.

Recommendations

As an indie author, I will shamelessly promote and recommend some other amazing books that I have had the privilege of reading over the years, written by other indie authors.

The Strange Hour by R.G. Wesley
The Lost Deer Queen by H.J. Nichols
A Realm of Fury by R.D. Baker
The Frangatelli Mirror by G.R. Thomas
Heretic Behaviour by E.C. Glynn
The Origins Daughter by Alexandra St Pierre
Whispers of the Blood by SK May

All of these amazing novels are available on Amazon in paperback and ebook formats. And if you love their stories as much as I do, head on over to Goodreads and give them some love.